Oliver Byrne

Dual Arithmetic

A new art

SALZWASSER
VERLAG

Oliver Byrne

Dual Arithmetic

A new art

Reprint of the original, first published in 1863.

1st Edition 2022 | ISBN: 978-3-37500-649-5

Verlag (Publisher): Salzwasser Verlag GmbH, Zeilweg 44, 60439 Frankfurt, Deutschland
Vertretungsberechtigt (Authorized to represent): E. Roepke, Zeilweg 44, 60439 Frankfurt, Deutschland
Druck (Print): Books on Demand GmbH, In de Tarpen 42, 22848 Norderstedt, Deutschland

DUAL ARITHMETIC.

A NEW ART.

INVENTED AND DEVELOPED

BY OLIVER BYRNE

LONDON

1863.

PREFACE.

In the most general sense, the peculiar system of developing and applying the power of numbers, which I have called Dual Arithmetic, is a new Art, and not merely a new method of obtaining results that might be found by arts previously known.

Dual Arithmetic unfolds the capabilities of numbers in an original manner, extends the boundaries of mathematical science, and establishes new rules by which many difficult problems of the greatest utility and importance are solved with ease without the aid of tables, cumbersome formulæ, or methods of approximation.

Those acquainted with the operations of common arithmetic can easily acquire a sufficient knowledge of Dual Arithmetic to understand the solutions of the following introductory examples.

In developing the elements of this new art, I have purposely disregarded the most obvious arithmetical abridgments, in order that each process may appear without the least disguise.

The Introductory Examples are for the purpose of showing the accomplished mathematician the power of this art. The learner who wishes to acquire it practically, is recommended to pass them over until he has mastered the work, when he will be able fully to appreciate their value.

I have applied the numerical operations of Dual Arithmetic to a variety of developments, so that in each particular inquiry the best method to connect actual calculation with algebraic language and symbolical expressions may be applied. In my works on Algebra and the Calculus, which are being prepared for publication, the whole subject and its different applications will be treated in a general and exhaustive manner. My work on the Calculus, to be termed the "Calculus of Form," unfolds a new science and establishes modern analysis on a purely Mathematical basis, rejecting the reasoning of the Differential and other methods.

OLIVER BYRNE.

CONTENTS.

PART III.

EVOLUTION AND INVOLUTION OF DUAL ARITHMETIC p. 29.

PART IV.

OF ANGULAR MAGNITUDES AND TRIGONOMETRICAL LINES, p. 59.

PART V.

FORMULÆ AND RULES FOR THE SOLUTION OF PLANE TRIANGLES, WITHOUT THE USE OF TABLES, p. 87.

PART VI.

DUAL ARITHMETIC APPLIED TO THE SOLUTION OF THE DIFFERENT CASES OF SPHERICAL TRIANGLES.

IMPORTANT MISCELLANEOUS PROBLEMS SOLVED BY DUAL ARITHMETIC.

GENERAL SOLUTION OF ALGEBRAICAL EQUATIONS OF ALL DEGREES, p. 173

GENERAL DEVELOPMENTS.

APPENDIX.

ERRATA.

Page 5,	line 5,	from top,	*for*	"$54{\cdot}247 \times (1{\cdot}06)$," *read* "$54{\cdot}247 \times (1{\cdot}01)$."
,, 21,	,, 6,		,,	"divide by 1, $(1{\cdot}01)^3$," *read* "divide 1 by $(1{\cdot}01)^3$."
,, 22,	,, 19,		,,	"negative," *read* "positive."
,, 22,	,, 20,		,,	"positive," *read* "negative."
,, 38,	,, 11,		,,	"sixth root," *read* "fifth root."
,, 72,	,, 14,		,,	"minutes," *read* "minutes, &c."
,, 117,	,, 9,		,,	"THE AREA," *read* "THE AREAS."

INTRODUCTORY EXAMPLES.

1. *The radius of the earth at the equator* = 20921185 *feet; and the area of circle whose diameter is unity* = ·78539816.

Required the value of $\left(\frac{78539{\cdot}816}{20921{\cdot}18{\cdot}5}\right)^{\frac{1}{7}}$

$78539{\cdot}816 = 10^4 \times 7 \downarrow 1,1,9,8,5,4,4,7, = \downarrow \overline{1127192741,}$

$2092118{\cdot}5 = 10^6 \times 2 \downarrow 0,4,5,2,3,1,2,0, = \downarrow \overline{1455441914,}$

$$\begin{array}{rl} & +\ 1127192741 \\ & -\ 1455441914 \\ \hline 7\ )\ - & 328249173 \\ \hline - & 46892739 = \tfrac{1}{10} \downarrow 0,4,2,1,2,1,4,8, = {\cdot}625687758. \end{array}$$

2. *Required the hyperbolic logarithm of* 3·141592654 = π, *or find the value of x in the equation*

$$\epsilon^x = \pi;$$

$$\epsilon = 2{\cdot}718281828.$$

$$\epsilon = \downarrow 10,4,7,1,0,0,3,8, = \downarrow \overline{100005025,}$$

$$\pi = \downarrow 12,0,1,0,0,8,2,3, = \downarrow \overline{114478742,}$$

Then by common division 114478742 divided by 100005025, gives 1·14472989, the hyperbolic logarithm of π.

The divisor 100005025, which is a whole number, remains constant in calculating hyperbolic logarithms. The division by 100005025 = $\downarrow$ 0,0,0,0,5,0,2,5, = $\downarrow$ 0,0,0,0,5,0,0,25, may be performed by Dual Arithmetic as follows:

$$114478742 \div \downarrow 0,0,0,0,5,0,0,25, = 114478742 \downarrow 0,0,0,0,\bar{5},0,0,\overline{25},$$

$$\begin{array}{r|l}
11447 & 8742 \,.\, + \\
 & 5724 \,.\, - \\
\hline
11447\,301 & 8 \,.\,.\,.\,.\,.\,.\,.\, + \\
2 & 9 \,.\,.\,.\,.\,.\,.\,.\, - \\
\hline
1\cdot 1447\,298 & 9
\end{array}$$

3. *Required the hyperbolic logarithm of* 1·25, *retaining the common divisor* 100005025, *or multiplier* $\downarrow 0,0,0,0,\bar{5},0,\overline{25},$

$$1\cdot 25 = \downarrow 2,3,2,6,7,3,2,3, = \downarrow \overline{22315476,}$$

$$\begin{array}{r|l}
22315 & 476 \,.\,. \\
1 & 116 \,.\,. \\
\hline
22314\,360 & \,.\,.\,.\,.\,.\,.\,.\,. \\
6 & \,.\,.\,.\,.\,.\,.\,.\,. \\
\hline
\end{array}$$

$$\text{Hyp. log. } 1\cdot 25 = \cdot 22314\,354$$

4. *Find the logarithm of* $\pi = 3\cdot 141592654$, *or the value of* x *in the equation,*

$$10^x = 3\cdot 141592654$$

$$10 = \downarrow 24,1,5,1,9,2,9,5. = \downarrow \overline{230270081,}$$

$$\pi = \downarrow 12,0,1,0,0,8,2,3, = \downarrow \overline{114478742,}$$

Then, by common division, 114478742 divided by 230270081 gives ·49714987 the logarithm of π.

In calculating common logarithms by this new art, 230270081 = 23 $\downarrow 0,0,1,1,7,4,0,8$ is constant, and may be retained, and the division performed thus,

$$497 \times 23 = 11431$$

$$11431 \downarrow 0,0,1,4,7,6,5,1, = 114478742\cdot$$

$$\therefore \frac{497 \times 23 \downarrow 0,0,1,4,7,5,6,1,}{23 \downarrow 0,0,1,1,7,4,0,8,} = 497 \downarrow 0,0,0,3,0,1,5,3, = \cdot 497149876.$$

5. *The distance of the earth from the sun* = 95364768 *miles, find the common logarithm of this number, or solve the equation,*

$$10^x = 95364768$$

$$9\,)\,\underline{95364768}$$
$$10596085{\cdot}33 = \downarrow 0,5,8,1,5,1,8,8,$$

$\downarrow$ 0,5,	=	4975415
0,0,8,	=	799640
and,		15188
9.	=	219733500
		225523743 ÷ 230270081 = ·97938795

∴ The common logarithm of 95364768 = 7·97938795.

This result may be found without the use of common division, thus:—

$$23 \times 98 = 2254$$

$$2254 \downarrow 0,0,0,5,5,\bar{1},\bar{1},\bar{2}, = 225523743$$

$$\therefore \frac{98 \times 23 \downarrow 0,0,0,5,5,\bar{1},\bar{1},\bar{3},}{23 \downarrow 0,0,1,1,7,4,0,8,} = 98 \downarrow 0,0,\bar{1},4,\bar{2},\bar{5},\bar{1},\overline{11},$$

$$\cdot 9793879598 = 98 \downarrow 0,0,\bar{1},3,7,4,7,9,$$

The log. of this constant number is wrong in Baron Von Vega's Tables, by Fischer, published at Berlin, 1857.

6. *How many degrees, minutes, &c. are contained in an arc of a circle, length* = ·34567895, *radius* = 1 ?

RULE.

Multiply double the length of the given arc by 100000, and then by $\downarrow 0,3,1,0,0,\bar{7},0,\bar{5},$

```
69|1 3|5 ·7|90
 2|0 7|4  0|74
  |  2|0  7|41        0,3,1,0,0,7̄,0,5̄,
   |       |69
---------------
71 2|3 0  6|74
    |7 1  2|31
---------------
71 3 0 1  9|05 ....
          4|99| ........ }
            4| ........ } minus
---------------
19° 48′ 21″·402 = 71 3 0 1″.4 02
```

7. *What is the length of an arc that contains* 19° 48′ 21″·402 = 71301·″402, *radius* = 1?

RULE.

Subtract twice the number of seconds from half the number of seconds with two cyphers affixed; the remainder, multiplied by ↓0,1,0,0,2,8,2,2, gives 100000 times the length of the given arc.

```
2 ) 71 30 1″·40 2 00
    ----------------
    35 65 0  70 1 00
     1 42 6  02 8 04        Constant.
    ----------------
  ·34|22 4  6|7 2|96
     |34|2  2|4 6|73      ↓0,1,0,0,2,8,2,2,
    ----------------
  ·34 56 6|9 1 9 69
          |6|9 1 34 ..
          2|7|6 54 ....
            |6|91 ......
              |69 ......
    ----------------
Length of arc = ·34 56 7 8 94 97
```

8. *Given the obliquity of the Elliptic* = 23° 27′ 25″·42 = 84445″·42, *to find the natural sine, and the log. sin of this angle.*

```
2 ) 84445″·4200
    -----------
    42222 ·7100
     1688 ·9084       Constant.
    -----------
Length of arc = ·40533 ·8016 ↓0,1,0,0,2,8,2,2, = ·409402949
```

$$\cdot 409402949 = \cdot 4 \downarrow 0,2,3,3,3,6,1,8, = \cdot 4 \downarrow \overline{2323649,}|$$

This last result may be found by a single operation, since the constant $\downarrow \overline{0,1,0,0,2,8,2,2,}|$ is given.

$$\begin{array}{rl} & \cdot 4 \downarrow 0,1,3,3,0,7,9,6, = \cdot 405338016 \\ \text{Constant} = & \quad \downarrow 0,1,0,0,2,8,2,2, \\ \hline & \cdot 4 \downarrow 0,2,3,3,3,6,1,8, \end{array}$$

Length of arc, which put $= x$. It is well-known that

$$\sin x = x - \frac{x^3}{2.3} + \frac{x^5}{2.3.4.5} - \ldots\ldots$$

$$\begin{array}{lrl} 4^{\cdot} = & 138636402 & \\ & 2323649 & \\ \hline & 140960051 & = 4 \downarrow \overline{2323649,}| \\ & 3 & \\ \hline \text{cube} \ldots & 422880153 & \\ & 179184951 & = 2.3 \\ \hline & 243695202 & \\ 11^{\cdot} \ldots\ldots & 239801578 & \\ \hline & 3893624 & \\ \downarrow 0,3, \ldots\ldots & 2985249 & = 3\text{B} \\ \hline & 908375 & \\ \downarrow 0,0,9, \ldots & 899595 & = 9\text{C} \\ \hline & 0,8,7,8,0, & \end{array}$$

Dividing by $(10)^8$; $11 \downarrow 0,3,9,0,8,7,8,0, = \cdot 011436724$ minus

$$\begin{array}{lrl} & 140960051 & \\ & 5 & \\ \hline \text{Fifth power} \ldots\ldots & 704800255 & \\ & 478773232 & = 2.3.4.5 \\ \hline & 226027023 & \\ 9^{\cdot} = & 219733500 & \\ \hline & 6293523 & \end{array}$$

```
                        6293523
↓0,6, . . .             5970498 = 6B
                        -------
                         323025
↓0,0,3, . . . .          299865 = 3C
                         ------
                        2,3,1,6,0,
```

∴ Dividing by $(10)^5$; 9 ↓0,6,3,2,3,1,6,0, = ·000095846 plus.

```
                   140960051
                           7
                   ---------
                   986720357
                   852558978 = 2.3.4.5.6.7
                   ---------
                   134161379
3· . . . . . . . . 109866750
                   ---------
                    24294629
↓2, . . .           19062994 = 2A
                    --------
                     5231633
↓0,5, . . . .        4975415 = 5B
                     -------
                      256220
↓0,0,2, . . .         199910 = 2C
                      ------
                     5,6,3,1,0,
```

Dividing by $(10)^7$; 3 ↓2,5,2,5,6,3,1, ·= 000000382 minus.

```
                              ·409402949 +
                                11436724 −
                                   95846 +
                                     382 −
                              ----------
Nat. sin 23° 27′ 25″·42 = ·398061689
```

```
3 ) 3·98061689
    1·32687229 = ↓2,9,2,6,5,2,2,1, = ↓28283872,
                                 3· = ↓109866750,
                  ∴ 3·98061686 = ↓138150622,
```

Then 138150622, divided by the constant 230270081, gives ·59995038.

∴ Log. sin 23° 27′ 25″·42 = 9·59995038.

9. *Find the degrees minutes, seconds, &c. in an arc to radius* 1, *whose sine* = ·226941796 = 2 ↓ **1,3,1,2,1,5,5,5,** = $\overline{81956457,}|$

```
                    81956457
                           3
                   ---------
cube . . . . . .   245869371
                   179184951 = 1./2.3
                   ---------
                    66684420
↓6, . . . .         57188982 = 6A
                    --------
                     9495438
↓0,9, . . . . .      8955747 = 9B
                    --------
                      539691
↓0,0,5, . . .         499775 = 5C
                     -------
                      3,9,9,1,6,
```

Dividing by $(10)^8$ ↓ **6,9,5,3,9,9,1,6,** becomes ·001948014

```
                        81956457
                               5
                       ---------
fifth power . . . .    409782285
                       259039732 = 1.3/2.4.5
                       ---------
                       150742553
4· . . . . . .         138636402
                       ---------
                        12106151
↓1,                      9531497 = A
                        --------
                         2574654
↓0,2, . . .              1990166 = 2B
                        --------
                          584488
↓0,0,5, . . .             499775 = 5C
                         -------
                          8,4,7,1,3,
```

Dividing $(10)^5$ 4 ↓ **1,2,5,8,4,7,1,3,** gives ·000045146.

$$
\begin{array}{lrl}
 & 81956457 & \\
 & 7 & \\
\hline
 & 573695199 & \\
 & 310921720 & = \dfrac{1.3.5}{2.4.6.7} \\
\hline
 & 262773479 & \\
10^{\cdot}\ldots\ldots & 230270081 & \\
\hline
 & 32503398 & \\
\downarrow 3,\ldots\ldots & 28594491 & = 3\,A \\
\hline
 & 3908907 & \\
\downarrow 0,3,\ldots & 2985249 & = 3\,B \\
\hline
 & 923658 & \\
 & 899595 & = 9\,C \\
\hline
 & 2,4,0,6,3, &
\end{array}
$$

Dividing by $(10)^7$ 10 ↓ **3,3,9,2,4,0,6,3,** becomes ·000001384.

$$
\begin{array}{lr}
\text{sine} & \cdot 22694\,1796 \\
 & \cdot 00194\,8014 \\
 & \cdot 00004\,5146 \\
 & \cdot 00000\,1384 \\
\hline
\text{arc} & \cdot 22893\,6340 \\
 & 2 \\
\hline
\end{array}
$$

seconds in arc = 45787·2680 ↓ $\mathbf{0,3,1,0,0,\overline{7},0,\overline{5},}$

45787·27 ↓ $\mathbf{0,3,1,0,0,\overline{7},}$ will give the seconds sufficiently correct, $= 47221''\cdot 42 = 13^\circ\ 7'\ 1''\cdot 42$.

10. *Find the area of the curve whose equation is*

$$y = \frac{2}{\sqrt{\pi}}\,\varepsilon^{-x^2}$$

$\pi = 3 \downarrow$ **0,4,6,3,1,9,3,0,** $= \overline{114478742,}|$

$\varepsilon = \downarrow$ **10,4,7,1,0,0,3,8,** $= \overline{100005025,}|$

$10\,y = 4{\cdot}2087962 = 4 \downarrow$ **0,5,1,1,3,1,2,0,** $= \downarrow \overline{\mathbf{143724892,}}|$

or $y = \cdot 42087962$. being given.

$$\varepsilon^{x^2} = \frac{2}{y\sqrt{\pi}} = \frac{20}{10y\sqrt{\pi}}.$$

$$\begin{array}{rl}
10 = & 230270081 \\
2 = & \;\;69318201 \\
\hline
 & 299588282 \\
 & \;\;57239371 \ldots\ldots\ldots \sqrt{\pi} \\
\hline
 & 242348911 \\
10y = & 143724892 \\
\hline
 & \;\;98624019
\end{array}$$

When required, x is readily found; for 98624019 divided by 100005025, gives x^2. $\therefore\ x = \cdot 99307$.

$$x^2 = \frac{98624019}{100005025} = \frac{9 \downarrow 0,9,2,0,4,7,0,0,}{10 \downarrow 0,0,0,0,5,0,2,5,} = \frac{\overline{\downarrow 228884457,}|}{\overline{\downarrow 230275106,}|}$$

$$= -\overline{1390649,}|$$

$$\therefore\ x = -\overline{695325,}|$$

The area between the limits $x = 0$ and $x = x$, may be expressed by

$$\frac{2}{\sqrt{\pi}}\left(x - \frac{1}{1}\frac{x^3}{3} + \frac{1}{1.2}\frac{x^5}{5} - \frac{1}{1.2.3}\frac{\;}{7} + \frac{1}{1.2.3.4}\frac{x^9}{9} - \frac{1}{1.2.3.4.5}\frac{x^{11}}{11} + \ldots\right)$$

$$\begin{array}{rl}
2 \ldots\ldots\ldots + & 69318201 \\
- & 57239371 \ldots\ldots \sqrt{\pi} \\
\hline
\frac{2}{\sqrt{\pi}} \ldots\ldots\ldots & 12078830 \\
- & \;\;\;695325 \ldots\ldots x \\
\hline
\frac{2}{\sqrt{\pi}} x \ldots\ldots + & 11383505 = \downarrow 1,1,8,5,7,2,8,5, = 1\cdot 119983 + \\
 & \;\;9531497 \\
\hline
 & \;\;1852008 \\
 & \;\;\;995083 \\
\hline
 & \;\;\;856925 \\
 & \;\;\;799640 \\
\hline
 & \;\;\;5,7,2,8,5,
\end{array}$$

3 . . . . − 109866750
x^3 . . . . . − 2085975

− 111952725
$\frac{2}{\sqrt{\pi}}$ . . . . . + 12078830

− 99873895
10 . . . . . + 230270081

130396186 = 3 ↓ 2,1,4,7,1,5,3,9, . . . ·368362 −

5 . . . . − 160951879
2 . . . − 69318201
x^5 . . . . − 3476625

− 233746705
+ 12078830 . . . $\frac{2}{\sqrt{\pi}}$

− 221667875
10 . . . . + 230270081

8602206 = ↓ 0,8,6,6,1,8,1,2, ... ·1090044 +

7 . . . . . . − 194600795
1.2.3 − 179184951
x^7 . . . − 4867275

− 378653021
+ 12078830 . . . . $\frac{2}{\sqrt{\pi}}$

− 366574191
$(10)^2$ . . . . + 460540162

+ 93965971
2 . . . . − 69318201

+ 24647770 = ↓ 2,5,6,0,9,6,3,1, ... ·025590 −

9 . . . . − 219733500
1.2.3.4 . . . . . − 317821353
x^9 . . . . − 6257925

− 543812778
+ 12078830 . . . . $\frac{2}{\sqrt{\pi}}$

− 531733948
$(10)^3$ . . . . . + 690810243

159076295

```
              159076295 = 4↓2,1,3,8,1,9,5,1,
4 .......     138636402
              ---------
               20439893
```

Divide by $(10)^8$, the result will be + ·004907, the next term.

```
       11 ....... − 23980 1 5 7 8
1.2.3.4.5 .... − 47877 3 2 3 2
      x^11 ..... −    7648 5 7 5
                 ---------------
               − 72622 3 3 8 5
             . +  1207 8 8 3 0 ....... 2/√π
                 ---------------
               − 71414 4 5 5 5
      10^4 ... + 92208 0 3 2 4
                 ---------------
               + 20793 5 7 6 9 = 8↓0,0,0,1̄,8̄,8̄,3̄,5̄, = ·000800
        8 ... − 20795 4 6 0 4
                 ---------------
  negative            1,8,8,3,5,
```

7·9986 divided by 10^4 gives ·000800 −

The next step gives ·000111 +

```
                    1·119983 +
                      368362 −
                    --------
                     ·751621
                     ·109004 +
                    --------
                     ·860625
                      025590 −
                    --------
                     ·834035
                     ·004907 +
                    --------
                     ·838942
                     ·000800 −
                    --------
                     ·838142
                     ·000111 +
                    --------
Area of curve =     ·838253
```

11. *Find the ordinate y, and area of the curve whose equation is*

$$y = \frac{2}{\sqrt{\pi}} \epsilon^{-x^2} = \frac{2}{\sqrt{\pi}\,\epsilon^{x^2}}$$

between the limits $x = 0$, *and* $x = 2{\cdot}12084$.

$x^2 = 4{\cdot}497962 = 4 \downarrow 1,2,2,1,2,0,3,0, = \downarrow \overline{150370005,}|$

$2 \ldots\ldots + 69318201$

$\sqrt{\pi} \ldots\ldots - 57239371$

$+ 12078830$

$\epsilon^{x^2} \ldots\ldots - 449818802 = 4{\cdot}497962 \times 100003025$

$- 437739972 = \downarrow \overline{y,}|$

$10^2 \ldots + 460540162$

$22800190 = \downarrow 2,3,7,5,2,1,6,2, = 1{\cdot}25607209$

$\therefore\; y = {\cdot}0125607209$

The area of this curve between the limits $x = 0$, and $x = x$ may be expresed by

$$1 - \frac{1}{x\sqrt{\pi}\,\epsilon^{x^2}}\left(1 - \frac{1}{2x^2} + \frac{1.3}{2^2 x^4} - \frac{1.3.5}{2^3 x^6} + \ldots\right)$$

$\frac{1}{x\sqrt{\pi}\,\epsilon^{x^2}} = - 582243176$

$10^8 = + 690810243$

$108567067 = 2 \downarrow 4,1,1,2,7,8,4,0, = 2{\cdot}9612632$

$\therefore$ First term $= {\cdot}0029613$

$\frac{1}{2x^3\sqrt{\pi}\,\epsilon^{x^2}} = - 801931382$

$+ 921080324 = 10^4$

$119148942 = 3 \downarrow 0,9,3,2,6,5,8, = 3{\cdot}2917839$

$\therefore$ Second term $= {\cdot}0003292$.

$$\frac{1.3}{2^2 x^5 \sqrt{\pi}\, \epsilon^{x^2}} = -\ 911752838$$
$$+\ 921080324 = 10^4$$
$$9327486 = \downarrow 0,9,3,7,1,8,7,3, = 1{\cdot}0977584$$

∴ Third term = ·0001098.

$$\frac{1.3.5}{2^3 x^7 \sqrt{\pi}\, \epsilon^{x^2}} = -\ 970489165$$
$$+\ 1151350405 = 10^5$$
$$180861240 = 6 \downarrow 0,1,6,8,1,4,7,6,$$
$$= (1{\cdot}0169034) \times 6$$

∴ Fourth term = ·0000610.

The fifth term will be = ·0000474577; hence

$$\begin{array}{rl} 1{\cdot}0000000 & + \\ {\cdot}0029613 & - \\ \hline {\cdot}9970387 & \\ 3292 & + \\ \hline {\cdot}9973679 & \\ 1098 & - \\ \hline {\cdot}9972581 & \\ 610 & + \\ \hline \end{array}$$

Area = ·9973191, nearly.

12. *The apparent distance of the centres of the planet Venus and the moon* = 76° 14′ 47″ (*D*), *the apparent altitude of the moon's centre* = 46° 36′ 27″ (*A*), *the true altitude* = 47° 12′ 47″ (*a*), *the apparent altitude of Venus* = 20° 25′ 10″ (*B*), *and her true altitude* = 20° 22′ 54″ (*b*); *determine the true distance* (*d*), *so that the longitude of the place of observation may be found.*

$$\cos d = \left\{\cos D + \cos (A + B)\right\} \frac{\cos a \cos b}{\cos A \cos B} - \cos (a + b).$$

$$\cos(A+B) = \cdot 3902982 \qquad \cos(a+b) = \cdot 3811556$$
$$\cos D = \cdot 2377471$$
$$\overline{\cdot 6280453}$$

$$\cos a = \cdot 6792741 \qquad \cos b = \cdot 9373934$$
$$\cos A = \cdot 6869924 \qquad \cos B = \cdot 9371636$$

$$\cos a \downarrow 0,1,1,3,4,8,7, = \cos A$$
$$\cos B \downarrow 0\ 0\ 0,2,4,5,2, = \cos b$$

$$\therefore \quad \cos d = \cdot 6280453 \frac{\downarrow 0,0,0,2,4,5,2,}{\downarrow 0,1,1,3,4,8,7} - \cdot 3811556$$

$$= \cdot 6280453 \downarrow 0,\overline{1,1,1,0,3,5}, - \cdot 3811556$$
$$= \cdot 2399859 \text{ cos of } 76^\circ\ 6'\ 51''\cdot 4, \text{ the true distance.}$$

13. *Find the value of x in the equation*

$$347\cdot 6392\, x^3 - 84\cdot 35216\, x^2 + 413\cdot 6645\, x = 4582575\cdot 36\,;\ (R).$$

Omitting the decimals, and examining the equation

$$347\, x^3 - 84\, x^2 + 413\, x = 4500000,$$

it is easily observed that a value of x lies between 10 and 30. If 20 be substituted for x, the result will be

$$+ 2781113\cdot 6 - 33740\cdot 864 + 8273\cdot 29 = 2755646\cdot 026\,;\ (r).$$

The result (r) is sufficiently near to (R) to effect the solution, for it is possible to render $r \downarrow a_1, a_2, a_3, a_4 \ldots = R$.

278	once	+ 2|78	
2	$\frac{2}{3}$	− | 3	
0	$\frac{1}{3}$	+ |	
276		2|75	take
		4|58	from (R)
		2|76) 1|83 (↓6,	

The quotient $\downarrow$ 6, may be found by mere observation, without setting down any figures, and the process may be continued by operating with $\downarrow$ 5, for x^8.

$\downarrow$ 5,	$\downarrow$ 3,3,1,9,1,9,6,2,	$\downarrow$ 1,6,3,8,3,9,6,8,
+ 278111360	− 3374086	+ 827329
+ 447901127	− 4635874	+ 969763

44|79 +	once	+ 44|79 . . . . .
|30 −	$\frac{2}{3}$ of	− |46 . . . . .
| 3 +	$\frac{1}{3}$ of	+ | 9 . . . . .
44|52		44|42 . . . . . take
		45|82 . . . . . from (*R*)
		1|40 ($\downarrow$ 0,3,

$\downarrow$ 0,3,	$\downarrow$ 0,2,	$\downarrow$ 0,1,
+ 447901127	− 4635874	+ 969763
+ 461472979.	− 4729065	+ 979461

46 |4 +	once	+ 461|47 . . . .
|2 −	$\frac{2}{3}$ of	− 4|72 . . . .
|3 +	$\frac{1}{3}$ of	+ |97 . . . .
458|5.		457|72 . . . . take
		458|25 . . . . from (*R*).
		|53 . . . . ($\downarrow$ 0,0,1,

$\downarrow$ 0,0,1,	$\downarrow$ 0,0,0,6,6,6,3,7,	$\downarrow$ 0,0,0,3,3,3,1,8,
+ 461472979	− 4729065	+ 979461
+ 461934452	− 4732216	+ 979787

+ 4619|34 . . .
− 47|32 . . .
+ 9|79 . . .

4581|82 . . . take
4582|57 . . . from (*R*)

|75 ($\downarrow$ 0,0,0,1,

↓ 0,0,0,1,	↓ 0,0,0,0,6,6,6,6,	↓ 0,0,0,0,3,3,3,3
+ 461934452	− 4732216	+ 979787
+ 461980645	− 4732531	+ 979819

46198 +	once	+ 46198|0645
315 −	⅝ of	− 473|2531
		45724|8114
32 +	⅓ of	+ 97|9819
45915)		45822|7933 take
		45825|7536 from (*R*)
		2|9603
		2|7549 (↓ 0,0,0,0,6,4,4,7,
		2054
		1837
		217
		184
		33
		32

$\therefore\ x^3 = (20)^3$ ↓ 5,3,1,1,6,4,4,7,

$\therefore\ x = (20)$ ↓ 1,7,4,2,2,7,6,9, $= 23{\cdot}6868595$ (*R*).

14. *Given,* $x^2 + 1{\cdot}41421356\,x = 1{\cdot}73205081$, *to find the value of* x.

As x is situated between ·1 and 1·, operations may be commenced with either ·5, ·6, or ·7. When $x = {\cdot}7$, the equation becomes

$$+\ {\cdot}490000000 + {\cdot}989949492 = 1{\cdot}479949492$$

9|80 +	twice	+ 4|90 . . . . . .
9|89 +	once	+ 9|89 . . . . . .
19|69		14|79 . . . . . . take
		17|32 . . . . . . from (*R*)
		2|53 (↓ 1,

↓ 2,

+ 490000000

+ 592900000

```
 11|858 +     twice
 10|889 +     once
 ------
 22|747
```

↓ 1,

+ 989949492

+ 1088944441

```
+  5|929 . . . . .
+ 10|889 . . . . .
  ---------
   16|818 . . . . . take
   17|320 . . . . . from (R)
  ---------
     |502  (↓ 0,2,
```

↓ 0,4,

+ 592900000

+ 616974118

```
123|38 +     twice
111|08 +     once
-------
234|46
```

↓ 0,2,

+ 1088944441

+ 1110832224

```
+  61|69 . . . . .
+ 111|08 . . . . .
  ---------
   172|77 . . . . . take
   173|20 . . . . . from (R)
  ---------
      |43  (↓ 0,0,1,
```

↓ 0,0,2,

+ 616974118

+ 618208683

```
12364 +     twice
11119 +     once
-------
23483
```

↓ 0,0,1,

+ 1110832224

+ 1111943056

```
+  618|208683
+ 1111|943056
  -------------
   1730|151739 take
   1732|050810 from (R)
  -------------
      1|899071
      1|87864   (↓ 0,0,0,8,0,8,6,
     ----------
        2043
        1879
       ------
         164
```

$\therefore\ x = \cdot 7$ ↓ 1,2,1,8,0,8,6, $= \cdot 7868982.$

15. *Find a value of x in the equation*

$$2{\cdot}7634x^5 + 12{\cdot}349x^4 - 542{\cdot}36x^3 - 7621{\cdot}3x = -174859{\cdot}34\ (R).$$

A value of x evidently lies between 1 and 10; 5, 6, or 7, may be substituted for x, but 7 is most convenient. 7 being substituted, the equation becomes

$$+46444{\cdot}4638 + 29649{\cdot}949 - 186029{\cdot}48 - 53349{\cdot}7 = -163284{\cdot}13872.$$

Working to three places of decimals to find x^5, the first factor may be found thus:—

+ 4|64 +	once	+ 4|64	
+ 2|37 +	$\frac{4}{8}$ of	+ 2|96	
− 11|16 −	$\frac{3}{8}$ of	− 18|60	
− 1|06 −	$\frac{1}{8}$ of	− 5|33	
5|21		− 16|32	take
		− 17|48	from (R)
		− 1 16 (↓2,	

↓2,	↓1,5,7,4,3,7,9,8,	↓1,1,9,1,1,6,2,1,	↓0,3,8,2,7,7,1,
+ 46444464	+ 29649949	− 186029480	− 53349100
+ 56197802	+ 34534427	− 208570554	− 55422253

+ 56|1 +	once	+ 56|197 . . .	
+ 27|6 +	$\frac{4}{8}$ of	+ 34|534 . . .	
− 125|1 −	$\frac{3}{8}$ of	− 208|570 . . .	
− 11|0 −	$\frac{1}{8}$ of	− 55|422 . . .	
− 52|4		− 173|260 . . .	take
		− 174|859 . . .	from (R)
		− 1|598 . . . (↓0,3,	

↓0,3,	↓0,2,3,9,8,1,6,8,	↓0,1,7,9,6,3,8,1,	↓0,0,5,9,7,2,7,5,
+ 56197802	+ 34534427	− 208570554	− 55422253
+ 57900651	+ 35369063	− 212339831	− 55754126

+ 579	once	+ 579|00 . . .
+ 282	$\frac{4}{5}$ of	+ 353|69 . . .
− 1274	$\frac{3}{5}$ of	− 2123|39 . . .
− ·111	$\frac{1}{5}$ of	− 557|54 . . .
− 523		1748|24 . . .
		1748|59 . . .
		|35 . . . (↓0,0,0,6,

↓0,0,0,6,	↓0,0,0,4,8,	↓0,0,0,3,6,	↓0,0,0,1,2,
+ 579006511	+ 35369063	− 212339831	− 55754126
+ 57935400	+ 35386044	− 212416283	− 55760816

+ 57935	once	+ 57935|400
+ 28309	$\frac{4}{5}$ of	+ 35386|044
+ 86244		+ 93321|444
− 127449	$\frac{3}{5}$ of	− 212416|283
− 41205		− 119094|839
− 11152	$\frac{1}{5}$ of	− 55760|816
− 52357		− 174855|655 take
+		− 174859|340 from (*R*)
		3|685
		3|665 (↓0,0,0,0,7,

$\therefore\ x^5 = 7^5$ ↓2,3,0,6,7,0,0,0,

$\therefore\ x = 7$ ↓0,4,4,4,2,8,9,6, $= 7{\cdot}31654917$

16. *Find the value of x to eight places of figures in the equation*

$$789x^7 - 678x^6 + 567x^5 + 456x^4 - 345x^3 - 234x^2 + 123x$$
$$= 9654321012345 67. \quad (R).$$

A value of x lies between 0, and 100; take $x = 50$, then the result will be

$$616406250000000 - 10593750000000 + 177187500000$$
$$+ 2850000000 - 43125000 - 585000 + 6150$$
$$= 605992493796150.$$

Since the value of x is only required to eight places of figures, the numbers to be operated upon will be

↓4.	↓3,4,1,0,4,6,4,	↓2,8,1,0,9,3,	↓2,2,7,3,
+ 616406250	− 10593750	+ 177188	+ 2850
	↓1,7,		
	− 43 − 1	= 605992494	
↓0,8,	↓0,6,8,5,3,2,8,8,	↓0,5,7,1,1,	↓0,4,5,7,
+ 902480319	− 14688162	+ 232416	+ 3544
	↓0,3,		
	− 50 − 1	= 888028066	
↓0,0,3,	↓0,0,2,5,7,1,1,7,	↓0,0,2,1,4,3,	↓0,0,1,7,
+ 977256943	− 15725329	+ 246014	+ 3709
	− 52 − 1	= 961781284	
↓0,0,0,7,	↓0,0,0,6,	↓0,0,5,	↓0,0,0,4,
+ 980191647	− 15765797	+ 246542	+ 3716
	− 52 − 1	= 964676055	
+ 980877877	− 15775258	+ 246665	+ 3717
	− 52 − 1	= 965352948	

The divisor that determines the next operating numbers, may be employed to find the remaining figures that compose the root; the work will stand as follows:

+ 98088	once	+ 98087	7877
− 1352	$\frac{6}{7}$ of	− 1577	5258
96736		96510	2619
18	$\frac{5}{7}$ of	+ 24	6665
0	$\frac{4}{7}$ of	+	3717
96754		96535	3001
·∸†			53
		96535	2948

$$\begin{array}{r|l}
96535 & 2948 \text{ take} \\
96543 & 2101 \text{ from } (R) \\
\hline
7 & 9153 \\
7 & 7403 \ (8, \\
\hline
 & 1750 \\
 & 968 \ (1, \\
\hline
 & 782 \\
 & 774 \ (8, \\
\hline
 & 8 \\
 & 9 \ (1, \\
\hline
\end{array}$$

$$x^7 = (50)^7 \downarrow 4,8,3,7,8,1,8,1,$$

$$\therefore \quad x = 50 \downarrow 0,6,6,6,7,5,8,6,$$

$$\therefore \quad x = 53{\cdot}4313588$$

17. *Given* $x_x = 72{\cdot}69517$, *to find the value of* x.

$$72{\cdot}69517 = 10{\cdot}7 \downarrow 0,3,7,9,3,2,2,6, = \downarrow \overline{428649036,}|$$

Because $3 = \downarrow \overline{109866750,}|$ and $4 = \downarrow \overline{138636402,}|$ the value of x must lie between 3 and 4; for if $\downarrow \overline{X,}|$ represents the reduction of x, in the same way that $\downarrow \overline{109866750,}|$ represents 3, then

$$x \times X = 428649036.$$

Consequently $\quad 3 \times 109866750$ is too small

and $\quad 4 \times 138636402$ is too great

$\therefore$ The first part of the expression for x may be represented by $3 \downarrow 1$, Putting A for 9531497, B for 995083, and C for 99955, D for 10000, &c., the value of x may be found as follows :—

$$\downarrow \overline{428649036,}| \ (n)$$

```
 3 = 109866750
↓1 =   9531497(A)
     ---------
     119398247
             3
     ---------
     3|5|8|1|9|4|7|4|1
      |3|5|8|1|9|4|7|4
     -----------------
  (o)394014215
       1313·50964(b)
     ------------
     40|7 1|49|3 1|1.
      1|6 2|8 5|9 7|2.
          2|4 4|2 9|0.
             1|6 2|9.
                  |4.
     ------------
  (p)423681206
       2059470 6(c)
     ------------
     425|740|676
       2|554|444
           6|386
               9
     ------------
  (q)428301515
        138188 4(d)
     ------------
     428439703...
        171376...
            26...
     ------------
  (r)428611105 take
  (n)428649036 from
     ------------
7742)    37931
 ....    30968 (4
         -----
          6963
          6194 (8
          ----
           769
           697 (9
           ---
            72
            70 (9
            --
```

```
(o) 394...  (n)  4286...
(b) 328...  (o)  3940...
    ----         -------
    722)         346(↓0,4,

(p) 4236... (n)  42864...
(c) 3432... (p)  42368...
    ----         --------
    7668)        496(↓0,0,6,

(q) 428301... (n) 428649...
(d) 34547     (q) 428301...
    ------        ---------
    773771)       348(↓0,0,0,4,

(r) 4286
(d) 3456
    ----
    7742
```

```
  995083(B)
       3
  -------
  2|9|8|5|2|4|9
   |2|9|8|5|2|5
  -------------
  3283774(b)

  99955(c)
      3
  -----
  2|9|9|8|6|5
   |2|9|9|8|7
  -----------
  329852
   13194
     198
       1
  ------
  343245(C)

  10000(D)
      3
  -----
  3|0|0|0|0
   |3|0|0|0
  ---------
  33|000.
   1|320.
      20.
  -------
  34340.
    206.
      1.
  ------
  34547

  1000 (E)
     3
  ----
  3|0|0|0
   |3|0|0
  -------
  3300
   132
     2
  ----
  343|4 ..
    2|1 ..
  --------
  3455|....
     1|....
  ---------
  3456 (d)
```

$\therefore \quad x = 3\downarrow\mathbf{1,4,6,4,4,8,9,9,} = 3{\cdot}45620015$

As an independent and direct solution of the equation $x^x = a$ has not been attempted by any mathematician, the work of this first general and direct solution is given at length, with exception of that which determined $\downarrow$**1,** ; and although this part of the root may he found by mere inspection, yet it may be desirable to find $\downarrow$**1,** in a formal manner.

```
(m) 329.....*   (n) 428...        3 = 109866750,   ↓428649036,| (n)
(a) 285.....    (m) 329...                    3
    614)            99 (↓1,  (m) 329600250         9531497 (A)
                                                         3
                                                  28594491 (a)
```

18. *Given*

$x^x = 8722{\cdot}83528 = 10^{3}{\cdot}8\downarrow 0,8,6,9,0,3,2,0, = \downarrow \overline{907415561,}|$

to find the value of x.

$6 = \downarrow \overline{179184951,}|$

$5 = \downarrow \overline{160951879,}|$

Hence x must be situated between 5 and 6.

```
(m) 804|7....*   (n) 9074.....        160951879    907415561 (n)
(a) 476|5....    (m) 8047.....                5
    1281|2           1027        (m) 804759395     9531497 (A)
                                                         5
                                                  47657485 (a)
```

Since 1281 is contained in 1027, no times the first part of the root must be 5 $\downarrow$ 0,

```
(m) 8|04....**   (n) 907......        160951879      907415561, (n)
(b) 4|97....     (m) 804......                5
    13|01 )          103 (↓0,7,  (m) 804759395          995083 (B)
                                     34827905 7(b)           5
                                    839587300 ↓7|      4975415 (b)
                                (p) 900151226
```

(*b*), (*m*), and (*n*), being found, the next part of the root ↓0,7, becomes known, because 13 is contained in 103 seven times. Seven times (*b*) is then added to (*m*), and the sum multipled by ↓0,7, (written ↓7,|) when (*p*) is produced.

```
(p) 900...***        (n) 9074.....          (p) 900151226
(c)  535...          (p) 9001.....                2679135   5 (c)
    ------               ---------          -------------
    1435)                    73 (↓0,0,5,        902830361   ↓|5,|
                                            (q) 907353550

                     99955   (C)
                         5
                     ------
                    499775   ↓7,|
                    535827   (c)
```

(*c*) being found, and (*n*) and (*p*) being known, the next figure of the root is found to be ↓0,0,5, (written ↓|5,|); then 5 (*c*) is added to (*p*), and the sum multiplied by ↓|5,| which gives (*q*).

```
(q) 9073|.****       (n) 9074|155..         (q) 907353550
(d) 5387|.           (q) 9073|535..
    -----                -----------
    14460|.                  |620..  ↓,0,0,0,0,

                     10000   (D)
                         5
                     -----
                     50000   ↓0,7,5,
                     53876   (d)
```

This step gives ↓0,0,0,0, for the next part of the root, which is now determined as far as 5↓0,7,5,0,

```
(q) 9073*****        (n) 9074155..          (q) 907353550
(e)  5388            (q) 9073535..                  21552   4 (e)
    ------               ---------          -------------
    14461)                  620.. (↓4,|         907375102   ↓4,|
                                            (r) 907411402

                      1000   (E)
                         5
                      ----
                      5000   ↓0,7,5,0,
                      5388   (e)
```

It is evident that the divisor 14461 remains constant, and that the remainder of the root may be found by common division.

```
                    (n)  907415561,
                    (r)  907411402
                         ---------
14461                         4159  (2,
  ··†                         2892
                              ----
                              1267  (8,
                              1156
                              ----
                               111  (8,
                               115
                              ----
```

$$\therefore\quad x = 5\downarrow 0,7,5,0,4,2,8,8, = 5{\cdot}38776485$$

The operations of each step are particularized to show that the process is conducted with certainty, and not depending on conjecture.

19. *Required the value of x in the equation*
$(\sin x)^{\log. x} = 2{\cdot}69919746 = 2\downarrow 3,1,3,9,2,8,7,2, = \downarrow\overline{99300512,}|$, (n),
supposing the logarithms to be hyperbolic and the radius = 10.

Put $e =$ 100005025, $\downarrow\overline{x,}| = x$, $\downarrow\overline{s,}| =$ sine x, reduced to the extent of (n) or $\downarrow\overline{99300512,}|$; and let $1 \frown 3$ represent the continued product 1.2.3, $1 \frown 5$ the continued product 1.2.3.4.5, and so on.

Then because $(\log. x)\ (\log. \sin x) = \log. n$.

$$\therefore\quad \frac{\downarrow\overline{x,}|}{e} \times \frac{\downarrow\overline{s,}|}{e} = \frac{n}{e}$$

$$\text{or } \downarrow\overline{x,}| \times \downarrow\overline{s,}| = \frac{n \times e}{e} = 9930552, \ (m).$$

In the sequel it will be shown that

$$\downarrow\overline{x,}| = \downarrow\overline{100274740,}| = \downarrow 0,0,2,7,4,4,6,7,$$

$$\text{and } \downarrow\overline{s,}| = \overline{99033417,}| \text{ ; then}$$

$$99033417 \downarrow 0,0,2,7,4,4,6,7, = 99305502. \ (m)$$

Since $\downarrow\overline{x,}| \times \downarrow\overline{(x - \frac{x^3}{1 \frown 3} + \frac{x^5}{1 \frown 5} - \frac{x^7}{1 \frown 7} + \ldots),}|$ $= 99305502$, (m) it is easily observed that the square root of $(m), = 99652110$, is very little greater than $\downarrow\overline{(x - \frac{x^3}{1 \frown 3} + \frac{x^5}{1 \frown 5} - \ldots),}|$ but not as great as $\downarrow\overline{x,}|$. If $\downarrow\overline{100000000,}|$ be taken $= \downarrow\overline{x,}|$ the corresponding value of $\downarrow\overline{(x - \frac{x^3}{1 \frown 3} + \frac{x^5}{1 \frown 5} - \ldots),}|$ will be found $= 98770506$, then

993	993|055|02	(m)
987	987|705|06	(r)
1980	5|349|96	$(\downarrow 0,0,2,7,.$
	3 960|	
	1 389	
	1 386	

Putting $\downarrow \ldots$ for the required expression, then because ultimately

$$r \downarrow \ldots = \frac{m}{\downarrow \ldots}$$

$$\text{or } r + \downarrow \ldots = m - \downarrow \ldots$$

$$\therefore \ 2 \downarrow \ldots = m - r$$

which establishes the method of obtaining the consecutive numbers of the expression $\downarrow 0,0,2,7, \ldots$; the whole of this result might be employed as part of the value of $\downarrow\overline{x,}|$, but for the purpose of illustration, only $\downarrow 0,0,2,$ will be next employed.

100000000 ↓ 0,0,2, = ↓ 100200100, = 2 ↓ 3,2,2,9,7,3,3,2,
= 272358946.

+ 100200100
10 = − 230270081
− 130069981
3
− 390209943
1.2.3 − 179184951
− 569394894
+ 690810243
121415349 = ·003 ↓ 1,2,0,2,6,9,3,6, = ·003367237

− 130069981
5
− 650349905
1 ⌒ 5 = − 478773232
− 1129123137
10^5 = + 1151350405
22227268 = ·00001 ↓ 2,3,1,7,9, . . . = ·000012489

− 130069987
7
− 910489867
1 ⌒ 7 = − 852558978
− 1763048845
10^8 = + 1842160648
79111803 = ·00000002 ↓ 1,0,2, . . . = ·000000022

·272358946 +
·003367237 −
12489 +
22 −
269004176 = 2 ↓ 3,1,0,5,2,8,7,0, = ↓ 98969045,

98960645 ↓ **0,0,2,** =	9915|8665 take	
	9930|5502 (m) from	
9915	14|6837	
9930	13|8915	(↓ **0,0,0,7,4,**
19845 ...	7922	
	7938	

Again, if ↓ **0,0,2,7,** = ↓ $\overline{\textbf{100270261,}}$| be substituted for ↓ $\overline{x}$,| the result 99296696 is obtained; then

99305 ...	99305|502 (m)	
99296 ...	99296|696	
198601	8|806	(↓ **0,0,0,0,4,4,**
†	7|944	
	862	
	794	

If greater accuracy be required, ↓ **0,0,2,7,4,4,** when substituted for ↓ $\overline{x}$,| gives ↓ **002,7,4,4,6,7,** = 100274740, the value of ↓ $\overline{x}$,| to nine places of figures.

But ↓ $\overline{\textbf{100274740,}}$| = 2 ↓ **3,2,3,7,2,0,1,7,** = 2·725623, which is the length of an arc of 15° 37′ to radius 10.

DUAL ARITHMETIC.

PART I.

DEFINITIONS AND ELEMENTARY PROPOSITIONS.

BECAUSE this system of Arithmetic requires numbers to be viewed under two aspects, and to distinguish it from other systems of operating upon numbers, I have called it DUAL ARITHMETIC. By this new art, a number representing any given magnitude, or the function of any given magnitude, may be made to assume a form composed of factors of whole numbers having a known relation to one another; and these derived whole numbers may be readily made to assume a variety of forms, each form always reducible to the given number or magnitude; and hence the derived numbers, by a peculiar arrangement, may be developed to suit different operations; and the factors produced after such operations are performed, are easily converted into natural numbers expressing the required results.

The more general development of this system will be given in the Author's works on Algebra and the Calculus; in the propositions that follow, the object is rather to establish new Arithmetical processes than to perform operations with conciseness.

PROPOSITION I.

TO MULTIRLY ANY GIVEN NUMBER BY ANY GIVEN POWER OF 1·1, 1·01, 1·001, 1·0001, 1·00001, ETC.

When the powers are whole-numbers, the multiplication is performed by the aid of the co-efficients of any binomial $(x + y)$ raised to the proposed power.

$(x + y)^1 = x + y$, the co-efficients are 1, 1.

$(x + y)^2 = x^2 + 2xy + y^2$, the co-efficients are 1, 2, 1.

$(x + y)^3 = x^3 + 3x^2y + 3xy^2 + y^3$, the co-efficients are 1, 3, 3, 1.

The co-efficients of $(x + y)^4$ are 1, 4, 6, 4, 1.
" " $(x + y)^5$ " 1, 5 10, 10, 5, 1.
" " $(x + y)^6$ " 1, 6, 15, 20, 15, 6, 1.
" " $(x + y)^7$ " 1, 7, 21, 35, 35, 21, 7, 1.
" " $(x + y)^8$ " 1, 8, 28, 56, 70, 56, 28, 8, 1.
" " $(x + y)^9$ " 1, 9, 36, 84, 126, 126, 84, 36, 9, 1.

The co-efficients of $(x + y)$, in any power, say the 20th, may be at once set down, without knowing the co-efficients of any other power, thus: the co-efficient of the first term is 1, and that of the second term 20, or

$x^{20} + 20x^{19}y$, are the two first terms of the development,

$\frac{20 \times 19}{2} = 190$, the co-efficient of the third term;

hence the three first terms of the development are

$$x^{20} + 20x^{19}y + 190x^{18}y^2.$$

Again, to find the co-efficient of the fourth term,

$\frac{190 \times 18}{3} = 1140$, co-eff. of 4th term.

$\frac{1140 \times 17}{4} = 4845$, co-eff. of 5th term.

$\frac{4845 \times 16}{5} = 15504$, co-eff. of 6th term.

In practice the co-efficients of such high powers are seldom required, but it will be found convenient to be able to set down the co-efficients without being obliged to refer to tables.

$$1, \quad 10, \quad \frac{10 \times 9}{2} = 45, \quad \frac{45 \times 8}{3} = 120, \quad \frac{120 \times 7}{4} = 210,$$

are the first five co-efficients of $(x + y)^{10}$, and set down with little mental exertion.

This method of finding the co-efficients of

$$(x+y)^n = x^n + nx^{n-1}y + \frac{n(n-1)}{1 \cdot 2}x^{n-2}y^2 + \frac{n(n-1)(n-2)}{1 \cdot 2 \cdot 3}x^{n-3}y^3 + \&c.$$

will be found more convenient, than by direct substitution. For example, when $n = 10$, the co-efficient of the 6th term, according to the series just given, is

$$\frac{n(n-1)(n-2)(n-3)(n-4)}{1 \cdot 2 \cdot 3 \cdot 4 \cdot 5} = \frac{10 \cdot 9 \cdot 8 \cdot 7 \cdot 6}{1 \cdot 2 \cdot 3 \cdot 4 \cdot 5} = 252.$$

Examples.

1. *Let it be required to multiply* 54247 *by* $(101)^6$, *true to ten places of figures.*

The number must be divided into

Single digits, when the multiplier is 11,
Periods of two figures „ „ 101,
„ three „ „ „ 1001,
„ four „ „ „ 10001,
and so on.

e	d	c	b	a			
	54	24	70	00	00	⌣ 1	
	3	25	48	20	00	⌣ 6	beginning at *a*
		8	13	70	50	⌣ 15	„ *b*
			10	84	94	⌣ 20	„ *c*
				8	14	⌣ 15	„ *d*
					3	⌣ 6	„ *e*

$54247 \times (101)^6 = 57\,58\,42\,83\,61$, true to ten places of figures.

Since the multipliers for the 6th power are

1, 6, 15, 20, 15, 6, 1;

begin at a, a period in advance, and multiply by 6; then commence at b, two periods in advance, and multiply by 15; at c, three periods in advance, and multiply by 20; at d, four periods in advance (counting from the right to the left), and multiply by 15; the period e should be multiplied by 6, but, as it is blank, only set down 3, which is obtained by multiplying d, or rather the first figure of d, by 6.

As it is very easy to operate with the co-efficients

1, 5, 10, 10, 5, 1,

the multipliers for the 5th power, it may be more convenient to multiply the given number by $(101)^5$, and then by $(101)^1$.

To multiply any number, as 54247, *by* 5, *affix a cypher, or suppose one affixed, half this number will be* 5 *times the given one,*

half of 542470 = 271235 = 5 times 54247.

e	d	c	b	a				
	54	24	70	00	00	⌣ 1		
	2	71	23	50	00	⌣ 5	beginning at	a
		5	42	47	00	⌣ 10	"	b
			5	42	47	⌣ 10	"	c
				2	71	⌣ 5	"	d
					1	⌣ 1	"	e

$54247 \times (101)^5 = 57|01|41\ 42\ 19|$

$|57|01|41|42|$

$57\ 58\ 42\ 83\ 61 = 54247 \times (101)^6.$

To render the operation clear, the decimal points are omitted, but the result is easily pointed, for

$$\cdot 54247 \times (1\cdot 01)^6 = \cdot 5758428361,$$
$$54\cdot 247 \times (1\cdot 01)^6 = 57\cdot 58428361,$$
$$\&c. \quad = \quad \&c.$$

The correctness of such results may be proved by common multiplication.

The multipliers for the different powers may be operated with in many ways: the present example will illustrate this remark:

6	15	20	15	6	1	
e	*d*	*c*	*b*	*a*		
	54	24	70	00	00	⌣ 1
	3	25	48	20	00	⌣ 6 . . . *a*
		8	13	70	50	⌣ 15 . . . *b*
			10	84	94	⌣ 20 . . . *c*
				8	14	⌣ 15 . . . *d*
					3	⌣ 6 . . . *e*

325482000 is found by multiplying the first line by 6, beginning with the period *a*; the next line may be obtained by multiplying the first line by 15, beginning at the period *b*, but it is known that 6 times the first line, beginning at the period *b*, is 3254820; 60 times it must therefore be 32548200, the quarter of which is 8137050 = 15 times the first line, beginning at the period *b*; so that the 15 line is found by little more than dividing the 6 line by 4. 20 times the first line, beginning at the period *c*, is found by doubling the first line, and adding a cypher. It seldom happens, in practice, that more than seven or eight places of figures are required, but these elementary examples are extended to a greater number of places, to make the simplicity of the method more apparent. Different plans of obtaining the same result, without altering the laws that govern the system, give proof and dexterity to the operator.

Without changing the example, let it be required to multiply by another method, 54247 by $(101)^6$, true to 12 places of figures.

				*			
54	24	70	00	00	00	put	= A
3	25	48	20	00	00	$6 \times A$	= B, beginning under *
	8	13	70	50	00	$\frac{5 \times B}{2}$	= C, ,, *
		10	84	94	00	$\frac{4 \times C}{3}$	= D, ,, *
			8	13	71	$\frac{3 \times D}{4}$	= E, ,, *
				3	25	$\frac{2 \times E}{5}$	= F, ,, *
					1	$\frac{1 \times F}{6}$	= G, ,, *

57 58 42 83 60 97, true to 12 places of figures.

If only six places of figures are required, the work is short and the calculations simple:

	*		
54	24	70	Put = A
3	25	48	$6 \times A \div 1 = B$
	8	14	$5 \times B \div 2 = C$
		11	$4 \times C \div 3 = D$

57 58 43

$5424{\cdot}7 \times 6 = 32548{\cdot}2.$
$325{\cdot}48 \times 5 \div 2 = 813{\cdot}70$, put down 814.
$8{\cdot}14 \times 4 \div 3 = 10{\cdot}85$, put down 11.

The next line is rejected, because the result obtained would not increase the required product a unit in sixth place of figures, reckoning from the left to the right.

c	*b*	*a*		
54	24	70	⌣ 1	
3	25	48	⌣ 6 times, beginning at the period	*a*
	8	14	⌣ 15 ,, ,, ,,	*b*
		11	⌣ 20 ,, ,, ,,	*c*

$5424{\cdot}7 \times 6 = 32548{\cdot}2$
$54{\cdot}24 \times 15 = 813{\cdot}6$, put down 814.
$\cdot 54 \times 20 = 10{\cdot}80$, put down 11.

2. *Multiply* 34567812 *by* $(10001)^8$, *so that the result may be true to* 12 *places of figures.*

The multipliers for the 8th power are 1, 8, 28, 56, 70, 56, 28, 8, 1.

d	*c*	*b*	*a*		
	3456	7812	0000	....	⌣ 1
	2	7654	2496	....	⌣ 8 times, *a*
		9	6790	....	⌣ 28 times, *b*
			19	....	⌣ 56 times, *c*
	3459	5475	9305		

A blank period of dots may be affixed to facilitate the operation; with dots 56 times the first line, beginning at *c*, is thus found, 56 times 6 gives a dot, 56 times 5 gives a dot, 56 times 4 gives a dot and carry 22, 56 times 3 gives 168, to which add 22 = 190, put down a dot, and place 19 under the next period.

The work is very easy when 28 times is found, as 9·67, &c. is found for 28 times, the double of which is 19·34, put down 19.

28 times the first line, beginning at *b*, is readily found, when 8 times is known. Double the first line, with 0 affixed, gives 691356240, putting dots for 4 of the figures.

69136	20 times,	beginning at	*b*
27654	8	„ „	*b*
96790	28	„ „	*b*

Hence, when 8 times is found, 28 times and 56 times may be obtained by little more than inspection. However, results are seldom required to more than 7 or 8 places of figures; if the product of 34567812 by $(10001)^8$ is only required to 7 places of figures, the work is much contracted, and may be arranged as follows:—

	*		
3456	7812	....	⌣ Put = A.
2	7654	....	⌣ $8 \times A \div 1 = B$, beginning under *
	10	....	⌣ $7 \times B \div 2 = C$, „ *

3459 548, true to 7 places of figures.

$8 \times A \div 1$, beginning under *, is worked thus: 8 times 2 gives a dot, 8 times 1 gives a dot, 8 times 8 gives a dot, but carry 6; 8 times 7 are 56, and 6 are 62, put down a 4th dot and carry 6; then 8 times 6 are 48, and 6 are 54, put down 4 and carry 5, and continue the multiplication in the common way. $7 \times B \div 2$, beginning under *, is readily found, thus: 7 times 4 gives a dot, 7 times 5 gives a dot, 7 times 6 gives a dot, but carry 4; 7 times 7 and 4 gives a dot, but carry 5; 7 times 2 and 5 = 19, the half of which is 9·5 and may be counted 10. So that but little mental labour is employed, although it takes many words to explain the operation.

To find the first 12 figures of the product of 34567812 by $(10001)^8$, the remaining multipliers, 70, 56, 28, 8, 1, are not required. Perhaps the required result might be obtained with greater ease by first multiplying 34567812 by $(10001)^5$, and the product thus found by $(10001)^3$; by this plan the work may be arranged as follows :—

c	*b*	*a*	
3456	7812	0000	◡ 1
1	7283	9060	◡ 5, *a*
	3	4568	◡ 10, *b*
		3	◡ 10, *c*
3458	5099	3631	◡ 1,
1	0375	5298	◡ 3, *a*
	1	0376	◡ 3, *b*
		0	◡ 1, *c*

3459 5475 9305, result as before.

With a blank period of dots the work will stand thus:

c	*b*	*a*	
3456	7812	0000	. . . . ◡ 1
1	7283	9060	. . . . ◡ 5, *a*
	3	4568	. . . . ◡ 10, *b*
		3	. . . . ◡ 10, *c*
3458	5099	3631	. . . . ◡ 1
1	0375	5298	. . . . ◡ 3, *a*
	. 1	0376	. . . . ◡ 3, *b*
		0	. . . . ◡ 1, *c*

3459 5475 9305

3. *Required the continued product of* 1·2345678, $(1·01)^4$, $(1·001)^5$, *and* $(1·0001)^6$, *true to 7 places of figures.*

```
|12|34|56|78 ◡ 1
   |49|38|27 ◡ 4
      |74|07 ◡ 6
         |49 ◡ 4
----------------
 128|469|6 . . ◡  1
    |642|3 . . ◡  5
    |  1|3 . . ◡ 10
----------------
 1291|132 . ◡  1
     |775 . ◡  6
        0 . ◡ 15
----------------
 1·291907 =
```

1·291907 = the first seven figures of the continued product of $1·2345678 \times (1·01)^4 \times (1·001)^5 \times (1·0001)^6$; which may be written,

$$1·2345678 \downarrow 0,4,5,6, \doteq 1·291907.$$

The arrow ↓ divides the co-efficient 1·2345678 and the powers of 1·1, 1·01, 1·001, 1·0001, &c. 0, immediately follows the arrow, because no power of 1·1 is employed; 6, is in the fourth place after ↓, and shows that this power operated upon periods of four figures each; 5 being in the third place after ↓, shows, by its position, that its influence is over periods of three figures each; and 4 occupies the second place after ↓, and reminds the operator that its influence is over periods of two figures each.

4. *Required the first* 9 *figures of the continued product of* 32·808992, $(1·01)^7$, *and* $(1·001)^9$; *or, according to the notation just adopted, the value of*

$$32·808992 \downarrow 0,7,9,$$

is required to nine places of figures.

Dots take the place of figures not required in the last period.

e	d	c	b	a				
	32	80	89	92	0 .	1		
	2	29	66	29	4 .	7 times,	beginning at	a
		6	88	98	9 .	21 „	„	b
			11	48	3 .	35 „	„	c
				11	5 .	35 „	„	d
					1 .	21 „	„	e
	35	17	56	80	2			

The way in which this result may be found is worth noting; but little mental labour is necessary, the co-efficients or multipliers being

1, 7, 21, 35, 35, 21, 7, 1,

when 7 times the first line (commencing with the period marked *a*) is found, 21 times the same line (commencing with the period marked *b*) may be determined by multiplying the second line by 3, beginning under *a*. Again, 35 times the first line, commencing with the period *c*, gives the same result as multiplying the second line by 5, commencing under *b*; but 5 times a number may be found by moving the decimal point one figure to the right, and then take the half.

22966·3 ◡ 7 times, beginning at *b*.
half = 114831, ◡ 35 times.
= 11483· putting a dot for the figure not required. Since the example requires that 351756802, is to be again multiplied by $(1·001)^9$, the remainder of the work may stand as follows :—

c	b	a				
	351	756	802	◡ 1,		
	3	165	811	◡ 9	beginning at	a
		12	663	◡ 36	„	b
			30	◡ 84	„	c
	354	935	306			

The 9 times line, beginning at *a*, may be found by subtraction, thus,

351756·8	has to be multiplied by 9;
3517568	ten times
351757	once
3165811	9 times.

The line 36 times begins at *b*, observing to carry from the preceding figure as if it were a decimal, and making the usual allowance when the number is followed by 5, 6, 7, 8, or 9.

$$351·76 \times 36 = 12663 = 3165·8 \times 4.$$

To multiply by 84, beginning at *c*: the period *c*, or ·351, may be called ·352, as 7 follows the last figure,

$$84 \times ·352 = 29·568 = 30,$$

after the usual allowance is made.

Or the work may stand thus :—

351	756	802	put = A	
3	165	811	9 × A ÷ 1 = B beginning under	*
	12	663	8 × B ÷ 2 = C " "	*
		30	7 × C ÷ 3 = D " "	*
354	935	306		

$$\therefore\ 32·808992 \downarrow 0,7,9, = 35·4935306.$$

In operating with the co-efficients or multipliers many contractions will suggest themselves to the operator.

5. *Required the first 7 figures of the continued product of* 106, $(1·1)^2$, $(1·01)^6$, $(1·001)^7$, $(1·0001)^1$, $(1·00001)^6$, *and* $(1·000001)^2$; *or, which is the same thing, find the first 7 figures of* 106 ↓ **2,6,7,1,6,2,**

```
|1|0|6|0|0|0|0
   |2|1|2|0|0|0
     |1|0|6|0|0
_______________
|1 2|8 2|6 0|0 .
    |7 6|9 5|6 .
       1|9 2|4 .
           2|6 .
_________________
|1 3 6|1 5 0|6 . .
      |9 5 3|1 . .
           2|9 . .
___________________
 1 3 7 1|0 6 6 .   .
        |1 3 7 .
___________________
 1 3 7 1 2|0 3 . . .
           8 2 . . .
_____________________
 1 3 7 1 2 8|5 . . . . .
_______________________
 1 3 7 1 2 8|5 . . . . .
             3 . . . . .
_______________________
 1 3 7 1 2 8 8
_______________________
```

∴ 106 ↓ 2,6,7,1,6,2, = 1371288, true to 7 places of figures as required. To balance the last period dots may be put to represent numbers; this plan involves no additional labour, but secures accuracy. Operating for the last 2, which is in the sixth place, 2 complete periods of 6 figures each are represented by placing 5 dots after 1371285; it then becomes,

```
     Q     P
137128|5 . . . . .
     1|0 . . . . .
```

Suppose the period of 6 figures Q, had to be multiplied by 7, and placed under the period P:—say, 7 times 8 is something to which carry something, for which put down a dot; and then say, 7 times 2 is something to which carry something, and, regardless of the result, put down a second dot; then 7 times 1, to which some number may have to be carried, the result is again disregarded, and only a third dot is set down; 7 times 7,.

&c. only gives a fourth dot; 7 times 3, with all carried, only produces a fifth dot; but, because the number 5 requires a number under it:—7 is multiplied by 1, to which 3 is carried, making the result 10, which is set down. 7 times 3 is only 21, because something has to be carried that makes the result more than 25. If 2 were carried, 9 should be placed under the 5; 9 is too small, and the number set down, 10, is too great, yet the true result is nearer to 10 than it is to 9; but in either case the difference is not unit in the seventh place. So that, to multiply the period marked Q, and place the result under P, is reduced to the simple operation of making five dots, and saying 7 times $1 + 3 = 10$. Those who wish to understand what follows, and operate with ease, should be well acquainted with this process of operating with dots.

While explaining the Elements of Dual Arithmetic, the work is spread out, to render the explanations clear; in practice, however, the numbers employed may be set down in a very compact form. The last example may stand thus:—

```
1|0 6|0 0|0 0
 |2 1|2 0|0 0
 .  1|0 6|0 0
-------------
1 2|8 2|6 0|0 .
   |7 6|9 5|6 .
   |  1|9 2|4 .
       |  2|6 .
-------------
1 3 6|1 5 0|6 . .
     |9 5 3|1 . .
     |    2|9 . .
-------------
1 3 7 1|0 6 6 .
       |1|3 7 . . .
         |8|2 . . . . .
           |3 . . . . .
-------------
1 3 7 1 2 8 8   =   106↓2,6,7,1,6,2,
-------------
```

When a period takes up half the required number of figures, or more than half, then one of the co-efficients or multipliers is only required, and that multiplier is the index of the power operated with.

6. *Required the first 8 figures of* 3↓3,4,5,6,7,8,9,10, *when developed.*

```
3|0|0|0|0|0|0|0|
 |9|0|0|0|0|0|0|
   |9|0|0|0|0|0|
     |3|0|0|0|0|
─────────────────
3 9|9 3|0 0|0 0    = 3↓3,
  1|5 9|7 2|0 0
   | 2|3 9|5 8
       |  1|6 0
─────────────────
4 1 5|5 1 3|1 8 .  = 3↓3,4,
    2|0 7 7|5 7 .
     |    4|1 6 .
─────────────────
4 1 7 5|9 4 9 1    = 3↓3,4,5,
      2|5|0 5 5 . .            6,
         2|9|2 5 . . . .           7,
           3|3|4 . . . . . .          8,
             3|7| . . . . . . . .         9,
               4| . . . . . . . .            10,
─────────────────
4 1 7 8 7 8 4 6 = 3↓3,4,5,6,7,8,9,10,
```

Every figure employed in this operation is set down; 6 numbers added together produce 41787846; the first partition line, to the left, divides 4175|9491 into periods of 4 figures each, then the number 25055 is found in the usual way. The second partition line divides

```
41759|491
    25|055 . .
```

into 2 periods of 5 figures each, counting the dots as 2 figures; the third partition line divides

```
41759491
   25055 . .
     29|25 . . . .        8,
```

into 2 periods of 6 figures each, counting the 4 dots as figures. In this case, and in cases of similar nature, the sum is not required. In operating at the step above exhibited, the left hand period has to be multiplied by 8, and the result placed under the right hand period; 8 times the sum of 9,0,4, and all that has to be carried, produce only a dot; 8 times the sum of 2,5,9, and all to be carried from the last operation, produce only another dot; 8 times the sum of 2,5, with what has to be carried, produce a third dot; 8 times 7 = 56, so that it is safe to place down a fourth dot and carry 6; then 8 times 1 + 6 = 14, put down 4 and carry 1; 8 times 4 + 1 = 33; the number 334 .... is found with little mental labour when the partition line and the required dots are properly placed:

```
41759491
  25055 . .
   29|25 . . . .
  · 3|34 . . . .     8,
```

PROPOSITION II.

TO FIND THE POWERS OF (1·1), (1·01), (1·001), (1·0001), ETC. SO THAT WHEN ONE GIVEN NUMBER IS MULTIPLIED BY THEM, THE CONTINUED PRODUCT WILL BE ANOTHER GIVEN NUMBER.

Examples.

1. *What powers of* (1·1), (1·01), (1·001), *&c. must* 23 *be continually multiplied by, so that the continued product may be* 2345678?

```
2345678.
-------
23|00|00|0.
  |23|00|0.
-------------
232|3 00|0..    = 23 ↓ 0,1,
   2|0 90|7..
    |    8|4..
-------------
2343|991.       = 23 ↓ 0,1,9,
   1|641.
-------------
23456|32...     = 23 ↓ 0,1,9,7,
     |47...
-------------
2345679         = 23 ↓ 0,1,9,7,2,
-------------
∴ 2345678       = 23 ↓ 0,1,9,7,2,
```

To find any of the operating figures as ↓ 0,0,9,

```
From 23|456...
Take 23|230...
     ----------
 23)    |226...   (↓ 0,0,9,
        |207
```

23 ↓ 0,1, shows that no periods of single figures are involved.

2. *Required the multipliers that will bring* 880091 *to* 886327.

```
Put n = 880|091
          6|160
           | 18
        ---------
        886 269.. = n ↓ 0,0,7,
```

It is evident, that if the left hand period 8862, be placed under the right one 69.. and added, the sum would be greater than 886327, hence no operation has to be performed on periods of 4 figures.

```
88626|9....      = n ↓ 0,0,7
    5|3|......             0,6
      5|......                  6,
----------
886327 = n ↓ 0,0,7,0 6,6,
```

∴ 880091 ↓ 0,0,7,0,6,6, = 886327.

3. *Required the multipliers that will bring* 663157 *to* 663312.

```
Put m = 6631|5 7 . .
           1|3|3 . . . . m ↓ 0,0,0,2,
            1|9| . . . . . .       3,
             3| . . . . . .           5,
       ---------------------
       6633 1 2 = m ↓ 0,0,0,2,3,5,
```

$$\therefore \frac{880091 \times 663312}{886327 \times 663157} = \frac{nm \downarrow 0,0,0,2,3,5,}{nm \downarrow 0,0,7,0,6,6,} = \frac{\downarrow 0,0,0,2,}{\downarrow 0,0,7,0,3,1,}$$

It is easily shown that

$$\frac{\downarrow 0,0,0,2,}{\downarrow 0,0,7,0,3,1,} = .993198.$$

```
                          100 0|00 0 .
                               |20 0 .
                         -------------------
1 ↓ 0,0,0,2,          =  100|0 20|0 . . +
                            |7 00|1 . . −
                            |   2|8 . . +
                         -------------------
↓ 0,0,0,2
---------             =   99 3 22|7 . . . . +
↓ 0,0,7                          2|9 . . . . −
                         -------------------
↓ 0,0,2,
-------------         =   99 3 19 8
↓ 0,0,7,0,3,1,
```

Division by the powers of 1·1, 1·01, 1·001, &c. will be explained presently; the process differs but little from that of multiplication. The numbers employed in this example are the cosines of the 4 angles, 27° 35′ 5″; 48° 27′ 32″; 28° 20′ 48″; 48° 26′ 49″, to six places of decimals. In the next example, it is proposed to operate on the cosines of the same angles, continued to seven places of decimals.

4. *Reduce the compound fraction* $\frac{8800909 \times 6633134}{8863271 \times 6631572}$; *to powers of* ↓ 1,; ↓ 0,1,; ↓ 0,0,1,: *&c.*

```
                   6633 1 3 4
                  -----------
                   6631|5 7 2 .
↓ 0,0,0,2,            1|3|2 6 . . .            (A).
        3,             1|9|9 . . . . .
           5,           3|3| . . . . . . .
            6            4| . . . . . . .
```

```
                886 32 7 1
               ------------
               880|09 0|9 . .
                 6|16 0|6 . .
                    1 8|5 . .
               --------------
 ↓0,0,7,       886 27,0 0 . . .
       0,6,         5 3|2 . . . . .            (B).
           4,         3|5| . . . . . . .
             4,         4| . . . . . . .
```

$$\frac{\downarrow 0,0,0,2,3,5,6,}{\downarrow 0,0,7,0,6,4,4,}$$

or $$\frac{\downarrow 0,0,0,2,0,1,2,}{\downarrow 0,0,7,0,3,} = \text{the given fraction.}$$

The details of the process have been so fully discussed, it is presumed that the work will be understood without entering into further detail.

In (A) and (B), the last additions are omitted, as unnecessary; it is easily observed, that if the additions were performed, the required results 6633134 and 88663271, set down merely to show the numbers to be made up, would be obtained. It is easily shown that the difference of the results (A) and (B), is equal to the given fraction. For, put $n = 6631572$, and $m = 8800909$,

$$\therefore \frac{8800909 \times 6633134}{8863271 \times 6631572} = \frac{mn \downarrow 0,0,0,2,3,5,6,}{nm \downarrow 0,0,7,0,6,4,4,} = \frac{\downarrow 0,0,0,2,0,1,2,}{\downarrow 0,0,7,0,3,}$$

the numerical value of which is easily found, thus,

```
                       100 0|00 0 0
                            |20 0 0
                       ------------
 1 ↓0,0,0,2,           100 0 20|0 0 . . . .
           0,1,                |1|0 . . . . . .
              2,                 |2 . . . . . .
                       -----------------
                       100|0 20|1 2 . +
                          |7 00|1 4 . −
                              2|8 0 . +
                               |  1 . −
                       -----------------
 Divided by ↓0,0,7,     99 3 22|7 7 . . . +
                 0,3,         2|9 8 . . . −
                       -----------------
 ∴ ↓0,0,0,2,0,1,   =    99 3 1979
   ------------        ----------
    ↓0,0,7,0,3,
```

It may be proper here to state, that the co-efficients employed, when dividing by the 7th power, are 1, − 7, + 28, − 84, + &c.

5. *Required the value of the compound fraction*

$$\frac{8126236 \times 9867261}{8124229 \times 9891787},$$

in terms of the powers of **↓1,**; **↓0,1,**; **↓0,0,1,** *&c.*

8126236 = cosine of 35° 38′ 49″; 9867261 = cos 9° 20′ 45″; 8124229 = cos 35° 40′; 9891787 = cos 8° 26′ 13″.

```
                      8126236
                   ------------
                      8124|229 .
↓0,0,0,2,                1|6|25 . . .
         4,                3|2|5 . . . . .
          7,                 5|7 . . . . .
                      9891787 . .
                   ------------
                      986|726|1 . .
                        1|973|5 . .
                             1|0 . .
                   ------------
↓0,0,2,               988 7|006 .
                         3|955 .
                              1 .
                   ------------
        4,            98909|02 . . .
         8,               7|9|1 . . . . .
          3,               3|0| . . . . . . .
           4,               4| . . . . . . .
```

$$\therefore \frac{\downarrow 0,0,0,2,4,7,}{\downarrow 0,0,2,4,8,3,4,} = \frac{\downarrow 0,0,0,0,0,4,}{\downarrow 0,0,2,2,4,0,4,}.$$

6. *The natural cosine of* 6° 26′ 23″·5 = 9936901; *the cosine of* 37° 39′ 49″·5 = 7916103; *required the value of* 9936901 × 7916103, *true to seven places of figures.*

9936901 ≐ 99 **↓0,0,3,7,2,2,**

∴ 7916103 × 99 **↓0,0,3,7,2,2,** = the required product.

To multiply a number by 99 is a simple matter.

```
                 791610300 ◡ 100 times,
                   7916103 ◡      once,
                 ---------
Difference       7836942.. ◡  99 times.
                 ---------
```

$\therefore 7916103 \times 9936901 = \dot{7}836942 \downarrow 0,0,3,7,2,2, = 7866153.$

WORK.

```
783|694|2 . .
  1|3 5 1|1 . .
        2|4 . .
-------------
7860|4 7 7 .
     5|5 0 2 .
           2 .
-------------
7865 9|8 1 . . .
      1|5|7 . . .
        1|6 . . .
-------------
7866153
-------------
```

7916103×9936901 gives 78661531816803 by common multiplication, and hence the first seven figures of the product are found true to the last figure.

PART II.

DIVISION OF DUAL ARITHMETIC.

THE method of division is more readily established by particular examples than by generalization; this being granted, let it be required to divide by 1 $(1{\cdot}01)^3$. The decimal point may be omitted during the operation, and $(1{\cdot}01)^3$ written $(101)^3$.

The co-efficients of $(x+y)^{-3}$, developed by the binomial theorem, are readily found; the first term is x^{-3}, the second term is $-3\,x^{-4}y$; the co-efficient -3, the same as the power, and, like it, negative; x^{-4} has a power (1) less than the power of x^{-3}. $-3\times-4\div2=+6$, hence the third term will be $+6\,x^{-5}y^2$, the index of x is decreased by unity, while the index of y is increased by unity: -3×-4 is divided by 2, because $-3\,x^{-4}y$, is the second term, from which is deduced $+6\,x^{-5}y^2$, the third term. $+6\times-5\div3=-10$, the co-efficient of the fourth term, $-10\,x^{-6}y^3$; so that $(x+y)^{-3}$ is developed in the same way as $(x+y)^3$.

$$\therefore (x+y)^{-3}=x^{-3}-3\,x^{-4}y+6\,x^{-5}y^2-10\,x^{-6}y^3+15\,x^{-7}y^4-\ldots.$$

which, when compared with $\left(1+\frac{1}{100}\right)^{-3}=\frac{1}{(1{\cdot}01)^3}$, gives

$$\left(1+\frac{1}{100}\right)^{-3}=1-3\times\frac{1}{100}+6\times\frac{1}{(100)^2}-10\times\frac{1}{(100)^3}+\ldots..$$

observing that every power of 1 is 1. The multipliers or co-efficients for the division by $(1{\cdot}01)^{-3}$ are

$$1;\ -3;\ +6;\ -10;\ +15;\ -\ \&c.$$

The co-efficient of the fifth term being + 15, and − 7 the index of x, therefore the co-efficient of the sixth term

$$= + 15 \times - 7 \div 5 = - 21.$$

Though it seldom happens that many of these multipliers or co-efficients are employed, in these elementary examples the work is extended beyond the limits required in practice, so that the laws which govern the operations may be easily detected.

The work may be arranged under the form established in Part I., as follows:—

	e	*d*	*c*	*b*	*a*				
+		10	00	00	00	00		+ 1,	
−			30	00	00	00	Mult. by	− 3,	beginning at *a*.
+				60	00	00	"	+ 6,	" *b*
−				1	00	00	"	− 10,	" *c*
+					1	50	"	+ 15,	" *d*
−						2	"	− 21,	" *e*
						9705901 48			

Sum of the negative terms = 1000600150 by inspection.
Sum of the positive terms = 30010002 "

970590148

In many cases, the difference of the positive and negative terms may be found without summing each class, and taking the difference. When this simple example is understood, what follows will appear easy. However, it may be asked, how − 21 times the first line, beginning under *e*, produces − 2, as no number exists under *e*: the − 2 is carried from the next term, when multiplied by − 21.

2. *Divide* 123 *by* $(10001)^7$, *true for the first ten places of figures.*

$123 \div (1{\cdot}0001)^7$, may be written $123 \downarrow 0,0,\bar{7}$, the negative sign being placed over the figure 7; for $123 \div (10001)^7$ equal

$$\frac{123}{(10001)^7} = 123 \times (10001)^{-7}.$$

Set down $123 \downarrow 0,0,0,\bar{7}$, for $123 \div (10001)^7$.

The first multiplier for the seventh power is 1, the second -7,

$$\text{the third} = \frac{-7 \times -8}{2} = +28;$$

$$\text{the fourth} = \frac{+28 \times -9}{3} = -84;$$

$$\text{the fifth} = \frac{-84 \times -10}{4} = +210;$$

&c. &c.

	c	*b*	*a*			
+		1230	0000	00	. . + 1,	
−			8610	00	. . − 7,	beginning at *a*
+			3	44	. . + 28,	„ *b*
−					. . − 84,	„ *c*
		1229	1393	44		

This result is instantly found, as 28 = 4 times 7, and 84 = 3 times 28; but the multiplier − 84, gives a result that does not affect the first ten places of figures, and is therefore omitted.

$$\therefore 123 \downarrow 0,0,0,\overline{7}, = 1229139344.$$

As in multiplication, when the factors are large, each step is readily obtained from the one preceding, thus:

		*		
+	1230	0000	00	. . call + A
−		8610	00	. . − 7 + A ÷ 1 = − B begin under *
+		3	44	. . − 8 × − B ÷ 2 = + C begin under *
				. . − 9 × + C ÷ 3 = − D begin under *
	1229	1393	44	

3. *Divide* 3425 *by the* 9*th power of* (10001), *or, which is the same thing, according to our notation, find the value of* $3425 \downarrow 0,0,0,\bar{9}$, *and give the first twelve figures of the quotient.*

	c	*b*	*a*		
+		3425	0000	0000 +	1
−		3	0825	0000 −	9 *a*
+			15	4125 +	45 *b*
−				57 −	165 *c*
		3421	9190	4068	

Or the required result may be found according to the second method, thus:

			*		
+	3425	0000	0000	call	+ A
−	3	0825	0000 ⌣	9 × + A ÷ 1 =	− B
+		15	4125 ⌣	10 × − B ÷ 2 =	+ C
−			57 ⌣	11 × + C ÷ 3 =	− D

The second line is found by multiplying the first by − 9, beginning under *; the third line is found by multiplying the second − 5 = − 10 × − B ÷ 2, beginning under *; the fourth line, or − 57, is found by multiplying the third line + 15·4 by − 11, and dividing by 3, beginning under *,

$$+ 15{\cdot}41 \times - 11 = 169{\cdot}51$$

$$- 169{\cdot}51 \div 3 = - 56{\cdot}5, \text{ or } - 57.$$

4. *Divide* 6436 *by* $(1{\cdot}1)^2$, *and give the first eight figures of the quotient.*

$$+ 1; - 2; + 3; - 4; - 5; \text{ \&c.}$$

are the multipliers, when dividing by the square, or second power,

	h g f e d c b a	Mult.	begin at
+	6 4 3 6 0 0 0 0 0 0	+ 1	begin at
−	1 2 8 7 2 0 0 0 0	− 2	" a
+	1 9 3 0 8 0 0 0	+ 3	" b
−	2 5 7 4 4 0 0	− 4	" c
+	3 2 1 1 8 0	+ 5	" d
−	3 8 8 6 2	− 6	" e
+	4 5 1	+ 7	" f
−	5 1	− 8	" g
+	6	+ 9	" h

66 3 2 3 4 3 7, sum of positive terms.
1 3 1 3 3 3 5 3, sum of negative terms.

Quotient = 5 3 1 9 0 0 8 4 = $6436\downarrow\overline{2}$,

The quotient just found may be shown to be correct by multiplying it by $(11)^2$, according to the methods explained in Part I. The multipliers for the square being 1, 2, 1;

5 3 1 9 0 0 8 4	− 1
1 0 6 3 8 0 1 6	− 2
5 3 1 9 0 0	− 1

Proof, 6 4 3 6 0 0 0 0

5. *Divide* 3141593 *by* $(101)^1$, *and give the first seven figures of the quotient.*

The multipliers for the first power are

+ 1 ; − 1 ; + 1 ; − 1 ; + 1 ; &c.

+	31 41 59 3 .	+ 1
−	31 41 6 .	− 1
+	31 4 .	+ 1
−	3 .	− 1

31 41 90 7, sum of positive terms.
31 41 9, sum of negative terms.

∴ 31 10 48 8 = $3141593\downarrow 0,\overline{1}$,

To divide by 11, 101, 1001, 10001, &c. the multipliers for the different powers are,

1st power,	+ 1,	− 1,	+ 1,	− 1,	+ 1, ...
2d power,	+ 1,	− 2,	+ 3,	− 4,	+ 5, ...
3d power,	+ 1,	− 3,	+ 6,	− 10,	+ 15, ...
4th power,	+ 1,	− 4,	+ 10,	− 20,	+ 35, ...
5th power,	+ 1,	− 5,	+ 15,	− 35,	+ 70, ...
6th power,	+ 1,	− 6,	+ 21,	− 56,	+ 126, ...
7th power,	+ 1,	− 7,	+ 28,	− 84,	+ 210, ...
8th power,	+ 1,	− 8,	+ 36,	− 120,	+ 330, ...
9th power,	+ 1,	− 9,	+ 45,	− 165,	+ 495, ...

The multipliers for other divisions are readily found: for example, let it be required to divide a given number by the 20th power of 11, 101, 1001, &c. The first multiplier will be + 1, the second − 20, the third − 20 × − 21 ÷ 2 = + 210, the fourth + 210 × − 22 ÷ 2 = − 1540, and so on in other cases.

6. *Required the value of* 7854↓3,$\overline{2}$,2, *which is the same as saying, multiply* 7854 *by* $(11)^8$ *and then* $(1001)^2$, *and divide by* $(101)^2$.

```
|7|8|5|4|0|0|0
|2|2|5|6|2|0|0        ↓3,
  |2|2|5|6|2|0
    |7|8|5|4
--------------
1 0 3|4 3 6|7 4 .
     |2 0 6|8 7 .      ↓3,0,2,
           |1 0 .
--------------
1 0 3 6 4 3 7 1 +
    2 0 7 2 8 7 −
        3 1 0 9 +      ↓3,2̄,2,
            4 1 −
--------------
1 0 1 6 0 1 5 2, the first eight figures.
```

7. *Find the first seven figures of the quotient of* 360 *by* 57·2957795.

$$57{\cdot}2957795 \downarrow 0,0,0,7,3,6,6, = 57{\cdot}3$$

$$\therefore 57{\cdot}3 \downarrow 0,0,0,\overline{7},\overline{3},\overline{6},\overline{6}, = 57{\cdot}2957795$$

$\therefore \dfrac{360,\downarrow 0,0,0,7,3,6,6,}{57\cdot3}$ gives the required quotient;

$$\text{but } \frac{360}{57\cdot3} \doteq \frac{1200}{191} = 6\cdot2827225$$

```
                    6·2827|2 2 5 . .
↓0,0,0,7,                4|3|9 8 . . . .
        3,                1|8|9 . . . . . .
         6,                 3|7| . . . . . . . .
          6,                  4| . . . . . . . .
                   ________________
                    6·2831 8 5 3, quotient.
```

8. *Divide* 70710678 *by* 39269908, *and give the first seven figures of the quotient.*

$$39269908\downarrow 0,0,1,8,4,7,4,6 = 4000000\dot{0};$$

then, according to the reasoning employed in the last example,

$$70710678 \div 4 \doteq 17677669$$

$$\therefore 17677669\downarrow 0,0,1,8,4,7,4,6 = 1\cdot8006314, \text{ the quotient.}$$

9. *Divide* 3·1415927 *by* 1·4142136, *and give the first seven figures of the quotient.*

Divide 1·414 into 3·1415927 by common division, and the quotient is 2·2217770.

```
                  1·414|00 00
↓0,0,0,1,              |14 14 . .
       5,             7|07 . . . .
        1,             | 4 . . . .
                ______________
                 1·414 2 1 25

                2·221|7 7 70
↓0,0,0,1̄,            |2|2 22 . .
       5,            1|1|11 . . . .
        1,             |22 . . . .
                ______________
                2·221 4 4 15, required quotient.
```

Another Method.

Divide 3·1415927 by 1·41, and the three first figures of the quotient will be 2·22; then

$$222 \times 141 = 31302.$$

Again, it is easily shown, that

$$31302 \downarrow 0,0,3,6,3,4,5, = 31415927$$

and

$$141 \downarrow 0,0,2,9,8,5, = 14142136$$

$$\therefore \frac{31415927}{14142136} = \frac{3{\cdot}1302 \downarrow 0,0,3,6,3,4,5,}{1{\cdot}41 \downarrow 0,0,2,9,8,5,} = 222 \downarrow 0,0,1,\bar{3},\bar{5},\bar{1},5,$$

$$\begin{array}{ll}
 & 222|000|00\,. \\
\downarrow 0,0,1, & \quad\;\; |222|00\,. \\
\hline
 & 222\,2\,2\,2\,0|0\,\ldots\ldots \\
 & \qquad\qquad 1|1\,\ldots\ldots \\
\hline
\downarrow 0,0,1,0,0,0,5, & 222\,2|2\,2\,1\,1\,+ \\
 & \qquad |6\,6\,6\,7\,- \\
 & \qquad\qquad\quad 1 \\
\hline
\downarrow 0,0,1,\bar{3}, & 222\,1\,5|54\,5\,+ \\
\qquad\quad \bar{5}, & \qquad 1|1|1\,1\,- \\
\qquad\quad\; \bar{1} & \qquad\quad |2\,2\,- \\
\hline
\end{array}$$

$$\therefore\; 222 \downarrow 0,0,1,\bar{3},\bar{5},\bar{1},\bar{5}, = \underline{2{\cdot}22\,1\,4\,4\,1\,2} = \text{quotient.}$$

Third Method.

$$3{\cdot}14159265 = 3 \downarrow 0,4,6,3,1,9,2,9, = \downarrow \overline{114478741,}$$

$$1{\cdot}41421356 = \;\downarrow 3,6,0,9,4,1,1,1, = \downarrow \overline{34659100,}$$

$$\begin{array}{rl}
 & 114478741 \\
 & \;\;\underline{34659100} \\
\downarrow & \;\;79819641, = 2 \downarrow 1,0,9,7,0,3,4,8, = 2{\cdot}22144147.
\end{array}$$

This method, which is independent of the rules of common arithmetic, will be explained presently.

PART III.

EVOLUTION AND INVOLUTION OF DUAL ARITHMETIC.

1. *Required the first eight figures of the cube of* ·4852.

$$·48 \times ·48 \times ·48 = ·110592$$

may be taken from a table of cubes, &c. or found by common multiplication.

$$48 \downarrow 0,1,0,8,2,4,7,8, = 4852.$$

$$(48)^3 \downarrow 0,3,0,24,6,12,21,24, = (4852)^3.$$

```
                         (48)³ = 1 1|0 5|9 2|0 0
                                    |3 3|1 7|7 6        ↓0,3,
                                        |3 3|1 8
   3                                        |1 1
                               ________________
 34182915|                      1 1 3 9|4 3 0 5| . . . .
 27346....| −8                        2|7 3 4 6| . . . . = A
                                       |   3 2| . . . . = A × 23 ÷ 2
                               ________________
 ↓0,3,0,24,                     1 1 4 2 1|6 8 3  . .
          6,                             |6|8 5  . . . .
           12,                          1|3|7  . . . . . .
              21,                         2|4| . . . . . . . .
               24,                         3| . . . . . . . .
                               ________________
                               ·1 1 4 2 2 5 3 2 = cube of ·4852, true
```

to the last figure.

2. *What is the fourth power of* ·88, *true to eight places of figures?*

$$(\cdot 8)^3 = \cdot 4096$$

and $$.8 \downarrow \mathbf{1,} = \cdot 88$$

$$\therefore\ (\cdot 8)^4 \downarrow \mathbf{4,} = (\cdot 88)^4$$

```
(·8)⁴ = 4|0|9|6|0|0|0|0
        1|6|3|8|4|0|0|0
         |2|4|5|7|6|0|0     ↓4,
           |1|6|3|8|4|0
               |4|0|9|6
        ----------------
(·88)⁴ = ·5 9 9 6 9 5 3 6
```

3. *Required the first seven figures of the cube of* ·0176325.

$(\cdot 017)^3 = \cdot 000004913$, which may be called ·0000049, as the result is only required to seven places of decimals.

$$17 \downarrow \mathbf{0,3,6,6,8,} = 176325$$

$$\therefore\ (\cdot 017)^3 \downarrow \mathbf{0,9,18,18,24,} = (\cdot 0176324)^3.$$

```
  3  |
 17  | − 3    49| . .       ↓0,9,
 4 . |           4| . .
                -----
 169 .|          53 .| . . .   ↓0,9,18,
 1 . . . .| − 6    1 .| . . .
                -------
                 54
```

$\therefore$ ·0000054 = cube of ·0176325.

Another Method.

```
 49| . . ↓0,11,
  6| . .
-----------
```

·0000055 = cube of ·0176325.

Since one figure only is required,

$(\cdot 017)^3 \downarrow \mathbf{0,11,}$ is put for $(\cdot 017)^3 \downarrow \mathbf{0,9,18,18,24,}$

because, as is readily shown, $\downarrow \mathbf{0,0,18,}$ is nearly equal $\downarrow \mathbf{0,2,}$

```
 |100|00 0|0 0 0|0 0 0
     1|00 0|0 0 0|0 0 0        ↓0,0,10,
          4|5 0 0|0 0 0
             1 2|0 0 0
                  2 1
 ------------------------
+ 101 00|4 5 1 2 0|2 1 . . .
-       |4 0 4 0 1|8 0 . . . ↓0,0,10,0,4̄,
+                1|0 1 . . .
 ------------------------
  101 000|4 7 1 9 4 2
-        |4 0 4 0 0 2      ↓0,0,10,0,4̄,4̄,
+                   1
 ------------------------
  101 0000|6 7 9 4 1 . .
-         |6|0 6 0 0 . . . .
-           |7|0 7 0 . . . . . .
-             |2|0 2 . . . . . . . .
-               |7 0 . . . . . . . .
```

∴ ↓0,0,10,0,4̄,4̄,6̄,7̄,2̄,7̄, = ↓0,1,

∴ $(1\cdot001)^{10}$ is nearly equal $(1\cdot01)$.

```
  1000|000 0|0 0 0 0
     1|000 0|0 0 0 0
           4|5 0 0 0      ↓0,0, ,10,
               1 2
 ------------------------
+ 1001 000|4 5 0 1 2 . .
-         |4|0 0 4 0 . . . .
-           |4|0 0 4 . . . . . .
-             |9|0 1 . . . . . . . .
-               |6|0 . . . . . . . . . .
-                 |7 . . . . . . . . . .
 ------------------------
  1001 000 00000
 ------------------------
```

∴ ↓0,0,0,10,0,0,4̄,4̄,9̄,6̄,7̄, = ↓0,0,1,

∴ $(1\cdot0001)^{10}$ nearly equal $(1\cdot001)$.

```
  10000|0000 0|00 . . .
      1|0000 0|00 . . .   ↓0,0,0,0,10,
              4|50 . . .
 ------------------------
+ 10001 0000|4 50
-           |4|00
-             |50
 ------------------------
  10001 0000 0 00
```

$$\therefore \downarrow 0,0,0,0,10,0,0,0,0,\bar{4},\bar{5}, = \downarrow 0,0,0,1,$$

$$\therefore (1{\cdot}00001)^{10} \text{ nearly equal } (1{\cdot}0001).$$

Working to seven places of decimals,

$$\downarrow 0,0,0,0,10,0,0, = \downarrow 0,0,0,1,$$

$$\downarrow 0,0,0,10,0,0,\bar{4}, = \downarrow 0,0,1,$$

$$\downarrow 0,0,10,0,\bar{4},\bar{4},\bar{7}, = \downarrow 0,1,$$

$$\downarrow 0,10,\bar{4},\bar{1},\bar{9},\bar{5},\bar{1}, = \downarrow 1,$$

The following arrangement may be more convenient :—

$$\begin{aligned}
\downarrow 1, \quad & = \downarrow 0,10,\bar{4},\bar{1},\bar{9},\bar{5},\bar{1}, \\
\downarrow 0,1, \quad & = \downarrow 0,0,10,0,\bar{4},\bar{4},\bar{7}, \\
\downarrow 0,0,1, \quad & = \downarrow 0,0,0,10,0,0,\bar{4}, \\
\downarrow 0,0,0,1, \quad & = \downarrow 0,0,0,0,10,0,0, \qquad \text{(B)}. \\
\downarrow 0,0,0,0,1, \quad & = \downarrow 0,0,0,0,0,10,0, \\
\downarrow 0,0,0,0,0,1, \quad & = \downarrow 0,0,0,0,0,0,10, \\
\text{\&c.} \quad & = \quad \text{\&c.}
\end{aligned}$$

To illustrate this property, take an example. It may be found by common arithmetic, that

$$({\cdot}0176325)^3 = {\cdot}000005482033404328125.$$

For the purpose in view, twelve of these figures will suffice,

548203340433.

```
          548203340430
          ============
(17)³ =   4913
          4913                  ↓1,
          54|04|3 0|00
            |5 4|04|3 0         ↓1,1,
          545|8 3 4|3 00|000
            2|1 8 3|3 3 7|200   ↓1,1,4,
                  3|2 7 5|006
                       2|1 8 3
          5480|2 0 9 1|4 3 8 9
              1|6 4 4 0|6 2 7 4
                     1|6 4 4 1   ↓1,1,4,3,
                             1
          54818|5 3 3 7 1|0 5 . . .
               1|6 4 4 5 5|6 0 . . . ↓1,1,4,3,3,
                          1|6 4 . . .
          548201|7 8 2 8 2 9
                1|0 9 6 4 0 4     ↓1,1,4,3,3,2,
                            1
          548 028|7 9 2 3 4 . .
                4|3|8 5 6 2 . . . .          8,
                 2|1|9 2 8 . . . . . .         4,
                    5|4 8 . . . . . . . .        1,
                    1|0|9 . . . . . . . . . .      2,
                      4|9 . . . . . . . . . .        9,
          548203340430
```

∴ ('017)³ ↓ 1,1,4,3,3,2,8,4,1,2,9, = . . . ('0176325)³. (A).

```
          0176325000000
          17|0 0|00|00|0 0|00
            |5 1|00|00|0 0|00   ↓0,3,
                |5 1|00|0 0|00
                    |1 7|0 0|00
          175|1 5 1|1 7 0|0 00
            1|0 5 0|9 0 7|0 20
                  2|6 2 7|2 68  ↓0,3,6,
                        3|5 03
                             3
          176204707794
```

```
                 1762|0470|7794
                    1|0572|2824 ↓0,3,6,6,
                     |   2|6531
                     |    |   4
             ____________________
                 17631|04570|53...
                     1|41048|36...  ↓0,3,6,6,8,
                      |    4|94...
             ____________________
↓0,3,6,6,8,      17632456238 3
          2,          3|52649..
           4,          |7|0530....
            8,         1|4|106......
             1,          |1|76........
              8,         1|4|1..........
                           1|4..........
             ____________________
                 176325.000000
```

∴ (·017)³ ↓0,9,18,18,24,6,12,24,3,24,24, = (·0176325)³. (D).

(A) being equal (D),

∴ ↓1,1,4,3,3,2,8,4,1,2,9, = ↓0,9,18,18,24,6,12,24,3,24,24,

Although these expressions appear unequal, they, as factors, effect the same purpose; each of the indices on the left is less than 10, while some of the indices on the right amount to 18 and 24.

The equality of such multipliers is at once established by equations (B), for, if

↓0,0,0,20,0,0,$\overline{8}$, be subtracted, ↓0,0,2, may be added without disturbing the equality. In the same way, if

↓0,0,20,0,$\overline{8}$,$\overline{8}$,$\overline{14}$, be subtracted, ↓0,1, must be added to maintain the equality. It is easily shown that the following six expressions are equal to one another:—

(I.) ↓0,9,18,18,24,6,14,

(II.) ↓0,9,18,20,4,7,4,

(III.) ↓0,9,20,0,4,7,12,

•(IV.) ↓0,11,0,0,12,15,26,

(V.) ↓1,1,4,1,21,20,27,

(VI.) ↓1,1,4,3,3,2,7,

In subtracting a factor like ↓0,0,10,0,$\bar{4}$,$\bar{4}$,$\bar{7}$, the negative numbers $\bar{4}$,$\bar{4}$,$\bar{7}$, have to be added.

It is easily perceived, that as far as seven places of figures, the multiplier ↓0,9,18,18,24,6,12, is exactly equal ↓1,1,4,3,3,2,7,. As each of the indices of the former expression can be divided by 3, the cube root of any number compounded with the latter, is readily found. The same general principle holds good with other powers and roots. An example will render this remark plain.

$$8 = 2^3;$$

```
↓1,          8000000            ↓0,3,      20|0 0|0 0|0 .
              800000                         |6 0|0 0|0 . .
             -------                              |6 0|0 .
↓1,1,        88|0 0|0 0|0 .                           |2 .
               |8 8|0 0|0 .                ---------------
             ---------------               20 6|0 6 0|2 . .
↓1,1,4,      88 8|8 0 0|0 . .   ↓0,3,6,       1|2 3 6|4 . .
                3|5 5 5|2 . .                        3|1 . .
                       5|3 . .             -----------------
             ---------------               2072|9 9 7 .
 3,          89 2 3|6 0 5 .        6,            1|2|4 4 . . .
   3,             2|6|7 7 . . .      8,            1|6 6 . . . . .
     2,             2|6|8 . . . . .    2,              |4| . . . . . . .
       7,             1|7| . . . . . . .  4,            1| . . . . . . .
                         6| . . . . . . .
             ------------------------      ------------------------
             8926573                       2074412
```

∴ 8·926573 = 8↓1,1,4,3,3,2,7, = 8↓0,9,18,18,24,6,12, the cube root of which is 2↓0,3,6,6,8,2,4, which, when developed, gave 2·074412. ∴ 2·074412 = cube root of 8·926573.

This example has not for its object the extracting of the cube root of a number, to effect which, as I will presently show, is an easy operation by this system of Arithmetic.

My design here is to illustrate a principle. The process is extremely simple, and requires little mental labour, yet it takes considerable space to explain the matter fully. However, I prefer prolixity to obscurity, ordinary examples to wonderful developments, lengthy work to contracted operations. When the method is understood, the operator may contract as much as he pleases; develop all that his fancy dictates by the most dark and difficult symbols, never to be read or understood by any one after him.

4. *Required the cube root of* 577385·261, *true to nine places of figures.*

$$(80)^3 = 512000.$$

```
   3 times                                            *
 153600000|0                           51|20|00|00|0. ‿  1
 61440000.| ‿4                          6|14|40|00|0. ‿ 12         =A
                                       33|7 9|2 0|0. ‿ 11×A÷2=B
                 ↓0,12,                 1|1 2|6 4|0. ‿ 10×B÷3=C
                                            2|5 3|4. ‿  9×C÷4=D
   3 times                                       4|1. ‿  8×D÷5=E
                                       ----------------
 1|7308|0324|5                         57 69|3 4 4 1|5 ...
 3|4616|1....| ‿2 ↓0,12,0,6,                3|4 6 1 6|1 ...
                                                    8|7 ...
   3 times                             ----------------
 1|73184|1989                          57·7 2 8|0 6 6 3. ‿  1
10|3911.|     ‿6· ↓0,12,0,6,18,          1 0|3 9 1 1. ‿ 18      =A
                                                    9. ‿ 17×A÷2=B
   3 times                             ----------------
  1732....|                            57 73 8 4 5|8 3.....
  520 .....| ‿3                                 5|2|0.......
  3 times                                          |
 1732.....|                                        |
 155........| ‿9                              1 5|5.......
                                       ----------------
                                       57 73 8 52 5 8
                                       ----------------
```

$512 \downarrow$ **0,12,0,6,18,0,9,27,** = 577385·258;

the cube root of which will be represented by

8 ↓ 0,4,0,2,6,0,3,9,

```
                 80|00|0 0|0 0|0 .
↓ 0,4,            3|20|0 0|0 0|0 .
                     4|8 0|0 0|0 .
                          3|2 0|0 .
                                |8 .
                 ________________
                 83 24|8 3 2 0|8 . . .
↓ 0,4,0,2,           1|6 6 4 9|7 . . .
                                |8 . . .
                 ________________
                 83 26 4|9 7 1 3 .
↓ 0,4,0,2,6,            4|9 9 5 9 .
                                  1 .
                 ________________
                 83 26 9 9 6|7 3 . . . . .
        0,3,                2|5|0 . . . . . . . .
          9,                7|5 . . . . . . .
                 ________________
     ∴ 83·2699998 is the cube root of 577385·261.
```

5. *Required the first six figures of the fourth root of* 3527·63.

$7^4 = 2401$.

```
                        3 5 2 7 6 3
   4 times              ___________
  96040|0               2|4|0|1|0|0
  96040| ᴗ 1             |9|6|0|4|0         ↓ 4,
                         |1|4|4|0|6
                               |9|6|0
                                 |2|4
   4 times             ___________
  14061|20              3 5 1 5|3 0 . .
 1125 ..|   ᴗ 8            1 1|2 5 . .     ↓ 4,0,0,32,
                                  2 . .
   4 times             ____________
 141062|8               3 5 2 6 5|7 . . . .
 99 . . . .| ᴗ 7               9|9| . . . . . .         28,
                                 7| . . . . . . .          20,
                       ____________
 Given number           3 5 2 7 6 3
```

The fourth root of 2401 ↓ 4,0,0,32,28,20, = 7 ↓ 1,0,0,8,7,5,

```
7000 0 0
 700 0 0        ↓1,
─────────
7700|0 0 . .
   6|2|6 . . . .   0,0,8,
     5|4| . . . . . .     7,
       4| . . . . . .       5,
─────────
7706 8 4
```

∴ 7·70684 = fourth root of 3527·63.

6. *Required the first six figures of the sixth root of* 3856700.

$20^6 = 3200000$.

```
                      3856700
5 times               ───────
1600000|0             32|0 0|00|0 .  1
48000..|  ⌣ 3          4|8 0|00| . . 15            = A
                         3 3|60| . . 14 × A ÷ 2 = C
                           1|46| . . 13 × C ÷ 3 = D
5 times                       4| . . 12 × D ÷ 4 = E
                      ─────────
1857|550              37 1|5 1 0    1
13003|     ⌣ 7          1 3|0 0 3   35             = A
                             2 2 1  34 × A ÷ 2 = B
5 times                          2  33 × B ÷ 3 = C
                      ─────────
19236|80              3847|3 6. . .  1
769..|    ⌣ 4            7|6 9 . . 20
                             1 . . 19 × A ÷ 2
5 times               ─────────
193...|               3855 0|6 . . . .
154....|  ⌣ 8            1 5|4| . . . . . . .
5 times
193....|
9......|  ⌣ 5               1 0| . . . . . .
                      ─────────
                      38567|0
```

∴ 20 ↓ 0,3,7,4,8,5, expresses the required fifth root.

20|00|00
|60|00 $\quad\downarrow 0,3,$
|60
___
206|060
1|442 $\quad\downarrow 0,3,7,$
4
___
2075|06..
|83.... $\quad$ 4,
1|7|...... $\quad$ 8,
1|...... $\quad$ 5,
___

$\therefore$ 20·7607 = the fifth root of 3856700.

7. *Required the cube root of* ·5236 = $\sqrt[3]{\frac{\pi}{6}}$, *the side of a cube equal the solidity of a sphere whose diameter* = 1.

$(\cdot 8)^3 = \cdot 512$

3 times
1536|00
1075.| ⌣7

3 times
157..|
63...|⌣4

3 times
157...|
11.....|⌣7

·52360
___
512|00.⌣1
10|75.⌣21 $\quad$ = A
|11.⌣20 × A ÷ 2
___
5228|6...
6|3...
___
52349|.....
11|.....
___
52360

$\therefore$ (·8) $\downarrow$ 0,0,7,4,7, expresses the required number;

800|00.
5|60. $\quad\downarrow 0,0,7,$
0| 2.
___
8056|2...
3|2|..... $\quad$ 4,
6|..... $\quad$ 7,
___

$\therefore (\cdot 5236)^{\frac{1}{3}} = \cdot 80600$ nearly.

8. *Let it be required to find the* $\frac{17}{43}$ *power of* 3·141593 *true to five places of decimals.*

$$1 \downarrow 12,0,1,0,0,8,6 = 3{\cdot}141593.$$

It is necessary to have 1, to the left of ↓, because $\frac{17}{43}$ power of 1 = 1. One or two trials show that 1 ↓ **11**, is too small, and 1 ↓ **13**, exceeds 3141593.

```
                                  *
                      1|0|0|0|0|0|0      1
                      1|2|0|0|0|0|0      12             = A
                        6|6|0|0|0|0      11 × A ÷ 2 = B
 ↓12,                   2|2|0|0|0|0      10 × B ÷ 3 = C
                          4|9|5|0|0       9 × C ÷ 4 = D
                            7|9|2|0       8 × D ÷ 5 = E
                              9|2|4       7 × E ÷ 6 = F
                                7|9       6 × F ÷ 7 = G
                                  5       5 × G ÷ 8 = H
                     ----------------
                      3 1 3|8 4 2|8 ..
 ↓12,0,1,                  |3 1 3|8 ..
                     ----------------
                      3 1 4 1 5 6|6 .....
        0,0,8,                  2|5| .......
              6,                  2| .......
                     ------------------------
∴ 1 ↓12,0,1,0,0,8,6, = 3 1 4 1 5 9 3
```

The 17th power of 1 ↓ **12,0,1,0,0,8,6,** = 1 ↓ **204,0,17,0,0,136,102,** which has to be divided by 43 for the required result.

By means of expressions (B) all the indices to the right of ↓, in the last expression, may be reduced until they are divisible by 43.

43 into 204, goes 4 times and 32 over,

now, ↓ **32,** = ↓ **0,320,$\overline{128}$,$\overline{32}$,$\overline{288}$,$\overline{160}$,$\overline{32}$,**

$$\therefore \text{(B)}\ 1{\downarrow}204,0,17,0,0,136,102 = 1{\downarrow}172,320,\overline{111},\ \overline{32},\overline{288},\ \overline{24},\ 70,$$
$$= 1{\downarrow}172,301,\ 79,\ \overline{32},\overline{364},\overline{100},\ \overline{63},$$
$$= 1{\downarrow}172,301,\ 43,328,\overline{364},\overline{100},\overline{207},$$
$$= 1{\downarrow}172,301,\ 43,301,\ \overline{94},\overline{100},\overline{207},$$
$$= 1{\downarrow}172,301,\ 43,301,\overline{106},\ 0,\ \overline{7},$$
$$= 1{\downarrow}172,301,\ 43,301,\ \overline{86},\overline{172},\overline{258},$$

All the indices can, in this reduced form, be divided by 43. Consequently, the $\frac{17}{43}$ power, or root of 3·141593, is represented by

$$1{\downarrow}4,7,1,7,\overline{2},\overline{4},\overline{6},$$

```
1|0|0|0|0|0|0
 |4|0|0|0|0|0
   |6|0|0|0|0
     |4|0|0|0
       |1|0|0
-------------
1 4|6 4|1 0|0 .
  1|0 2|4 8|7 .
     3,0 7|4 .
         5|1 .
-------------
1 5 6|9 7 1|2 . .
      |1 5 7|0 . .
-------------
1 5 7 1|2 8 2 .
      1|1 0 0 .
-------------
1 5 7 2 3|8 2
         |3|2 minus.
           |6 minus.
-------------
1 5 7 2 3 4 4
```

$$\therefore\ 1{\cdot}572344 = (3{\cdot}141593)^{\frac{17}{43}}.$$

9. *Express* $\downarrow$ **0,1,** *in positive terms of the indices that follow in succession.*

```
            100|000|000|000
               |900|000|000
                  3|600|000   ↓0,0,9,
                      8|400
                         13
            _______________
            1009|0360|8413
                |9081|3247
                    3|6325   ↓0,0,9,9,
                         8
            _______________
            10099|445799|3...
                 |50497|23...
                      1|01...
            _______________
↓0,0,9,9,5,   100999|507817
          4,         |403998
           8,         |80800
            7,         |7070
             3,         |303
              1,         |10
```

∴ ↓01, = ↓0,0,9,9,5,4,8,7,3,1,

The following equalities, found in the same manner, may be made useful in reducing one set of indices to another:

↓1,	=	↓0,9,5,7,5,9,7,3,5,7,1,2,5,9,4,7,7,
↓0,1,	=	↓0,0,9,9,5,4,8,7,3,1,0,4,4,5,5,1,9,
↓0,0,1,	=	↓0,0,0,9,9,9,5,4,5,7,8,4,6,0,5,7,3,
↓0,0,0,1,	=	↓0,0,0,0,9,9,9,9,5,4,5,4,8,7,5,7,5,
↓0,0,0,0,1,	=	↓0,0,0,0,0,9,9,9,9,9,5,4,5,4,5,8,4,
↓0,0,0,0,0,1,	=	↓0,0,0,0,0,0.9,9,9,9,9,9,5,4,5,4,5,
↓0,0,0,0,0,0,1,	=	↓0,0,0,0,0,0,0,9,9,9,9,9,9,9,5,4,5,
↓0,0,0,0,0,0,0,1,	=	↓0,0,0,0,0,0,0,0,9,9,9,9,9,9,9,9,5,
&c.	=	&c.

10. *What power must* 1·251853 *be raised to, so that the result may be* 1·571653?

Or, $(1{\cdot}251853)^x = 1{\cdot}571653$, *find* x.

It is readily found that ɪ ↓2,3,4,1,5,6,0, = 1·251853,
and that ɪ ↓4,7,1,2,3,6,0, = 1·571653.

The co-efficients ɪ, to the left of ↓, in future operations will be omitted, ɪ ↓2,3,4,1,5,6,0, is the same as ↓2,3,4,1,5,6,0,

In the succeeding reduction, the following equalities, before given, are employed:—

$\downarrow 1, \quad = \downarrow 0,\ 10,\ \bar{4},\ \bar{1},\ \bar{9},\ \bar{5},\ \bar{1},$

$\downarrow 0,1, \quad = \downarrow 0,\ 0,\ 10,\ 0,\ \bar{4},\ \bar{4},\ \bar{7},$ (K).

$\downarrow 0,0,1, = \downarrow 0,\ 0,\ 0,\ 10,\ 0,\ 0,\ \bar{4},$

$$\left.\begin{array}{l} \downarrow 2,3,4,1,5,6,0, = \downarrow 0,\ 23,\ \bar{4},\ \bar{1},\ \overline{13},\ \bar{4},\ \bar{2}, \\ \qquad = \downarrow 0,\ 0,\ 226,\ \bar{1},\ \overline{105},\ \overline{96},\ \overline{163}, \\ \qquad = \downarrow 0,\ 0,\ 0,\ 2259,\ \overline{105},\ \overline{96},\ \overline{1067}, \end{array}\right\}$$

$$\begin{array}{r} 22590 \\ 105 \\ \hline 224850 \\ 96 \\ \hline 2247540 \\ 1067 \\ \hline 2246473 \end{array}$$

With (K) this reduction requires no mental labour, for when ↓2, is taken away, and 0, put in its place, $\downarrow 0,20,\bar{8},\bar{2},\overline{18},\overline{10},\bar{2},$ is added.

$$\begin{array}{lllllll} 0, & 3, & 4, & 1, & 5, & 6, & 0, \\ 0, & 20, & \bar{8}, & \bar{2}, & \overline{18}, & \overline{10}, & \bar{2}, \\ \hline \downarrow 0, & 23, & \bar{4}, & \bar{1}, & \overline{13}, & \bar{4}, & \bar{2}, \\ 0, & 0, & 230, & 0, & \overline{92}, & \overline{92}, & \overline{161}, \\ \hline 0, & 0, & 226, & \bar{1}, & \overline{105}, & \overline{96}, & \overline{163}, \end{array}$$

where $0,0,230,0,\overline{92},\overline{92},\overline{161}, = 23$ times $0,0,10,0,\bar{4},\bar{4},\bar{7},$

It will be found unnecessary to set down these figures to effect this continued reduction.

$$
\begin{array}{rrrrrrrr}
 & \downarrow 4, & 7, & 1, & 2, & 3, & 6, & 0, \\
= & \downarrow 0, & 47, & \overline{15}, & \overline{2}, & \overline{33}, & \overline{14}, & \overline{4}, \\
 & \downarrow 0, & 0, & 455, & \overline{2}, & \overline{221}, & \overline{202}, & \overline{333}, \\
 & \downarrow 0, & 0, & 0, & 4548, & \overline{221}, & \overline{202}, & \overline{2153},
\end{array}
$$

$$
\begin{array}{r}
45480 \\
221 \\ \hline
452590 \\
202 \\ \hline
4523880 \\
2153 \\ \hline
4521727
\end{array}
$$

∴ 4521727 divided by 2246473 gives 2·012812 the value of x. Consequently 1·251853 raised to the 2·012812 power produces 1·571653.

11. *What power must* 10 *be raised to, so that the result may be* 7? *Or in other terms, given* $10^x = 7$, *find* x.

It is easily shown that 1 ↓ 24,1,5,1,9,2,5,9, = 10,
and that 1 ↓ 20,3,9,8,6,0,1,2, = 7.

The following reduction is readily made by employing the equalities (K):—

$$
\begin{array}{rrrrrrrr}
10 = & \downarrow 24, & 1, & 5, & 1, & 9, & 2, & 9, \\
= & 0, & 241, & \overline{91}, & \overline{23}, & \overline{207}, & \overline{118}, & \overline{15}, \\
= & 0, & 0, & 2319, & \overline{23}, & \overline{1171}, & \overline{1082}, & \overline{1702}, \\
= & 0, & 0, & 0, & 23167, & \overline{1171}, & \overline{1082}, & \overline{10978},
\end{array}
$$

$$
\begin{array}{r}
231670 \\
1171 \\ \hline
2304990 \\
1082 \\ \hline
23039080 \\
10978 \\ \hline
23028102
\end{array}
$$

$$
7 = \begin{array}{rrrrrrr}
\downarrow 20, & 3, & 9, & 8, & 6, & 0, & 1, \\
0, & 203, & \overline{71}, & \overline{12}, & \overline{174}, & \overline{100}, & \overline{19}, \\
0, & 0, & 1959, & \overline{12}, & \overline{986}, & \overline{912}, & \overline{1440}, \\
0, & 0, & 0, & 19578, & \overline{986}, & \overline{912}, & \overline{9276},
\end{array}
$$

$$
\begin{array}{r}
195780 \\
986 \\
\hline
1947940 \\
912 \\
\hline
19470280 \\
9276 \\
\hline
19461004 \\
\hline
\end{array}
$$

∴ 19461004 divided by 23028102 gives ·8450980, the logarithm of 7 true to the last figure.

If the logarithm be only required to five places of figures, but five factors are necessary.

$$
10 = \begin{array}{rrrrr}
\downarrow 24, & 1, & 5, & 1, & 9, \\
0, & 241, & \overline{91}, & \overline{23}, & \overline{207}, \\
0, & 0, & 2319, & \overline{23}, & \overline{1171},
\end{array}
$$

$$
\begin{array}{r}
23190 \\
23 \\
\hline
231670 \\
1171 \\
\hline
230499
\end{array}
$$

$$
7 = \begin{array}{rrrrr}
\downarrow 20, & 3, & 9, & 8, & 6, \\
0, & 203, & \overline{71}, & \overline{12}, & \overline{174}, \\
0, & 0, & \overline{1959}, & \overline{12}, & \overline{986},
\end{array}
$$

$$
\begin{array}{r}
19590 \\
12 \\
\hline
195780 \\
986 \\
\hline
194794
\end{array}
$$

194794 divided by 230499 gives ·845099, the logarithm of 7, to six decimal places, and differs but a unit from the truth; the logarithm of 7 taken from a table is ·845098.

12. *Find in a direct manner the logarithm of* 8.

$$\frac{10}{8} = 1·25 \text{ and } 1 \downarrow 2,3,2,6,7,3,2, = 1·25.$$

But ↓**2,3,2,6,7,3,2,** by (K) may be reduced to 2231653. In the last problem it was found that 10 = ↓**24,1,5,1,9,2,9,** =23028102, then 2231653 divided by 23028080, by common division, gives ·09690999, the logarithm of 1·25.

$$\begin{aligned} \log 10 &= 1·0000000 \\ \log 1·25 &= ·0969100 \\ \hline \log \text{ of } 8 &= ·9030900 \end{aligned}$$

true to seven places of decimals. To seven places of decimals ·09690999 is represented by ·0969100.

The cube root of 8 = 2,

∴ log 2 = ·3010300.

	1·1 = 1	↓**1,**	**0,**	**0,**	**0,**	**0,**	**0,**	**0,**
(K)	=	↓**0,**	**10,**	$\overline{4}$,	$\overline{1}$,	$\overline{9}$,	$\overline{5}$,	$\overline{1}$,
	=	↓**0,**	, **0,**	**96,**	$\overline{1}$,	$\overline{49}$,	$\overline{45}$,	$\overline{71}$,
	=	↓**0,**	**0,**	**0,**	**959,**	$\overline{49}$,	$\overline{45}$,	$\overline{455}$,

$$\begin{array}{r} 9590 \\ 49 \\ \hline 95410 \\ 45 \\ \hline 953650 \\ 455 \\ \hline 953195 \end{array}$$

953195 divided by 23028102 gives ·0413927, the logarithm of 1·1; and therefore the logarithm of 11 = 1·0413927.

The reason of this rule is evident, for $\downarrow 2,3,5,4,8,2,4,$ from the properties (K), may be reduced to the form $\downarrow 0,0,0,0,0,0,$ N,; and any other expression, as $\downarrow 1,3,6,2,5,7,2,$ may, in the same way, be represented by $\downarrow 0,0,0,0,0,0,$ M,:

N is an index of the factor 10000001, and M is an index of the same factor; any other factor may be employed.

Let a = the extreme factor; in the case before us a = 10000001. Let it be required to find the power $\downarrow 2,3,5,4,8,2,4,$ must be raised to, to produce $\downarrow 1,3,6,2,5,7,2,$; if x = the required power; then

$$(\downarrow 0,0,0,0,0,0,\ \mathrm{N},)^x = \downarrow 0,0,0,0,0,0,\ \mathrm{M},$$

$$\therefore (a^{\mathrm{N}})^x = a^{\mathrm{M}}$$

$$\therefore x \log (a^{\mathrm{N}}) = \mathrm{M} \log a,$$

$$\therefore \mathrm{N}\, x \log a = \mathrm{M} \log a,$$

$$\therefore x = \frac{\mathrm{M}}{\mathrm{N}}$$

13. *The reciprocal of ·743383 is 1·3452, what are the logarithms of both these numbers?*

$$1{\cdot}34520 = \downarrow 3,\ 1,\ 0,\ 6,\ 6,\ 0,$$
$$= \downarrow 0,\ 31,\ \overline{12},\ \overline{3},\ \overline{21},\ \overline{15},$$
$$\doteq \downarrow 0,\ 0,\ 298,\ 3,\ \overline{145},\ \overline{170},$$

The equalities (K) are only employed to six figures.

$$\left.\begin{aligned} \downarrow 1, &= \downarrow 0,\ 10,\ \overline{4},\ \overline{1},\ \overline{9},\ \overline{5},\\ \downarrow 0,1, &= \downarrow 0,\ 0,\ 10,\ 0,\ \overline{4},\ \overline{5},\\ \downarrow 0,0,1, &= \downarrow 0,\ 0,\ 0,\ 10,\ 0,\ 0,\end{aligned}\right\}$$

$$\begin{array}{r} 29830 \\ 145 \\ \hline 296850 \\ 170 \\ \hline 296680 \end{array}$$

296680 divided by 2302810, the constant before used, gives ·128786, the logarithm of 1·3452.

$$\begin{array}{rl} \log 10 = & 1{\cdot}000000 \\ \log 1{\cdot}3452 = & {\cdot}128786 \\ \hline & {\cdot}871214 = \log \text{ of } 743383. \end{array}$$

10, is the base of the common system of logarithms, and 2·718281828459, is the base of the hyperbolic system, which is by most writers represented by ϵ.

14. *Required the hyperbolic logarithm of* $\pi = 3{\cdot}14159265359$, *true to seven places of decimals.*

$$\epsilon^x = \pi$$

is the equation to be solved.

$$\begin{array}{ll} \pi \text{ is found} & = \downarrow 12,0,1,0,0,8,2,3, \\ \epsilon \quad ,, & = \downarrow 10,4,7,1,0,0,3,8, \end{array}$$

$$\begin{array}{rrrrrrrr} & \downarrow 12, & 0, & 1, & 0, & 0, & 8, & 2, \\ = & \downarrow 0, & 120, & \overline{47}, & \overline{12}, & \overline{108}, & \overline{52}, & \overline{10}, \\ = & \downarrow 0, & 0, & 1153, & \overline{12}, & \overline{588}, & \overline{532}, & \overline{850}, \\ = & \downarrow 0, & 0, & 0, & 11518, & \overline{588}, & \overline{532}, & \overline{5462}, \end{array}$$

$$\begin{array}{r} 115180 \\ 588 \\ \hline 1145920 \\ 532 \\ \hline 11453880 \\ 5462 \\ \hline 11448418 \end{array}$$

$$
\begin{array}{rrrrrrrr}
 & \downarrow 10, & 4, & 7, & 1, & 0, & 0, & 4, \\
= & \downarrow 0, & 104, & \overline{33}, & \overline{9}, & \overline{90}, & \overline{50}, & \overline{6}, \\
 & \downarrow 0, & 0, & 1007, & \overline{9}, & \overline{506}, & \overline{466}, & \overline{734}, \\
 & \downarrow 0, & 0, & 0, & 10061, & \overline{506}, & \overline{466}, & \overline{4762},
\end{array}
$$

$$
\begin{array}{r}
100610 \\
506 \\
\hline
1001040 \\
466 \\
\hline
10005740 \\
4762 \\
\hline
10000978
\end{array}
$$

Then 11448418 divided by 10000978 by common division gives 1·1447297, the hyperbolic logarithm of π. This example may be more readily solved by taking the square roots of π and ϵ, for the determination of $\downarrow 12$, and $\downarrow 10$, requires more skill than the finding of $\downarrow 6$, and $\downarrow 5$, : the fourth, eighth, or any other convenient roots of π and ϵ, may be operated with in the same manner.

$$\sqrt{\epsilon} = 1{\cdot}6487213 \;\; = \downarrow 5,2,3,5,5,0,0,$$
$$\sqrt{\pi} = 1{\cdot}77245385 = \downarrow 6,0,0,5,0,3,9,$$

$$
\begin{array}{rrrrrrrr}
 & \downarrow 5, & 2, & 3, & 5, & 5, & 0, & 0, \\
= & \downarrow 0, & 52, & \overline{17}, & 0, & \overline{40}, & \overline{25}, & \overline{5}, \\
= & \downarrow 0, & 0, & 503, & 0, & \overline{248}, & \overline{233}, & \overline{369}, \\
= & \downarrow 0, & 0, & 0, & 5030, & \overline{248}, & \overline{233}, & \overline{2884},
\end{array}
$$

$$
\begin{array}{r}
50300 \\
248 \\
\hline
500520 \\
233 \\
\hline
5002870 \\
2381 \\
\hline
5000489
\end{array}
$$

$$
\begin{array}{rrrrrrr}
\downarrow 6, & 0, & 0, & 5, & 0, & 3, & 9, \\
= \downarrow 0, & 60, & \overline{24}, & \overline{1}, & \overline{54}, & \overline{27}, & \overline{3}, \\
= \downarrow 0, & 0, & 576, & \overline{1}, & \overline{294}, & \overline{267}, & \overline{417}, \\
= \downarrow 0, & 0, & 0, & 5759, & \overline{294}, & \overline{267}, & \overline{2721},
\end{array}
$$

$$
\begin{array}{r}
57590 \\
294 \\
\hline
572960 \\
267 \\
\hline
5726930 \\
2721 \\
\hline
5724209
\end{array}
$$

Divide 5000489 into 5724209 by common division, the quotient = 1·1447298, the hyperbolic logarithm of π, true to the last figure: the equalities used in this latter method are,

$$
\begin{array}{llrrrrrrl}
\downarrow 1, & = \downarrow 0, & 10, & \overline{4}, & \overline{1}, & \overline{9}, & \overline{5}, & \overline{1}, & \\
\downarrow 0,1, & = \downarrow 0, & 0, & 10, & 0, & \overline{4}, & \overline{4}, & \overline{7}, & \\
\downarrow 0,0,1, & = \downarrow 0, & 0, & 0, & 10, & 0, & 0, & \overline{5}, & \text{(K)}. \\
\downarrow 0,0,0,1, & = \downarrow 0, & 0, & 0, & 0, & 10, & 0, & 0, &
\end{array}
$$

The following equations of condition are composed of positive number, and may be often employed with advantage, when only seven decimal places are required:—

$$
\begin{array}{llrrrrrrl}
\downarrow 1, & = \downarrow 0, & 9, & 5, & 7, & 5, & 9, & 7, & \\
\downarrow 0,1, & = \downarrow 0, & 0, & 9, & 9, & 5, & 4, & 9, & \\
\downarrow 0,0,1, & = \downarrow 0, & 0, & 0, & 9, & 9, & 9, & 5, & \text{(L)}. \\
\downarrow 0,0,0,1, & = \downarrow 0, & 0, & 0, & 0, & 10, & 0, & 0, &
\end{array}
$$

Example.

Reduce $\epsilon = \downarrow 10,4,7,1,0,0,4,$ to a representative number, standing in the seventh position by the equations (L).

$$\downarrow 10, = \downarrow 0,90,50,70,50,90,70,$$

subtract the left-hand member of this equation, and add the right-hand member, the result will be—

$$\epsilon = \downarrow 0,94,57,71,50,90,74,$$

Again, $\quad \downarrow 0,94 = \downarrow 0,0,846,846,470,376,846,$

take the left-hand member away, and add the right-hand member;

$$\begin{array}{rrrrrrrrr}
\text{Then} & \epsilon = \downarrow 0, & 0, & 903, & 917, & 520, & 466, & 920, \\
\downarrow 0,0,903, & = \downarrow 0, & 0, & 0, & 8127, & 8127, & 8127, & 4515, \\
\therefore & \epsilon = \downarrow 0, & 0, & 0, & 9044, & 8647, & 8593, & 5435, \\
\therefore & \epsilon = \downarrow 0, & 0, & 0, & 0, & 0, & 0, & 10000065,
\end{array}$$

$$\begin{array}{r}
90440 \\
8647 \\
\hline
990870 \\
8593 \\
\hline
9994630 \\
5435 \\
\hline
10000065
\end{array}$$

The values of (K) may be found reduced to the seventh position, as follows:—

$$\begin{array}{lll}
& \downarrow 1, & = \downarrow 0,10,\bar{4},\bar{1},\bar{9},\bar{5},\bar{1}, = \downarrow 0,0,0,0,0,0,953195, \quad (a) \\
& \downarrow 0,1, & = \downarrow 0,\ 0,10,\ 0,\ \bar{4},\bar{4},\bar{7}, = \downarrow 0,0,0,0,0,0,\ 99513, \quad (b) \\
(\text{K}), & \downarrow 0,0,1, & = \downarrow 0,\ 0,\ 0,10,\ 0,0,\bar{4}, = \downarrow 0,0,0,0,0,0,\ 9996, \quad (c) \\
& \downarrow 0,0,0,1, & = \downarrow 0,\ 0,\ 0,\ 0,10,0,0, = \downarrow 0,0,0,0,0,0,\ 1000, \quad (d)
\end{array}$$

$$\underline{\underline{\downarrow 0,0,0,\ 1}}, = 1000,\ (d)$$

$$\text{Then, } \downarrow 0,0,0,10, = (d) \times 10 = 10000,$$

$$\text{and, } \downarrow 0,0,0,\ 0,0,0,\bar{4}, \qquad = \quad -4,$$

$$\therefore \underline{\underline{\downarrow 0,0,\ 1}}, = \downarrow 0,0,0,10,0,0,\bar{4}, \qquad = \underline{9996},\ (c).$$

$$\text{Then, } \downarrow 0,0,10, = (c) \times 10 = 99960,$$

$$\text{and, } \downarrow 0,0,\ 0,0,\bar{4},\bar{4},\bar{7}, \qquad = \underline{-447},$$

$$\underline{\underline{\downarrow 0,\ 1}}, = \downarrow 0,0,10,0,\bar{4},\bar{4},\bar{7}, \qquad = \underline{99513},\ (b).$$

$$\text{Then, } \downarrow 0,10, = (b) \times 10 = 995130,$$

$$\text{and, } \downarrow 0,\ 0,\bar{4}, = (c) \times -4 = -39984,$$

$$\downarrow 0,\ 0,0,\bar{1},\bar{9},\bar{5},\bar{1}, \qquad = \underline{-1951},$$

$$\downarrow 1, = \downarrow 0,10,\bar{4},\bar{1},\bar{9},\bar{5},\bar{1}, \qquad = \underline{953195},\ (a).$$

The final values of $\downarrow 1$, $\downarrow 0,1$, $\downarrow 0,0,1$, &c. are also readily found from their positive equalities.

$$\downarrow 1, \quad = \downarrow 0,9,5,7,5,9,8, = \downarrow 0,0,0,0,0,0,953195,\ (a).$$

$$(\text{K}),\ \downarrow 0,1, \quad = \downarrow 0,0,9,9,5,4,9, = \downarrow 0,0,0,0,0,0,\ 99513,\ (b).$$

$$\downarrow 0,0,1, = \downarrow 0,0,0,9,9,9,6, = \downarrow 0,0,0,0,0,0,\ \ 9996,\ (c).$$

$$\underline{\underline{\downarrow 0,0,1}}, = 9996,\ (c).$$

$$\text{Then, } \downarrow 0,0,9, = c \times 9 = 89964,$$

$$\text{and, } \downarrow 0,0,0,9,5,4,9, \quad = \quad 9549,$$

$$\therefore \underline{\underline{\downarrow 0,1}}, \quad = \downarrow 0,0,9,9,5,4,9, \quad = \underline{99513},\ (b).$$

$$\text{Then, } \downarrow 0,9, \quad = (b) \times 9 = 895617,$$

$$\text{and, } \downarrow 0,0,5, = (c) \times 5 = 49980,$$

$$\text{and, } \downarrow 0,0,0,7,5,9,8, \quad = \quad 7598,$$

$$\therefore \downarrow 1, = \downarrow 0,9,5,7,5,9,8, \quad = 953195,\ (a).$$

By a similar process, the values of $\downarrow$1, $\downarrow$0,1, $\downarrow$0,0,1, &c. are readily reduced to the eight, or any other position.

$\downarrow$1, = $\downarrow$0,9,5,7,5,9,7,4, = $\downarrow$0,0,0,0,0,0,0,9531497, (A).
$\downarrow$0,1, = $\downarrow$0,0,9,9,5,4,8,8, = $\downarrow$0,0,0,0,0,0,0, 995083, (B).
$\downarrow$0,0,1, = $\downarrow$0,0,0,9,9,9,5,5, = $\downarrow$0,0,0,0,0,0,0, 99955, (C).

$\downarrow$0,0,1, = 99955, (C).
Then, $\downarrow$0,0,9, = (C) × 9 = 899595
and $\downarrow$0,0,0,9,5,4,8,8, = 95488
∴ $\downarrow$0,1, = $\downarrow$0,0,9,9,5,4,8,8, = 995083, (B).
Then, $\downarrow$0,9, = (B) × 9 = 8955747,
and $\downarrow$0,0,5, = (C) × 5 = 499775,
and $\downarrow$0,0,0,7,5,9,7,4, = 75974,
∴ $\downarrow$1, = $\downarrow$0,9,5,7,5,9,7,4, = 9531496, (A).

It will be found convenient to register from 1 to 9 times the values of (A), (B), and (C).

	A.	B.	C.
1	9531497	995083	99955
2	19062994	1990166	199910
3	28594491	2985249	299865
4	38125988	3980332	399820
5	47657485	4975415	499775
6	57188982	5970498	599730
7	66720479	6965581	699685
8	76251976	796c664	799640
9	85783473	8955747	899595

While operating on magnitudes, developed as far as the eight position, the succeeding collection of simple equalities will also be found useful.

2 = ↓ 7,2,6,0,7,8,2,6,	= 69318201,	in the eight position.	
3 = ↓ 11,5,0,4,4,8,6,8,	= 109866750,	,,	,,
4 = ↓ 14,5,2,2,0,1,1,9,	= 138636402,	,,	,,
5 = ↓ 16,8,4,8,7,4,4,3,	= 160951879,	,,	,,
6 = ↓ 18,7,6,5,2,6,9,4,	= 179184951,	,,	,,
7 = ↓ 20,3,9,8,6,0,1,0,	= 194600794,	,,	,,
8 = ↓ 21,7,8,2,7,9,4,6,	= 207954604,	,,	,,
9 = ↓ 23,0,5,0,9,2,9,4,	= 219733500,	,,	,,
10 = ↓ 24,1,5,1,9,2,9,5,	= 230270081,	,,	,,

It may be observed, that the whole number 69318201, to which 2 is reduced, is half the number 138636402, to which 4 is reduced, and one third the number 207954604, to which 8 is reduced, because $2^2 = 4$, and $2^3 = 8$. Again, the number 109866750, to which 3 is reduced, is half 219733500, the number to which 9 is reduced, because $3^2 = 9$. Further, since $2 \times 3 = 6$, the numbers representing 2 and 3 added together = the number to which 6 is reduced; and because $2 \times 5 = 10$, the numbers representing 2 and 5 added together = the number to which 10 is reduced, and so on with other numbers. Hence, the only numbers to be calculated, before forming the last collection, are the representatives of 2, 3, 5, and 7.

From what has been previously explained, it is easily found that

2 = ↓ 7,2,6,0,7,8,2,6, ..

Then, 7 (A) =	66720479
2 (B) =	1990166
6 (C) =	599730
To which add 0,7,8,2,6, =	7826
∴ 2 =	69318201,

Again, $\frac{3}{2}$ = 1·50000000 = ↓4,2,4,3,2,5,7,4,

Then, 4 (A) = 38125988,
2 (B) = 1990166,
4 (C) = 399820,
To which add 3,2,5,7,4, = 32574,
$\frac{3}{2}$ = 40548548,
2 = 69318201,
∴ 3 = 109866749 = ↓11,5,0,4,4,6,7,
95314970 ⌣ 10 (A);
14551779
9531497 ⌣ 1 (A),
5020282
4975415 ⌣ 5 (B),
0,4,4,8,6,7,

$\frac{5}{4}$ = 1·25000000 = ↓2,3,2,6,7,3,2,4,

Then, 2 (A) = 19062994,
3 (B) = 2985249,
2 (C) = 199910,
and 6,7,3,2,4, = 67324,
$\frac{5}{4}$ = 22315477
4 = 138636402
∴ 5 = 160951879, = ↓16,8,4,8,7,4,4,3,
95314970
65636909
57188982
8447927
7960664
487263
399820
8,7,4,4,3,

$$\frac{7}{6} = 1{\cdot}16666667 = \downarrow 1,5,9,0,9,3,3,4,$$

Then 1 (A) = 9531497,
5 (B) = 4975415,
9 (C) = 899595,
and 09335,
add 6. = 179184951,
194600793, $= \downarrow 20,3,9,8,6,0,0,9,$
190629949 ⌣ 20 (A),
3970853
2985249 ⌣ 3 (B),
985604
899595 ⌣ 9 (C),
8,6,0,0,9, and.

Examples in Reduction.

1. *Express* 88888·8888 *in the eight position,*

$$88888{\cdot}8888 = 10^4 \times 8 \times 1{\cdot}11111111$$
$$= 10^4 \times 8 \downarrow 1,1,0,1,0,0,0,1,$$

10 = 230270081
4
10^4 = 921080324
8 = 207954604
9531497 ⌣ 1 (A),
995083 ⌣ 1 (B),
10001 and.

$\therefore$ 88888·8888 = $\downarrow \overline{1139571509,}$

This notation will be explained hereafter.

2. *Reduce ·0066666666 to the eight position.*

$$·0066666666 = \frac{1}{10^3} \times 6 \times 1·1111111,$$

$$= \frac{1}{10^3} \times 6 \downarrow 1,1,0,1,0,0,0,0,$$

$$\begin{array}{rrl} 6 = & 179184951 & \\ & 9531497 & 1\,(A) \\ & 995083 & 1\,(B) \\ & 10000 & \\ \hline & +\,189721531 & \\ \frac{1}{10^3} = & -\,690810243 & \\ \hline \end{array} \qquad \begin{array}{rl} 10 = & 230270081 \\ & 3 \\ \hline 10^3 = & 690810243 \end{array}$$

$$\therefore ·0066666666 = \downarrow -\overline{501088712,}|$$

3. *What number answers to* 1139571509, *written* $\downarrow\overline{1139571509,}|$ *standing in the eight position?*

Four times 230270081 = 921080324, is a multiple of the value of 10, nearest the given number, but not exceeding the given number.

$$\begin{array}{rr} & 1139571509 \\ 10^4 = & 921080324 \\ \hline & 218491185 \\ 8 = & 207954604 \\ \hline & 10536581 \\ 1\,(A) = & 9531497 \\ \hline & 1005084 \\ 1\,(B) = & 995083 \\ \hline & ·10001 \end{array}$$

$$\therefore 10^4 \times 8 \times \downarrow 1,1,0,1,0,0,0,1, = 88888·8888.$$

4. *What is the corresponding number of* $-$ 501088712, *written* $\downarrow -\overline{501088712,}|$?

Three times 230270081 = 690810243 is the nearest multiple of the value of 10 exceeding the given number.

$$
\begin{array}{rr}
10^{9} = & +\,690810243, \\
 & -\,501088712, \text{ given number.} \\
\hline
 & 189721531 \\
6 = & 179184951 \\
\hline
 & 10536580 \\
1\ (A) = & 9531497 \\
\hline
 & 1005083 \\
1\ (B) = & 995083 \\
\hline
 & 0,1,0,0,0,0,
\end{array}
$$

$$\therefore \frac{1}{10^{8}} \times 6 \downarrow 1,1,0,1,0,0,0,0, = \cdot 0066666666.$$

5. *What is the* $\frac{17}{43}$ *root of* π, *to nine places of figures?*

$\pi = 3 \downarrow 0,4,6,3,1,9,2,9,5, = 114478742$ reduced to the eight position,

$$
\begin{array}{rr}
3 = & 109866750 \\
4\ (B) = & 3980332 \\
6\ (C) = & 599730 \\
\text{And} & 31930 \\
\hline
 & 114478742 = \\
\text{Multiply by} & 17 \\
\hline
43\ ) & 1946138614 \\
\hline
\end{array}
$$

$$45259038 = \downarrow 4,7,16,7,5,1,4, = 1\cdot 57234422.$$

PART IV.

OF ANGULAR MAGNITUDES AND TRIGONOMETRICAL LINES.

To seven places of decimals, $\pi = 3{\cdot}1415927$; π is generally put for the length of an arc of a circle of 180°, radius = 1.

```
312|000|00 .
  1|872|00 .   ↓0,0,6,9,
      4|68 .
          1 .
-----------
313 876 69
    282 49
        11
-----------
314 159 29
```

When the radius is not equal to 1, its length will be mentioned; when the length of the radius is not specified, it is assumed = 1.

Arc of	180°	may be	represented by	3·12 ↓0,0,6,9,
„	45°	„	„	·78 ↓0,0,6,9,
„	60°	„	„	1·04 ↓0,0,6,9,
„	30°	„	„	·52 ↓0,0,6,9,
„	15°	„	„	·26 ↓0,0,6,9,
„	7½°	„	„	·13 ↓0,0,6,9,
„	22½°	„	„	·39 ↓0,0,6,9,
„	90°	„	„	1·56 ↓0,0,6,9,
„	37½°	„	„	·65 ↓0,0,6,9,

The succeeding combinations are also readily established.

Length of an arc of		30° =	·52 ↓0,0,6,9,
"	"	3° =	·052↓0,0,6,9,
"	"	6° =	·104↓0,0,6,9,
"	"	9° =	·156↓0,0,6,9,
"	"	12° =	·208↓0,0,6,9,
"	"	15° =	·26 ↓0,0,6,9,
"	"	18° =	·312↓0,0,6,9,
"	"	21° =	·364↓0,0,6,9,
		&c. =	&c.

The length of an arc $(a)^\circ$ may be found by saying

$$\text{As } 180^\circ : \pi :: (a)^\circ : \frac{\pi(a)^\circ}{180^\circ}.$$

Other methods to find the length of an arc of a circle corresponding to any number of degrees, minutes, &c. will be given hereafter.

It is well known that if x be the length of an arc of a circle to radius 1, then

$$\sin x = x - \frac{x^3}{2.3} + \frac{x^5}{2\cdot3\cdot4\cdot5} - \frac{x^7}{2\cdot3\cdot4\cdot5\cdot6\cdot7} + \ldots.$$

$$\cos x = 1 - \frac{x^2}{2} + \frac{x^4}{2\cdot4} - \frac{x^6}{2\cdot3\cdot4\cdot5\cdot6} + \ldots.$$

Examples.

1. *Find the length of the sine and cosine of an arc of* 15°, *to seven places of decimals.*

Length of 15° = ·26↓0,0,6,9,

$(\cdot 26)^2 = \cdot 0676000$
$(\cdot 26)^3 = \cdot 0175760$
$(\cdot 26)^4 = \cdot 0045698$
$(\cdot 26)^5 = \cdot 0011881$
$(\cdot 26)^6 = \cdot 0003089$

2	3	4	5	6	↓0,0,36,54
3089	1546	515	129	26	4

2
45698

3
22849

4
761|6
46..| ⌣6

7800|
7....|⌣9

↓0,0,24,36,
190|4..
4|6..

195 0|....
7|....

195 7

2
676|000
4056| ⌣6

6841|56
616..| ⌣9

↓0,0,12,18,
338|0 00
4|0 56 which call A
22 = 11 × A ÷ 2

342 6|78..
6|16.. call A
1.. = 17 × A ÷ 2

342 695

1·0000000 +
1957 +
342695 −
4 −

·9659258 = cosine of 15°.

In finding the cosine, the length of the arc is not required except under the form

·26↓0,0,6,9,

2	3	4	5		↓0,0,30,45,
11881	5940	1980	495 ·		99 · | . . .
			3 . . . . | ◡ 6		3 · | . . .
					102

2	3	↓0,0,18,27,
175760	878 | 80	292 | 9 3 ·
	527 · | ◡ 6	5 | 2 7 · = A
		4 · = 17 · × A ÷ 2
	8947 | 2	298 2 | 4 . . .
	80 . . | ◡ 9	8 | 0 . . .
		299 0 4

Length of arc = ·2617994 +
102 +
·2618096
29904 −
·2588192, sine of 15°.

RADIUS = 1.

	Length of an arc of 1°, 2°, 3°, 4°, &c.	Length of an Arc of 1′, 2′, 3′, 4′, &c.	Length of an Arc of 1″, 2″, 3″, &c.
1	·017453293	·000290888	·000004848
2	·034906585	·000581776	·000009696
3	·052359878	·000872664	·000014544
4	·069813170	·001163552	·000019393
5	·087266463	·001454440	·000024241
6	·104719755	·001745329	·000029089
7	·122173048	·002036216	·000033937
8	·139626340	·002327105	·000038785
9	·157079633	·002617993	·000043633

Examples.

2. *Required the length of an arc of a circle to radius* 1, *of* 8° 26′ 13″ *and its cosine.*

·13962634
·00581776
·00174533
·00004848
·00001454

True to seven places of decimals, ·1472525 = arc of 8° 26′ 13″.

1472525 = 147 ↓ 0,0,1,7,1,7,
(·147)² = ·0216090
(·147)⁴ = ·0004669

2 | 3 | 4 | ↓ 0,0,4,28,4,28,
4669 | 2335 | 778 | 195 | . . .
1 . . . | ⌣ 1 | 1 | . . .
784 . | 196 . | . . . .
6 . . . . | ⌣ 7 | 1 . | . . . .
197

2 | ↓ 0,0,2,14,2,14,
216 | 0 90 | 108 | 0 4 5
216 | ⌣ 1. | | 2 1 6
216 5 | 22 | 108 2 | 6 1 . .
152 . . | ⌣ 7 | 1 | 5 2 . . . .
| 2 | . . . . . .
| 2 | . . . . . .
108 4 1 7

1·0000000
108417 −
·9891583
197 +
·9891780 = cosine 8° 26′ 13″, exact to the last figure.

Examples of Transformations of the Equations of condition.

1. *It is required to put* $\downarrow 3,\overline{17},8,\overline{28},\overline{12},6,\overline{41},$ *in a positive convenient form to extraet the seventh root of it.*

$$\begin{array}{lllllll}
\downarrow 1, & = \downarrow 0,10, & \overline{4}, & \overline{1}, & \overline{9},\overline{5},\overline{1}, & = \downarrow 0,10, & \overline{4}, \; 0, \; 0,0,\overline{1951}, \\
\downarrow 0,1, & = \downarrow 0, & 0,10, & 0, & \overline{4},\overline{4},\overline{7}, & = \downarrow 0, & 0,10, \; 0, \; 0,0, \; \overline{447}, \\
\downarrow 0,0,1, & = \downarrow 0, & 0, & 0,10, & 0,0,\overline{4}, & = \downarrow 0, & 0, \; 0,10, \; 0,0, \; \overline{4}, \\
\downarrow 0,0,0,1, & = \downarrow 0, & 0, & 0, & 0,10,0,0, & = \downarrow 0, & 0, \; 0, \; 0,10,0, \; 0,
\end{array}$$

$$\begin{array}{lllll}
 & \downarrow 0,10, & \overline{4}, & 0,0,0,\overline{1951}, & +\,4470 \\
= & \downarrow 0, & 0,96, & 0,0,0,\overline{6421}, & +\;\;384 \\
= & \downarrow 0, & 0, & 0,960,0,0,\overline{6805}, &
\end{array}$$

$$\begin{array}{r}
960000 \\
6805 \\
\hline
953195
\end{array}$$

$$\downarrow 0,0,10, \quad 0,0,0,\overline{447},$$
$$\downarrow 0,0, \; 0,100,0,0,\overline{487},$$

$$\begin{array}{r}
100000 \\
487 \\
\hline
99513
\end{array}$$

In this manner the following equalities may also be established:

$$\begin{array}{llll}
\therefore \; \downarrow 1, & = \downarrow 0,0,0,0,0,0,953195, & 7 \text{ times} = & 6672365 \\
\downarrow 0,1, & = \downarrow 0,0,0,0,0,0, \; 99513, & 7 \text{ times} = & 696591 \\
\downarrow 0,0,1, & = \downarrow 0,0,0,0,0,0, \; 9996, & 7 \text{ times} = & 69972 \\
\downarrow 0,0,0,1, & = \downarrow 0,0,0,0,0,0, \; 1000, & 7 \text{ times} = & 7000
\end{array}$$

$$\begin{aligned}
\text{Given,}\quad & \downarrow 3,\overline{17},\ 8,\ \overline{27},\overline{12},\ 6,\ \overline{41},\\
&= \downarrow 0,13,\ \overline{4},\ \overline{30},\overline{39},\ \overline{9},\ \overline{44},\\
&= \downarrow 0,\ 0,126,\ \overline{30},\overline{91},\overline{61},\overline{135},\\
&= \downarrow 0,\ 0,\ 0,1230,\overline{91},\overline{61},\overline{639},
\end{aligned}$$

```
                12300
                   91
               ------
               122090
                   61
              -------
              1220290
                  639
             --------
696591 )  1219651 (↓0,1,7,4,7,5,1,
           696591
           ------
 69972 )   523060
           489804
           ------
  7000 )    33256
            28000
            -----
   700 )     5256
             4900
             ----
    70 )      356
              350
              ---
     7 )        6
                7 nearly.
```

∴ $\downarrow 0,1,7,4,7,5,1,$ = the seventh root of $\downarrow 3,\overline{17},8,\overline{27},\overline{12},6,\overline{41},$

or, $\downarrow 0,7,49,28,49,35,7, = \downarrow 3,\overline{17},8,\overline{27},\overline{12},6,\overline{41},$

$= \downarrow 0,0,0,0,0,0,1219651,$ which may readily be reduced to

$\downarrow 1,2,6,7,4,5,4,$

```
953195 ) 1219651 (1,
          953195
          ------
          266456
```

$$99513\,)\,266456\,(\,2,$$
$$\underline{199026}$$
$$9996\,)\,67430\,(\,6,$$
$$\underline{59976}\;.$$
$$7,4,5,4,$$

2. *Put* $\downarrow 3,\overline{17},8,\overline{27},\overline{12},6,\overline{41},$ *in a form so that the square root of it is represented in whole numbers.*

953195 × 2 = 1906390; 99513 × 2 = 199026; 9996 × 2 = 19992.

The given expression, when reduced to the seventh place, becomes

$$\downarrow 0,0,0,0,0,0,1219651,$$

$$199026\,)\,1219651\,(\downarrow 0,6,1,$$
$$\underline{1194156}\;.$$
$$19992\,)\,25495$$
$$\underline{19992}$$
$$2\,)\,\underline{5503}$$
$$2,7,5,1,$$

$\downarrow 0,6,1,2,7,5,1,$ represents the square root of $\downarrow 3,\overline{17},8,\overline{27},\overline{12},6,\overline{41}$

Find the cosine of 6° 26′ 23″·5.

$$\begin{aligned} 10471976 &= 6^\circ \\ 00581776 &= 20' \\ 00174533 &= 6' \\ 00009696 &= 20'' \\ 00001454 &= 3'' \\ 00000242 &= ''\cdot 5 \\ \hline \cdot 1123968 &= \text{arc of } 6^\circ\, 26'\, 23''\cdot 5 \end{aligned}$$

$$1123968 = 112 \downarrow 0,0,3,5,3,8,$$
$$\cdot 112^2 = \cdot 0125440$$
$$\cdot 112^4 = \cdot 0001574$$

2	3	4		$\downarrow 0,0,12,20,12,32,$
1574	787	262 . |		66 . | . . .
		1 . . . . |	⌣ 3	1 . | . . .
				67

2 divided into 1574, gives 787; 3 divided into 787, gives 262; and 4 divided into 262, gives 65·5 or 66. Then, ↓0,0,12,20,12,32, operates on 66; the extent to which the operation is carried only requires the use of one of these factors, namely ↓0,0,12,.

```
   2                          ↓0,0,6,10,6,16,
1254|40                     ·627|20 .
376.|   ⌣ 3                    3|76 .
                                  1 .
                           ----------------
1261|94                     6309|7 . . .
63...|  ⌣ 5                    6|3| . . . . .
                               4| .| . . . . . .
                               1| .| . . . . . .
                           -------------
                            63165
                           -------------
```

```
1·0000000
    63165
---------
·9936835
       67
---------
·9936902 = cos 6° 26′ 23″·5
```

3. *What is the length of an arc of* 9° 20′ 45″, *and its sine and cosine, radius* = 1?

```
       1570796 –  9°
         58178 – 20′
          1939 – 40″
           242 –  5″
         ---------
163↓0,0,0,7,0,8, = 1631155
```

The numbers employed to find the square, cube, &c., of ·163 may be taken from the following line containing from 1 to 9 times 163. It may be observed that only 15 numbers are required to be taken this line.

1	2	3	4	5	6	7	8	9
163	326	489	652	815	978	1141	1304	1467

```
   489
  978
 163
---------
·0265690 = (·163)²

          1467
         978
        815
       978
      326
   ---------
   ·004330747
   ·0043307 = (·163)³

     1141
    4890
    489
   652
  ---------
  ·0007059041
  0007059 = (·163)⁴

          1467
          815
         11410.
   ----------
   ·0001150617
   ·0001151 = (·163)⁵

   2         3         4         5
 1151       576       192,      48        10

   2            3              ↓0,0,0,21,0,24,
 43307        21654             7218| . . . .
              15 . . . . ⌣ 7      15| . . . .
                                -----------
                                 7233

Length of arc = 1631155
                   7233 −
                     10 +
                -------
                1623932 = sin 9° 20′ 45″.

   2            3            4            ↓0,0,0,28,0,32,
 7059         3530         1177 .|          294 .| . . . .
                           8 . . . .| ⌣ 7     1 .| . . . .
                                           ---------
                                            295

       2                   ↓0,0,0,14,0,16,
   2656|9 0                 1328|45 . .
   186 . .|  ⌣ 7               1|86 . .
                            -----------
   26606 2|                 1330 31| . . . . . .
   2 . . . . . . .| ⌣ 8            2| . . . . . .
                            -----------
                            1330 33
```

```
 1·0000000
   133033 −
 ─────────────
  ·9866967
       295 +
 ─────────────
  ·9867262 = cos 9° 20′ 45″.
```

4. *The length of an arc of* 35° 40″ = ·6225008; *find the cosine.*

62 ↓ 0,0,4,0,2,7,5, = 6225008.

```
               62
               62
             ─────
              124
             372
             ─────
Square       3844 ⌣ 1
             7688 ⌣ 2
            11532 ⌣ 3
            15376 ⌣ 4
            19220 ⌣ 5
            23064 ⌣ 6
            26908 ⌣ 7
            30752 ⌣ 8
            34596 ⌣ 9
            ─────
```

The following are taken from the above column :—

```
   1537|6               1|5376              1|1532
  15376|               11|532            3075|200
 30752 |              230|64            23064|
·11532·|             2690|8             19220|
────────            26908|             ──────────────
·1477634 fourth.   15376 |             0218340 eighth.
                   3844  |
                  ──────────
                  ·0568003 sixth.
```

```
   2        3        4       5      6     7    8
218340   109170   36390   9098   1820   304   43   5
```

The 5 in the seventh decimal place, here produced by dividing 218340 continually by 1 ⌣ 8 when operated upon by ↓ 0,0,32, ... is not increased a unit, so the operation is omitted.

```
   2         3        4       5        6     · ↓0,0,24,0,12,
568003    284002   94667   23667    4733|          789| . . .
                                    19. . .| ⌣ 4    19| . . .
                                                   ----
                                                   808

       2          3        4          ↓0,0,16,0,8,28,20,
   1477634   738817   2462|72            615|68 ..
                       985 .|    ⌣ 4        9|85 .
                                               7 .
                                         ------
                                         625 60| . . . . .
                                              5| . . . . .
              250260 .|                  625 65 .| . . . . . .
              2 . . . . . . .| ⌣ 7             2 .| . . . . . .
                                         ------
                                         625 67

        2                      ↓0,0,8,0,4,14,10,
   384400|0 . .                  192|20 0|0 . .
   15376 . .|        ⌣ 4           1|53 7|6| . .
                                        5|4| . .
                                 ------------
                                 193 74|3 0| . . .
                                       |7|8 . . . . .
                                        2|5| . . . . . . .
                                          2| . . . . . . .
                                 ------------
                                 193 75 3 5
```

```
 1·0000000 +
   1937535 −
 ---------
  ·8062465
     62567 +
 ---------
  ·8125032
       808 −
 ---------
  ·8124224
         5 +
 ---------
  ·8124229 = cos 35° 40′.
```

5. *It is readily found that the length of an arc of* 35° 38′ 49″ = 6221566, *find the cosine.*

62 ↓ 0,0,3,4,7,4, = 6221566.

Many of the results, and the column of the last example may be employed here, as 62 are the two first figures.

```
       6                    ↓ 0,0,18,24,42,
     4734|                        789| . . .
    14...|  ⌣ 3                    14| . . .
                                  ---------
    4818.|                        803 .| . . . .
   2.....|  ⌣ 4                     2 .| . . . .
                                  -----------
                                  805 . . | . . . . .
```

```
      4                     ↓ 0,0,12,16,28,16,
    2462|72                   615|68 .
    739.|     ⌣ 3               7|39 .
                                    4 .
                             ----------
   24924|4                   623 1|1 . . .
   100...|   ⌣ 4                1 0|0| . . .
                                  1 7|.| . . . . . .
                                    1|.| . . . . . .
                             ---------------------
                             62429
```

```
                            ↓ 0,0,6,8,14,8,
                            192|2 0 0|0 . .
                              1|1 5 3|2 . .
                                    2|9 . .
                            ---------------
                            193 3|5 6 1 .
                                1|5 4 7 .
                                      1 .
                            ---------------
   38702|26                 193 5 1|0 9 . . .
   271...|     ⌣ 7                2|7|1 . . . . .
                                  1|5 . . . . .
                            ---------------
                            1935395
```

```
1·0000000 +
  1935395 −
 ─────────
 ·8064605
    62429 +
 ─────────
 ·8127034
      805 −
 ─────────
 ·8126229
        5 +
 ─────────
 ·8126234 = cos 35° 38′ 49″.
```

6. *What is the cosine* 37° 39′ 49″·5, *the length of the arc being* = ·6573565?

To calculate the length of an arc of any number of degrees, minutes, the following table is easily constructed, and readily applied;

·0000048481368 being the length of an arc of 1″, to radius unity:

```
·0000048481368 ◡ 1
·0000096962736 ◡ 2
·0000145444104 ◡ 3
·0000193925472 ◡ 4
·0000242406840 ◡ 5
·0000290888208 ◡ 6
·0000339369576 ◡ 7
·0000387850944 ◡ 8
·0000436332312 ◡ 9
```

37° 39′ 49″·5 = 135589″·5.

```
                  ·4848137 = 100000″
                  ·1454441 =  30000
                    242407 =   5000
                     24241 =    500
                      3879 =     80
                       436 =      9
                        24 =      ·5
                  ─────────
657 ↓ 0,0,0,5,4,2,4, = ·6573565
```

The numbers whose sums give the square, cube, &c. of ·657, may be found by inspection, when the following line is formed.

1	2	3	4	5	6	7	8	9
657	1314	1971	2628	3285	3942	4599	5256	5913

```
  4599
 3285
3942
·4316490 square.
```

```
     59|13
    262|8
   3942|
   657 |
  1971 |
 2628  |
·2835934| cube
```

```
      2|628
     19|71
    591|3
   3285|
  1971 |
 5256  |
1314   |
·1863209| fourth.
```

```
      5|913
    131|40
   1971|
  3942 |
 5256  |
657    |
.1224128| fifth.
```

```
      5|256
     13|14
     65|7
   2628|
  1314 |
 1314  |
657    |
·0804252| sixth.
```

```
      1|314
     32|85
    131|4
   2628|
  52560|
·0528394| seventh.
```

```
      2|628
     59|13
    197|1
   5256|
  1314 |
 3285  |
·0347155| eight.
```

```
   2         3        4       5      6     7    8
347155    173578   57859   14465   2893   482   69   9.

   2         3        4       5      6     ↓0,0,0,5,4,2,4,
804252    402126   134042  33510   6702      1117|....
                                  3....         3|....
                                              ----
                                              1120

   2             3            4           ↓0,0,0,20,16,8,16,
1863209       931605       31053|5          7763|4...
                            155...|  ⌣5       15|5...
                                             --------
                           311156|          7778 9|.....
                            12.....| ⌣4          1 2|.....
                                             --------
                           311204.|         7780 1 .|......
                           6......|              1 .|......
                                             --------
                                             77802

              2                ↓0,0 0,10,8,4,8,
          4316|490               2158|245 .
          2158.|     ⌣5             2|158 .
                                        1 .
                                 ------------
                                 2160 4|04 . .
                                      1|7|3 . . . . .
                                         |9|. . . . . . .
                                         1|. . . . . . .
                                 ------------
                                 |2160587

        1·0000000 +
          2160587 −
        ---------
         ·7839412
            77802 +
        ---------
         ·7917214
             1120 −
        ---------
         ·7916094
                9 +
        ---------
         ·7916103 =  cos 37° 39′ 49″·5.
```

PROBLEM.

7. *Given the apparent altitude of the moon's centre* 8° 26′ 13″ (a), *the true altitude,* 9° 20′ 45″ (A), *the apparent altitude of a star* 35° 40′ ($a_{,}$), *the true altitude,* 35° 38′ 49″ ($A_{,}$), *and the apparent distance* 31° 13′ 26″ (d); *required the true distance, so as to find the longitude at sea.*

Put D = the true distance.

$A, A_{,}$ = the true altitudes

d = the apparent distance.

$a, a_{,}$ = apparent altitudes.

It is established by writers on Spherical Trigonometry, that,

$$\cos D = [\cos d + \cos (a + a_{,})] \frac{\cos A \cos A_{,}}{\cos a \cos a_{,}} - \cos (A + A_{,}).$$

```
       d  31° 13′ 26″  cos = ·8551482
(a + a,)  44   6  13   cos = ·7180824
                             ---------
                             1·5732306
```

```
(A) 9° 20′ 45″ cos = ·9867261
(a) 8  26  13  cos = ·9891779
                     ---------
                      986726|1 ..   ↓0,0,2,4,8,2,8,
                        1|9735|5 ..
                         |   1|0 ..
                     ---------
                      9887|006 .
                         3|9|55 ...
                          7|9|1 .....
                           1|9| .......
                             8| .......
                     ---------
                      9891779
```

$$
\begin{array}{ll}
(A_{,})\ 35^\circ\ 38'\ 49''\ \cos = \cdot 8126236 \\
(a_{,})\ 35\ \ 40\ \ 0\ \ \cos = \cdot 8124229.
\end{array}
$$

$$
\begin{array}{r}
8124|229. \\
1|6|25\ldots \downarrow 0,0,0,2,4,7,0, \\
3|2|5\ldots\ldots \\
5|7\ldots\ldots \\
\hline
8126236
\end{array}
$$

$$\therefore \frac{\downarrow 0,0,0,2,4,7,0,}{\downarrow 0,0,2,4,8,2,8,} = 0,0,\bar{2},\bar{2},\bar{4},5,\bar{8},$$

Then,

$$
\begin{array}{ll}
15732306 \downarrow 0,0,\bar{2},\bar{2},\bar{4},5,\bar{8}, = 1\cdot 5697186 & \\
\quad \cdot 7071959 \cos (A + A_{,})\ 44^\circ\ 59'\ 34''. & \\
\hline
\cdot 8625227 \cos (D) \qquad 31^\circ\ 23'\ 56''\cdot 3. &
\end{array}
$$

8. *The apparent distance of the moon's centre from the star Regulus was* 63° 35′ 14″ (*d*), *the apparent altitude of the moon's centre,* 24° 29′ 44″ (*a*), *the apparent altitude of the star,* 45° 9′ 12″ ($a_{,}$), *the true altitude of the moon's centre,* 25° 17′ 45″ (A), *and the true altitude of the star,* 45° 8′ 15″ ($A_{,}$); *required the true distance* (D), *so as to find the longitude at sea.*

$$\cos D = [\cos d + \cos (a + a_{,})] \frac{\cos A \cos A_{,}}{\cos a \cos a_{,}} - \cos (A + A_{,}).$$

$$
\begin{array}{ll}
(d)\ 63^\circ\ 35'\ 14''\ \cos = \cdot 4448349 \\
(a + a_{,})\ 69\ \ 38\ \ 56\ \ \cos = \cdot 3477722 \\
\hline
\cdot 7926071
\end{array}
$$

$$
\begin{array}{l}
(A)\ 25^\circ\ 17'\ 45''\ \cos = \cdot 9041135 \\
(a)\ 24^\circ\ 29'\ 44''\ \cos = \cdot 9099935 \\
(A_{,})\ 45^\circ\ \ 8'\ 15''\ \cos = \cdot 7054078 \\
(a_{,})\ 45\ \ \ 9\ \ 12\ \ \cos = \cdot 7052119
\end{array}
$$

$\therefore \cos A \downarrow 0,0,6,4,8,5,6, = \cos a$, and $\cos a_{,} \downarrow 0,0,0,2,7,7,9, = \cos A_{,}$;

$$\frac{\downarrow 0,0,0,2,7,7,9,}{\downarrow 0,0,6,4,8,5,6,} = 0,0,\bar{6},\bar{2},\bar{1},2,3,$$

·792607|1 . . . . .
1|6| . . . .
2| . . . .

$\downarrow 0,0,0,0,0,2,3, =$ 792|608|9 . . + 1
4|755|6 . . − 6 = β
16|6, . . + 7 × β ÷ 2

$\downarrow 0,0,\bar{6},0,0,2,3, =$ 7878|699 .
1|5|76 . . . . − 2
|78 . . . − 1

$\downarrow 0,0,\bar{6},\bar{2},\bar{1},2,3, =$ ·7877045 = cos 63° 4′ 35″, (D).

When half the indices to the right of ↓ are found, the remainder may be determined by common division.

From 7054078
take 7052119

705|2 1959
1410 (2

70|5 549 (7
494

7|1 56 (7
50

6 (9
6

9. *Suppose the apparent distance between the centres of the sun and moon to be* 83° 57′ 33″ (*d*), *the apparent altitude of the moon's centre,* 27° 34′ 5″ (*a*), *the apparent altitude of the sun's centre,* 48° 27′ 32″ ($a_{,}$), *the true altitude of the moon's centre,* 28° 20′ 48″ (A), *and the true altitude of the sun's centre,* 48° 26′ 49″ ($A_{,}$); *find the true distance* (D), *so as to determine the longitude at sea.*

$$\cos D + [\cos d + \cos (a + a_{,})] \frac{\cos A \ \cos A_{,}}{\cos a \ \cos a_{,}} - \cos (A + A_{,}).$$

(d) 83° 57′ 33″ cos = ·1052372
($a + a_{,}$) 76 1 37 cos = ·2414656

·3467028

(A) 28° 20′ 48″ cos = ·8800909
(a) 27 34 5 cos = ·8864618

```
880|090|9 ..   ↓0,0,7,2,1,6,3,
  6|160|6 ..
   |  18|5 ..
8862|700 .
   1|7|73 ...
      |8|9 .....
      5|3| .......
        3| .......
 884618
```

(A,) 48° 26′ 49″ cos = ·6633133   ↓0,0,0,2,3,5,3,

```
(a,) 48 27 32 cos = ·6631|573 .
                         1|3|26 ...
                          1|9|9 .....
                            3|3| .......
                              2| .......
·6633133
```

$$\frac{\downarrow 0,0,0,2,3,5,3,}{\downarrow 0,0,7,2,1,6,3,} = \downarrow 0,0,\bar{7},0,2,\bar{1},0,$$

```
346|702|8 .. +
  2|426|9 .. −
   |  9|7 .. +
34428|56 ...
     |6|9 ..... +
      |3 ..... −
3442922
```

(A + A,) 76° 47′ 37″ cos = 2284592

True distance, (D) 83 20 53·98 cos = ·1158330

This is one of the model examples given by writers on the Longitude.

10. *The natural cosine of an angle is given equal* ·1158330; *how many degrees, minutes, and seconds are contained in the arc?*

It is well known, if c be the length of a circular arc to radius 1, and s its sine, then

$$c = s + \frac{1}{2}\frac{s^3}{3} + \frac{1}{2}\frac{3}{4}\frac{s^5}{5} + \frac{1}{2}\frac{3}{4}\frac{5}{6}\frac{s^7}{7} + \&c.$$

1158330 = 115 ↓0,0,7,2,2,

The square of ·115 = ·013225; once, twice, three times, &c. of 13225, or of any other number, may be found without much mental exertion, as follows:

1 ◡	13225		
2 ◡	26450	◡ 39675	◡ 3
4 ◡	52900	79350	◡ 6
8 ◡	105800	119025	◡ 9
	13225	52900	
7 ◡	92575	66125	◡ 5

Twice one = 2, twice 2 = 4, twice 4 = 8; take 1 from 8, and 7 remains; 1 and 2 make 3, twice 3 = 6; 6 plus 3 = 9; and finally, 9 minus 4 = 5; or, 5 times 13225 = half 132250 = 66125.

$$·013225 \times ·115 = (·115)^3$$

661	25
1322	5
13225	

·0015209 . . = $(·115)^3$, true to seven places of decimals.

The numbers added together are taken from the multiples of 13225, so easily found above.

$$\cdot 0015209 \times (\cdot 013225) = (\cdot 115)^5$$

	119025
2	64500
66	125
132	25

$\cdot 0000201 \ldots\ldots = (\cdot 115)^2$

$\frac{1}{2}$	3	↓0,0,21,6,6,
15209	760|5	253|5 ..
	53 ..| ⌣7	5|3 ..
		258 8| ....
		2| ....
		2590

Operating with ↓0,0,0,0,6, would not increase the result 2590 by a unit, so it was only necessary to employ ↓0,0,21,6,

$\frac{1}{2}$	$\frac{3}{4}$	5	↓0,0,35,10,10,
201	101	75|	15 .| ...
		5 ...| ⌣7	1 | ...
			16

·1158330
2590
16

·1160936 arc of 6° 39′ 6″

From 90° 0′ 0″
take 6 39 6

83 20 54, true distance.

The degrees, &c. corresponding to the length of an arc, may be found by any of the given rules or by the small tables, pages 62, 72, or by direct calculation, thus:—

As 3·1415927 : 180° : : ·1160936 : 6° 39′ 6″.

Because $3{\cdot}12 \downarrow 0,0,6,9,$ = 3·1415927, nearly.

$$\therefore \quad \frac{180}{3{\cdot}12} \times {\cdot}1160936 \downarrow 0,0,\bar{6},\bar{9},$$ = degrees, and decimal parts of a degree, in the arc. This expression may be reduced to

$$\frac{18000}{312} \times {\cdot}1160936 \downarrow 0,0,\bar{6},\bar{9},$$

$$= \frac{750}{13} \times {\cdot}1160036 \downarrow 0,0,\bar{6},\bar{9},$$

In general terms, if L be the length of an arc to radius 1, the degrees, and decimal parts of a degree, in this arc will be expressed by

$$\frac{750}{13} \times \mathrm{L} \downarrow 0,0,\bar{6},\bar{9},$$

$$\begin{array}{rrl}
4) & 116{\cdot}0936 & 1000 \text{ times} \\
 & 29{\cdot}0234 & 250 \text{ times} \\
\hline
13) & 87{\cdot}0702 & 750 \text{ times} \\
\hline
 & 6{\cdot}69|77\,. & + \\
 & {\cdot}4|02\,. & -6 = \mathrm{A} \\
 & 1\,. & +7 \times \mathrm{A} \div 2 \\
\hline
 & 6{\cdot}657|6\,\ldots & + \\
 & 5|9\,\ldots & -9 \\
\hline
 & 6{\cdot}6517 & \\
 & 60 & \\
\hline
 & 39{\cdot}1020 & \\
 & 60 & \\
\hline
6°\ 39'\ 6'' & 6{\cdot}1200, & \text{as before found.}
\end{array}$$

This method will be found useful when tables are not convenient.

11. *The length of a circular arc is* ·165433; *how many degrees, &c. does it contain?*

```
     4 ) 165·43 3
          41·35 8
    ——————————————
   13 ) 124·07 5
    ——————————————
           9·54|4   . .
              5|7|  . . . . ᵕ 6
               8|   . . . . ᵕ 9
          ————————
           9°·47 9
               60
          ————————
          28′·7 40
                60
          ————————
          44″·400
```

9° 28′ 44″ nearly in an arc whose length is ·165433. The most lengthy and accurate calculation makes the degrees in this arc 9° 28′ 43″. It is easily observed, that the simple method here introduced gives the degrees, &c. in an arc with considerable accuracy, even when only three places of decimals are employed, as in the last example.

12. *The sine of an arc is given* = ·342025; *find the degrees, &c. contained in the arc.*

342 ↓ 0,0,0,0,6, = ·342025.

By the help of the following line, which may be computed in the usual manner before explained, the cube, fifth, seventh, and ninth powers of ·342 are readily determined.

1	2	3·	4	5	6	7	8	9
342	684	1026	1368	1710	2052	2394	2736	3078

·0400017 cube.
·0046788 fifth.
·0005472 seventh.
·0000640 ninth.

$\frac{1}{2}$	$\frac{3}{4}$	$\frac{5}{6}$	$\frac{7}{8}$	9	↓0,0,0,0,54,
640	320	240	200	175	19 . . . | . . . . .
					. . | . . . . .

$\frac{1}{2}$	$\frac{3}{4}$	$\frac{5}{6}$	7	↓0,0,0,0,42,
5472	2736	2052	1710	244 . . | . . . . .
				. . | . . . . .

$\frac{1}{2}$	$\frac{3}{4}$	5	↓0,0,0,0,30,
46788	23394	17546	3509 . | . . . . .
			1 . | . . . . .
			3510

$\frac{1}{2}$	3	↓0,0,0,0,18,
400017	200009|	66670| . . . . .
	12 . . . . . | ⌣ 6	12| . . . . .
		66682

```
                3420205
                  66682
                   3510
                    244
                     19
                -------
Length of arc = ·3490660
                ·3490658 arc of 20°.
```

When the sine of the required arc is greater than ·3, perhaps it is better to find the sine of half the arc by the well-known formula of verification.

$$2 \sin \theta = \sqrt{1 + \sin 2\theta} - \sqrt{1 - \sin 2\theta}, \qquad \text{(I.)}$$

suppose $\sin 2\theta = \cdot 3420205$

$\sqrt{1 \cdot 3420205} = 1 \cdot 1584561$

$\sqrt{\cdot 6579795} = \cdot 8111594$

$2 \,)\, \cdot 3472967$

$\sin \theta = \cdot 1736484$

$$\cdot 1736484 = 173 \downarrow 0,0,3,7,5,$$
$$\cdot 173 \times \cdot 173 = \cdot 0299290.$$
$$(\cdot 173)^3 = \cdot 0051777$$
$$(\cdot 173)^5 = \cdot 0001550$$

```
 ½              3                  ↓0,0,9,21,15,
51777         2588|8                862|9 . .
               78..|   ⌣3            7|8 . .
                                   ---------
              26121|               8707|. . . .
              18....|  ⌣7             18|. . . .
                                   ---------
              26175.|              8725 .|. . . . .
              1......|  ⌣5              1 .|. . . . .
                                   ---------
                                    8726

 ½          ¼·          5           ↓0,0,15,35,25,
1550        775        581|           116|. . .
                      2...|  ⌣3          2|. . .
                                     -----
                                      118
```

$$\begin{array}{r} \cdot 1736484 \\ 8726 \\ 118 \\ \hline \cdot 1745328 \end{array} = \text{an arc of } 10^\circ \text{ very nearly.}$$

The seventh power of ($\cdot 173$) would give $\cdot 0000002$, which may be added. If the sine of $2\,\theta$ be given to find the cosine of θ, then the formula is

$$2 \cos \theta = \sqrt{1 + \sin 2\,\theta} + \sqrt{1 - \sin 2\,\theta}, \quad \text{(II.)}$$

In the last example,

$$\sqrt{1\cdot 3420205} = 1\cdot 1584561$$
$$\sqrt{\cdot 6579795} = \cdot 8111594$$
$$2)\ 1\cdot 9696155$$
$$\cdot 9848078 = \cos 10^\circ = \sin 80^\circ.$$

To these formulæ may be added the following well-known expressions, namely,

$$\sin 2\theta = 2 \sin \theta \cos \theta; \qquad \text{(III.)}$$

$$\cos 2\theta = 2\cos^2\theta - 1 = 1 - 2\sin^2\theta, \qquad \text{(IV.)}$$

$$\cos \theta = \sqrt{\frac{1 + \cos 2\theta}{2}}, \qquad \text{(V.)}$$

$$\sin \theta = \sqrt{\frac{1 - \cos 2\theta}{2}}, \qquad \text{(VI.)}$$

13. *Given the cosine of an angle* = ·88888, *find the degrees and minutes contained in the arc, working to five places of decimals by* (VI.).

```
    1·00000
     ·88888
  ----------
  2 ) ·11112
  ----------
   √·05556 = ·23571          = 23 ↓ 0,2,4,6,3,
              ------
              23|00|0 .
                |46|0 .
                   |2 .
              ------
              234|62 .
                 |9|4 . . .
                 1|4| . . . . .
                  1| . . . . .

          (·23)² = ·05290
          (·23)³ = ·01217
          (·23)⁵ = ·00064

   ½          ¾          5
   64         32         24          5
```

½ of 64 = 32; ¾ of 32 = 24, &c.; 5 operated upon by $\downarrow$ 0,10, . . . is not increased a unit.

$\frac{1}{2}$
1217

3
60|9
12.| ◡ 2

645|
3...| ◡ 4

↓0,6,12,18, &c.
20|3 .
1|2 .
215|...
3|...
218

·23571
218
5

4) ·237·94 length of arc
59·48

13) 178·46

13·7|3 ..
8|.... ◡ 6
1|.... ◡ 9

13·64
60

38·40

13° 38′ doubled = 27° 16′, the angle whose cosine = ·88888.

If S be the seconds in an arc whose length is L, radius = 1,

Then, $$S = L\,200000 \times \downarrow 0,3,1,0,0,\bar{7},0,\bar{5},$$

and $$L = \frac{4S}{1000000} \downarrow 2,0,2,\bar{3},\bar{2},0,7,.$$

PART V.

FORMULÆ, AND RULES FOR THE SOLUTION OF PLANE TRIANGLES, WITHOUT THE USE OF TABLES.

Examples.

Fig. 1.

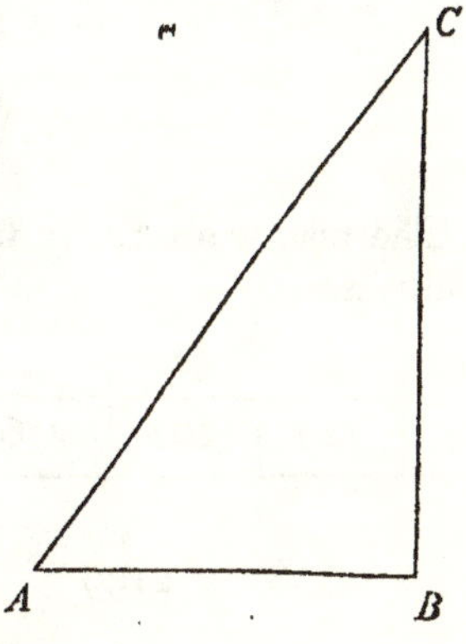

1. *In a right-angled plane triangle ABC given the angle CAB* = 53° 8′, *and the base AB* = 288; *find the perpendicular CB and the hypothenuse AC.*

Since the angle CAB + angle $ACB = 90°$,

$$\begin{array}{rll} & 90° & 0' \text{ from} \\ \therefore \quad CAB = & 53 & 8 \text{ take} \\ \hline ACB = & 36 & 52 \\ & 60 & \\ \hline = & 2212 \text{ minutes.} & \end{array}$$

Length of an arc of 1000′ = ·29089
" " 2000 = ·58178
" " 3000 = ·87267
" " 4000 = 1·16355
" " 5000 = 1·45444
" " 6000 = 1·74533
" " 7000 = 2·03622
" " 8000 = 2·32711
" " 9000 = 2·61799

2000′ = ·58178
200 = ·05818
10 = ·00291
2 = ·00058

·64345 Length of an arc of 36° 52′.

·640 ↓ **0,0,5,3,7,** = ·64345

$(\cdot 64)^2$ = ·40960
$(\cdot 64)^3$ = ·26214
$(\cdot 64)^4$ = ·16777
$(\cdot 64)^5$ = ·10737
$(\cdot 64)^6$ = ·06872
$(\cdot 64)^7$ = ·04398

The results are easily found by means of the following line of multipliers.

1	2	3	4	5	6	7	8	9
64	128	192	256	320	384	448	512	576

2	3	4	5	6	7	
4398	2199	733	184	37	6	1

2	3	4	5	6	
6872	3436	1145	286	57	10

2	3	4	5		↓ **0,0,25,15,35,**
10737	5369	1789	447 . |		89 . | . . .
			2 . . . . |	◡ 5	2 . | . . .
					91

```
  2        3          4        ↓0,0,20,12,28,
16777    8389       2796|        699| . . .
                    14...| ⌣ 5    14| . . .
                                 ------
                                 713 .| . . . .
                                   1 .| . . . .
                                 ------
                                 714

      2        3          ↓0,0,15,9,21,
    26214    1310|7         436|9 . .
             66..|  ⌣ 5       6|6| . . . .
                               |4| . . . .
                           ---------
                            443 9

     2        ↓0,0,10,6,14,
   40960      204|8 0 .
                2|0 5 .  = A
                 |  1 .  = A × 9 ÷ 2
              ----------
              206 8|6 . . .
                  1|2| . . . . .
                    3| . . . . .
              ----------
              207 0 1
```

```
1·00000 +                      ·64345 +
 ·20701 −                        4439 −
    714 +                          91 +
     10 −                           1 −
-------                        ------
 ·80013 = sine of 53° 8′.      ·59996 = sine of 36° 52′.
```

The value of any term, as $+\dfrac{x^9}{1\cdot2\cdot3\cdot4\cdot5\cdot6\cdot7\cdot8\cdot9}$ may be found independently; for example, the length of an arc of 36° 52′ $= \cdot643444724 = \dfrac{6}{10}$ ↓0,7,0,2,5,4,1,6, $= \dfrac{6}{10}$ ↓6990997,. Then,

```
     6990997+     − 396847197
 6=179184951+     −1280247082=1·2·3·4·5·6·7·8·9
   ---------       ----------
   186175948+     −1677094279
10=230270081−     −1842160648=10⁸
   ---------      ------------
    44094133−      165066369=5↓0,4,1,3,4,2,0,3,=5·2100046.
           9
   ---------
   396847197−
```

$$\therefore \frac{x^9}{1\cdot2\cdot3\cdot4\cdot5\cdot6\cdot7\cdot8\cdot9} = (\cdot643444724)^9 \div 362880 = \cdot000000052100046.$$

As sin 36° 52 : 288 :: sin 90° : *A C.*

∴ ·59996 : 288 :: 1·00000 : 480·036 = *A C.*

Again, as sin 36° 52′ : 288 :: sin 53° 8′ : *CB.*

∴ ·59996 : 288 :: ·80003 : 384·045 = *CB.*

2. *Given the two perpendicular sides to find the hypothenuse and angles, that is to say, $AB = 472$; $BC = 765$; find $A\,C$ and the angles CAB, $A\,CB$.*

$$\sqrt{472^2 + 765^2} = 898{\cdot}8933\,;$$

$$\frac{472}{898{\cdot}8933} = \sin ABC = {\cdot}52498,$$

$$\sqrt{1{\cdot}5249789} = 1{\cdot}234901$$

$$\sqrt{{\cdot}4750211} = {\cdot}689218$$

$$2\,)\;{\cdot}545683$$

$$\quad{\cdot}272842$$

·272 ↓ 0,0̇,3,0,9, ← ·272842

Square of ·272 = ·073984

Cube of ·272 = ·020124

Fifth power of ·272 = ·001489

Seventh power of ·272 = ·000110

$\frac{1}{2}$	$\frac{3}{4}$	$\frac{5}{6}$	7	
110	55	42	35	5

$\frac{1}{2}$	$\frac{3}{4}$	5	↓ 0,0,15,0,45,
1489	745	559 |	112 | . . .
		2 . . . | ⌣ 3	2 | . . .
			114

$\frac{1}{2}$	3		↓ 0,0,9,0,27,
20124	10062		335 | 4 . .
			3 | 0 . .
		10152 . |	3384 . | : . . . .
		1 . . . . . . | ⌣ 9	1′ . | . . . . .
			3385

$$
\begin{array}{r l}
 & \cdot 272842 \\
 & 3385 \\
 & 114 \\
 & 5 \\
\hline
 & \cdot 276346 \text{ length of arc.} \\
900' = & \cdot 261799 \\
\hline
 & \cdot 014547 \\
50' = & \cdot 014544 \\
\hline
950' = & 15^\circ\ 50' \\
\therefore & 31\ \ 40 = \text{angle } ACB.
\end{array}
$$

$$
\begin{array}{l r}
\text{From} & 90^\circ\ \ 0' \\
\text{take} & 31\ \ 40 \\
\hline
 & 58^\circ\ 20' = \text{angle } CAB.
\end{array}
$$

If the angles be required to seconds, the decimals must extend to seven places.

Fig. 2.

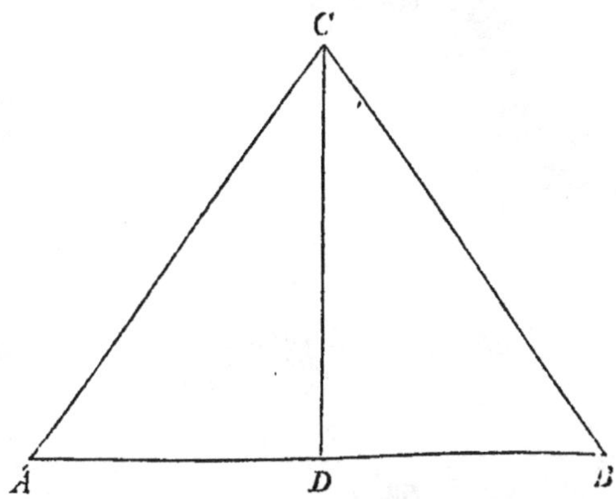

3. *Given two sides and the included angle of an isosceles triangle ACB, to find the other parts.* $AC = CB = 288$, $ACB = 78^\circ\ 12'$.

Draw CD perpendicular to AB, then

$$\begin{aligned} ADC &= 90^\circ \ \ 0' \\ ACD &= \underline{39 \ \ \ 6} \\ CAD &= 50^\circ\ 54' = CBD. \end{aligned}$$

The work of this example is only extended to four decimal places.

$39^\circ\ 6' = 2346'$, length of arc $= {\cdot}6824$.

$6 \downarrow 1,3,3,6, = {\cdot}6824$

$({\cdot}6)^3 = {\cdot}2160$

$({\cdot}6)^5 = {\cdot}0778$

2	3	4	5	$\downarrow$ 5,15,15,30
778	389	130	33	7|·
				4|·
				11|· ·|· ·
				2|· ·|· ·
				13

2	3		$\downarrow$ 3,9,9,18,
2160	1080		3|6|0|·
			1|0|8|·
			1|1|·
			47|9 ·
			4|3 ·
			|2 ·
			524|· · ·
			5|· · ·
		1587·|	529·|· · · ·
		1· · · · ·|⌣6	1·|· · · ·
			530

6824 +
530 −
6294
13 +
$\cdot$6307 = sin 39° 6′.

$$\sin ADC : AC :: \sin ACD : AD,$$
$$\text{or as } \sin 90^\circ : 288 :: {\cdot}6307 : AD,$$
$$\therefore 1 : 288 :: {\cdot}6307 : 181{\cdot}64.$$

$$AD = 181{\cdot}64 \qquad \therefore AB = 363{\cdot}28.$$

4. *In the triangle ABC are given $AB = 137$, $AC = 153$, and angle $CBA = 78^\circ\ 13'$, to find the other parts.*

Draw CD perpendicular to AB, then $DCB = 11^\circ\ 47' = 707'$; arc of $707' = {\cdot}205658$.

Fig. 3.

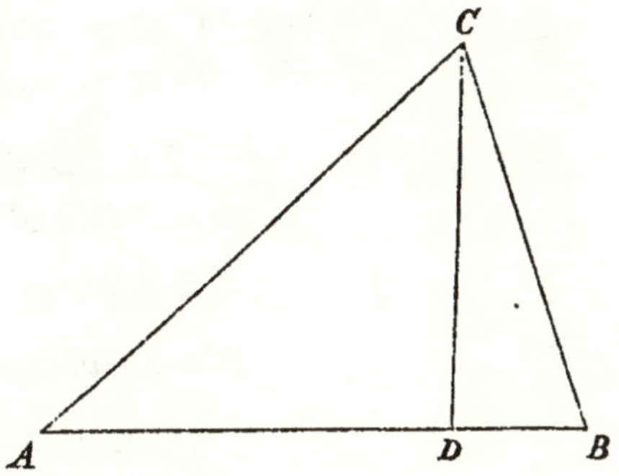

205 ↓0,0,3,2, = 205658.

$({\cdot}205)^2 = {\cdot}042025$

$({\cdot}205)^3 = {\cdot}008615$

$({\cdot}205)^4 = {\cdot}001766$

$({\cdot}205)^5 = {\cdot}000362$

2	3	4	5	
362	181	60	15	3

2	3	4	↓0,0,12,8,
1766	883	294 · | 8 . . . | ⌣ 3	74 · | . . . 1 . | . . . 75

2	3	↓0,0,9,6,
8615 .	430 | 8 13 . . | ⌣ 3	143 | 6 . . 1 | 3 . . 144 9 | . . . . 1 | 145 0

```
     2                ↓0,0,6,4,
  420|25               210|1 3 .
  126.|   ⌣3              1|2 6 .
                      ---------
                       211 3|9 . . .
                            |8 . . .
                      ---------
                       21147
```

```
1·000000              ·205658
 ·021147 −               1450 −
--------              -------
 ·978853              ·204208
      75 +                  3 +
--------              -------
 ·978928              ·204211
```

∴ sine 11° 47′ = ·204211, which put = n,
sine 78 13 = ·978928, „ = m.

Let $CB = x$, then
$nx = BD$, and $mx = CD$.

Put $AB = b$ and $AC = h$. $AD = b - nx$.

$$\therefore \quad b^2 - 2bnx + x^2n^2 + x^2m^2 = h^2.$$

Because $m^2 + n^2 = 1$,

$$x = nb \pm \sqrt{(h + mb)(h - mb)}, = 101{\cdot}616.$$

153 : ·978928 :: 101·616 : sin CAB = ·650161.

Again, sin $ABC : AC$ :: sin $ACB : AB$,

$$\therefore \quad \frac{137 \times {\cdot}978928}{153} = \sin ACB = {\cdot}876556.$$

To find the sine of half this angle:

```
  √ 1·876556 = 1·369875
  √  ·123446 =  ·351336
              ---------
            2) 1·018529
              ---------
sine of half ACB =  ·509265
```

$$\sqrt{1\cdot509265} = 1\cdot228522$$
$$\sqrt{\cdot490735} = \cdot700525$$
$$2)\ \underline{\cdot527997}$$

sin of $\frac{1}{4}$ of $ACB =$ ·263998

263 ↓0,0,3,7,6, = 263998

$(\cdot263)^3 = \cdot018191$

$(\cdot263)^5 = \cdot001258$

$(\cdot263)^7 = \cdot000087$

$\frac{1}{2}$· 87 $\frac{3}{4}$· 44 $\frac{5}{6}$ 33   7 28   4

$\frac{1}{2}$ 1258 $\frac{3}{4}$ 629   5 472 .| 1 ....| ⌣3   ↓0,0,15,35,30, 94 .| ... 1 .| ... 95

$\frac{1}{2}$ 18191   · 3 909:6 27 ..| ⌣3 9177| 6....| ⌣7 9195 .| 5.....| ⌣6   ↓0,0,9,21,18, 303|2 .. 2|7 .. 305 9| .... 6| .... 306 5 .| ..... • 1 .| 3066

263998
3066
95
4

Length of arc = ·267163, and will be found to correspond to 918′ 27″ = 15° 18′ 27″, which, when multiplied by 4, gives 61° 13′ 48″ for the angle ACB.

	61°	13′	48″
	78	13	0
Take	139°	26′	48″
from	180	0	0
	40°	33′	12″ = angle CAB.

5. *In the plane triangle ABC or ACD, are given $AC = 216$, CB or CD 117, angle $CAB = 22° 37'$, to find the remaining parts.*

Let $AC = b$, CB or $CD = a$, $AB = n$, $AD = m$, and angle $CAB = \theta$.

Fig. 4.

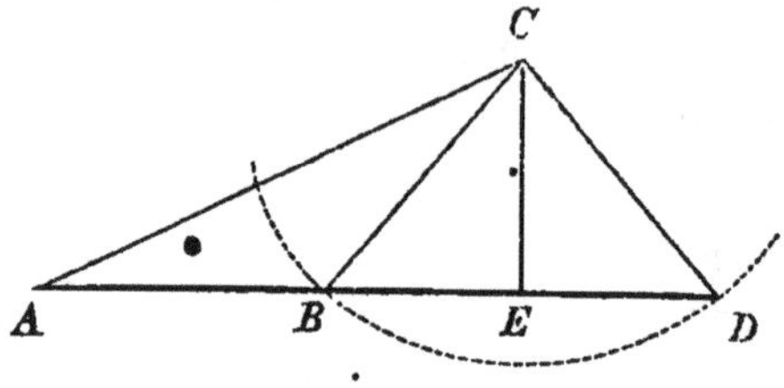

$$\text{Then, } CE = b \sin \theta$$

$$AE = b \cos \theta$$

$$BE^2 = ED^2 = a^2 - b^2 \sin^2 \theta$$

$$\therefore AB = n = b \cos \theta - \sqrt{a^2 - b^2 \sin^2 \theta}$$

$$AD = m = b \cos \theta + \sqrt{a^2 - b^2 \sin^2 \theta}$$

$$(a + b \sin \theta)(a - b \sin \theta) = a \; - b^2 \sin^2 \theta.$$

$22° 37' = 1357'$, length of this arc $= \cdot 394734$.

$$394 \downarrow 0,0,1,8,6, = 394734$$

$$(\cdot 394)^2 = \cdot 155236$$

$$(\cdot 394)^3 = \cdot 061163$$

$$(\cdot 394)^4 = \cdot 024098$$

$$(\cdot 394)^5 = \cdot 009495$$

$$(\cdot 394)^6 = \cdot 003741$$

2	3	4	5	
9495	4748	1583	396	79

2   3   ↓0,0,3,24,18,
61163   30582   101|94..
|31.

3067|5   102 2|5....
25...| ⌣8   2|5...

30750| 102 5 0|.....
2.....| ⌣6   2|.....

102 5 2

·394734 +
10252 −
·384482
79 +
·384561 = sin 22° 37′.

216 × ·384561 = 83·065.

117·000
83·065
33·935 diff.
200·065 sum.

$\sqrt{200·065 \times 33·935} = 82·396.$

To find the cosine of 22° 37′.

2   3   4   5   6
3741   1872   624   156   31   5

2   3   4   ↓0,0,4,32,24,
24098   12049   4016   100|4..
|4..

4032| 100 8|....
3....| ⌣8   3|....

101 1

0

2	↓0,0,2,16,12,
155236	776 | 18 .
	1 | 55 .
15554 | 6	7777 | 3 . . .
124 . . . | ◡8	12 | 4 . . .
155794 |	77897 | . . . . .
9 . . . . . | ◡6	9 | . . . . .
	77906

1·000000 +
77906 −

·922094
1011 +

·923105
5 −

·923100 = cos 22° 37′.

216 × ·9231 = 199·3896
82·396

281·7856 sum = *AD*,
116·9936 diff. = *AB*.

Fig. 5.

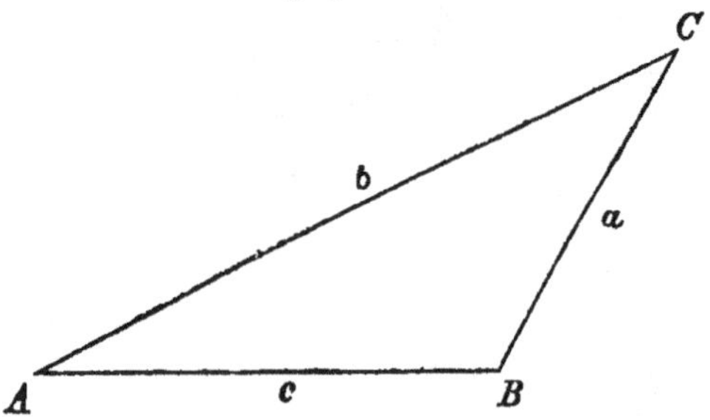

Let *ABC* be any plane triangle, and denote the angles by the letters *A*, *B*, *C*, at their vertices, and the sides opposite to them by the small letters *a*, *b*, *c*; represent $a+b+c$ by $2s$.

Then
$$\sin\frac{A}{2} = \sqrt{\frac{(s-b)(s-c)}{bc}};$$
$$\sin\frac{B}{2} = \sqrt{\frac{(s-a)(s-c)}{ac}};$$
$$\sin\frac{C}{2} = \sqrt{\frac{(s-a)(s-b)}{ab}};$$

$$\begin{array}{r} 116{\cdot}994 \\ 216{\cdot}000 \\ 117{\cdot}000 \\ \hline 2\,)\ 449{\cdot}994 \\ \hline 224{\cdot}997 = s \end{array} \qquad \begin{array}{r} 224{\cdot}997 \\ 117{\cdot}000 \\ \hline 107{\cdot}997 = s - a \end{array} \qquad \begin{array}{r} 224{\cdot}997 \\ 216{\cdot}000 \\ \hline 8{\cdot}997 = s - b. \end{array}$$

$$\sqrt{\frac{107{\cdot}997 \times 8{\cdot}997}{117 \times 216}} = {\cdot}196081$$

$$196\downarrow 0,0,0,4,2, = 196081$$

$$({\cdot}196)^3 = {\cdot}007530$$
$$({\cdot}196)^5 = {\cdot}000289$$

$$\begin{array}{cccc} \frac{1}{2} & \frac{3}{4} & 5 & \\ 289 & 144 & 108 & 22 \end{array}$$

$$\begin{array}{ccc} \frac{1}{2} & 3 & \downarrow 0,0,0,12,6, \\ 7530 & 3765 & 1255 \\ & 2\ldots\ \smile 4 & 2 \\ & & \overline{1257} \end{array}$$

$$\begin{array}{r} {\cdot}196081 \\ 1257 \\ 22 \\ \hline {\cdot}197360 \end{array} = \text{arc of } 678'\ 28''{\cdot}6 = 11^\circ\ 18'\ 28''{\cdot}6,$$

the double of which is $22^\circ\ 36'\ 57''{\cdot}2 = ACB$.

$$\begin{array}{lrrr} & 22^\circ & 36' & 57'' \\ & 22 & 37 & 0 \\ \hline \text{Take} & 45^\circ & 13' & 57'' = CDE \text{ (fig. 4.)} \\ \text{from} & 180 & 0 & 0 \\ \hline & 134^\circ & 46' & 3'' = ABC \end{array}$$

$$\begin{array}{lrrr} & 45^\circ & 13' & 57'' \\ & 22 & 37 & 0 \\ \hline \text{Take} & 67^\circ & 50' & 57'' \\ \text{from} & 180 & 0 & 0 \\ \hline & 112^\circ & 9' & 3'' = ACD \text{ (fig. 4.)} \end{array}$$

6. *In the plane triangle ABC, are given AB* = 408 *yards, B* = 74° 14′, *A* = 49° 23′; *to find the other sides.*

Fig. 6.

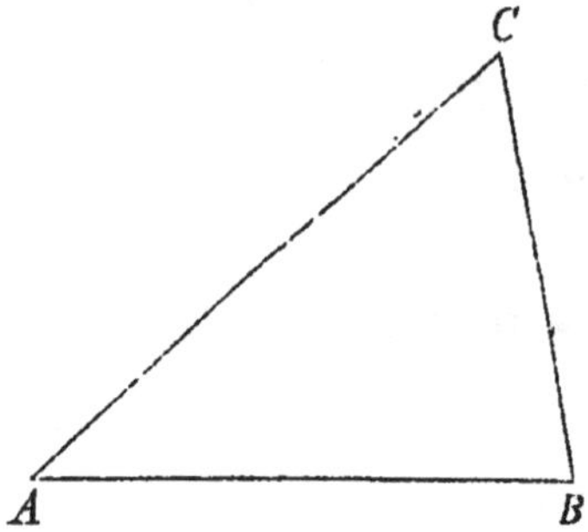

As the three angles taken together make 180°,

$\therefore\ C = 56° 23'$.

Sin 56° 23′ = cosine 33° 37′.

Length of arc of 33° 37′ = ·586721.

586↓0,0,1,2,3, = 586721.

$(\cdot586)^2 = \cdot343396$
$(\cdot586)^4 = \cdot117921$
$(\cdot586)^6 = \cdot040494$

```
.2        3        4        5        6
40494     20247    6749     1687     337      56

2         3        4                 ↓0,0,4,8,12,
117921    58960    19653              491|3 . .
                                        2|0 . .
                                      493 3| . . . .
                                          4| . . . .
                   19748 .|           493 7 .| . . . . .
                   6.....|⌣ 3             1 .| . . . . .
                                      493 8

          2                ↓0,0,2,4,8,
          343396        171|698 . . .
                           |343 . . .
                        172 0|41 . .
                             |69 . .
                        172 1 1|0 . . . .
                              1|0 . . . .
                        172 1 2 0
```

```
                1·000000 +
                  172120 −
                ---------
                  827880
                    4938 +
                ---------
                  832818
                      56 −
                ---------
sin 56° 23′ =    ·832762 = cos 33° 37′.
```

Length of arc of 15° 46′ = ·275180.

275 ↓ 0,0,0,6,6, = 275180

(·275)² = ·075625

(·275)⁴ = ·005719

```
  2        3         4               ↓ 0,0,0,24,24,
5719     2860       953 .|             238 .| . . . .
                   6 . . . .| ⌣ 6 −      1 .| . . . .
                                     -----
                                       239

      2                     ↓ 0,0,0,12,12,
   7562|5                    3781|3 . . .
 45 . . .|  ⌣ 6 −               4|5 . . .
                             ---------
   75716|                    3785 8| . . . . .
 45 . . . .| ⌣ 6 −                5| . . . . .
                             ---------
                             3786 3

                1·000000 +
                   37863 −
                ---------
                  962137
                     239 +
sin 74° 14′ =    ·962376 = cos 15° 46′.

                90°  0′
                49  13
               --------
Length of arc of 40° 47′ = ·711803

711 ↓ 0,0,1,1,3, = ·711803
          (·711)² = ·505521
          (·711)⁴ = ·255551
          (·711)⁶ = ·129186
          (·711)⁸ = ·065306
```

2)	3)	4)	5)	6)	7)	8)	
65306	32653	10884	2721	544	91	13	2

2)	3)	4)	5)	6)
129186	64593	21531	5383	1077

↓0,0,6,6,18,
179| . . .
1| . . .
180

2)	3)	4)
255551	127776	42592

↓0,0,4,4,12,
106|48 .
|43 .
1069|1 . . .
|4 . . .
10695| . . . . .
1| . . . . .
10696

2)
505521

↓0,0,2,2,6,
252|762| . . .
|506| . . .
2532|68 . . . .
|5|1 . . . .
1|5 . . . .
253334

1·000000 +
253334 −
·746666
10696 +
·757362
180 −
·757182
2 +

sin 49° 13′ = ·757184 = cos 40° 47′ :

sin 56° 23′ : 408 :: sin 74° 14′ : AC.

$$\therefore \quad \cdot 832762 : 408 :: \cdot 962376 : 471{\cdot}5 = AC$$

$$\therefore \quad \cdot 832762 : 408 :: \cdot 757184 : 371{\cdot}9 = BC.$$

Fig. 7.

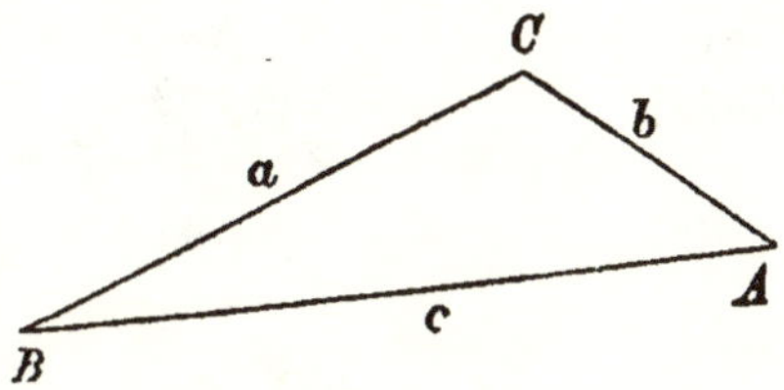

7. *Given the two sides* (a = 562, b = 320) *and the included angle* (C = 128° 4′), *to find the third side* (c), *and the remaining angles* (B, A).

Fig. 8.

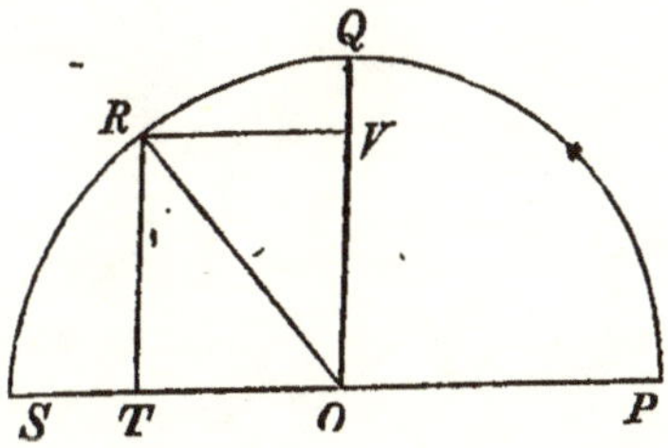

Let OP (fig. 8) be radius = 1, and the arc PQR one of 128° 4′, the cosine of this arc is = TO = VR, and is negative. But VR is the sine of the arc QR = 128° 4′ − 90° 0′ = 38° 4′ = 2284′; the length of this arc = ·664389.

The well-known formula,

$$c^2 = a^2 + b^2 - 2\ ab \cos C \text{ (fig. 7)},$$

in this example becomes

$$c^2 = a^2 + b^2 + 2\,ab \cos C.$$

$$\therefore \quad c^2 = (562)^2 + (320)^2 + 2 \times 320 \times 562 \times \cos C.$$

Now c is readily found when cos C becomes known; the length of the arc QR is given = ·664389 to find RV.

664 ↓ 0,0,0,5,8,6, ≐ 664389
$(664)^3$ = ·292755
$(664)^5$ ≐ ·129075
$(664)^7$ = ·037787

2)	3)	4)	5)	6)	7)	
37787	18894	6298	1575	315	53	8

```
   2)       3)      4)        5)          ↓0,0,0,25,40,30,
129075   64538   21513      5378|          1076| . . . .
                            27 . . .| ⌣5 −     3| . . . .
                                          ----
                                          1079

   2)               3)                    ↓0,0,0,15,24,18,
292755           14637|8                   4879|3 . . .
                 73 . . .| ⌣5 −               7|3 . . .
                                          -----
                 146598|                   48866| . . . .
                 12 . . . . .| ⌣8 −           12| . . . .
                                          -----
                 146634 .|                 48878 .| . . . . . .
                 8 . . . . . .| ⌣6 −           1 .| . . . . . .
                                          -----
                                           48879
```

```
 664389 +
  48879 −
 ------
 615510
   1079 +
 ------
·616589
      8 −
 ------
```

$$\sin 38^\circ 4' = \cdot 616581$$

$$\therefore \quad \cos 128^\circ 4' = \text{negative } \cdot 616581.$$

$$\therefore \quad c^2 = 562^2 + 320^2 + 2 \times 320 \times 562 \times \cdot 616581$$

$$\therefore \quad c = 800\cdot 009 = AB.$$

To find B, the lesser of the remaining angles:

$$\sin \frac{B}{2} = \sqrt{\frac{(s-a)(s-c)}{ac}}$$

$$\therefore \quad \sin \frac{B}{2} = \sqrt{\frac{279 \times 41}{562 \times 800}} = \cdot 15908$$

To find the arc and angle corresponding to this sine:

$$159 \downarrow 0,0,3,2, = \cdot 159508$$

$$(\cdot 159)^2 = \cdot 025281$$

$$(\cdot 159)^3 = \cdot 004020$$

$$(\cdot 159)^5 = \cdot 000102$$

$\frac{1}{2}$ 102 $\frac{3}{4}$ 51 5) 38 8

$\frac{1}{2}$ 4020 3) 2010| 6...|⌣3⌣ ↓0,0,9,6, 670| 6| 676

```
   159508
      676
        8
   ------
   160192
9°⌣ 157080
   ------
   003112
10⌣ 002909
   ------
   000203
40″⌣ 000194
```

9° 10′ 40″ doubled gives 18° 21′ 20″ = angle B.

∴ Angle A = 33° 34′ 40″.

8. *In a plane triangle, ABC, given the side* (*a*), *opposite the angle A* = 7891·23456; *the side* (*b*), *opposite the angle B*, = 12345·67891; *and the side* (*c*), *opposite the angle C*, = 8912·34567, *to find the area and also the angle A.*

Put $2s = a + b + c$. It is well known that the area $= \sqrt{s(s-a)(s-b)(s-c)}$.

s = 14574·62957 = 10^4 × ↓3,9,1,2,1,4,2,2, = ↓958751939,).

$s-a$ = 6683·39501 = 10^3 × 6 ↓1,1,2,6,0,7,1,5, = ↓880782399,).

$s-b$ = 2228·95066 = 10^3 × 2 ↓1,1,3,1,2,4,7,4, = ↓770967363,).

$s-c$ = 5662·28390 = 10^3 × 5 ↓1,2,9,1,8,3,0,8, = ↓864201688,).

2) 3474703389

1737351695

$+ 1737351695 = 10^7 \times 3 \downarrow \mathbf{1,6,0,9,2,3,8,3,} = 35062539{\cdot}6$, area.
$- 161189056 7 \smile 10^7$

$\;\;125461128$
$\;\;109866750 \smile 3$

$\;\;\;15594378$
$\;\;\;9531497 \smile (1,$

$\;\;\;6062881$
$\;\;\;5970498 \smile (6,$

$\;\;\;\;9,2,3,8,3,$

$$\sin\frac{A}{2} = \sqrt{\frac{(s-b)(s-c)}{bc}}$$

$b = 12345{\cdot}67891 = 10^4 \times \;\downarrow \mathbf{2,2,0,2,0,0,0,2,} = \downarrow \overline{\mathbf{942153486,}}$

$c = 8912{\cdot}34567 = 10^3 \times 8 \downarrow \mathbf{1,1,2,7,3,6,4,5,} = \downarrow \overline{\mathbf{909564982,}}$

$\qquad 1851718468$

$s - b = 770967363$
$s - c = 864201688$

$\qquad + 1635169051$
$bc = - 1851718468$

$2) - 216549417$

$\div\; 108274709 = \downarrow \overline{z,}$ to be referred to presently.
$10 \smile +\; 230270081$

$+\; 121995372 = 3 \downarrow \mathbf{1,2,6,0,7,2,2,9,} = 3{\cdot}38682336$
$3 \smile \;\; 109866750$

$\;\;12128622$
$\;\;9531497\;(1,$

$\;\;2597{\cdot}125$
$\;\;1990166\;(2,$

$\;\;606959 \qquad \therefore\; {\cdot}338682336 = \sin\frac{A}{2}.$
$\;\;599730\;(6,$

$\;\;0,7,2,2,9,$

If x be the length of a circular arc, and z its sine, to radius 1 (it may be repeated here), then

$$x = z + \frac{1}{2.3} z^3 + \frac{1.3}{2.4.5} z^5 + \frac{1.3.5}{2.4.6.7} z^7 + \frac{1.3.5.7}{2.4.6.8.9} z^9 + \dots.$$

By adding the corresponding values of 1,3,5,7, ... reduced to the eight position, and subtracting the values of 2,4,6, ... reduced to the same position, the following arrangement is readily formed, and may be applied in similar cases.

$$\frac{1}{2.3} = -\ 179184951$$

$$\frac{1.3}{2.4.5} = -\ 259039733$$

$$\frac{1.3.5}{2.4.6.7} = -\ 310921720$$

$$\frac{1.3.5.7}{2.4.6.8.9} = -\ 349408234$$

$$\frac{1.3\ 5.7.9}{2.4.6.8.10.11} = -\ 380012893$$

$$\begin{array}{rl}
\downarrow\overline{z,}| = - & 108274709 \\
 & \underline{\qquad\qquad 3} \\
- & 324824127 \\
\frac{1}{2.3} = - & \underline{179184951} \\
- & 504009078 = \frac{6}{10^3} \downarrow 0,7,6,5,0,9,0,3, = \cdot 00647480.
\end{array}$$

$$\begin{array}{rl}
\downarrow\overline{z,}| = - & 108274709 \\
 & \underline{\qquad\qquad 5} \\
- & 541373545 \\
\frac{1.3}{2.4.5} = - & \underline{259039733} \\
- & 800413278 = \frac{3}{10^4} \downarrow 1,1,2,7,3,8,0,6, = \cdot 00033421.
\end{array}$$

$$\begin{array}{rl}
\downarrow\overline{z,}| = - & 108274709 \\
 & \underline{\qquad\qquad 7} \\
- & 757922963 \\
\frac{1.3.5}{2.4.6.7} = - & \underline{310921720} \\
- & 1068844683 = \frac{2}{10^5} \downarrow 1,3,6,7,1,0,4,5, = \cdot 00002282.
\end{array}$$

$$\downarrow \overline{z,|} = - \quad 108274709$$
$$9$$
$$- \quad 974472381$$
$$\frac{1.3.5.7}{2.4.6.8.9} = - \quad 349408234$$
$$- \quad 1323880615 = \frac{1}{10^8} \downarrow 6,0,5,5,1,1,1,4. = \cdot 00000178.$$

$$\downarrow \overline{z,|} = - \quad 108274709$$
$$11$$
$$- \quad 1191021799$$
$$\frac{1.3.5.7.9}{2.4.6.8.10.11} = - \quad 380012893$$
$$- \quad 1571034692 = \frac{1}{10^7} \downarrow 4,2,7,4,0,0,3,6, = \cdot 00000015.$$

Approximate value of next step $= \dfrac{15 \times 11 \times 11 \times (\cdot 33)^2}{12 \cdot 13} = 1.$

$$\begin{array}{rr} \text{Sine} = & \cdot 33868234 \\ & 647480 \\ & 33421 \\ & 2282 \\ & 178 \\ & 15 \\ & 1 \\ \hline \text{Arc} = & \cdot 34551611 \end{array} \text{ of } 19^\circ\ 47'\ 47''\cdot 8122$$

$$\therefore \text{ Angle } A = 39^\circ\ 35'\ 35''\cdot 6244$$

PART VI.

DUAL ARITHMETIC APPLIED TO THE SOLUTION OF THE DIFFERENT CASES OF SPHERICAL TRIANGLES.

RIGHT-ANGLED SPHERICAL TRIANGLES.

Fig. 9.

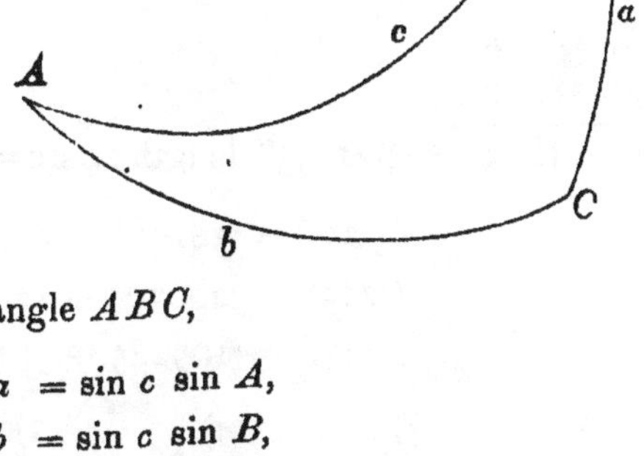

The angles of the spherical triangle may be represented by the letters at their vertices A, B, C; and the sides opposite to them by the small letters a, b, c.

In any right-angled triangle ABC,

$$\begin{aligned} \sin a &= \sin c \sin A, \\ \sin b &= \sin c \sin B, \\ \cos c &= \cos a \cos b, \\ \cos A &= \cos a \sin B, \\ \cos B &= \cos b \sin A. \end{aligned}$$

1. *In the right-angled spherical triangle ABC are given,* $a = 48° \; 24' \; 16''$; $b = 59° \; 38' \; 27''$; *to find the hypothenuse c.*

It is a question for the operator to decide, whether the sine or cosine of an arc ought to be found at once, or by employing two operations; if a table of the squares and cubes of numbers be convenient, perhaps one operation is more easily managed. It is easily observed, when the three first figures of the length of an arc are raised to a power sufficiently high, from the following continued products,

$$2 = 2$$
$$2 \times 3 = 6$$
$$2 \times 3 \times 4 = 24$$
$$2 \times 3 \times 4 \times 5 = 120$$
$$2 \times 3 \times 4 \times 5 \times 6 = 720$$
$$2 \times 3 \times 4 \times 5 \times 6 \times 7 = 5040$$
$$2 \times 3 \times 4 \times 5 \times 6 \times 7 \times 8 = 40320$$
$$2 \times 3 \times 4 \times 5 \times 6 \times 7 \times 8 \times 9 = 362880.$$

The decimal should be very great, when the ninth power of the first three figures has to be taken.

90° 0′ 0″
48 24 16

41° 35′ 44″ = 2495′ 44″, length of arc = ·725979 = ·725↓0,0,1,3,5,

90° 0′ 0″
59 38 27

30° 21′ 33″ = 1821′ 33″, length of arc = ·529868 = ·529↓0,0,1,6,4,

$$(\cdot725)^3 = \cdot381078 \div 6 \quad = 63513$$
$$(\cdot725)^5 = \cdot200304 \div 120 \quad = \quad 1669$$
$$(\cdot725)^7 = \cdot105285 \div 5040 = \quad .. \; 21$$

2)	3)	4)	5)	6)	7)	
105285	52643	17548	4387	877	149	21

The nearest whole number to the quotient of 105285 divided by $2 \times 3 \times 4 \times 5 \times 6 \times 7 = 5040 = 21$.

```
  2)        3)        4)       5)          ↓0,0,5,15,25,
200304    100152    33384     834|6          166|9 . .
                              8 . .|  ᵕ 1       |8 . .
                                            ---------
                              8385|          167 7|. . . .
                             3 . . . .| ᵕ 3        3|. . . .
                                            ---------
                                             168 0

  2)                    3)                 ↓0,0,3,9,15,
381078               1905|39              635|1 3 .
                     191 .|    ᵕ 1 ᵕ        1|9 1 .
                                          ----------
                     19111|2              637 0|4 . . .
                     57 . . .|  ᵕ 3 ᵕ          5|7 . . .
                                          ----------
                     191283|              637 6 1|. . . . .
                     10 . . . . .| ᵕ 5 ᵕ       1 0|. . . . .
                                          ----------
                                          637 7 1
```

Length of arc = ·725979
63771 minus

·662208
1680 plus

·663888
21 minus

sin 41° 35′ 44″ = ·663867 = cos 48° 24′ 16″.

Again, ·529 ↓0,0,1,6,4, = ·529868

$(·529)^3$ = ·148036 ÷ 6 = 24673
$(·529)^5$ = ·041427 ÷ 120 = 345
$(·529)^7$ = ·011593 ÷ 5040 = 2

345 ↓0,0,5,30,20, = 348
24673 ↓0,0,3,18,12, = 24795.

Length of arc = ·529868
24795 minus

·505073
348 plus

·505421
2 minus

cos 59°.38′ 27″ = ·505419 = sin 30° 21′ 33′.

∴ ·663867 × ·505419 = ·335532 = ·335 ↓0,0,1,5,9, = cosine of c, the required side; from which the degrees, minutes, &c. in c has to be found.

$$(\cdot 335)^3 = \cdot 037595$$
$$(\cdot 335)^5 = \cdot 004219$$
$$(\cdot 335)^7 = \cdot 000473$$

```
½        ¾        ⅚        7        
473      237      178      148      21

½        ¾        5                 ↓0,0,5,25,45,
4219     2109     1582|             316|...
                  2...| ⌣ 1 ⌣         2|...
                                    ----------
                  1590.|            318 .|....
                  1.....| ⌣ 5 ⌣       1 .|....
                                    ----------
                                    319

½                 3                 ↓0,0,3,15,27,
37595             1879|8            626|6..
                  19..| ⌣ 1 ⌣         1|9..
                                    ----------
                  18855|            628 5|....
                  9....| ⌣ 5 ⌣          9|....
                                    ----------
                  18882.|           6294 .|.....
                  2......| ⌣ 9 ⌣       2 .|.....
                                    ----------
                                    6296
```

Length of sine = ·335532
6296
319
21

Length of arc = ·342168 = 1176′ 18″ = 19° 36′ 18″

∴ c = 70° 23′ 42″.

2. *In a spherical triangle ABC, right-angled at C, are given* b = 46° 18′ 23″, A = 34° 27′ 39″, *to find the other angle B.*

$$\cos B = \cos b \sin A.$$

$$
\begin{array}{r}
90^\circ \;\; 0' \;\; 0'' \\
46 \;\; 18 \;\; 23 \\
\hline
43^\circ\, 41'\, 37''
\end{array}
= 2621'\, 37'', \text{ length of arc}
$$

= ·762597 = 762 ↓ 0,0,0,7,8,4,

$(·762)^3$ = ·442451 ÷ 6 = 73742 ; ↓ 0,0,0,21,24,12, = 73916
$(·762)^5$ = ·256907 ÷ 120 = 2141 ; ↓ 0,0,0,35,40,20, = 2149
$(·762)^7$ = ·149171 ÷ 5040 = 30 ; ↓ 0,0,0,49,56,28, = 30

As a matter of form, ↓ 0,0,0,49,56,28, is affixed to 30, the nearest whole number to the quotient of 149171 divided by $2 \times 3 \times 4 \times 5 \times 6 \times 7 = 5040$. It is evident that 30 multiplied by ↓ 0,0,0,49,56,28, will not amount to 31, which is easily shown:

7)
210 . . |
14 . . . . | ⌣ 7 ⌣

↓ 0,0,0,49,56,28,
30 . . | . . . .
. . | . . . .
30

Length of arc = ·762597
73916 minus
·688681
2149 plus
·690830
30 minus

sin 43° 41′ 37″ = ·690800 = cos 46° 18′ 23″

34° 27′ 39″, arc of which = ·601454 = ·600 ↓ 0,0,2,4,2,

$(·6)^3$ = ·216000 ÷ 6 = 36000, mult. by ↓ 0,0,6,12,6, gives 36262.
$(·6)^5$ = ·077760 ÷ 120 = 648, mult. by ↓ 0,0,10,20,10, gives 655.
$(·6)^7$ = ·027994 ÷ 5040 = 6, which has not to be multiplied;

∴ Length of arc = ·601454
36262 minus
·565192
655 plus
·565847
6 minus

sine of 34° 27′ 39″ = ·565841

$\therefore$ ·565841 × ·6908 = ·390883 = cos B = 39 ↓ 0,0,2,2,6,5,

$$(\cdot 39)^3 = \cdot 059319$$
$$(\cdot 39)^5 = \cdot 009022$$
$$(\cdot 39)^7 = \cdot 001372$$
$$(\cdot 39)^9 = \cdot 000209$$

$\frac{1}{2}$	$\frac{3}{4}$	$\frac{5}{6}$	$\frac{7}{8}$	9)	
209	105	79	66	58	6;

$\frac{1}{2}$	$\frac{3}{4}$	$\frac{5}{6}$	7)	
1372	686	515	429	61;

61 ↓ 0,0,14,14,42,35, = 62.

All the factors except the first may be neglected, as the employment of the other factors will not increase 62 a single unit in the sixth decimal place. This is easily shown.

```
 7)                    ↓0,0,14,
427.|                  61 .| . . .
8...| ◡ 2               1 .| . . .
                       ----
                       62
```

$\frac{1}{2}$	$\frac{3}{4}$	5)	↓ 0,0,10,10,30,25,
9022	4511	3383	677

$\therefore$ 677 ↓ 0,0,10,10, = 685.

$\frac{1}{2}$	3	↓ 0,0,6,6,18,15,
59319	29660	9887

$\therefore$ 9889 ↓ 0,0,6,6,18, = 9954.

```
·390883
   9954
    685
     62
      6
-------
·401590 = arc of 1380′ 34 = 23° 0′ 34″,
```

which taken from 90° gives 69° 59′ 26″ = the angle B.

3. *In an oblique spherical triangle the three sides are*

$$a = 68^\circ\ 46'\ \ 2''$$
$$b = 43\ \ 37\ \ 38$$
$$c = 37\ \ 10\ \ \ 0$$

required the angle A.

It is well known that, if s be half the sum of the three sides, then:

$$\sin\frac{A}{2} = \sqrt{\frac{\sin(s-b)\sin(s-c)}{\sin b \sin c}}$$

$$\cos\frac{A}{2} = \sqrt{\frac{\sin s \sin(s-a)}{\sin b \sin c}}.$$

In this example, $s = 74^\circ\ 46'\ 50''$ sin = ·964938.

sin a = ·932117, sin b = ·689964, sin c = ·604136.

$s - b = 31^\circ\ \ 9'\ 12''$ sin = ·517330;
$s - c = 37\ \ 36\ \ 50$ sin = ·610337;
$s - a = \ \ 6\ \ \ 0\ \ 48$ sin = ·104760.

$$\therefore \quad \cos\frac{A}{2} = \sqrt{\frac{\cdot 964938 \times \cdot 104760}{\cdot 689964 \times \cdot 604136}}.$$

The object of working out this example, is to dispense altogether with the common and laborious operations of multiplication, division, and of the square root. From a table of the squares of numbers, or otherwise, it is readily found that

·964938 stands between		$(\cdot 982)^2$ and $(\cdot 983)^2$,
·104760	,,	$(\cdot 323)^2$ and $(\cdot 324)^2$,
·689964	,,	$(\cdot 830)^2$ and $(\cdot 831)^2$,
·604136	,,	$(\cdot 777)^2$ and $(\cdot 778)^2$.

It is also evident that

·77 is contained in ·924 exactly 1·2 times
·805 ,, ·322 ,, ·4 ,,

Now let P, Q, R, S, be factors with the following properties, namely :—

$$(\cdot 924)^2 \downarrow P^2 = \cdot 964938$$
$$(\cdot 322)^2 \downarrow Q^2 = \cdot 104760$$
$$(\cdot 77)^2 \downarrow R^2 = \cdot 604136$$
$$(\cdot 805)^2 \downarrow S^2 = \cdot 689964$$

$$\therefore \quad \cos\frac{A}{2} = \frac{\cdot 924 \downarrow P \times \cdot 322 \downarrow Q}{\cdot 77 \downarrow R \times \cdot 805 \downarrow S} = \frac{\cdot 48 \downarrow P \downarrow Q}{\downarrow R \downarrow S}$$

When the factors P, Q, R, S, are found, $\cos\frac{A}{2}$ becomes known without extracting the square root, and without multiplying and dividing the given cosines.

The work necessary to find P may be arranged as follows :—

2	964938 = $(\cdot 924)^2 \downarrow$ **0,12,2,8,18,12,**
17075 52	85|37|76 = $(924)^2$
102453| ◡ 6 ◡	10|24|53 = 12
	|56|35 = $\frac{11}{2}$
	1|88 = $\frac{10}{3}$
	|4 = $\frac{9}{4}$
1924|112	962|056
1924| ◡ 1 ◡	1|924 = 2
	1 = $\frac{1}{2}$
19279|62	9639|81 . .
771. .| ◡ 4 ◡	7|71 . .
192950|4	96475|2 . . . .
174 . . . .| ◡ 9 ◡	174 . . . .
1929852|	96492 6| . . . . . .
12 . . . . . .| ◡ 6 ◡	12| . . . . . .
	964938, the number required.

$$
\begin{array}{llllllll}
\therefore\ P = & \downarrow 0, & 6, & 1, & 4, & 9, & 6, & + \\
Q = & \downarrow 0, & 0, & 5, & 1, & 6, & 0, & + \text{ found in the same way.} \\
R = & \downarrow 0, & 0, & 9, & 3, & 9, & 0, & - \\
S = & \downarrow 0, & 3, & 1, & 5, & 0, & 4, & - \\
\hline
 & \downarrow 0, & 3, & \bar{4}, & \bar{3}, & 6, & 2, & = \dfrac{\downarrow P \downarrow Q}{\downarrow R \downarrow S}
\end{array}
$$

$$\cdot 48 \downarrow 0,3,\bar{4},\bar{3},6,2, = \cdot 492454 = \cos \frac{A}{2};$$

$$\therefore\ \frac{A}{2} = 60^\circ\ 29'\ 53''.$$

THE AREA OF SPHERICAL TRIANGLES AND THE SPHERICAL EXCESS.

Fig. 10.

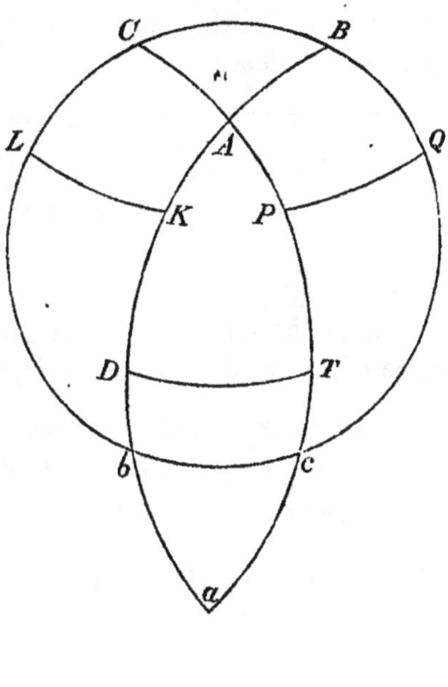

Let $BQcbLC$ represent the earth, a sphere, radius $= r$, and ABC a spherical triangle, formed by the three great circles BAb, CAc, CBc; and let $BL, BK; CQ, CP; AD, AT$, quadrants. The spherical angle A may be measured by the arc DT, the spherical angle B by the arc LK, and the spherical angle C by the arc PQ, being all arcs of great circles. The spherical triangle abc, part of the lune Aa, is supposed to be unwrapped from the obverse hemisphere.

The triangle *abc* is equal to the triangle *ABC*, because the spherical angle A is equal to the spherical angle a, and

$$Ab + AB = \text{semicircle} = Ab + bc,$$
$$Ac + AC = \text{semicircle} = Ac + ac,$$
$$\therefore \quad AB = ab$$
$$AC = ac.$$

Then it is evident that the area of the lune *AbacA*, that is, the lune *Aa*, is equal to the area of *ABC* + area of *Abc*; and the sum of the areas of the lunes *Aa*, *Bb*, *Cc*, is equal to the area of the hemisphere *BcbC*. On these considerations the following calculations depend. It is well known and easily proved, that the surface of a sphere is equal to four times the area of any one of its great circles;

$$\therefore \quad 2\pi r^2 = \text{area of the hemisphere } BCLb'cQ.$$

Let A° represent the degrees, &c. in the spherical angle A, and put $A_{,}$ = the length of the arc that measures this angle, radius = unity; and let the same notation be applied to the spherical angles B, C; hence,

$$\left.\begin{array}{llll} \text{length of arc } A_{,} & \text{to radius } r & = rA_{,} & = DT, \\ \quad ,, \quad B_{,} & \quad ,, \quad r & = rB_{,} & = LK, \\ \quad ,, \quad C_{,} & \quad ,, \quad r & = rC_{,} & = PQ, \end{array}\right\} \text{(see fig. 10.)}$$

It is easily perceived, that the circumference of the sphere ($2r\pi$) is to the length of the arc $LK = rB$; so is the area of the surface of the whole sphere ($4\pi r^2$), to the area of the lune *Bb*, or

$$2\pi r : rB_{,} :: 4\pi r^2 : 2B_{,}r^2 = \text{area of } BLbKB;$$
$$2\pi r : rC_{,} :: 4\pi r^2 : 2C_{,}r^2 = \text{area of } CQcPC;$$
$$2\pi r : rA_{,} :: 4\pi r^2 : 2A_{,}r^2 = \text{area of } ADaTA.$$

Hence, $2r^2B_{,} + 2r^2C_{,} + 2r^2A_{,}$ = half the surface of the sphere + twice the area of the triangle *ABC*, fig. 10.

Putting E for the area of the spherical triangle, then,

$$2\pi r^2 + 2E = 2r^2B_{,} + 2r^2C_{,} + 2r^2A_{,};$$
$$\therefore\ E = (A_{,} + B_{,} + C_{,} - \pi)\, r^2, \quad (1.)$$

Let E be represented by e, when $r = 1$, and suppose the angles to be measured in degrees, then (1) becomes

$$e = (A^\circ + B^\circ + C^\circ - 180^\circ), \quad (2.)$$

(2) is Girard's Theorem, and shows that the area of a spherical triangle may be represented by e, the excess of the sum of its three angles above two right angles. e is technically termed the *Spherical Excess.*

$$\text{From (1), } A_{,} + B_{,} + C_{,} - \pi = \frac{E}{r^2}, \quad (3.)$$

(3) expresses the spherical excess, in the lengths of arcs to radius unity; $A_{,} B_{,} C_{,}$ being the lengths of the arcs that measure the angles $A\ B\ C$ to radius unity.

$\pi : 180 \times 60 \times 60 :: A_{,} + B_{,} + C_{,} - \pi :$ the seconds in the spherical excess

$\therefore\ \pi : 180 \times 60 \times 60 :: \frac{E}{r^2} : \frac{180 \times 60 \times 60 \times E}{\pi r^2} =$ the seconds in the spherical excess. If the area E be expressed in square feet, the radius r must be given in feet also. If l be the length of a degree on the surface of the earth, supposing it to be a sphere, then $r = \frac{180\, l}{\pi}$ for,

$\pi : 180^\circ :: 1 : \frac{180}{\pi} =$ length of radius 1, in degrees and decimal parts of a degree; hence the length of radius r, in degrees, $= \frac{180}{\pi}$ also, but these degrees are measured on a great circle of the earth, the length of each being $= 365154{\cdot}6$ feet, which put $= l$.

$$\therefore\ r = \frac{180 l}{\pi}, \text{ and } r^2 = \frac{180^2 l^2}{\pi^2}.$$

∴ The spherical excess in seconds

$$= \frac{180 \times 60 \times 60 \times E}{\pi r^2} = \frac{60 \times 60 \times \pi E}{180 l^2}.$$

$$\therefore \text{ The spherical excess in seconds, } = \frac{20 \pi E}{l^2}, \quad (4.)$$

If (4) be put in a logarithmic form it gives Dalby's rule.

E, the area of the spherical triangle ABC, being in square feet.

4. *Given* E = 124797955000, *square feet, the area of the spherical triangle* ABC, *fig.* 10, *to find the spherical excess.*

$$l = 365154{\cdot}6 = 10^5 \times 3 \downarrow \mathbf{2,0,5,9,2,0,5,5},$$
$$E = 12479795500 = 10^{11} \downarrow \mathbf{2,3,1,0,5,5,0,3},$$
$$\pi = 3 \downarrow \mathbf{0,4,6,3,1,9,3,0},$$

(4), may be written

$$\frac{10^{11} \times 20 \times 3 \downarrow \overline{\pi',} \downarrow \overline{E',}}{10^{10} \times 9 \downarrow \overline{2l',}} = \tfrac{2}{3}\ \frac{10^2 \downarrow \overline{\pi',} \downarrow \overline{E',}}{\downarrow \overline{2l',}}$$

$E' = \downarrow \mathbf{2,3,1,0,5,5,0,3,}$ = 221537 0 1 reduced to the eight position.
$\pi' = \downarrow \mathbf{0,4,6,3,1,9,3,0,}$ = 461 1992 " " "
10^2 = 460540162 " " "

487305855

$l' = \downarrow \mathbf{2,0,5,9,2,0,5,5,}$ $= \downarrow \overline{\mathbf{19654824,}}$; $2l'$ } = 39309648

447996207 = 10 × 8 $\downarrow$ **1,0,2,4,0,1,1,5,**
230270081 ⌣ 10

217726126
207954604 ⌣ 8

9771522
9531497 ⌣ $\downarrow$**1,**

240025
199910 ⌣ (0,2,

4,0,1,1,5

$$\begin{array}{rr}
\downarrow 1,0,2,4,0,1,1,5, = & 1\cdot 10264332 \\
 & 80 \\
\hline
 & 88\cdot 21146560 \\
 & 2 \\
\hline
3\ ) & 176\cdot 42293120 \\
\hline
 & 58\cdot 80764373
\end{array}$$

$\therefore$ The spherical excess $= 58''\cdot 80764373$.

The same result may be found in the following manner, by continued reductions :—

$$\begin{array}{rcccccccc}
E' = & \downarrow 2, & 3, & 1, & 0, & 5, & 5, & 0, & 3, \\
\pi' = & \downarrow 0, & 4, & 6, & 3, & 1, & 9, & 3, & 0, \\
\hline
 & \downarrow 2, & 7, & 7, & 3, & 6, & 14, & 3, & 3, \\
2l' = & \downarrow 4, & 0, & 10, & 18, & 4, & 0, & 10, & 10, \\
\hline
 & \downarrow \overline{2}, & 7, & \overline{3}, & \overline{15}, & 2, & 14, & \overline{7}, & \overline{7}, \quad (5.) \\
= & \downarrow \overline{2}, & 0, & 67, & \overline{15}, & \overline{26}, & \overline{14}, & \overline{49}, & \overline{56}, \\
= & \downarrow \overline{2}, & 0, & 0, & 655, & \overline{26}, & \overline{14}, & \overline{317}, & \overline{391},
\end{array}$$

$\therefore$ (5) is reduced to $\downarrow \overline{2},6,5,\dot{4},8,7,6,6,$

$$\begin{array}{l}
6550 \\
\quad 26 \\
\hline
65240 \\
\quad\ 14 \\
\hline
652260 \\
\quad\ 317 \\
\hline
6519430 \\
\quad\ 391 \\
\hline
6519039 = \downarrow 0,6,5,4,8,7,\dot{6},6,
\end{array}$$

WORK UNABRIDGED.

```
          1|0|0|0|0|0|0|0|0|0| 0| 0
           |2|0|4|0|6|0|8|0|10| 0 minus
          -|7|9|5|9|3|9|1|9| 0| 0
           | |3|0|5|0|7|0|9| 0|11 plus
↓2̄, =    8 2|6 4|4 6|2 8|1   1 ◡  1
           4|9 5|8 6|7 7|7   . ◡  6
             |1 2|3 9|6 6|9   . ◡ 15
                 |1 6|5 2|9   . ◡ 20
                     |1 2|4   . ◡ 15
         8 7 7|2 8 9|3 8 0 ◡  1
             4|3 8 6|4 4 7 ◡  5
                   8|7 7 3 ◡ 10
                         9 ◡ 10
         8 8 1 6|8 4 6 0|9 . . . ◡ 1
               3|5 2 6 7|4 . . . ◡ 4
                      5|3 . . . ◡ 6
         8 8 2 0 3|7 3 3 6
                 7|0|5 6 3 ◡ 8
                   6|1|7 4 ◡ 7
                     5|2|9 ◡ 6
                      5|3 ◡ 6
         8 8 2 1 1 4 6 5 5
```

```
        8·82114655
               200
  3 ) 176·422931000
       58·8076437
```

The spherical excess the same as before found.

IMPORTANT MISCELLANEOUS PROBLEMS,

SOLVED BY

DUAL ARITHMETIC.

1. *Find the hyperbolic logarithm of* 1·95 *to seven places of decimals.*

$$
\begin{array}{rrrrrrrrr}
\epsilon = & \downarrow 10, & 4, & 7, & 1, & 0, & 0, & 3, & 8, \\
= & \downarrow 0, & 104, & \overline{33}, & \overline{9}, & \overline{90}, & \overline{50}, & \overline{7}, & \overline{22}, \\
= & \downarrow 0, & 0, & 1007, & \overline{9}, & \overline{506}, & \overline{466}, & \overline{631}, & \overline{750}, \\
= & \downarrow 0, & 0, & 0, & 10061, & \overline{506}, & \overline{466}, & \overline{4659}, & \overline{5785},
\end{array}
$$

$$
\begin{array}{r}
100610 \\
506 \\
\hline
1001040 \\
466 \\
\hline
10005740 \\
4659 \\
\hline
100010810 \\
5785 \\
\hline
100005025
\end{array}
$$

This reduction is made by employing the property:

$$
\begin{array}{lrrrrrrrr}
\downarrow 1, & = \downarrow 0, & 10, & \overline{4}, & \overline{1}, & \overline{9}, & \overline{5}, & \overline{1}, & \overline{3}, \\
\downarrow 0,1, & = \downarrow 0, & 0, & 10, & 0, & \overline{4}, & \overline{4}, & \overline{6}, & \overline{7}, \\
\downarrow 0,0,1, & = \downarrow 0, & 0, & 0, & 10, & 0, & 0, & \overline{4}, & \overline{5}, \\
\downarrow 0,0,0,1, & = \downarrow 0, & 0, & 0, & 0, & 10, & 0, & 0, & 0, \\
\&c. & = & & & \&c. & & & &
\end{array}
$$

$$\begin{array}{rrrrrrrrr}
1\cdot95 = & \downarrow 7, & 0, & 0, & 6, & 5, & 8, & 1, & 4, \\
& \downarrow 0, & 70, & \overline{28}, & \overline{1}, & \overline{58}, & \overline{27}, & \overline{6}, & \overline{17}, \\
& \downarrow 0, & 0, & 672, & \overline{1}, & \overline{338}, & \overline{307}, & \overline{426}, & \overline{507}, \\
& \downarrow 0, & 0, & 0, & 6719, & \overline{338}, & \overline{307}, & \overline{3114}, & \overline{3867}.
\end{array}$$

$$\begin{array}{r}
67190 \\
\underline{338} \\
668520 \\
\underline{307} \\
6682130 \\
\underline{3114} \\
66790160 \\
\underline{3867} \\
66786293
\end{array}$$

If 66786293 be divided by 100005025, the quotient is ·6678293, the hyperbolic log. of 1·95, as required.

2. *Required the hyperbolic logarithm of* 1·95 *to five places of decimals.*

$$\begin{array}{rrrrrrr}
1\cdot95 = & \downarrow 7, & 0, & 0, & 6, & 5, & 8, \\
= & \downarrow 0, & 70, & \overline{28}, & \overline{1}, & \overline{58}, & \overline{27}, \\
= & \downarrow 0, & 0, & 672, & \overline{1}, & \overline{338}, & \overline{307},
\end{array}$$

$$\begin{array}{r}
6720 \\
\underline{1} \\
67190 \\
\underline{338} \\
668520 \\
\underline{307} \\
668213
\end{array}$$

$$\begin{array}{rrrrrrr}
\epsilon = & \downarrow 10, & 4, & 7, & 1, & 0, & 0, \\
= & \downarrow 0, & 104, & \overline{33}, & \overline{9}, & \overline{90}, & \overline{50}, \\
= & \downarrow 0, & 0, & 1007, & \overline{9}, & \overline{506}, & \overline{466}, \\
= & \downarrow 0, & 0, & 0, & 10061, & \overline{506}, & 466,
\end{array}$$

$\therefore$ ϵ in the sixth position = 1000574.

Then 668213 divided by 1000574 gives ·66783, the hyperbolic logarithm of 1·95, true to five places of decimals as required.

3. *Required the hyperbolic logarithm of* 2 *to seven places of decimals.*

$$
\begin{array}{lrrrrrrrr}
2 = & \downarrow 7, & 2, & 6, & 0, & 7, & 8, & 2, & 8, \\
= & \downarrow 0, & 72, & \overline{22}, & \overline{7}, & \overline{56}, & \overline{27}, & \overline{5}, & \overline{13}, \\
= & \downarrow 0, & 0, & 698, & \overline{7}, & \overline{344}, & \overline{315}, & \overline{437}, & \overline{517}, \\
= & \downarrow 0, & 0, & 0, & 6973, & \overline{344}, & \overline{315}, & \overline{3229}, & \overline{4007},
\end{array}
$$

$$
\begin{array}{r}
69730 \\
344 \\ \hline
693860 \\
315 \\ \hline
6935450 \\
3229 \\ \hline
69322210 \\
4007 \\ \hline
69318203
\end{array}
$$

69318203 divided by 100005025 gives ·6931472 the hyperbolic logarithm of 2 to seven places of decimals.

Because 100005025 = $\downarrow$0,0,0,0,5,0,2,5, the quotient may be found by a simple subtraction, without the use of common division.

$$
\begin{array}{lr}
 & 69318|203\,.\,. \\
\text{half} & 3|46|6\,.\,.\smile\ 5 \\
\text{half} & 1|7\,.\,.\smile 25 \\ \hline
 & 3483 \\ \hline
\text{Hyp. log. } 2 = & \cdot 69314720
\end{array}
$$

It must be observed, that this rule only applies, when reductions are carried to the eight position.

4. *Required the hyperbolic logarithm of* 10.

Since $\epsilon = 2{\cdot}718281828459\ldots$ and it was before shown that the value of x may be found in a direct way, from the equation

$$\epsilon^x = 10;$$

then x is the hyperbolic logarithm of 10; $2x$ will be the hyperbolic logarithm of 100; $3x$ the hyperbolic logarithm of 1000, and so on. The square roots, fourth roots, eight roots, &c. of e and 10, may be found by common arithmetic; the bases will then be reduced nearer and nearer to 1, and the operation simplified.

Let $\qquad v^8 = e, \text{ and } a^8 = 10,$

then $\qquad v^{8x} = a^8;$

$$\therefore\ v^x = a.$$

$$
\begin{array}{rrrrrrrrr}
\text{But } v = & \downarrow 1, & 2, & 9, & 7, & 9, & 3, & 6, & 9, \\
= & \downarrow 0, & 12, & 5, & 6, & 0, & \bar{2}, & 5, & 6, \\
= & \downarrow 0, & 0, & 125, & 6, & \overline{48}, & \overline{50}, & \overline{67}, & \overline{78}, \\
= & \downarrow 0, & 0, & 0, & 1256, & \overline{48}, & \overline{50}, & \overline{567}, & \overline{703},
\end{array}
$$

$$
\begin{array}{r}
12560 \\
48 \\
\hline
125120 \\
50 \\
\hline
1250700 \\
567 \\
\hline
12501330 \\
703 \\
\hline
12500627
\end{array}
$$

$$
\begin{array}{rrrrrrrrr}
a = & \downarrow 3, & 0, & 1, & 8, & 9, & 3, & 1, & 4, \\
= & \downarrow 0, & 30, & \overline{11}, & 5, & \overline{18}, & \overline{12}, & \bar{2}, & \bar{5}, \\
= & \downarrow 0, & 0, & 289, & 5, & \overline{138}, & \overline{132}, & \overline{182}, & \overline{215}, \\
= & \downarrow 0, & 0, & 0, & 2895, & \overline{138}, & \overline{132}, & \overline{1338}, & \overline{1660},
\end{array}
$$

$$
\begin{array}{r}
28950 \\
138 \\
\hline
288120 \\
132 \\
\hline
2879880 \\
1338 \\
\hline
28785420 \\
1660 \\
\hline
28783760
\end{array}
$$

Then 28783760 divided by 12500627 gives 2·302585093, the hyperbolic logarithm of 10.

$\therefore\ 2x =$ hyp. log. 100 = 4·6051702
$3x =$ „ „ 1000 = 6·9077553
$4x =$ „ „ 10000 = 9·2103404, &c. &c.

5. *Required the hyperbolic log. of* 3, 4, 5, ... *the log. of* 2 *being given* = ·693147, *to five places of decimals.*

2) 3·000000
1·500000

$= \downarrow 4,\ 2,\ 4{,}3,\ 3,\ 2,$
$= \downarrow 0{,}42,\ \overline{12},\overline{1},\ \overline{33},\ \overline{18},$
$= \downarrow 0,\ 0{,}408,\overline{1},\overline{201},186,$

4080
1
40790
201
405890
186
405704

$\epsilon = \downarrow 10,\ 4,\ 7{,}1,\ 0,\ 0,$
$= \downarrow\ 0{,}104,\ \overline{33},\overline{9},\ \overline{90},\ \overline{50},$
$= \downarrow\ 0,\ 0{,}1007,\overline{9},\overline{506},\overline{466},$
= 1000574, a result before found.

405704 divided by 1000574 gives ·40547 = log. of 1·5.

·40547
·69315
hyp. log. of 3 = 1·09862 to five places of decimals.

·693147
2
hyp. log. 4 = 1·386294

To find the hyperbolic log. of 5;

4) 5·000000
1·250000

$$
\begin{aligned}
&= \downarrow 2, &&3, &&2, &&6, &&7, &&5,\\
&= \downarrow 0, &&23, &&\overline{6}, &&4, &&\overline{11}, &&\overline{5},\\
&= \downarrow 0, &&0, &&224, &&4, &&\overline{103}, &&\overline{97},
\end{aligned}
$$

$$
\begin{array}{r}
2240\\
4\\
\hline
22440\\
103\\
\hline
223370\\
97\\
\hline
223273
\end{array}
$$

Then 22327 ÷ 1000574

gives ·22314 log. of 1·25;

log. 4 = 1·38629

log. 5 = 1·60943

In the same manner the hyperbolic logarithms of the remaining consecutive numbers 6, 7, 8, &c., may be determined.

When it is required to find the hyperbolic logarithm of a number greater than 10; suppose all the figures after the first to be decimals, then find the hyperbolic logarithm, and afterwards add 2·3025851, for two places of figures; 4·6051702 for three places of figures; 6·9077553 for four places of figures, and so on. The following example illustrates this matter.

6. *Required the hyperbolic log. of* 345·678.

First find the hyperbolic log. of 3·45678.

$$
3\,)\,\underline{3{\cdot}45678}\\
1{\cdot}15226
$$

$$
\begin{aligned}
&= \downarrow 1, &&4, &&6, &&6, &&1, &&7,\\
&= \downarrow 0, &&14, &&2, &&5, &&\overline{8}, &&2,\\
&= \downarrow 0, &&0, &&142, &&5, &&\overline{64}, &&\overline{54},
\end{aligned}
$$

$$\begin{array}{r} 14250 \\ 64 \\ \hline 141860 \\ 54 \\ \hline 141806 \end{array}$$

141806 divided by 1000574 gives the log. of

$$\begin{array}{lrl} & 1{\cdot}15226 = & {\cdot}14172 \\ \text{log. of } 3 & = & 1{\cdot}09861 \\ \hline \text{log. of } 3{\cdot}45678 & = & 1{\cdot}24033 \\ \text{log. of } 100 & = & 4{\cdot}60517 \\ \hline \text{log. of } 345{\cdot}678 & \doteq & 5{\cdot}84550 \end{array}$$

In calculating the log. of 345·678 by this method, it was supposed that the log. of 3 was known.

7. *Required the hyp. log. of 345·678, without knowing the log. of any number except the log. of* 10 (=2·3025851); *the base* ϵ = 2·718281828 *being also given.*

The square root of 3·45678 may be reduced to ↓ **6,4,8,5,1,0,7,** which may be reduced to 6202297, in the seventh position.

Again the square root of 2·718281828 may be reduced to ↓ **5,2,3,5,4,9,9,** which may be reduced to 5000488, in the seventh position.

Then 6202297 ÷ 5000488 gives 1·240338, hyp. log. of 3·45678.

$$\begin{array}{lr} & 1{\cdot}240338 \\ \text{twice log. } 10 \ldots\ldots & 4{\cdot}605170 \\ \hline \text{hyp. log. } 345{\cdot}678 \ldots & 5{\cdot}845508 \end{array}$$

8. *Required the hyperbolic logarithm of* 7635·214 *by direct calculation to seven places of decimals, having only given the base and the hyperbolic logarithm of* 10.

10000 ÷ 7365·214 = 1·30972098

```
100000000
 20000000
  1000000
---------
12|10|00|00|0 . +  1
  |96|80|00|0 . +  8
    3|38|8 0|0 . + 28
       6|7 7|0 . + 56
           8|5 . + 70
            |1 . + 56
---------
13 10|25 66|2 . . . +  1
     |52 4 1|0 . . . −  4
            1|3 . . . + 10
---------
13 09 73|2 6 5 . . .
        1|1 7 9 . . . −  9
---------
13 09 72 0|8 6
          |1 3        +  1
```

∴ 1·30972098 = $\downarrow 2,8,0,\bar{4},0,\bar{9},1$, which is easily reduced to 2698405 = $\downarrow 0,0,0,0,0,0,2698405$,

$\epsilon = \downarrow 10,4,7,1,0,0,4$, when reduced in the same manner becomes 10000978.

∴ 2698405 ÷ 10000978 gives ·2698141, the hyperbolic log. of 1·30972098;

log. of 10000	= 9·2103404
log. of 1·30972098	= ·2698141
log. of 7365·214	= 8·9405263

9. *Required the number corresponding to the hyperbolic logarithm* 8·9405263, *by a direct calculation, the log. of* 10, = 2·3025851, *being given.*

Four times is the first multiple of the log. of 10, that exceeds the given logarithm,

4 times 2·3025851	= 9·2103404
given log.	- 8·9405263
	·2698141

$$
\begin{aligned}
\epsilon &= \downarrow 10,\ 4,\ 7,\ 1,\ 0,\ 0,\ 4, \\
&= \downarrow 0,\ 0,\ 0,\ 0,\ 0,\ 0,\ 10000978,
\end{aligned}
$$

$\cdot 2698141 \times 10000978 = 2698405$, the decimal part being rejected.

$$
\begin{aligned}
\text{Then}\quad & \downarrow 0,\ 0,\ 0,\ 0,\ 0,\ 0,\ 2698405, \\
&= \downarrow 2,\ 0,\ 0,\ 0,\ 0,\ 0,\ 792015, \\
&= \downarrow 2,\ 7,\ 0,\ 0,\ 0,\ 0,\ 95424, \\
&= \downarrow 2,\ 7,\ 9,\ 0,\ 0,\ 0,\ 5460, \\
&= \downarrow 2,\ 7,\ 9,\ 5,\ 4,\ 6,\ 0,
\end{aligned}
$$

This reducing is simple enough, since

$$
\begin{aligned}
\downarrow 1, &= \downarrow 0,\ 10,\ \bar{4},\ \bar{1},\ \bar{9},\ \bar{5},\ \bar{1}, \\
&= \downarrow 0,\ 0,\ 0,\ 0,\ 0,\ 0,\ 953195, \\
\downarrow 0,1, &= \downarrow 0,\ 0,\ 10,\ 0,\ \bar{4},\ \bar{4},\ \bar{7}, \\
&= \downarrow 0,\ 0,\ 0,\ 0,\ 0,\ 0,\ 99513, \\
\downarrow 0,0,1, &= \downarrow 0,\ 0,\ 0,\ 10,\ 0,\ 0,\ \bar{4}, \\
&= \downarrow 0,\ 0,\ 0,\ 0,\ 0,\ 0,\ 9996,
\end{aligned}
$$

$$
\begin{array}{r}
953195\ )\ 2698405\ (\ 2 \\
\underline{1906390} \\
99513\ )\ 792015\ (\ 7 \\
\underline{696591} \\
9996\ )\ 95424\ (\ 9 \\
\underline{89964} \\
5460
\end{array}
$$

In this way the resulting numbers are found, and afterwards arranged in the usual form.

$$\downarrow 2,7,9,5,4,6,0,$$

It is evident that $\downarrow 2,0,0,0,0,0,0,$ must be added when $\downarrow 0,0,0,0,0,0,190639,$ is subtracted; that $\downarrow 0,7,0,0,0,0,0,$ must be added when ↓0,0,0,0,0,0,696591, is subtracted; and that 0,0,9,0,0,0,0, must be added when ↓0,0,0,0,0,0,89964, is subtracted.

```
 100000000
  20000000
   1000000
 ----------
 12|1 0|0 0|0 0|0 .      ⌣  1
   |8 4|7 0|0 0|0 .      ⌣  7
      2|5 4|1,0|0 .      ⌣ 21
           4|2 3|5 .     ⌣ 35
               4|2 .     ⌣ 35
 ----------
 129|7 2 8|3 7 7         ⌣  1
   1|1 6 7|5 5 5         ⌣  9
        4|6 7 0          ⌣ 36
             1 1         ⌣ 84
 ----------
 1309|006|1|3 . .        ⌣  1
     |6 4 4|5|0 . .      ⌣  5
             |1|3 . .    ⌣ 10
 ----------
 13096,6076 .
      |5|2 3 8 . . .     ⌣  4
        |7 8 6 . . .     ⌣  6
 ----------
 130972100
```

∴ 10000 divided by 1·309721 gives 7365·214, the number required.

10. *Required the number corresponding to the hyperbolic logarithm of* 2·1972245.

It is evident that the required number must be less than 10.

$$\begin{array}{rl} \text{From} & 2{\cdot}3025851 \\ \text{take} & 2{\cdot}1972245 \\ \hline & {\cdot}1053606 = \log \frac{10}{x}, \end{array}$$

x being the required number.

$\cdot 1053606 \times 10000978 = 1053709$, neglecting decimals.

```
953195 ) 1053709 ↓ 1,
         953195
  99513 ) 100514 ( 1,
           99513
    9996 ) 1001 ( 0,
```

Find the number corresponding to

↓ 1,1,0,1,0,0,1,

```
10 00 00 000
 1 00 00 000
-------------
11|00|00|00|0 .
  |11|00|00|0 .
-------------
11|11 00 00|0 . . .
  |    11 1|0 . . .
-------------
11 11 11 1|1 0 . . . . .
          |1 11111
-------------
11 11 11 1 2
```

∴ 10 divided by 1·1111112 gives 9 very nearly.

∴ 2·1972245 is the hyp. log. of 9.

the reciprocal with respect to 10

```
4 ) 2·1972245
    ·5493061 log. of fourth root of the
```

required number.

5493061 × 10000978· = 5493598.

```
953195 ) 5493598 ↓ 5,
         4765975
  99513 ) 727623 ( 7,
          696591
    9996 ) 31032 ( 3
           29988
            1044
```

∴ ↓5,7,3,1,0,4,4, represents the fourth root of the required number.

```
1|0|0|0|0|0|0|0    ⌣  1
 |5|0|0|0|0|0|0    ⌣  5
 |1|0|0|0|0|0|0    ⌣ 10
   |1|0|0|0|0|0    ⌣ 10
       |5|0|0|0    ⌣  5
         |1|0|0    ⌣  1
-------------------
1 6|1 0|5 1|0 0    ⌣  1
  1|1 2|7 3|5 7    ⌣  7
   |  3|3 8|2 1    ⌣ 21
       |  5|6 4    ⌣ 35
           |  6    ⌣ 35
-------------------
1 7 2|6 6 8|4 8 .
    ,|5 1 8|0 1 .
           |5 2 .
-------------------
1 7 3 1|8 7 0 1
       |1 7|3 2 . . . .
           6|9 . . . . . .
            |7 . . . . . .
-------------------
1 7 3 2 0 5 0 9
```

∴ 1·7320509 is the fourth root of the required number, but 1·7320509 is the square root of 3, hence 9 is the required number.

In works on geometry, methods are sometimes given to find distances of inaccessible objects without the aid of instruments to measure angles; but such rules and directions can seldom be applied for want of sufficient suitable space to operate upon. It mostly happens that the distance required is great compared with the convenient base from which observations have to be made, besides the angles at the base approach right angles, one of them often greater than a right angle. The next problem shows how to find inaccessible distances with great accuracy from confined bases, the means of measuring a straight line being only required.

11. *An observer at A wishes to find the inaccessible distance AC: the base AB measures 8 chains; AD in a direct line to C measures* 10 *chains, and BE* 14; *then DB is found by measurement to be* 11 *chains, and AE* 17; *required all the angles of the triangle ACB and the distance AC.*

Fig. 11.

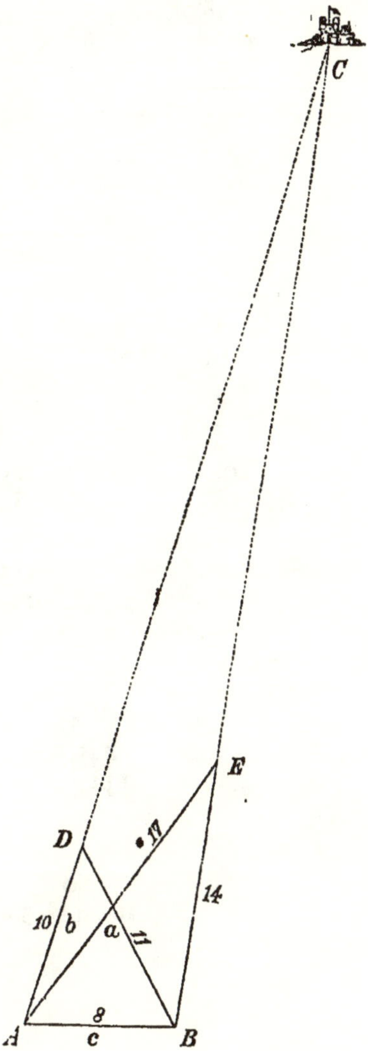

$$\cos DAB = \frac{b^2 + c^2 - a^2}{2bc}$$

$$= \frac{100 + 64 - 121}{160} = \cdot 26875000$$

$$\cos ABE = \frac{196 + 64 - 289}{224}$$

$$= - \cdot 13660714$$

The cosine of the angle ABE being negative, indicates the angle to be greater than a right angle.

$$\cdot 26875000 = \cdot 26 \downarrow 0,3,3,2,5,0,0,5,$$

$$\cdot 13660714 = \cdot 13 \downarrow 0,5,0,\overline{2},2,3,1,$$

$$(\cdot 26)^2 = \cdot 0676$$

1 ⌣ 676	3380 ⌣ 5
2 ⌣ 1352	2028 ⌣ 3
4 ⌣ 2704	4056 ⌣ 6
8 ⌣ 5408	6084 ⌣ 9
676	
7 ⌣ 4732	

It is easy to find 1, 2, 3, 4, 5, 6, 7, 8, and 9 times 676; then the required powers of (·26) are obtained by mere inspection.

```
      4056
     1352
     ------
·26³ = ·017576
```

```
     4|056                          |676
    47|32                          5|408
   338|0                          54|08
  4732|                           67|6
   676|                          676|
 ----------                   ----------
.0011881| fifth.              ·0000803| seventh.
```

```
         |2028
       54|080
  ------------
 ·0000054| ninth.
```

```
  ½     ¾     ⅚     ⅞     9)
  54    27    20    17    15     2
```

```
 ½     ¾     ⅚      7)                  ↓0,21,21,
803   402   302    252|               36| . . ⌣ 1
                   8 . .| ⌣ 3 ⌣        8| . . ⌣ 21 = A
                                       1| . . ⌣ A × 20 ÷ 2
                                     ----
                   315 .|             45 .| . . .
                   9 . . .| ⌣ 3 ⌣      1 .| . . .
                                     ----
                                      46
```

```
  ½       ¾        5)                ↓0,15,15,10, &c.
11881   5940     445|5             89|1 . ⌣ 1
                 134 .| ⌣ 3 ⌣      13|4 . ⌣ 15 = A
                                     |9 . ⌣ A × 14 ÷ 2 = B
                                         . ⌣ B × 13 ÷ 3
                                  ------
                 517|0            103|4 . . .
                 16 . .| ⌣ 3 ⌣      1|6 . .
                                  ------
                                  105 0| . . . .
                                      1| . . . .
                                  ------
                                  105 1
```

½	3)	↓0,9,9,6,15,0,
175760	87880	29|29|3 . ⌣ 1
		2|63|6 . ⌣ 9
		10|5 . ⌣ 36
		|2 . ⌣ 84
		320|36 . ⌣ 1
		2|88 . ⌣ 9
		1 . ⌣ 36
		3232|5 . . .
		1|9| . . . . .
		5| . . . . .
		32349

·2687500
32349
1051
46
2

·2720948, length of arc whose sine is ·2687500 ∴ arc = 15° 35′ 23″·6

∴ the angle $CAB = 74° \ 24' \ 36''·4$.

$(·13)^2 =$ ·0169

1 ⌣	169	845 ⌣	5
2 ⌣	338	507 ⌣	3
4 ⌣	676	1014 ⌣	6
8 ⌣	1352	1521 ⌣	9
	169		
7 ⌣	1183		

507
169

·0021970 cube;

1\|183
15\|21
16\|9
338\|

·0000371\|fifth;

```
        | 169
       1| 183
       5| 07
--------|--------
·0000006|seventh;
```
which may be neglected, as it will not, when reduced, give a unit in the seventh decimal place.

```
 ½        ¾         5)            ↓ 0,25,0,1̅0̅, &c.
371      186       140|          28| . . ⌣ 1
                   7 . .| ⌣ 5 ⌣   7| . . ⌣ 25 = A
                                  1| . . ⌣ A × 24 ÷ 2
                                 ----
                                 36

              3)                 ↓ 0,15,0,6̅,6, &c.
21970       10985|          36|62| . . ⌣ 1
            549 . .| ⌣ 5 ⌣    5|49| . . ⌣ 15 = A
                               |38| . . ⌣ A × 14 × 2 = B
                                  2| . . ⌣ B × 13 ÷ 3
                             ------
                             42 51| . . . .
                                  3| . . . . negative 6 times.
                             ------
                             42 48
```

```
 1366071
    4248
      36
--------
·1370355, length of arc whose sine is ·1366071.
```

∴ arc = 7° 51′ 5″·6

∴ angle ABC = 97° 51′ 5″·6, since its cosine is negative.

∴ The angle ACB = 7° 44′ 18″.

```
From  ·2720948
take  ·1370355
      --------
·13 ↓ 0,4,2̅,3, = ·1350593 length of arc of 7° 44′ 18″.
```

$(\cdot 13)^3 = \cdot 0021970$
$(\cdot 13)^5 = \cdot 0000371$

```
2)        3)        4)        5)             ↓0,20, &c.
371       186       62        15. |            3 .|. .
                              6.. | ◡4◡        1 .|. .
                                               ———
                                                4

2                   3         ↓0,12,6̄,9,
21970           109|85        36|62 ◡ 1
                   |  ◡4◡      4|40 ◡ 12 = A
                                 24 ◡ A × 11 ÷ 2
                              ———————
                              41 2|6 . . .
                                 2|5 . . . ◡6 minus
                              ———————
                              41 0 1|. . . .
                                   4|. . . .
                              ———————
                              41 0 5
```

```
1350593 +
   4105 −
———————
1346488
      4 +
———————
1346492 sine of 7° 44′ 18″.
```

∴ sin 7° 44′ 18″ : 8 :: sin 97° 51′ 5″·6 : *AC*, the distance required.

$$\{1 - (\cdot 13660714)^2\}^{\frac{1}{2}} = \cdot 9906244 = \sin 97^\circ\ 51'\ 5''\cdot 6.$$

∴ ·1346492 : 8 :: ·9906244 : 58·864 the required distance.

In solving this example, lengthened details are entered into, to prevent obscurity; the results are carried to a degree of accuracy seldom required in practice, to show the delicacy and powers of the method. It may also be observed, that, to find the distance it was not necessary to find the degrees, minutes, &c. contained in the arcs.

The work of this example, without superfluities, carried out to five places of decimals, may be arranged as follows :

$$\frac{100 + 64 - 121}{160} = \cdot 26875 = \cos CAB = \cdot 26 \downarrow 0,3,3,2,5,$$

$$\frac{196 + 64 - 289}{224} = - \cdot 13661 = \cos CBA = - \cdot 13 \downarrow 0,5,0,\bar{2},2,$$

$$(\cdot 26)^3 = \cdot 01758$$
$$(\cdot 26)^5 = \cdot 00119$$

$$\begin{array}{llll}
\frac{1}{2} & \frac{3}{4} & 5) & \downarrow 0,15,15 \\
119 & 60 & 45| & 9\cdot|\cdot\cdot \\
 & & 14\cdot|\ \smile 3 \smile & 1\cdot|\cdot\cdot \\
 & & & \overline{10}
\end{array}$$

$$\begin{array}{lll}
\frac{1}{2} & 3) & \downarrow 0,9,9, \\
1758 & 879 & 29|3\ \cdot \\
 & & 2|6\ \cdot \\
 & & |1\ \cdot \\
 & & \overline{320}|\cdot\cdot\cdot \\
 & & 3|\cdot\cdot\cdot \\
 & & \overline{323}
\end{array}$$

$$\begin{array}{r}
\cdot 26875 \\
\cdot 323 \\
10 \\
\hline
\end{array}$$

arc = ·27208 to sin 26875; cos CAB.

$$(\cdot 13)^3 = \cdot 00220$$

$$\begin{array}{lll}
\frac{1}{2} & 3) & \downarrow 0,15,0, \\
220 & 110 & 37|\cdot\cdot \\
 & 6\cdot\cdot\ \smile 5 \smile & 6|\cdot \\
 & & \overline{43}
\end{array}$$

$$\begin{array}{r}
\cdot 13661 \\
43 \\
\hline
\end{array}$$

arc = ·13704 to sin ·13661; cos CBA

$$\begin{array}{r}
\cdot 27208 \\
\cdot 13704 \\
\hline
\end{array}$$

$\cdot 13 \downarrow 0,4,\bar{2}, = \cdot 13504$ = arc of angle ABC.

$$(\cdot 13)^3 = \cdot 00220$$

```
2)          3          ↓0,12,6̄,
220         110          37|. .
                          4|. .
                         ——
                         41
```

```
·13504
    41
——————
·13463 sine of arc ·13504.
```

∴ ·13463 : 8 :: 99062 : 58·864 as before.

The length of an arc (·13704) to radius 1, and its sine (·13661) being known, and the cosine required: it is a question whether it is easier to find the cosine from the sine by the well known expression,

$$\sqrt{1 - \sin^2} = \cos,$$

or to find the cosine, by Dual Arithmetic, in a direct manner from the length of the arc. To square five or six figures, and afterwards to extract the square root of twice as many, appear to involve more mental labour than the following direct method:

·13704 = ·13 ↓ 0,5,3,

(·13)² = ·01690 to five decimal places

(·13)⁴ = ·00029.

```
   2)       3)       4)
   29       15       5        1
```

```
2)        ↓0,10,6,                  1·00000
1690       84|5 .                       939 −
            8|5 . ◡ 10 = A          ——————
             |4 . ◡ A × 9 ÷ 2        ·99061
          ——                              1 +
          934|. . .                 ——————
            5|. . .                  ·99062 = cosine.
          ——
          939
```

12. *Find the meridional parts answering to any given latitude* (35° 0′) *by a direct calculation.*

The meridional parts y for any latitude x, is given by the formula

$$y = 3437{\cdot}74679 \text{ log. tan } (45° + \tfrac{1}{2} x).$$

Hyperbolic logarithms are employed, and 3437·74679 are the nautical miles or minutes that in every circle is equal to its radius.

$$\begin{array}{r} 90°\ 0' \\ 35\ \ 0 \\ \hline 2\ )\ 125\ \ 0 \\ \hline \cos 27°\ 30' = \sin\ 62°\ 30' \end{array}$$

Length of arc of 27° 30′ = ·4799655.

$$\cdot4799655 = \cdot48 \downarrow 0,0,0,0,\overline{7},\overline{2},$$

$(\cdot48)^2 = \cdot2304000$. When necessary, the seven places.
$(\cdot48)^3 = \cdot1105920$
$(\cdot48)^4 = \cdot0530842$
$(\cdot48)^5 = \cdot0254804$
$(\cdot48)^6 = \cdot0122306$
$(\cdot48)^7 = \cdot0058707$

2)	3)	4)	5)	6)	7)	
58707	29354	9785	2446	489	82	12.

2)	3)	4)	5)	6)	
122306	61153	20384	5096	1019	170.

2) 254804 3) 127402 4) 42467 5 10617. | 7..... | ⌣7⌣ $\downarrow 0,0,0,0,\overline{35},$
2124. |.....
1. |..... minus
2123

2) 530842 3) 265421 4 88474 | 6..... | ⌣7⌣ $\downarrow 0,0,0,0,\overline{35},8,$
·22119 |.....
6 |.....
22113

```
2)                 3                ↓0,0,0,0,2̄1̄,6̄,
1105920          55296|0            18432|0....
                 39....|.  ⌣7⌣          3|9.... minus
                                    ─────────
                                    18428 1|.....
                                          1|...... minus
                                    ─────────
                                    18428 0

            2              ↓0,0,0,0,1̄4̄,4̄,
        23040|00·           115 20|00...
        161...|   ⌣7⌣            1|61... minus
                            ─────────
                            115183|9.....
                                  |5..... minus
                            ─────────
                            1151834

1·0000000                         ·4799655
 ·1151834 −                         184280 −
 ─────────                         ─────────
 ·8848166                          ·4615375
    22113 +                           2123 +
 ─────────                         ─────────
 ·8870279                          ·4617498
      170 −                             12
 ─────────                         ─────────
 ·8870109 = cosine 27° 30′         ·4617486 = sin 27° 30′.
```

Now ·8870109 is the sine of 62° 30′, and ·4617486 is the cosine, and since the sine divided by the cosine gives the tangent we may proceed as follows to find the hyperbolic log. of the tangent.

·8870109 multiplied by ↓**1,2,4,6,8,9,1,** = 1
·4617486 multiplied by ↓**8,1,0,3,0,3,0,** = 1

∴ ·8870109 divided by ·461748, will be represented by

```
           ↓8, 1, 0, 3, 0, 3, 0,
Divided by ↓1, 2, 4, 6, 8, 9, 1,
           ─────────────────────
           ↓7, 1̄, 4̄, 3̄, 8̄, 6̄, 1̄, represents the quotient,
```

which is readily reduced to 6529007, which, when divided by 10000978, gives ·6528368, the hyperbolic logarithm of the tangent of 62° 30′. Then 3437·74679 × ·6528368 = 2244·287, the meridional parts required.

The multiplication of any given number by 3437·74679, is a matter of mere inspection when 1, 2, 3, 4, 5, 6, 7, 8, 9, times 3437·74679 are first set down.

WORK WITHOUT CONTRACTION.

1 ◡	3437·74679	17188·73395	◡ 5
2 ◡	6875·49358	10313·24037	◡ 3
4 ◡	13750·98716	20626·48074	◡ 6
8 ◡	27501·96432	30939·72111	◡ 9
	3437·74679		
7 ◡	24064·22753		

2	750197432
20	62648074
103	1324037
2 750	197432
6 875	49358
171 887	3395
2062 648	074
2244·287	

This example is carried to an extent seldom required in practice. The whole theory of Mercator's sailing depends upon the accuracy of these meridional parts.

Since $\frac{10000}{3}$ ↓ 0,3,1, represents 3437·74679 nearly, then $\frac{10000}{3}$ × ·6528368 ↓ 0,3,1, gives the meridional part nearly.

WORK.

```
·65|2 8|3 6 8 .
  1|9 5|8 5|1 .
      1|9 5|9 .
           |7 .
---------------
·67 2|6 1 8|5 . .
     |6 7 2|6 . .
---------------
3 ) 67 3 2·9 1 1
---------------
    22 4 4·3
```

22443 meridional parts, lat. 35°, and near enough the truth for practice.

13. *Find without the use of tables of logarithms, or of sines and tangents, the true meridional parts corresponding to 80° of latitude, not the approximate meridional parts given by Mr. Wright.*

```
    90° 0′
    80  0
   -------
2 ) 170  0
   -------
    85° 0′
```

The cosine of 5° = sine of 85°.

The length of arc of 5° = ·087266.

By the method of calculation so fully explained and illustrated, the cosine of this arc is found to be ·996195, and the sine = ·0871557. The process is so simple for an angle so small, that it is unnecessary to insert the work.

```
8|7|1|5|5|7   ↓1,4,2,3,6,3,
 |8|7|1|5|6
-----------
9 5|8 7|1 3| . .
  3|8 3|4 9| . .
      5|7 5| . .
           4| . .
-----------
9 9 7 6 4 1 . . .
```

```
                ↓0,0,3,8,1,3,
996|1 9 5| . . .
  2|9 8 9| . . .
          3 . . .
---------------
999 1|8 7 . .
    8|0 0 . .
---------------
999 9 8 7 . . . .
```

```
997'641|...              99998|7 ....
   1995|...                  1|0| ......
      1|...                   |3| ......
---------
9996|3|7 ..
   3|0|0 ....
    |6|0| ......
       3| ......
```

$\therefore \quad \cdot 996195 \times \downarrow 0,0,3,8,1,3, = 1.$

and $\cdot 0871557 \times \downarrow 1,4,2,3,6,3, = \frac{1}{10}.$

$\cdot 996195$ is represented by $\dfrac{1}{\downarrow 0,0,3,8,1,3,}$

and $\cdot 0871557$ by $\dfrac{1}{10 \downarrow \bar{1},4,\bar{2},\bar{3},\bar{6},\bar{3},}$

$$\frac{\cdot 996195}{\cdot 0871557} = \frac{10 \downarrow 1,4,2,3,6,3,}{\downarrow 0,0,3,8,1,3,} = 10 \downarrow 1,4,\bar{1},\bar{5},5,0,$$

To render this method clear, every step is set down, figure by figure.

$$\begin{array}{rrrrrr} \downarrow 1, & 4, & \bar{1}, & \bar{5}, & 5, & 0, \\ = \downarrow 0, & 14, & \bar{5}, & \bar{6}, & \bar{4}, & \bar{5}, \\ = \downarrow 0, & 0, & 135, & \bar{6}, & \overline{60}, & \overline{75}, \end{array}$$

```
           1350
              6
           ------
           13440
              60
           ------
           133800
               75
           ------
1000470 )  133725 (quotient  ·13366
                            2·30259 hyp. log. 10.
                            -------
```

Hyp. log. tan (45° + half lat.) = 2·43625

This result must be multiplied by

$$\frac{10000}{3} \downarrow 0,3,1,$$

WORK.

```
   24|3 6|2 5
     |7 3|0 9
         |7 3
   ----------
   25 1|0 0 7
       |2 5 1
   ----------
3 ) 25 1 2 5·8
   ----------
    8 3 7 5·2
```

8375·2 meridional parts for latitude 80°. The number $3437{\cdot}74679 = \dfrac{180 \times 60}{3{\cdot}14159265\ldots}$; because rad. of earth × 3·14159265 . . = length of an arc of 180°, = length of arc of 10800 minutes or nautical miles.

$$\therefore \text{ Rad. of earth} = \frac{10800}{3{\cdot}14159265} = 3437{\cdot}74679 \text{ nautical miles.}$$

14. *The pressure of steam upon the piston is* 65 *lbs. to the square inch, the length of the stroke* = 11·6 *feet, the steam is cut off when* 2·4 *feet of the stroke is made; find the number of units of work done upon each square inch of the piston. The hyperbolic log. of* 10 = 2·3025851, *and the base of the system* (ϵ = 2·718281828) ϵ = ↓10,4,7,1,0,0,' = ↓0,0,0,0,0,1000470, *being given.*

RULE GIVEN BY WRITERS ON THE STEAM ENGINE.

Multiply the pressure at which the steam is admitted by the distance travelled by the piston before the steam is cut off; this gives the work done before expansion begins. Divide the whole length of the stroke by the above-mentioned distance, and find the hyperbolic logarithm of the quotient. Multiply this hyperbolic log. by the work done before expansion begins. Adding the work done after to that done before expansion, the whole work done upon one square inch of the piston in one stroke will be obtained.

Investigation.

Fig. 12.

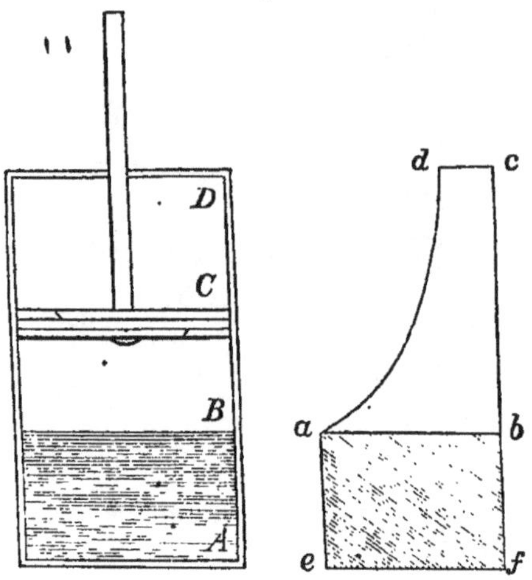

Let $x = AC$, the number of feet described at any part of the stroke, p_2 the pressure when that part is described; $a = AB$, the number of feet described before the steam is cut off, and $l = AD$, the length of the stroke in feet; then let p_1 be the pressure at which the steam is admitted; by Boyle's law,

$$p_2 : p_1 :: a : x$$

$$\therefore p_2 x = p_1 a,$$

that is, any height AC multiplied by the pressure at C, is equal to any height AB multiplied by the pressure at B; or, $p_2 = \frac{p_1 a}{x}$; the variable work equals the integral of $p_2 dx$ taken between the limits, $x = a$ and $x = l$, or

$$\int_a^l p_2 dx = \int_a^l p_1 a \frac{dx}{x} = ap_1 (\log. l - \log. a) = ap_1 \log. \frac{l}{a}.$$

This is the work done on the square inch during expansion; the work done before expansion is evidently represented by ap_1. Hence the whole work done on the square inch

$$= ap_1 + ap_1 \log \frac{l}{a};$$

therefore the rule is established.

Calculation.

It is desirable, to solve this question in the most independent way, and to this end, first calculate the hyperbolic log. of 2.

$$2^{10} = 1024$$

$$1{\cdot}024 = \downarrow 0,2,3,8,1,7, = \downarrow 0,0,0,0,0,23727$$

23727 divided by 1000470 gives ·023716, the hyp. log. of 1·024.

$$\begin{array}{r} \cdot 023716 \\ 6{\cdot}907754 \text{ three times the log of 10,} \\ \hline \end{array}$$

log. of 1024 = 6·931470 divided by 10, gives ·693147, the log. of 2.

11·6 divided by 2·4, gives 4·833333, the hyp. log. of which has to be found.

$$\begin{array}{r} 2\,)\,4{\cdot}833333 \\ \hline 2\,)\,2{\cdot}416666 \\ \hline 1{\cdot}208888 = \downarrow 2,0,\bar{1},0,8,0, \\ = \downarrow 0,0,0,0,0,189790, \end{array}$$

∴ 189790 divided by 1000470, gives ·189701, the hyp. log. of 1·208888.

$$\begin{array}{r} \cdot 189701 \\ 1{\cdot}386294 \text{ twice log. 2} \\ \hline \text{log. of } 4{\cdot}833333 = 1{\cdot}575995 \end{array}$$

$$\begin{array}{r} 65{\cdot} \times 2{\cdot}4 = 156{\cdot} \text{ units of work} \\ 1{\cdot}576 \times 156 = 245{\cdot}856 \\ \hline 401{\cdot}856 \text{ units of work required.} \end{array}$$

The work done on one square inch of the piston is sometimes termed the *load ;* in the present case the load will be

$$\frac{401{\cdot}856}{11{\cdot}6} = 34{\cdot}64 \text{ lbs.}$$

Suppose the cylinder to be 88 inches in diameter, then the area = 6082 square inches. If the piston makes 16 double strokes a minute, that is, 16 revolutions of the crank, the horse-power of the engine =

$$\frac{6082 \times 32 \times 401{\cdot}856}{33000} = 2370{\cdot} \text{ horse-power.}$$

15. *To find the time of oscillation of a circular pendulum.*

Let P, P_1, P_2, P_3, P_4, fig. 12, be a material point attached to a thread or rod without weight, and oscillating in the plane of the paper, about a fixed axis at X, the other extremity of the rod.

Fig. 13.

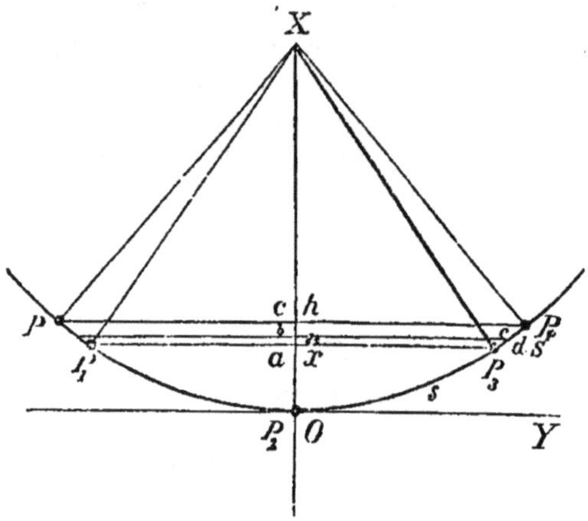

Taking O, the origin of the vertical and horizontal axes at the lowest point of the curve, put $r = OX$, $h = Oc$, $x = Oa$, $dx = ab$, $s = OP_3$, $ds = P_3e$, and since the object is to find the time it will take the body to move from the lowest point, O to P_4 . . . or, which is the same thing, to move from P to the lowest point O—either of these branches might be investigated—the ascending one, P_2, P_3, ... is selected, then the arc s increases with the time, and $\overline{|s}$ which represents ds, n the well-known formula (A), is positive.

$$t, \text{ time employed in describing the arc } PP_2 \text{ or } P_2P_4 \Big\} = \int \frac{\overline{|s}}{(2g(h-x))^{\frac{1}{2}}} \ldots\ldots (A).$$

It must also be borne in mind, that in plane curves referred to rectangular co-ordinates

$$\overline{|s} = \left(1 + \frac{\overline{|y}^2}{\overline{|x}^2}\right)^{\frac{1}{2}} \overline{|x} \ldots\ldots (B).$$

The equation of the path of P is $y^2 = 2rx - x^2$, putting $y = aP_1 = aP_3$.

$$\therefore \frac{\overline{|y}^2}{\overline{|x}^2} = \frac{(r-x)^2}{2rx - x^2}, \text{ and } \overline{|s} = \frac{r\,\overline{|x}}{(2rx - x^2)}$$

$$\therefore t = \int \frac{ds}{\{2g(h-x)\}^{\frac{1}{2}}} = \frac{r}{(2g)^{\frac{1}{2}}} \int \frac{dx}{\{(h-x)(2rx-x^2)\}^{\frac{1}{2}}}$$

$$= \frac{(r)^{\frac{1}{2}}}{2(g)^{\frac{1}{2}}} \int_0^h \frac{dx}{(hx-x^2)} \left(1 - \frac{x}{2r}\right)^{-\frac{1}{2}};$$

if the second factor be developed by the binomial theorem, the differential in question will be reduced to a series of others of the known integral form

$$\frac{x^m\, dx}{(hx-x^2)^{\frac{1}{2}}}.$$

Consequently, the value of $2t$, or the time of a complete oscillation,

$$= \pi \left(\frac{r}{g}\right)^{\frac{1}{2}} \left\{ 1 + \left(\frac{1}{2}\right)^2 \frac{h}{2r} + \left(\frac{1.3}{2.4}\right)^2 \left(\frac{h}{2r}\right)^2 + \left(\frac{1.3.5}{2.4.6}\right)^2 \left(\frac{h}{2r}\right)^3 \right.$$

$$\left. + \left(\frac{1.3.5.7}{2.4.6.8}\right)^2 \left(\frac{h}{2r}\right)^4 + \ldots\ldots \right\}.$$

In this expression h is the versine of the arc of half the whole path $P \ldots . P_4$, and $\frac{h}{r}$ is the versine of a similar arc to radius 1. Let the arc $POP_4 = 29° \; 14'$, for the sake of example, then $OP_4 = OP = 14° \; 37'$, the natural versine of $14° \; 37' = \cdot 0323642 = \frac{h}{r}$.

Suppose $r = 4{\cdot}35$ feet, then $h = \cdot 1407843$ feet $= 1{\cdot}6894116$ inches.

When $g = 32{\cdot}18$ feet, it is required to find the time of one oscillation.

$$\frac{h}{2r} = \cdot 0161821 = \cdot 016 \downarrow 0,1,1,\dot{3},5,$$

$(\cdot 016)^4$ does not give a unit in the seventh decimal place.

$$(\cdot 016)^3 = \cdot 0000041$$

$$\left(\frac{1.3.5}{2.4.6}\right)^2 = \left(\frac{5}{16}\right)^2 = \frac{25}{256}$$

$$41 \times \frac{25}{256} = 4$$

$$\downarrow 0,3,3,9,15,$$

```
 4 . | . .
   . | . .
 ---------
 4
```

So that $\left(\frac{1.3.5}{2.4.6}\right)^2 \left(\frac{h}{2r}\right)^3$ only gives ·0000004.

$$(\cdot 016)^2 = \cdot 0002560$$

$$\left(\frac{1.3}{2.4}\right)^2 = \frac{9}{64}, \text{ and } \frac{9}{64} \times 2560 = 360.$$

$$\downarrow 0,2,2,6,10,$$

```
 36|0 .
   |7 .
 -----
 36 7| . . .
    1| . . .
 -----
 36 8
```

$$\left(\frac{1.3}{2.4}\right)^2 \left(\frac{h}{2r}\right)^2 = \cdot 0000368$$

$$\left(\frac{1}{2}\right)^2 \frac{h}{2r} = \cdot 0040455$$

```
1·0000000
 ·0040455
      368
        4
---------
```

$\downarrow 0,0,4,0,7,6,4,$ = 1·0040827 = the sum of the series, exact to seven places of decimals.

$$g = 32\cdot 18 = (5.6)^2 \downarrow 0,\ 2,\ 6,\ 0,\ \bar{8},\ \bar{4},\ \overline{16},$$

$$r = 4\cdot 35 = (2)^2 \downarrow 0,\ 8,\ 4,\ 2,\ 8,\ 0,\ 8,$$

$$\pi = 3\cdot 12 \quad \downarrow 0,\ 0,\ 6,\ 9,\ 0,\ 0,\ \bar{2},$$

$$\pi\left(\frac{r}{g}\right)^{\frac{1}{2}} \times \text{the sum of series} = \frac{3 \cdot 12 \times 2}{5 \cdot 6} \downarrow 0,3,9,10,15,8,14,$$

$$= \frac{7 \cdot 8}{7} \downarrow 0,4,0,2,0,4,5,$$

$$\begin{array}{lrrrrrrr} \text{because} & \downarrow 0, & 3, & 9, & 10, & 15, & 8, & 14, \\ & = \downarrow 0, & 0, & 39, & 10, & 3, & \bar{4}, & \bar{7}, \\ & = \downarrow 0, & 0, & 0, & 400, & 3, & \bar{4}, & \overline{163}, \\ & = \downarrow 0, & 0, & 0, & 0, & 0, & 0, & 400097, \end{array}$$

Then by the method shown in Example 9 (page 131),

$$\begin{array}{rrrrrrr} = \downarrow 0, & 4, & 0, & 0, & 0, & 0, & 2045, \\ = \downarrow 0, & 4, & 0, & 2, & 0, & 4, & 5, \end{array}$$

$\frac{7 \cdot 8}{7} \downarrow 0,4,0,2,0,4,5, = 1 \cdot 1597672$ seconds, the time of one oscillation.

16. *By the direct application of Dual Arithmetic, and without the use of the well-known constant π, it is required to find the length of an arc to radius 1, corresponding to any number of degrees, minutes, and seconds, true to seven places of decimals, and give an example.* (*see* page 86.)

Let the arc whose length is required contain 12° 15′ 18″·2 = 44118″·2.

RULE :—The seconds multiplied by 4 and divided by 1000000, the result multiplied by $\downarrow 2,0,2,\bar{3},\bar{2},0,7,$ gives the length of the given arc.

```
  44118·2
        4
 ---------
·1|7|6|4|7|2|8 seconds × 4 and divided by 1000000
  |3|5|2|9|4|5
    |1|7|6|4|7
 ---------
 2 1 3,5 3 2|0 . .
      |4 2 7|1 . .
            |2 . .
 ---------
 2 1 3 9 5 9·3 ·
```

```
2139|593 .
    |6|42 ...          minus
       43| ........    minus
        1| ........    plus
·2138909 length of arc.
```

17. *Having given the length of an arc to radius* 1, *to find the degrees, minutes, &c. contained in it, without the direct use of the constant* π, *by Dual Arithmetic, and give an example.*

How many degrees, minutes, &c. are contained in an arc to radius 1, whose length = ·2138909?

RULE :—Multiply the length of the given arc by 200000, and then by ↓ **0,3,1,0,0,$\overline{7}$,0,$\overline{5}$**, the result gives the number of seconds contained in the arc.

```
        ·2138909
               2
        ------------
        42|77|8·1|8 . arc multiplied by 200000.
         1|28|33|5 .
          |  1|28|3 .
          |     |4 .
        ------------
        440|744|0 . .
           |440|7 . .
        ------------
        44118 4|7 . . . . .
        .     3|1 . . . . . minus
seconds 44118·16 = 12° 15′ 18″·16.
```

18. *Suppose the apparent distance between the centres of the sun and moon to be* 56° 56′ 31″ (*d*), *the apparent altitude of the moon's centre,* 23° 3′ 4″ ($a_{\prime}$); *the apparent altitude of the sun's centre,* 58° 4′ 35″ (*a*), *the true altitude of the moon's centre,* 23° 51′ 42″ ($A_{\prime}$), *and the true altitude of the sun's centre,* 58° 3′ 59″ (*A*); *find the true distance* (*D*), *so as to determine the longitude at sea.*

$$\cos D = [\cos d + \cos (a + a_{\prime})] \frac{\cos A \cos A_{\prime}}{\cos a \cos a_{\prime}} - \cos (A + A_{\prime}).$$

(*d*)	56° 56′ 31″	cos =	·5454885
($a + a_{\prime}$)	81 7 39	cos =	·1542362
			·6997247

```
(A)  58° 3′ 59″ cos = ·5289 3 63
(a)  58  4  35  cos = ·5287|8 82 . ↓0,0,0,3,2̄,0,0,
                          1|5 86 .
                     --------------
                      52894|68 . . .
                          1|06 . . . minus
                     --------------
                      5289 3 62

(a,) 23°  3′  4″ cos = ·920 1 5 5 9    ↓0,0,6,1,4,1,7,
(A,) 23  51  42  cos = ·914|5 2 4|8 . .
                          5|4 8 7|1 . .
                              1 3|7 . .
                     --------------
                      ·9200|2 5 6 .
                           |9 2 0 .
                     --------------
                      ·920 1 1|7 6 . . .
                             3|6 8 . . .
                     --------------
                      ·920·1 5 4|4 . . . . .
                                |9 . . . . .
                     --------------
                      ·920 1 5 5 3| . . . . . . .
                                 6| . . . . . . .
                     --------------
                      ·920 1 5 5 9
```

$$\frac{\downarrow 0,0,0,3,\bar{2},0,0,}{\downarrow 0,0,6,1,4,1,7,} = \downarrow 0,0,\bar{6},2,\bar{6},\bar{1},\bar{7},$$

```
                          699|7 2 4|7 . . +
                            4|1 9 8|3 . . −
                                1 4|7 . . +
                          ---------------
                          695 5|4 1 1 .
                              1|3 9 1 .
                          ---------------
                          695 6 8|0 2 . . .       +
                                4|1|7 . . . .     −
                                   |7| . . . . . . . −
                                    5| . . . . . . . +
                          ---------------
                          ·695 6 3 7 3
(A + A,) 81° 55′ 41″   cos = ·140 4 1 6 4
                          ---------------
(D) 56  16  26 ·6 cos = ·555 2 2 0 9
```

19. *To find the length of an arc of an ellipsis.*

Let $a = OP$, the semi-transverse axis,
$b = OR$, the semi-conjugate axis,
$x = ON$, and $y = NL$. $s =$ the length of the arc RL.

Fig. 14.

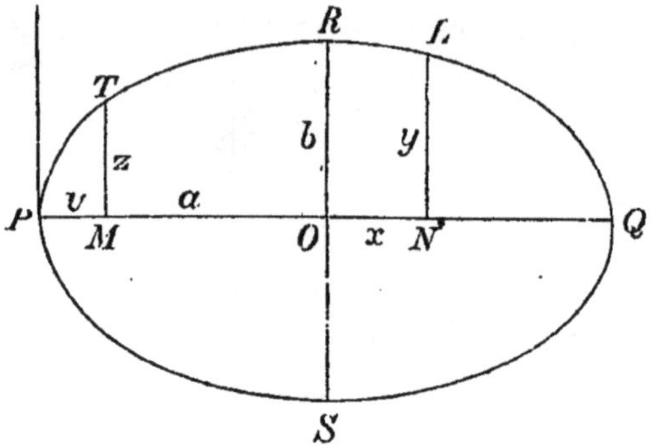

Then, $a^2 : b^2 :: a^2 - x^2 : y^2 = \frac{b^2}{a^2}(a^2 - x^2),\ y = \frac{b}{a}(a^2 - x^2)^{\frac{1}{2}}.$

(1) $$\therefore\ a^2y^2 + b^2 x^2 = a^2b^2$$

In plane curves referred to rectangular co-ordinates,

(2) $$s = \int \left(1 + \frac{|\overline{y}^2}{|\overline{x}^2}\right)^{\frac{1}{2}} |\overline{x}.$$

The differential of (1) gives $a^2y\,|\overline{y} + b^2x\,|\overline{x} = 0$,

$$\therefore\ \frac{|\overline{y}^2}{|\overline{x}^2} = \frac{b^4}{a^4}\frac{x^2}{y^2} = \frac{b^2x^2}{a^4 - a^2x^2}$$

$\therefore\ s = \int\left(1 + \frac{b^2x^2}{a^4 - a^2x^2}\right)^{\frac{1}{2}} |\overline{x}$, which, by converting $\frac{b^2x^2}{a^4 - a^2x^2}$ into an infinite series, becomes

(3) $$s = \int\left(1 + \frac{b^2}{a^4}x^2 + \frac{b^2}{a^6}x^4 + \frac{b^2}{a^8}x^6 + \frac{b^2}{a^{10}}x^8 + \dots\right)^{\frac{1}{2}} |\overline{x}.$$

Let the square root of the quantity enclosed in the brackets of (2) be represented by

$$(4)\ 1 + Ax^2 + Bx^4 + Cx^6 + Dx^8 + Ex^{10} + Fx^{12} + Gx^{14} + \dots.$$

The square of (4) will be represented by the sum of the following series:

$$1 + 2Ax^2 + 2Bx^4 + 2Cx^6 + 2Dx^8 + 2Ex^{10} + 2Fx^{12} + 2Gx^{14} + \dots.$$

$$A^2x^4 + 2ABx^6 + 2ACx^8 + 2ADx^{10} + 2AEx^{12} + 2AFx^{14} + \dots.$$

$$B^2x^8 + 2BCx^{10} + 2BDx^{12} + 2BEx^{14} + \dots.$$

$$C^2x^{12} + 2CDx^{14} + \dots.$$

$$\therefore\ 2A = \frac{b^2}{a^4} \quad A = \frac{b^2}{2a^4} \qquad \therefore\ \int \frac{b^2}{2a^4}\, x^2\,|\overline{x} = \frac{b^2}{a^2}\,\frac{x^2}{a^2}\,\frac{x}{6}$$

$$A^2 + 2B = \frac{b^2}{a^6};$$

$$2B = \frac{b^2}{a^6} - \frac{b^4}{4a^8};\ B = \frac{b^2}{2a^6} - \frac{b^4}{8a^8};$$

$$\int \left(\frac{b^2}{a^2} - \frac{b^4}{4a^4}\right) \frac{x^4\,|\overline{x}}{2a^4} = \left(\frac{b^2}{a^2} - \frac{b^4}{4a^4}\right) \frac{x^4}{a^4}\,\frac{x}{10}.$$

$$2AB + 2C = \frac{b^2}{a^8};$$

$$2C = \frac{b^2}{a^8} - \frac{b^4}{2a^{10}} + \frac{b^6}{8a^{12}};\ C = \frac{b^2}{2a^8} - \frac{b^4}{4a^{10}} + \frac{b^6}{16a^{12}};$$

$$\int \left(\frac{b^2}{a^2} - \frac{b^4}{2a^4} + \frac{b^6}{8a^6}\right) \frac{x^6\,|\overline{x}}{2\,a^6} = \left(\frac{b^2}{a^2} - \frac{b^4}{2a^4} + \frac{b^6}{8a^6}\right) \frac{x^6}{a^6}\,\frac{x}{14}.$$

$$B^2 + 2AC + D = \frac{b^2}{a^{10}};$$

$$D = \frac{b^2}{2a^{10}} - \frac{3b^4}{8a^{12}} + \frac{3b^6}{16a^{14}} - \frac{5b^8}{128a^{16}};$$

$$\int \left(\frac{b^2}{a^2} - \frac{3b^4}{4a^4} + \frac{3b^6}{8a^6} - \frac{5b^8}{64a^8}\right) \frac{x^8|x}{2a^8} = \left(\frac{b^2}{a^2} - \frac{3b^4}{4a^4} + \frac{3b^6}{8a^6} - \frac{5b^8}{64a^8}\right) \frac{x^8}{a^8}\,\frac{x'}{18}.$$

&c. = &c.

$$\therefore \quad s = x + \frac{b^2}{a^2}\frac{x^2}{a^2}\frac{x}{6}$$

$$+ \left(\frac{b^2}{a^2} - \frac{b^4}{4a^4}\right)\frac{x^4}{a^4}\frac{x}{10} + \left(\frac{b^2}{a^2} - \frac{b^4}{2a^4} + \frac{b^6}{8a^6}\right)\frac{x^6}{a^6}\frac{x}{14}$$

$$+ \left(\frac{b^2}{a^2} - \frac{3b^4}{4a^4} + \frac{3b^6}{8a^6} - \frac{5b^8}{64a^8}\right)\frac{x^8}{a^8}\frac{x}{18} + \ldots .$$

When the length of the arc RL is found, the length of LQ = the quadrant RQ minus RL.

Numerical Example.

Let $a = 41{\cdot}3245$; $b = 25{\cdot}1636$; $x = 12{\cdot}3456$; $x = 10{\cdot}\downarrow 2,2,0,2,0,\overline{6},$

$\frac{b}{a} = {\cdot}6089269 = {\cdot}6 \downarrow 0,1,4,8,2,0,3,$

$\frac{x}{a} = {\cdot}2987477 = {\cdot}3 \downarrow 0,0,\overline{4},\overline{2},1,5,$

$\frac{b^2}{a^2} = {\cdot}36 \downarrow 0,2,8,16,4,0,6,$

$= {\cdot}36 \downarrow 0,2,9,6,4,1,0,$

$= {\cdot}3707918$

$\frac{b^4}{a^4} = {\cdot}1296 \downarrow 0,4,16,32,8,0,12,$

$= {\cdot}1296 \downarrow 0,5,9,3,2,7,1,$

$= {\cdot}1374867$

$\frac{b^6}{a^6} = {\cdot}046656 \downarrow 0,6,24,48,12,0,18,$

$= {\cdot}046656 \downarrow 0,8,9,0,0,3,2,$

$= {\cdot}0509784$

$\frac{b^8}{a^8} = {\cdot}0167962 \downarrow 0,8,32,64,16,0,24,$

$= {\cdot}0167962 \downarrow 1,1,2,9,3,8,7,$

$= {\cdot}0187155$

$$\frac{b^2}{a^2} = \cdot 3707918 = k$$

$$\frac{b^2}{a^2} - \frac{b^4}{4a^4} = \cdot 3364201 = k \downarrow \bar{1},0,\bar{2},0,3,\bar{1}, = l$$

$$\frac{b^2}{a^2} - \frac{b^4}{2a^4} + \frac{b^6}{8a^6} = \cdot 3084207 = l \downarrow 0,\bar{8},\bar{7},\bar{3},0,3, = m$$

$$\frac{b^2}{a^2} - \frac{3b^4}{4a^4} + \frac{3b^6}{8a^6} - \frac{5b^8}{64a^8} = \cdot 2867937 = m \downarrow 0,\bar{7},\bar{3},0,\bar{5},\bar{1}, = n$$

From analogy it becomes apparent that the next terms are nearly $\left\{ \begin{array}{ll} = n \downarrow 0,\bar{6}, & = p \\ = p \downarrow 0,\bar{5}, & = q \end{array} \right.$

$$\begin{array}{rl} \dfrac{b^2}{a^2} = & \cdot 36 \downarrow 0, \ 2, \ 9, \ 6, \ 4, \ 1, \\ \dfrac{x^2}{a^2} = & \cdot 09 \downarrow 0, \ 0, \ \bar{8}, \ \bar{4}, \ 3, \ 0, \\ x = & 10 \cdot \downarrow 2, \ 2, \ 0, \ 2, \ 0, \ \bar{6}, \\ \hline & \cdot 324 \downarrow 2, \ 4, \ 1, \ 4, \ 7, \ \bar{5}, = k\dfrac{x^2}{a^2}x \end{array}$$

$$\therefore \frac{b^2}{a^2}\frac{x^2}{a^2}\frac{x}{6} = \cdot 054 \downarrow 2,4,1,4,7,\bar{5}, = \cdot 0680928.$$

$$\begin{array}{rr} k\dfrac{x^2}{a^2}x = & \cdot 324 \downarrow 2,4,1,4, \ 7,\bar{5}, \\ \dfrac{x^2}{a^2} = & \cdot 09 \downarrow 0,0,\bar{8},\bar{4}, \ 3,0, \\ & \downarrow \bar{1},0,\bar{2},0, \ 3,\bar{1}, \\ \hline l\dfrac{x^4}{a^4}x = & \cdot 02916 \downarrow 1,4,\bar{9},0,13,\bar{6}, \end{array}$$

$$\left(\frac{b^2}{a^2} - \frac{b^4}{4a^4}\right)\frac{x^4}{a^4}\frac{x}{10} = \cdot 002916 \downarrow 1,4,\bar{9},1,3,\bar{6}, = \cdot 0033081$$

$$l\frac{x^4}{a^4}x = \cdot 02916 \downarrow 1,4,\ \bar{9},0,13,\bar{6},$$
$$\frac{x^2}{a^2} = \cdot 09 \downarrow 0,0,\ \bar{8},\bar{4},\ 3,0,$$
$$\downarrow 0,\bar{8},\ \bar{7},\bar{3},\ 0,3,$$
$$m\frac{x^6}{a^6}x = \cdot 0026244 \downarrow 1,\bar{4},\overline{24},\bar{7},16,\bar{3},$$

$$\left(\frac{b^2}{a^2} - \frac{b^4}{2a^4} + \frac{b^6}{8a^6}\right)\frac{x^6}{a^6}\frac{x}{14} = \cdot 0001875 \downarrow 0,3,1,1,2,7, = \cdot 0001933$$

$$m\frac{x^6}{a^6}x = \cdot 0026244 \downarrow 0,3,\ 1,1,2,7,$$
$$\frac{x^2}{a^2} = \cdot 09 \downarrow 0,0,\ \bar{8},\bar{4},3,0,$$
$$\downarrow 0,\bar{7},\ \bar{3},0,\bar{5},\bar{1},$$
$$n\frac{x^8}{a^8}x = \cdot 0002362 \downarrow 0,\bar{4},\overline{10},\bar{3},0,6,$$

$$\left(\frac{b^2}{a^2} - \frac{3b^4}{4a^4} + \frac{3b^6}{8a^6} - \frac{5b^8}{64a^8}\right)\frac{x^8}{a^8}\frac{x}{18} = \cdot 0000131 \downarrow 0,\bar{4},\overline{10},\bar{3},0,6,$$
$$= \cdot 0000124.$$

$$n\frac{x^8}{a}x = \cdot 0002362 \downarrow 0,\ \bar{4},\overline{10},\bar{3},0,6,$$
$$\frac{x^2}{a^2} = \cdot 09 \downarrow 0,\ 0,\ \bar{8},\bar{4},3,0,$$
$$\downarrow 0,\ \bar{6},$$
$$p\frac{x^{10}}{a^{10}}x = \cdot 0000213 \downarrow 0,\overline{10},\overline{18},$$

$$p\frac{x^{10}}{a^{10}}\frac{x}{22} = \cdot 0000009 \downarrow \bar{1},\bar{1}, = \cdot 0000008$$

$$\begin{array}{rl} x = & 12\cdot3456000 \\ & \cdot0680928 \\ & \cdot0033081 \\ & \cdot0001933 \\ & \cdot0000124 \\ & \cdot0000008 \\ \hline & 12\cdot4172074 = \text{length of elliptic arc } RL. \end{array}$$

To render the mode of operating clear, the work of this example is given in detail. If the axes of co-ordinates be at P, the extremity of the major axis, then, putting $PM = v$ and $MT = z$, the equation to the ellipsis will be $z^2 = \frac{b^2}{a^2}(2av - v^2)$; and the length of the arc PT may be found in a similar manner in terms of a, b, and the ordinate z. The length of an elliptic arc measured from P, is often required.

20. *To determine the numerical value of elliptic and hyperbolic functions.*

Suppose the expression (1) has to be integrated,

$$\frac{AX^2 \lfloor X}{(BX^2 - X^4 - C)^{\frac{1}{2}}} \dots\dots (1)$$

Take (2) the equation to the ellipsis,

$$a^2y^2 + b^2x^2 = a^2b^2 \dots\dots (2)$$

the differential of the arc of the ellipse, by (2) of the last problem, is

$$\lfloor s = \frac{[a^4 - (a^2 - b^2)\, x^2]^{\frac{1}{2}} \lfloor x}{a\,(a^2 - x^2)^{\frac{1}{2}}} \dots\dots (3)$$

$$\text{Assume } [a^4 - (a^2 - b^2)\, x^2]^{\frac{1}{2}} = av \dots\dots (4)$$

solve (4) for x, then

$$x = \frac{a\,(a^2 - v^2)^{\frac{1}{2}}}{(a^2 - b^2)^{\frac{1}{2}}} \dots\dots (5)$$

Put the values of x and $|\overline{x}$ from (5) into (3), then

$$|\overline{s} = \frac{v^2 |\overline{v}}{[(a^2 + b^2)\, v^2 - v^4 - a^2 b^2]^{\frac{1}{2}}} \cdots\cdots (6)$$

(6) is the same form as (1). It is evident that the integral of (1) is the arc of an ellipse. To find the axes of the ellipse, equate the co-efficients of the like powers of x and v under the radicals of (6) and (1); that is, put

$$a^2 + b^2 = B \text{ and } a^2 b^2 = C,$$

from which the axes a and b may be found. The abscissa x, of the extremity of the elliptic arc (1) is given by (5). Again, suppose the integral of (7) is required:

$$\frac{A\ X}{X^2\, (BX^2 - X^4 - C)^{\frac{1}{2}}} \cdots\cdots (7).$$

Assume the numerator of (3) $= \dfrac{a^2 b}{v}$, that is,

$$[a^4 - (a^2 - b^2)\, x^2]^{\frac{1}{2}} = \frac{a^2 b}{v} \cdots\cdots (8).$$

From (8), (9) is readily obtained:

$$x = \frac{a^2\, (v^2 - b^2)^{\frac{1}{2}}}{v\, (a^2 - b^2)^{\frac{1}{2}}} \cdots\cdots (9).$$

This value of x, and its differential, substituted in (3), gives

$$|\overline{s} = \frac{-\, a^2 b^2\, |\overline{v}}{v^2\, [(a^2 + b^2)\, v^2 - v^4 - a^2 b^2]^{\frac{1}{2}}} \cdots\cdots (10)$$

Hence, the integral of (7) is an elliptic arc, the abscissa of whose extremity is the value of x in (9); the axes may be found as in the last case.

Take another example, and suppose the integral of (11) to be required:

$$\frac{AX^2 |\overline{X}}{(B X^2 + X^4 - C)^{\frac{1}{2}}} \cdots\cdots (11).$$

Take (12) as the equation of the hyperbola,

$$a y^2 - b^2 x^2 = -a^2 b^2 \ldots\ldots (12)$$

Then

$$|\overline{s} = \frac{[(a^2 + b^2)x^2 - a^4]^{\frac{1}{2}} \, |\overline{x}}{a^2 (x^2 - a^2)^{\frac{1}{2}}} \ldots\ldots (13)$$

$$\text{Assume } (a^2 + b^2)x^2 - a^4 = a^2 z^4 \ldots\ldots (14),$$

then (13) becomes, in terms of z, reduced to (15):

$$|\overline{s} = \frac{z^2 \, |\overline{z}}{[(a^4 - b^2)z^2 + z^4 - a^2 b^2]^{\frac{1}{2}}} \ldots\ldots (15).$$

(15) is of the same form as (11), ∴ (11) is the differential of an arc of an hyperbola, whose axes and abscissa are found as in the case of the elliptic arc.

Lastly, suppose the form (16) has to be integrated:

$$\frac{A \, |\overline{X}}{X^2 (BX^2 - X^4 + C)^{\frac{1}{2}}} \ldots\ldots (16).$$

By assuming $(a^2 + b^2)x^2 - a^4 = \frac{a^2 b^2}{z^2} \ldots\ldots (17)$, then $|\overline{s}$ becomes of the same form as (16), which is therefore the differential of an arc of an hyperbola.

Example.

21. *Required the integral of* (18), *when* $x = 28$, *neglecting the constant.*

$$\frac{200 x^2 \, |\overline{x}}{(1000x^2 - x^4 - 130000)} \ldots\ldots (18).$$

$$a^2 + b^2 = 1000, \text{ and } a^2 b^2 = 130000, \text{ by } 6.$$

$$\therefore \quad (a^2 - b^2)^2 = 480000,$$

$$a^2 - b^2 = 692{\cdot}82032.$$

$a^2 = 846{\cdot}41016$, $a = 29{\cdot}093129$; $b^2 = 153{\cdot}58984$, $b = 12{\cdot}393137$.

The integral of (18) is 200 times an arc of an ellipse whose semi-transverse axis $= 29{\cdot}093129$, and semi-conjugate $= 12{\cdot}393137$, and the square of the abscissa (5) of the extremity of this elliptic arc equals

$$\frac{a^2(a^2 - x^2)}{(a^2 - b^2)}, \text{ which put } = Z^2.$$

$$a^2 = 29^2 \downarrow 0,0,6,4,0,16,0, \qquad a^2 - x^2 = (7{\cdot}9)^2 \downarrow 0,0,0,0,0,2,6,$$

$$a^2 - b^2 = (26)^2 \downarrow 0,2,4,6,8,0,\overline{10},$$

$$\therefore \quad Z = \frac{29 \times 7{\cdot}9}{26} \downarrow 0,\overline{1},1,\overline{1},\overline{4},9,8, = 8{\cdot}8115385 \downarrow 0,\overline{1},1,\overline{1},\overline{4},9,8,$$

$$Z = 8{\cdot}7318828 = 8{\cdot} \downarrow 0,9,\overline{2},0,\overline{2},5,5,$$

$$\frac{Z}{a} = \left(\frac{a^2 - x^2}{a^2 - b^2}\right)^{\frac{1}{2}} = \frac{7{\cdot}9}{26} \downarrow 0,\overline{1},\overline{2},\overline{3},\overline{4},1,8 = {\cdot}3001354 = {\cdot}3 \downarrow 0,0,0,4,5,1,$$

$$\frac{Z^2}{a^2} = {\cdot}09 \downarrow 0,0,0,9,0,2,$$

$$\frac{b^2}{a^2} = {\cdot}1814603 = {\cdot}18 \downarrow 0,0,8,0,8,0,4,$$

$$\text{Length of arc} = Z + \frac{b^2}{a^2}\frac{z^2}{a^2}\frac{Z}{6} + \left(\frac{b^2}{a^2} - \frac{b^4}{4a^4}\right)\frac{z^4}{a^4}\frac{Z}{10}$$
$$+ \left(\frac{b^2}{a^2} - \frac{b^4}{2a^4} + \frac{b^6}{8a^6}\right)\frac{z^6}{a^6}\frac{Z}{14}$$
$$+ \left(\frac{b^2}{a^2} - \frac{3b^4}{4a^4} + \frac{3b^6}{8a^6} - \frac{5b^8}{64a^8}\right)\frac{z^8}{a^8}\frac{Z}{18} + \ldots\ldots$$

$$\frac{b^2}{a^2} = {\cdot}18 \downarrow 0,0,8,0,8,0,4,$$

$$= {\cdot}1814603$$

$$\frac{b^4}{a^4} = \cdot 0324 \downarrow 0,0,16,0,16,0,8,$$
$$= \cdot 0324 \downarrow 0,1,6,2,0,5,5,$$
$$= \cdot 0329271$$

$$\frac{b^6}{a^6} = \cdot 005832 \downarrow 0,0,24,0,24,0,12,$$
$$= \cdot 005832 \downarrow 0,2,4,1,1,4,6,$$
$$= \cdot 0059737$$

$$\frac{b^8}{a^8} = \cdot 0010498 \downarrow 0,0,32,0,32,0,16,$$
$$= \cdot 0010498 \downarrow 0,3,2,4,5,6,3,$$
$$= \cdot 0010843$$

$$\frac{b^2}{a^2} = \cdot 1814603 \qquad = k.$$

$$\frac{b^2}{a^2} - \frac{b^4}{4a^4} = \cdot 1732285 = k \downarrow 0,\bar{5},3,3,2,7, = l.$$

$$\frac{b^2}{a^2} - \frac{b^4}{2a^4} + \frac{b^6}{8a^6} = \cdot 1657434 = l \downarrow 0,\bar{5},5,6,1,\bar{5}, = m.$$

$$\frac{b^2}{a^2} - \frac{3b^4}{4a^4} + \frac{3b^6}{8a^6} - \frac{5b^8}{64a^8} = \cdot 1590870 = m \downarrow 0,\bar{5},8,7,6,7, = n.$$

$$\ldots\ldots\ldots = n \downarrow 0,\bar{5},12, \qquad = p.$$

$$\ldots\ldots\ldots = p \downarrow 0,\bar{5},16, \qquad = q.$$

$$\frac{b^2}{a^2} = \cdot 18 \downarrow 0,0,8,0,8,0,4,$$
$$\frac{z^2}{a^2} = \cdot 09 \downarrow 0,0,0,9,0,2,$$
$$Z = 8 \cdot \downarrow 0,9,\bar{2},0,\bar{2},5,5,$$

$$\cdot 1296 \downarrow 0,9,6,9,6,7,9, = k \frac{z^2}{a^2} Z.$$

$$\therefore\ \frac{b^2}{a^2}\frac{Z^2}{a^2}\frac{Z}{6} = \cdot 0216 \downarrow 0,9,6,9,6,7,9, = \cdot 0233040.$$

$$k\frac{z^2}{a^2}Z = \cdot 1296 \downarrow 0,9,6,\ 9,6,\ 7,9,$$

$$\frac{z^2}{a^2} = \quad \cdot 09 \downarrow 0,0,0,\ 9,0,\ 2,$$

$$\downarrow 0,\bar{5},3,\ 3,2,\ 7,$$

$$\cdot 011664 \downarrow 0,4,9,21,8,16,9, = l\frac{z^4}{a^4}Z.$$

$$\therefore\ \left(\frac{b^2}{a^2} - \frac{b^4}{4a^4}\right)\frac{Z^4}{a^4}\frac{Z}{10} = \cdot 0011664 \downarrow 0,5,1,2,4,2,4, = \cdot 0012273.$$

$$l\frac{z^4}{a^4}Z = \cdot 011664 \downarrow 0,5,1,\ 2,4,2,4,$$

$$\frac{Z^2}{a^2} = \quad \cdot 09 \downarrow 0,0,0,\ 9,0,2,$$

$$\downarrow 0,\bar{5},5,\ 6,1,\bar{5},$$

$$\cdot 0010498 \downarrow 0,0,6,17,5,\bar{1},4, = m\frac{z^6}{a^6}Z.$$

$$\left(\frac{b^2}{a^2} - \frac{b^4}{2a^4} + \frac{b^6}{8a^6}\right)\frac{Z^6}{a^6}\frac{Z}{14} = \cdot 0000750 \downarrow 0,0,7,7,5,\bar{1},8, = \cdot 0000756.$$

$$m\frac{z^6}{a^6}Z = \cdot 0010498 \downarrow 0,0,\ 7,\ 7,\ 5,$$

$$\frac{Z^2}{a^2} = \quad \cdot 09 \downarrow 0,0,\ 0,\ 9,\ 0,$$

$$\downarrow 0,\bar{5},\ 8,\ 7,\ 6,$$

$$\cdot 0000945 \downarrow 0,\bar{5},15,23,11, = n\frac{z^8}{a^8}Z.$$

$$\left(\frac{b^2}{a^2} - \frac{3b^4}{4a^4} + \frac{3b^6}{8a^6} - \frac{5b^8}{64a^8}\right)\frac{Z^8}{a^8}\frac{Z}{18} = \cdot 0000053 \downarrow 0,\bar{4},7, = \cdot 0000051.$$

$$n\frac{z^8}{a^8}Z = \cdot0000945 \downarrow 0,\bar{4},\ 7,$$

$$\frac{z^2}{a^2} = \qquad \cdot09 \downarrow 0,0,\ 0,$$

$$\downarrow 0,\bar{5},12,$$

$$\overline{\cdot0000085 \downarrow 0,\bar{9},19,} = p\frac{z^{10}}{a^{10}}Z$$

$$p\frac{z^{10}}{a^{10}}\frac{Z}{22} = \cdot0000004 \downarrow 0,\bar{8},9, = \cdot0000004$$

$Z =$ 8·7318828 abscissa
·0233040
·0012273
·0000756
·0000051
·0000004
8·7564952 length of the elliptic arc.

Consequently the integral of (18) when $x = 28$, becomes 1751·29904, the constant not being taken into account.

22. *Find the true meridional parts corresponding to latitude* 83° 25′ 24″.

	90°	0′	0″
	83	25	24
2)	173	25	24
	86	42	42
	90	0	0
	3°	17′	18″

The length of an arc of 3° 17′ 18″ = ·057392242, the sine and cosine of this arc are readily calculated.

sin 3° 17′ 18″ = ·0573607 = cos 86° 42′ 42″.
cos 3 17 18 = ·9983465 = sin 86 42 42.

$\cdot 9983465 \downarrow 0,0,1,6,5,5,5,3, = 1.$

$$\therefore \quad \cdot 9983465 = \frac{1}{\downarrow 0,0,1,6,5,5,5,3,}$$

$$\cdot 0573607 = \frac{5}{10^2} \downarrow 1,4,2,2,2,5,9,1,$$

$$\frac{\sin}{\cos} = \tan = \frac{10^2}{5}\,\frac{1}{\downarrow 1,4,3,8,7,10,14,4,} = \frac{20}{\downarrow 1,4,3,8,8,1,4,4,}.$$

```
                9541497          230270081 ◡ 10
                3930332           69318201 ◡  2
                 289865          ---------
                  88144          299588282
↓1,4,3,8,8,1,4,4, = ↓13899838,    13899838
                                 ---------
                                 285688444
```

Then, 285688444 ÷ ·100005025 = 2·8567409, the hyperbolic logarithm of the tangent, or

```
        2·8568|84|44
half         1|42|84
half          |  |71
        ------------
           1 43 55  subtract
        ------------
        2·8567 40 89,
```

which has to be multiplied by

$$3437{\cdot}74679 = \frac{10000}{3} \downarrow 0,3,1,0,0,\bar{7},0,\bar{4},$$

OPERATION UNABRIDGED.

```
3 ) 285 6 7·40 89
    -------------
     95|2 2|46|96
      2|8 5|67|41
          2|85|67
            ▪|95
    -------------
     98 1,1 00|99 .
          |9 81|10 .
    -------------
     98 2 0 82|09
             6|87| minus ◡ 7
                4| minus ◡ 4
    -------------
```

Meridional parts 98 2 0·75 18 for lat. 83° 25′ 24″.

23. *Find the value of* $\left(\frac{1.3.5.7.9.11.13}{2.4.6.8.10.12.14}\right)^2 x^7$, *a term in the series that expresses the time of oscillation of a circular pendulum, when* $x = \cdot 113574657$.

By adding the values of 1.3.5. ..... and also the values of 2.4.6. ..... reduced to the eight position, and then taking the differences, the results will be

$$\frac{1}{2} = -\ 69318201\,; \qquad \frac{1.3.5.7}{2.4.6.8} = -\ 129674734\,;$$

$$\frac{1.3}{2.4} = -\ 98087853\,; \qquad \frac{1.3.5.7.9}{2.4.6.8.10} = -\ 140211315\,;$$

$$\frac{1.3.5}{2.4.6} = -\ 116320925\,; \qquad \frac{1.3.5.7.9.11}{2.4.6.8.10.12} = -\ 148912889\,;$$

$$\frac{1.3.5.7.9.11.13}{2.4.6.8.10.12.14} = -\ 156324061.$$

$$x = \cdot 113574657 = \frac{1}{10}\downarrow 1,3,2,1,4,7,6,5, = \downarrow -\ \overline{217538660,}$$

$$\begin{array}{rrl}
 & -\ 217538660 & \\
 & 7 & \\ \hline
 & -\ 1522770620 & \\
-\ 156324061 \times 2 = & -\ 312648122 & \\ \hline
 & -\ 1835418742 & = \frac{1}{10^8}\downarrow 0,6,7,7,1,7,2,3, \\
10^8 \smile & +\ 1842160648 & \\ \hline
 & 6741906 & \\
 & 5970498 & \smile \downarrow 0,6, \\ \hline
 & 771408 & \\
 & 699685 & \smile 7, \\ \hline
 & 7,1,7,2,3, &
\end{array}$$

$$\downarrow 0,6,7,7,1,7,2,3, = 1\cdot 06974005$$

∴ The value of the term will be ·000000106974005, true to the last figure. In this case the range of the pendulum would be a circular arc of 78° 46′ 42″·8.

24. *Let* $x = \cdot 113574657$, *the cosine of* $83^\circ\ 28'\ 42''\cdot 8$, *to find the sine, tangent, secant, versine, cotangent, cosecant, coversine, and their hyperbolic logarithms.*

$$\text{ver.} = 1 - x = \cdot 886425343 = \frac{8}{10}\downarrow 1,0,7,2,7,8,5,2, = \downarrow - \overline{12056443,}|$$

$$\text{cov.} = 1 + x = 1\cdot 113574657 = \downarrow 1,1,2,3,1,5,5,0, = \downarrow \overline{10758040,}|$$

$$\cos = x = \frac{1}{10}\downarrow 1,3,2,1,4,7,6,5, = \downarrow - \overline{217538660,}|$$

$$\begin{array}{r} -12056443 \\ +10758040 \\ \hline 2)-\ 1298403 \end{array}$$

$$\sqrt{(1+x)(1-x)} = \sqrt{1-x^2} = \downarrow - \overline{649202,}| = \frac{9}{10}\downarrow 1,0,3,5,6,0,1,7,$$

$$\begin{array}{rr} 10\smile & +230270081 \\ \hline & 229620879 \\ 9\smile & 219733500 \\ \hline & 9887379 \\ & 9531497\smile \quad \downarrow 1, \\ \hline & 355882 \\ & 299865\ (0,0,3, \\ \hline & 5,6,0,1,7, \end{array}$$

$$\therefore\ \sin = \frac{9}{10}\downarrow 1,0,3,5,6,0,1,7, = \cdot 993529332.$$

$$\frac{-649202}{100005025} = - \cdot 00649169 = \text{hyp. log. sin.}$$

$$\begin{array}{lr} & -21753|8660 \\ \text{half} & 1|08|77 \\ \text{half} & |54 \\ \hline & 1\,09\,31 \text{ subtract} \\ \hline & -\cdot 2175277\,29 \text{ hyp. log. cos.} \end{array}$$

```
−  12056|44 3
        |60|3
        |  |3
         60 6
−  ·12055 83 7 hyp. log. ver.

+  10758|04 0
        |53|8
        |  |3
         54 1
   ·10757 49 9 hyp. log. cov.
```

$$x : \sqrt{1 - x^2} :: 1 : \tan = \frac{\sqrt{1 - x^2}}{x}$$

```
−        64 92 02 from
− 2 1753 86 60 take
+ 2 1688|94 58 = 8↓0,8,9,7,4,5,9,5, = 8·747655 12 = tangent.
       1|08|44
        |  |54
       1 08 98
  2·1687 85 60 hyp. log. tan.
```

$$\sqrt{1 - x^2} : x :: 1 : \frac{x}{\sqrt{1 - x^2}} = \text{cot.}$$

```
− 2 1753 86 60 from
−        64 92 02 take
− 2 1688|94 58 = 2/10 ↓1,7,8,0,4,4,5,8, = ·237773952 = cotangent.
       1|08|44
        |  |54
       1 08 98
− 2·1687 85 60 = hyp. log. cot.
```

$$x : 1 :: 1 : \frac{1}{x} = \text{secant.}$$

```
    0 0000 00 00 from
  − 2 1753 86 60 take
  ──────────────
  + 2 1753|86 60 = 8↓1,0,0,6,1,5,5,9, = 8·80541864
           1|08|77
            |  |·54
       ──────────
         1 09 21
  ──────────────
  2·1752 77 39 = hyp. log. secant.
```

$$\sqrt{1 - x^2} : 1 :: 1 : \frac{1}{\sqrt{1 - x^2}} = \text{cosecant.}$$

```
    00000000 0 from
  −     64920 2 take
  ──────────────
  +     64920|2 = ↓0,0,6,4,9,4,7,2, = 1·00651282
            3|3
  ──────────────
  ·00649169 = hyp. log. cosecant.
```

$$\frac{-649202}{230270081} = -\ {\cdot}002819302$$

```
  10·000000000
     002819302
  ────────────
   9·997180698 = common log. sine of the given
```

arc. The com. log. cos. &c. may be determined in a similar manner.

GENERAL SOLUTION

OF

ALGEBRAICAL EQUATIONS OF ALL DEGREES.

To multiply a number by any of the factors ↓5,; ↓0,5,; ↓0,0,5,; &c. is an operation so simple, that future results in such cases will only be exhibited, the work being omitted.

(*A*) 132690018825
(*B*) 133354797147 |5|

Thus the number (*A*), multiplied by ↓0,0,5, produces the number (*B*). According to the following monogram, which is easily remembered, |5| is made to show that there are two zeros before the operating figure 5, or, which is the same thing, the number (*A*) operated upon is divided into periods of three figures each.

MONOGRAM.

one	two	three
four	five	six
seven	eight	nine

WORK WITHOUT CONTRACTION.

(*A*)	132	690	018	825	⌣	1
(*a*)		663	450	094	⌣	5
(*b*)		1	326	900	⌣	10
(*c*)			1	327	⌣	10
(*d*)				1	⌣	5
(*B*)	133	354	797	147		

(*A*) advanced a figure and divided by 2, gives (*a*), falling back a period to the right.

(*b*) is the same as (*A*), advanced a figure, and falling back two periods to the right.

(*c*) is the same as (*A*), advanced a figure, and falling back three periods to the right hand.

(*d*) is the same as (*a*), but for ·663 . . . neglected 1 is brought forward to the next period. The process becomes plain, when the nature of the multipliers 1, 5, 10, 10, 5, 1, are examined. This property of the factors ↓5, ↓0,5, ↓0,0,5, &c. was pointed out before.

```
12|50|00|00|00|00|00
13|13|76|25|62|62|50   5|
  |13|13|76|25|62|63|
---------------------
13 26 90 01 88 25 13   1| = ↓0,6,
```

Since the result at the end of each step is only required, the figures between the steps may be omitted in the general statement. Should the work require revision, the figures left out are easily made to reappear by a trifling calculation. The last example may stand thus :—

```
12|5·0|0 0|00|00|00|00
13|1·3|7|6|25|62|62|50   5|
13 2·69001 88 25 13      1| = 125·↓0,6,
```

Examples.

1. *Extract the root of the equation* $3x^2 + 4x = 21$, *to eight places of decimals.*

By substituting 2 for x, the result will approach 21 ; by this method 2 may, or not, be the first figure of the required root.

+	+
12·00000000	8·00000000

```
twice 12 = 24                    12·|00000000
once   8 =  8                     8·|00000000
          ---                    ---------------
           32                    20·|00000000 from
                                 21·|00000000 take
                                 ---------------
                           32 )   1·|00000000 ↓0,3,

      12|00|00|00|00   51         80|00|00|00|0 .
      12|61|21|20|60              82|42|40|80|0 .   31
      12|73|82|41|81   11 .

twice 2546                      12·73|8241 81
once   824                       8·24|2408 00
      ----                     --------------
      3370                      20·98|0649 81 take
                                21·00|0000 00 from
                               --------------
                      3370 )        1|9350|19 (↓0,0,0,5,

      1273|8241|81 . .             8242|4080|0 . . .
      1274|4612|20 . .   15        8246|5300|2 . . .   15
      1275|0985|78 . .   15 .

25500 twice                   12·750|98578
 8246 once                     8·246|53002
-----                         ------------
33746                         20·997|51580 take
                              21·000|00000 from
                              ------------
                  33746 )          2|48420 (↓0,0,0,0,7,3,6,1
                                   2|36222
                                    ------
                                    121980
                                    101238
                                    ------
                                     207420
                                     202476
                                     ------
                                      49440
                                      33746
                                      -----
```

$\therefore \quad x = 2 \downarrow 0,3,0,5,7,3,6,1,$

The last four figures being found by common division.

$\therefore \quad x = 2{\cdot}06178427$, true to the last figure.

2. *Extract a root of the equation* $x^3 + 2x^2 - 23x = 70$.

Substitute 5 for x, and the result approaches 70.

+	+	minus
125·00000000	50·00000000	115·00000000

3 times	37	5
2 times	10	0
	47	5
minus once	11	·5
	36	

	12	5·00000000
	5	0·00000000
	17	5·00000000
	11	5·00000000
	6	0·00000000 take
	7	0·00000000 from
36)	1	0·00000000 (↓0,2,

12	50	00	00	00	
13	13	76	25	63	5
13	26	90	01	89	1

50	00	00	00	0 .	
52	03	02	00	5 .	4

11	5·0	00	00	00	
11	7 3	11	50	00	2

3 times	+ 397	8
twice	+ 104	0
	+ 501	8
once	− 117	3
	384	5

	132·	6900189
	52·	0302005
	184·	7202194
	117·	3115000
	67·	4087194 take
	70·	0000000 from
384)	2·	5912806 (↓0,0,6

132	690	018	9 . .	
133	354	797	1 . .	15
134	022	906	0 . .	15
134	694	362	1 . .	15
135	098	849	4 . .	13

520	302	005	
522	908	723	15
525	528	501	15
526	580	084	12

117	311	500	0 . .	
117	899	231	8 . .	15
118	017	131	0 . .	11

+ 4052	3 times —	135·0	9884 94	
+ 1053	twice —	52·6	5800 84	
5105		187·7	5685 78	
− 1180	once —	118·0	1713 10	
3925		69·7	3972 68	take
		70·0	0000 00	from
	3925)	2	6027 32	(↓ 0,0,0,6,

1350	9884	94 . .			5265	8008	4 . . .			1180	1713	10 . .	
1351	6641	24 . .	15		5268	4342	6 . . .	15		1180	7615	14 . .	15
1352	3400	91 . .	15		5271	0690	1 . . .	15		1180	8796	90 . .	11
1353	0163	96 . .	15		5272	1232	7 . . .	12					
1353	4223	42 . .	13										

+ 40603 3 times		135·34	22342	
+ 10544 twice		52·72	12327	
51147		188·06	34669	
− 11809 once		118·08	79690	
39338		69·97	54979	take
		70·00	00000	from
	39338)	2	45021	(↓ 0,0,0,0,6,2,3,

∴ $x = 5 \downarrow 0,2,6,6,6,2,3, = 5·1345787$; the last three factors being found by common division.

3. *Extract a root of the biquadratic equation*

$$x^4 - 3x^3 + 75x = 1000.$$

If 8 be substituted for x, the result will approach 10000 near enough to commence operating.

4	2	1
plus	minus	plus
4096	192	600

```
16384     4 times      4|096
  384     twice         |192 –
-----                 -----
16000                  3|904
  600     once          |600 +
-----                 -----
16600                  4|504 take
                      10|000 from
                      -----
            16600 )    5|496        (↓2,
```

```
            plus                                minus
4|0|9|6·|0|0|0|0|0|0|0              1|9|2|·0|0|0|0|0|0|0
6|5|9|6 |6|4|8|9|6|0|0  ↓5,         2|8|1| 1|0|7|2|0|0|0  ↓4,
8|7|8|0 |1|3|9|7|6|5|8  ↓3,

                       plus
                6|0|0·|0|0|0|0|0|0|0|0
                7|2|6 |0|0|0|0|0|0|0|0–↓2.
```

```
351|2 +     4 times      87|80·1397658
  5|6 –     twice         2|81·1072000 –
-----                   --------------
345|6                    84|99·0325658
  7|3 +     once          7|26·0000000 +
-----                   --------------
352|9                    92|25·0325658 take
                        100|00·0000000 from
                        --------------
              353 )       7|74·9674342        (0,2,
```

```
         plus                      minus                    plus
87|80|13|97|65|8 .        28|11|07|20|00            72|60|00|00|00
92|28|01|51|35|2 . 51     29|25|21|27|95 41         74|05|92|60|00 21
95|07|63|32|21|8 . 31
```

```
3803| +     4 times      950|7·6332218 +
  59| –     twice         29|2·5212795 –
----                    ---------------
3744|                    921|5·1119423
  74| +     once           74|0·5926000 +
----                    ---------------
3818                     995|5·7045423 take
                        1000|0·0000000 from
                        ---------------
           3818 )          4|4·2954577        (↓0,0,1,
```

plus — minus — plus

950|763|322|18 .   292|521|279|5 . .   740|592|600|0 . .
954|572|083|85 . 4   293|106|614|6 . . 2   741|333|192|6 . . 1

3818|3 +   4 times   954|5·7208385 +
58|6 −   twice   29|3·1066146 −

3759|7   925|2·6142239
74|1 +   once   74|1·3331926 +

3833|8   999|3·9474165 take
1000|0·0000000 from

3834) |6·0525835   ($\downarrow$ **0,0,0,1,**

plus — minus — plus

9545|7208|385 .   2931|0661|46 . .   7413|3319|26 . .
9549|5396|995 . 4   2931|6523|88 . . 2   7414|0732|59 . . 1

38198| +   4 times   9549·|5396995 +
586| −   twice   293·|1652388 −

37612| 9256·|3744607
741| +   once   741·|4073259 +

38353   9997·|7817866 take
10000·|0000000 from

38353)   2·|2182134   ($\downarrow$ **0,0,0,0,5,7,8,3,**

$$\therefore\ x = 8 \downarrow \mathbf{2,2,1,1,5,7,8,3} = 9{\cdot}8860027\,;$$

the last four factors, 5, 7, 8, 3, were obtained by common division.

It may be observed that the work did not commence by operating with the first figure of the root, nor was any notice taken of the absent term of the equation.

4. *Extract a root of the equation*

$$x^5 + 4x^4 - 2x^3 + 10x^2 - 2x = 962.$$

If 3 be substituted for x, the number 962 will be approached, for

$$243 + 324 - 54 + 90 - 6 = 597.$$

```
 12|15 +     5 times      + 2|43
 12|96 +     4 times      + 3|24
 ------                   ------
 25|11                      5|67
  1|62 -     3 times      -  |54
 ------                   ------
 23|49                      5|13
  1|80 +     2 times      +  |90
 ------                   ------
 25|29                      6|03
   | 6 -     1 time       -  | 6
 ------                   ------
 25|23                      5|97 take
                            9|62 from
                          ------
            divisor 2523 )  3|65          ↓1,
```

```
            plus                                plus

2|4|3|0|0|0|0|0|0|0                 3|2|4|0|0|0|0|0|0|0
3|9|1|3|5|3|9|3|0|0   ↓5,           4|7|4|3|6|8|4|0|0|0   ↓4,

           minus                                plus

5|4|0|0|0|0|0|0|0                    9|0|0|0|0|0|0|0|0
7|1|8|7|4|0|0|0|0     ↓3,          10|8|9|0|0|0|0|0|0|0   ↓2,

                          minus

                   6|0|0|0|0|0|0|0
                   6|6|0|0|0|0|0|0    ↓1,
```

```
195|68 +     5 times     + 39|1·3|539300
189|74 +     4 times     + 47|4·3|684000
-------                  ----------------
385|42                     86|5·7|223300
 21|56 -     3 times     -  7|1·8|740000
-------                  ----------------
363|86                     79|3·8|483300
 21|78 +     2 times     + 10|8·9|000000
-------                  ----------------
385|64                     90|2·7|483300
   |66 -     1 time      -   |6·6|000000
-------                  ----------------
384|08                     89|6·1|483300 take
                           96|2·0|000000 from
                         ----------------
       divisor 384|98 )   6|5·8|516700        ↓0,1,
```

In these early examples, the array of figures employed to find the divisor, and the next factor to be operated with, may be omitted; for when the method is understood, the determination of each successive factor requires but little calculation.

plus

39	13	53	93	00	
41	13	16	91	35	5

minus

71	87	40	00	0 .	
74	05	18	54	1 .	3

plus

47	43	68	40	00	
49	36	29	65	92	4

plus

10	89	00	00	00	
11	10	88	89	00	2

minus

66	00	00	00	
66	66	00	00	1

205	658	+	5 times	+	41	1·31	69135	
197	451	+	4 times	+	49	3·62	96592	
403	109				90	4·94	65727	
22	215	−	3 times	−	7	4·05	18541	
380	894				83	0·89	47186	
22	217	+	2 times	+	11	1·08	88900	
403	111				94	1·98	36086	
	666	−	1 time	−		6·66	60000	
402	445				93	5·31	76086	take
					96	2·00	00000	from
			402)		2	6·68	23914	(↓ 0,0,6,

plus

411	316	913	5 . .	
413	377	615	4 . .	5
415	448	641	4 . .	5
417	530	043	3 . .	5
419	621	873	0 . .	5
421	724	182	8 . .	5
423	837	025	1 . .	5

plus

493	629	659	2 . .	
496	102	748	7 . .	5
498	588	228	4 . .	5
501	086	160	4 . .	5
503	596	607	1 . .	5
505	614	017	1 . .	4

minus			
740	518	541	
744	228	546	5
747	957	138	5
751	704	411	5
753	961	780	3

plus				
111	088	890	0 . .	
111	645	446	5 . .	5
112	204	791	3 . .	5
112	429	313	1 . .	2

minus			
666	600	00 .	
669	939	68 .	5
670	609	62 .	1

2119	2	5 times	+	423·	8370	251	
2022	5	4 times	+	505·	6140	171	
4141	7			929·	4510	322	
226	2	3 times	−	75·	3961	780	
3915	5			854·	0548	542	
224	9	2 times	+	112·	4293	131	
4140	4			966·	4841	673	
6	7	1 time	−	6·	7060	962	
4133	7			959·	7780	711	take
				962·	0000	000	from
			4134)	2·	2219	289	(↓ 0,0,0,5,3,7, by common division.

$\therefore \quad x = 3 \downarrow 1,1,6,5,3,7, = 3\ 354849.$

But for the purpose of rendering the process clear, this root might be found with less than one-third the figures exhibited.

5. *Required a root of the equation*

$$3{\cdot}01416x^5 - 28{\cdot}233x^4 + 923{\cdot}7x^3 + 1234x^2 - 1862x = 1609149128.$$

It is easily found that the root is between 10 and 100; 40 will reduce the final number considerably, but 50 approaches much nearer. However, the operation may be commenced with either 50 or 40. With 50 the following result is found:—

+ 46|0	5 times	+ 9|41925000 .
− 7|0	4 times	− 1|76456250 .
39|0		7|65468750 .
+ 4|6	3 times	+ 1|15462500 .
43|6		8|80931250 .
+ |0	2 times	+ |3085000 .
43|6		8|84016250
− |0	1 time	− |93100
43|6		8|83923150 take
		16|09149128 from
	44)	·7|25225978 (↓1,

plus

9\|4\|1\|9\|2\|5\|0\|0\|0
15\|1\|6\|9\|7\|9\|6\|3\|2 ↓5,

minus

1\|7\|6\|4\|5\|6\|2\|5\|0
2\|5\|8\|3\|4\|9\|5\|9\|6 ↓4,

plus

11\|5\|4\|6\|2\|5\|0\|0
15\|3\|6\|8\|0\|5\|8\|8 ↓3,

plus

3\|0\|8\|5\|0\|0\|0
3\|7\|3\|2\|8\|5\|0 ↓2,

minus

9\|3\|1\|0\|0
10\|2\|4\|1\|0 ↓1,

+ 75|85	5 times	+ 15|17	Omitting six figures.
− 10|32	4 times	− 2|58	" "
65|53		12|59	
+ 4|62	3 times	+ 1|54	
70|15		14|13	
+ |8	2 times	+ |4	
70|23		14|17	
− |0	1 time	− |0	
		14|17 take	
		16|09 from	
	70)	1|92 (↓0,2,	

plus

15\|16\|97\|96\|32
15\|94\|36\|08\|40 51
16\|75\|68\|92\|67 51

minus

25\|83\|49\|59\|6 .
27\|15\|28\|02\|2 . 51
27\|97\|55\|59\|3 . 31

```
plus                                  plus
15|36|80|58|8 .                       37|32|85|0 .
16|15|19|84|3 . 5|                    38|84|41|9 . 4|
16|31|35|04|1 . 1|

                  minus
                10|24|10|
                10|44|68| . 2|
```

```
+ 83785      5 times     + 167|57  Omitting five figures.
- 11192      4 times     -  27|98     ,,      ,,
  -----                    ------
  72593                    139|59     ,,      ,,
+  4893      3 times     +  16|31     ,,      ,,
  -----                    ------
  77486                    155|90     ,,      ,,
+    76      2 times     +     |38    ,,      ,,
  -----                    ------
  77562                    156|28     ,,      ,,
-     1      1 time      -     | 1    ,,      ,,
  -----                    ------
  77561                    156|27 take
                           160|91 from
                           ------
                   776)      4|64 (↓0,0,5,
```

```
plus                                  minus
167|568|926|7 . .                     279|755|593
168|408|448|7 . . 15|                 281|157|172 15|
169|252|176|7 . . 15|                 282|565|773 15|
170|100|131|8 . . 15|                 283|981|431 15|
170|952|335|2 . . 15|                 285|404|181 15|
171|808|808|1 . . 15|

plus                                  plus
163|135|041                           388|441|9 . .
163|952|349 15|                       390|388|0 . . 15|
164|773|753 15|                       392|343|8 . . 15|
165|599|272 15|

                  minus
                104|468
                104|991 15|
```

```
+ 8590|44      5 times    + 1718|0880|81
- 1141|62      4 times    -  285|4041|81
  -------                   --------------
  7448|82                   1432|6839|00
+  496|80      3 times    +  165|5992|72
  -------                   --------------
  7945|62                   1598|2831|72
+    7|85      2 times    +    3|9234|38
  -------                   --------------
  7953|47                   1602|2066|10
-      |10     1 time     -      |1049|91
  -------                   --------------
  7953|37                   1602|1016|19 take
                            1609|1491|28 from
                            --------------
                  7953 )       7|0475|09  (↓0,0,0,8,8,6,
```

$\therefore\ x = 50\downarrow 1,2,5,8,8,6, = 56{\cdot}43657$

6. *Find the value of x in the equation*

$$x^6 + 2x^5 + 3x^4 + 4x^3 + 5x^2 + 6x = 654321.$$

If 8 be substituted for x, the result will be as follows:

```
 15|7      6 times      2|62144 ◡  x^6
  3|2      5 times       |65536 ◡ 2x^5
   |5      4 times       |12288 ◡ 3x^4
   |.      3 times       |  2048 ◡ 4x^3
   |.      2 times       |   320 ◡ 5x^2
   |.      1 time        |    48 ◡ 6x
 -----                  ----------
 19|4                    3|42 ... from
                         6|54 ... take
                     ----------
                     19) 3|12     (↓1,
```

```
        plus                      plus                        plus
2|6|2|1|4|4|0|0|0          6|5|5|3|6|0|0|0            1|2|2|8|8|0|0|0
4|2|2|1|8|5|5|3|3 ↓5,     10|5|5|4|6|3|8|3 ↓5,        1|7|9|9|0|8|6|1 ↓4,
4|6|4|4|0|4|0|8|6 ↓1,

        plus                      plus                        plus
2|0|4|8|0|0|0              3|2|0|0|0|0                4|8|0|0|0
2|7|2|5|8|8|8 ↓3,          3|8|7|2|0|0 ↓2,            5|2|8|0|0 ↓1,
```

```
                                              omitting decimals
       278|          6 times                 46|4404
        52|          5 times                 10|5546
         7|          4 times                  1|7990
         1|          3 times                   |2725
         .|          2 times                   | 387
         .|          1 time                    |  52
      -----                                 --------
      34 .|                                  59|1 . . . take
                                             65|4 . . . from
                                            --------
                                       34 )   6|3 . . . (↓0,1,

46|44|04|08|6 .          10|55|46|38|3 .          17|99|08|61
48|80|93|36|1 . 51       11|09|30|30|8 . 51       18|72|13|61 41
49|29|74|29|5 . 11

   27|25|88|8 .             38|72|00                52|80|0 .
   28|08|48|6 . 31          39|49|83 21             53|32|8 . 11

          294                      49|2974
           55                      11|0930
            7                       1|8721
            1                        |2808
            .                        | 394
            .                        |  53
         -----                    --------
          357                      62|5880
                                   65|4321
                                  --------
                            36 )    2|8441 (↓0,0,7,

492|974|295            110|930|308 .          187|213|61 .
514|109|379 421        114|879|605 351        192|526|97 . 281

   280|848|6 . .          394|983             533|28 .
   286|805|8 . . 211      400|549 141         537|02 . 71
```

308	6 times	514|109 379
57	5 times	114|879 605
8.	4 times	19|252 697
1	3 times	2|868 058
.	2 times	|400 549
.	1 time	| 53 702
374		651|563·990 take
		654|321·000 from
	37)	2|757·010 ($\downarrow$ 0,0,0,7,

5141|0937|9 . . .
5162|7307|0 . . . 421

1148|7960|5 . . .
1152|8236|9 . . . 351

1925|2697
1930|6678 281

2868|058 .
2874|087 . 211

4005|49 . .
4011| 141

5370|2 . . .
5374|0 . . . 71

3097638420	5162|73 070
576411845	1152|82 369
77226712	193|06 678
8622261	28|74 087
802220	4|01 110
53740	|53 740
3760755198	6541|91·054 take
	6543|21·000 from
3761)	1|29 946 ($\downarrow$ 0,0,0,0,3,4,5,5,

$\therefore \quad x \doteq 8 \downarrow 1,1,7,7,3,4,5,5, = 8{\cdot}95697958.$

To reduce a number as 492974295 to 514109379 421 has been explained in the first part of this work; but the result may be found in one operation, which may be arranged as follows:

492|974|295 = 1
20|704|919 = 42 = a
|424|451 = 41 × a ÷ 2 = b
| 5|659 = 40 × b ÷ 3 = c
| | 55 = 39 × c ÷ 4 = d

514 109 379 421

Calculation, to find the line *a*:

```
 492974·259
         42
-----------
 ·985948 518
19718970 36
-----------
20704918·878
20704919 set down
```

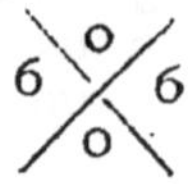

To find the line *b*:

```
2 ) 20704·919
-------------
    10352·46
         41
-------------
    10352 46
   414098 4
-------------
   424450·86
   424451 set down.
```

This direct method can be proved by casting out nines, which has an advantage, as the result may be relied on as correct. In working these examples, the most obvious arithmetical abridgments are not attended to, in order that this new method of extracting the roots of all equations may be presented without any disguise. The accomplished calculator can, at his pleasure, introduce many expedients to reduce numerical labour.

7. Find the value of x in the equation

$$421x^7 + 356{\cdot}2x^5 - 548x^4 - 298x = 9876543210.$$

Although it is not absolutely necessary to commence operating with the first figure of the root, yet the nearer we approach this number to commence with, the easier the required root is extracted. This example, set down at random, three of the terms absent, the coefficients large and irregular without any particular arrangement, will tend to establish the great power of this new and general method of solving numerical equations.

It will be found that $x = 10$, tends to approach the absolute number 9876543210, sufficiently near, to commence operating.

29	+ 7 times	4|210000009	$+ 421x^7$
	+ 5 times	| 35620000	$+ 356{\cdot}2x^5$
		4|245620000	
	− 4 times	| 5480000	$- 548x^4$
		4|240140000	
	− 1 time	| 29830	$- 2983x$
29		4|240110170 take	
		9|876543210 from	

29) 5|6 . . . . (↓1,

4|2|1|0|0|0|0|0|0|0
6|7|8|0|2|4|7|1|0|0 ↓5,
8|2|0|4|0|9|8|9|9|1 ↓2,

3|5|6|2|0|0|0|0
5|7|3|5|1|7|6|2 ↓5,

5|4|8|0 0|0|0|
8|0|2|3|2|6|8| ↓4,

2|9|8|3|0
3|2|8|1|3 ↓1,

57	+ 7 times	8|204098991
	+ 5 times	| 57351762
		8|261450753
	− 4 times	| 8023268
		8|253427485
	− 1 time	| 32813
57		8|253394672 take
		9|876543210 from

57) 1|62 . . . . (↓0,2,

82|04|09|89|91
94|30|40|02|33 14|

57|35|17|62
63|35|20|24 10|

80|23|26|8 .
86|88|04|8 . 8|

32|81|3 .
33|47|2 . 2|

6601	+ 7 times	943|0 . . . . . .
32	+ 5 times	6|3 . . . . . .
6633		949|3 . . . . . .
3	− 4 times	|8 . . . . . .
6630		948|5 . . . . . .
.	− 1 time	|. . . . . . .
6630		948|5 . . . . . . take
		987|6 . . . . . . from
	66)	39|1 . . . . . . (↓0,0,5,

943|040|023|4 . .	.633|520|25 .
976|613|754|9 . . |35|	649|552|71 . |25|
868|804|8 . .	334|72 .
886|346|9 . . |20|	336|39 . |5|

68363	+ 7 times	976|6137549
325	+ 5 times	6|4955271
68688		983|1092820
35	− 4 times	|8863469
68653		982|2229351
.	− 1 time	|33639
68653		982|2195712 take
		987|6543210 from
	68653)	5|4347498 (↓0,0,0,7,9,2,

$\therefore\ x = 10 \downarrow 1,2,5,7,9,2, = 11 \cdot 286252.$

8. *Find the value of x in the equation*

$$x^2 - 120x - 100x^{\frac{3}{2}} + 999x^{\frac{1}{2}} = 91000.$$

The value of x lies somewhere between 3 and 4 hundred; commencing with $x = 300$, then

```
180    twice    + 90|000·        = x²
 36    once     − 36|000·        = − 120x
───             ─────────
144               54|000·
  1    half     −  1|732·0508 = − 100x^½
───             ─────────
143               52|267.9492
  2    third    +  6|687·6352 = + 999x^⅓
───             ─────────
145               58|955·5844 take
                  91|000·0000 from
                ─────────
           145 ) 32|044 4156 (↓0,22,
                 29|0
                 ────
                  3 04
                  2 90
```

The nearest less number to 22 that can be divided by 2 and 3; or by 6, is 18.

```
 90|00·0·0|00|0 .                     36|00|0·0|00|0 .
128|76·9 1|90|5 . ↓0,36,              43|06|1·3|09|1 . ↓0,18,

 17|32·|05|08|0 .                     66|87·|63|52|0 .
 18|94·|31|84|5 . ↓0,9,               70|99·|05|95|2 . ↓0,6,
```

```
25754   twice    + 12876|9·1905
 4306   once     −  4306|1·3091
─────              ──────────
21448               8570|7·8812
   99   half     −   189|4·3185
─────              ──────────
21349               8381|3·5629
  236   third        709|9·0595
─────              ──────────
21585               9091|2·6224 take
                    9100|0·0000 from
                   ──────────
              2188)    8|7·3776 (↓0,0,0,0,40,
```

The nearest less number to 40 divisible by 6 is 36; therefore,

```
128769|1905 = 1                        43061|3091 . = 1
     9|27138 = 72 = a                     15|5021 . = 36 = a
      |  658 = 71 × a ÷ 2                   |  27 . = 35 × a ÷ 2
─────────────                          ─────────────
128861·9701                            43076·8139
```

18943	185 . .	1
3	410 . .	18
1894·6595		

70990	595 . .	= 1
8	519 . .	= 12 = a
	1 . .	= 13 × a ÷ 2
7099·9115		

25772	twice	+	12886|1·9701
4308	once	−	4307|6·8139
21464			8578|5·1562
99	half	−	189|4·6595
21365			8389|0·4967
236	third	+	709|9·9115
21601			9099|0·4082 take
			9100|0·0000 from
		216)	|9 5918

$(\downarrow 0,0,0,0,0,444, = \downarrow \boxed{444},$

$$\therefore \quad x = 300 \downarrow 0,18,0,0,36,444, = 358{\cdot}98937$$
$$= 300 \downarrow 0,18,0,0,36,42,24,$$

This value of x is given in a form so that the factors to the right of $\downarrow$ are divisible by 6; the work is easily proved by continuing the process two more steps.

$$\begin{aligned}
x = 300 &\downarrow 0,18, \ 0, \ 0,36,42, \ 24,\\
&= \downarrow 0, \ 0,180, \ 0,\overline{36},\overline{30}, \ \overline{102},\\
&= \downarrow 0, \ 0, \ 0,1800,\overline{36},\overline{30}, \ \overline{822},\\
&= \downarrow 0, \ 0, \ 0, \ 0, \ 0, \ 0,1795278, = \downarrow \boxed{\overline{1}795278},\\
&= \downarrow 1, \ 0, \ 0, \ 0, \ 0, \ 0, \ 842083,\\
&= \downarrow 1, \ 8, \ 0, \ 0, \ 0, \ 0. \ 45979,\\
&= \downarrow 1, \ 8, \ 4, \ 0, \ 0, \ 0, \ 5995,\\
&= \downarrow 1, \ 8, \ 4, \ 5, \ 9, \ 9, \ 5,
\end{aligned}$$

These reductions are instantly made by the following equalities so often employed :—

$$\downarrow 1, \qquad = \downarrow 0,10,\ \bar{4},\ \bar{1},\ \bar{9},\bar{5},\bar{1}, = \downarrow \lfloor\overline{9}53195,$$

$$\downarrow 0,1, \qquad = \downarrow 0,\ 0,10,\cdot 0,\ \bar{4},\bar{4},\bar{7}, = \downarrow \lfloor\overline{9}9513,$$

$$\downarrow 0,0,1, \qquad = \downarrow 0,\ 0,\ 0,10,\ 0,0,\bar{4}, = \downarrow \lfloor\overline{9}996,$$

$$\downarrow 0,0,0,1, = \downarrow 0,\ 0,\ 0,\ 0,10,0,0, = \downarrow \lfloor\overline{1}000,$$

The succeeding equations of condition are also easily adduced,

$$\downarrow 6, \qquad = \downarrow \lfloor\overline{5}719170,$$

$$\downarrow 0,6, \qquad = \downarrow \lfloor\overline{5}97078,$$

$$\downarrow 0,0,6, \qquad = \downarrow \lfloor\overline{5}9976,$$

$$\downarrow 0,0,0,6, \qquad = \downarrow \lfloor\overline{6}000,$$

$$\downarrow 0,0,0,0,6, \qquad = \downarrow \lfloor\overline{6}00,$$

$$\downarrow 0,0,0,0,0,6, \qquad = \downarrow \lfloor\overline{6}0,$$

$$\downarrow 0,0,0,0,0,0,6, = \downarrow \lfloor\overline{6},$$

Hyperbolic logarithms of $\downarrow 1,$; $\downarrow 2,$; $\downarrow 3,$; &c. of $\downarrow 0,1,$; $\downarrow 0,2,$; $\downarrow 0,3,$; &c. &c. are easily determined, for putting $c = 10000978$, then, because $\epsilon = \downarrow \lfloor\overline{1}0000978,$.

$$\log.\downarrow 1, \qquad \downarrow \lfloor\overline{9}53195, \div c = \cdot 0953102$$

$$\log.\downarrow 0,1, \qquad \downarrow \lfloor\overline{9}9513, \div c = \cdot 0099503$$

$$\log.\downarrow 0,0,1, \qquad \downarrow \lfloor\overline{9}996, \div c = \cdot 0009995$$

$$\log.\downarrow 0,0,0,1, \qquad \downarrow \lfloor\overline{1}000, \div c = \cdot 0001000$$

$$\log.\downarrow 0,0,0,0,1, \downarrow \lfloor\overline{1}00, \div c = \cdot 0000100$$

&c. &c. &c.

$$\therefore \log.\downarrow 12, = \cdot 0953102 \times 12 = 1\cdot 1437224$$

$$\log.\downarrow 0,9, = \cdot 0099503 \times 9 = \cdot 0895527$$

$$\log.\downarrow 0,0,5, = \cdot 0009995 \times 5 = \cdot 0049975$$

$$\log.\downarrow 0,0,0,1, = \cdot 0001000 \times 1 = \cdot 0001000$$

$$\log.\downarrow 0,0,0,0,0,1, = \cdot 0000010 \times 1 = \cdot 0000010$$

$$\log.\downarrow 0,0,0,0,0,0,5, = \cdot 0000001 \times 5 = 5$$

$$1\cdot 2383742$$

$$\therefore \log. \downarrow 12{,}9{,}5{,}1{,}0{,}1{,}5, = 1{\cdot}2383742$$

$$3{\cdot}4499997 = \downarrow 12{,}9{,}5{,}1{,}0{,}1{,}5,$$

Such transformations and equalities as these will be found useful, especially in solving problems like the following:—

9. *Find the value of x in the equation*

$$x^m = \epsilon^{ax}$$

$$m \log. x = ax$$

$\therefore \quad \frac{\log. x}{x} = \frac{m}{a} =$ suppose ·358949 since a and m are known quantities.

Very few trials will show that the required number is between $\downarrow$ **12,** and $\downarrow$ **13,**

1	0	0	0	0	0	0	0
1	3	0	0	0	0	0	0
	7	8	0	0	0	0	0
	2	8	6	0	0	0	0
		7	1	5	0	0	0
		1	2	8	7	0	0
			1	7	1	6	0
				1	7	1	6
					1	2	9
							7
3·	4	5	2	2	7	1	2

log. $\downarrow$ **13,** = 13 × 0953102
= 1·2390326

$$\therefore \frac{1{\cdot}2390326}{3{\cdot}4522712} = {\cdot}3589036$$

1	0	0	0	0	0	0	0	0
1	2	0	0	0	0	0	0	0
	6	6	0	0	0	0	0	0
	2	2	0	0	0	0	0	0
		4	9	5	0	0	0	0
			7	9	2	0	0	0
				9	2	4	0	0
					7	9	2	0
						4	9	5
							2	2
								7
3·	1	3	8	4	2	8	4	4

log $\downarrow$ **12,** = 12 × ·0953102
= 1·1437224

$$\therefore \frac{1{\cdot}1437224}{3{\cdot}13842844} = {\cdot}3633252$$

The number required will be found to be $\downarrow$ **12,9,5,1,0,1,6,** which is evidently nearer to $\downarrow$ **13,** than to $\downarrow$ **12,**

The nearest less digit found in solving the simple equation,

$$(3\cdot1|38|42|84|4' + 31384284 \times n) \times \cdot358949$$

$$= 1\cdot1436224 + n \times \cdot0099503$$

for n gives $n = 9$. Many of these figures may be omitted in finding n; in a similar way, 5, 1, 0, 6, may be ascertained, and ultimately

$$x = \downarrow 12{,}9{,}5{,}1{,}0{,}1{,}6, = 3\cdot45 \text{ nearly.}$$

Or the factors $\downarrow$ **0,9,** ; $\downarrow$ **0,0,5,** ; &c. may be found by division, for if n be made to represent the second factor, then the trial equation becomes

$$3\cdot1|38|42 + \cdot03138)n = (1\cdot1436224 + \cdot0099503)\,n \div \cdot358949$$

$$= 3\cdot160 \qquad + \cdot02772\,n$$

$$\therefore \ \cdot00366\,n = \cdot0476$$

Consequently, n must be 9; for although ·00366 is contained in ·0476, more than 9 times, yet n may be taken for certain 9, because x lies between $\downarrow$ **12,** and $\downarrow$ **13,** but $\downarrow$ **12,10,** would exceed $\downarrow$ **13,**. However, by continuing the process one step further, the truth is established:

$$\begin{array}{l} 31|38|42|84|4\,\cdot \\ 34|32|45|29|6\,\cdot\ \underline{9|} \end{array} \qquad \begin{array}{lr} \log. \downarrow 12, & = 1\cdot1437224 \\ \log. \downarrow\ 0{,}9, & \underline{\cdot0895527} \end{array}$$

$$\therefore \ \log. \downarrow 12{,}9, = 1\cdot2332751$$

$$\therefore \ \log. 3\cdot43245296 = 1\cdot2332751$$

$$\frac{1\cdot2332751}{3\cdot43245296} = \cdot3592985$$

Suppose m = the next factor, then

$$3\cdot43245296 + \cdot00343245\,m$$

$$= (1\cdot2332751 + \cdot0009995\,m) \div \cdot358949$$

$$= 3\cdot435795 \quad + \cdot00278452\,m$$

$$\therefore \cdot 00064793\, m = \cdot 003342$$

$$\therefore m = 5.$$

To continue and advance the work another step:

343|245|296
344|964|957 151

$$\begin{aligned} \log. \downarrow 12, &= 1\cdot 1437224 \\ \log. \downarrow 0,9, &= \cdot 0895527 \\ \log. \downarrow 0,0,5, &= \underline{\cdot 0049975} \\ \therefore \log. \downarrow 12,9,5, &= 1\cdot 2382726 \end{aligned}$$

$$\frac{1\cdot 2382726}{3\cdot 44964957} = \cdot 3589560$$

Let r represent the next factor, then

$$\begin{aligned} &3\cdot 44964957 + \cdot 000344965\, r \\ &= (1\cdot 2382726 + \cdot 0001000\, r) \div \cdot 358949 \\ &= 3\cdot 4497174 + \cdot 000278591\, r \end{aligned}$$

$$\therefore \cdot 000066374\, r = \cdot 0000678$$

$$\therefore r = 101$$

The three succeeding factors 1, 0, 1, may be determined in one operation; the required number is approached rapidly when the first two factors become known. In this manner, the required number is found to be $\downarrow 12,9,5,1,0,1,6, = 3\cdot 45$.

As in other cases, the details of the work of this example are given at great length, the more clearly to show that the factors comprising the required number are not guessed at, but determined by a well-defined law.

10. *Let* $y = \frac{2}{\sqrt{\pi}} \epsilon^{-x^2}$, *be the equation of the curve* $EARB$,

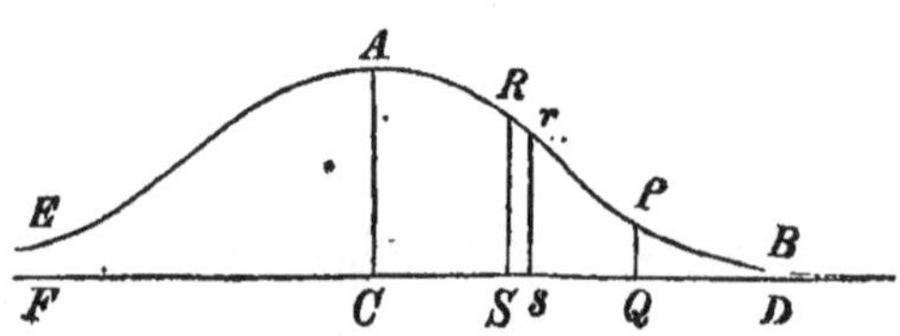

find the values of x *and* y, *when the area* $= \frac{1}{2}$.

By the integral calculus, it may be shown that

$$\int_0^x y\,dx = \frac{2}{\sqrt{\pi}} \int_0^x dx \left(1 - x^2 + \frac{x^4}{1.2} - \frac{x^6}{1.2.3} + \dots\right)$$

$$\therefore \text{ area} = \frac{2}{\sqrt{\pi}} \left(x - \frac{1}{1}\frac{x^3}{3} + \frac{1}{1.2}\frac{x^5}{5} - \frac{1}{1.2.3}\frac{x^7}{7} + \dots\right) = \tfrac{1}{2}$$

$$\therefore\ x - \frac{1}{1.3}x^3 + \frac{1}{1.2.5}x^5 - \frac{1}{1.2.3.7}x^7 + \frac{1}{1 \frown 4.9}x^9$$

$$- \frac{1}{1 \frown 5.11}x^{11} + \frac{1}{1 \frown 6.13}x^{13} = \frac{\sqrt{\pi}}{4} = \cdot 4431134627.$$

From this equation the value of x has to be found: call this equation (A). The following six values of the co-efficients are readily determined:

$$\frac{1}{1.3} = -\ 109866750\,. \qquad \frac{1}{1.2.3.4.9} = -\ 537554853\,.$$

$$\frac{1}{1.2.5} = -\ 230270081\,. \qquad \frac{1}{1.2.3.4.5.11} = -\ 718574810\,.$$

$$\frac{1}{1.2.3.7} = -\ 373785746\,. \qquad \frac{1}{1.2.3.4.5.6.13} = -\ 914466007\,.$$

It is evident that x is greater than ·4; then if ·4 be substituted for x in the left-hand member of (A), it becomes

+ ·4000000000 − ·0213333333 + ·0010240000 − ·0000390095
+ ·0000012136 − ·0000000318 + ·0000000007.

To effect the object in view, only a portion of these terms are required:

400 +	once	+ ·40000 . . . . .
64 −	3 times	− ·02133 . . . . .
5 +	5 times	+ ·00102 . . . . .
341		− ·00003 . . . . .
		·37966 take
		·44311 from, right mem. of (A).
		6345

```
341 ) 6345 (↓1,8,
      341
      ----
      2935
      2728
      ----
```

So that the first part of the value of

$$x = \frac{4}{10} \downarrow 1,8, = \downarrow - \overline{74141518,}|.$$

The succeeding results are obtained by substituting this value of x in the left member of (A):

```
47645 +  once     ᴗ + ·476 4569505 = x = 4/10 ↓1,8,
10816 −  3 times  ᴗ − ·036 0536904 = 1/(1.3) x³
 1228 +  5 times  ᴗ + ·002 4553777 = 1/(1.2.5) x⁵
   93 −  7 times  ᴗ − ·000 1327139 = 1/(1.2.3.7) x⁷
    5 +  9 times  ᴗ + ·000 0058581 = 1/(1.2.3.4.9) x⁹
-----
37969
                  − ·000 0002175 = 1/(1.2.3.4.5.11) x¹¹
                  + ·000 0000064 = 1/(1.2.3.4.5.6.13) x¹³
                  --------------
                    442|7315709 take
                    443|1134627 from, The right side of (A).
                    --------------
37969                  |3818918
                       |37969   (↓0,0,1,0,0,
                       --------
                         220
```

Hence, the value of x, as far as the fifth position, will be $\frac{4}{10} \downarrow 1,8,1,0,0,$. Before advancing the next step, it may be necessary to show how the values of the terms given above are found. Take, for example, $\frac{1}{1.2.3.4.5.11}x^{11}$:

$- \quad 74141518 = \frac{4}{10} \downarrow 1,8, = x.$

11

$- \quad 815556698$

$\frac{1}{1.2.3.4.5.11} = - \quad 718574810$

$- \quad 1534131508 = \frac{2}{10^7} \downarrow 0,8,4,8,0,3,7,4,$

$10^7 . \smile + 161189 0567 \qquad = \cdot 0000002175$

77759059

$2 . \smile \quad 69318201$

8440858

$7960664 \smile \downarrow 0,8,$

480194

$399820 \smile (4,$

8,0,3,7,4,

The part of the value of x, that is ↓ 0,0,1, found by the last process, being small, is best to be operated with alone.

↓ 0,0,1,	↓ 0,0,3	↓ 0,0,5,
+ ·4764569505	− ·0360536904	+ ·0024553777
+ ·4769334075	− ·0361619597	+ ·0024676792

↓ 0,0,7,	↓ 0,0,9,	↓ 0,0,11,
− ·0001327139	+ ·0000058581	− ·0000002175
− ·0001336457	+ ·0000059110	− ·0000002198

↓ 0,0,13,

+ ·0000000064.

+ ·0000000065.

47693 +	once	+ ·476933 4075
10848 −	3 times	− ·036161 9597
1234 +	5 times	+ ·002467 6792
93 −	7 times	− ·000133 6457
5 +	9 times	+ ·000005 9110
		− ·000000 2198
37991		+ ·000000 0065 .

·443111|1790 take
·443113|4627 from, (A).

37991   2|2837   (↓0,0,0,0,0,6,0,1,1,
2|2795

42
38

4
4

$$\therefore \quad x = \frac{4}{10} \downarrow 1,8,1,0,0,6,0,1,1,$$

476933|4075
··2|8616 ◡ 6,
48 ◡ 0,1,
·5 ◡ 0,0,1,

$x =$ ·476936 2744

Since $y = \dfrac{2}{\sqrt{\pi}} \epsilon^{-x^2}$, and it was before shown that ϵ reduced to the eight position, or $\downarrow \overline{\epsilon'}| = 100005025$; $\downarrow \overline{2',}| = 69318201$; $\downarrow \overline{\pi',}| = 114478742$, then,

$$-x^2 = -\frac{16}{10^2} \downarrow 2,16,2,0,0,12,0,2,$$

and $-100005025 \times \dfrac{16}{100} \downarrow 2,16,2,0,0,12,0,2, = -22747964$

$\sqrt{\pi} = \downarrow \frac{1}{2} \overline{\pi',}| = -57239371$

-79987335

$2 \smile = +69318201$

$\dfrac{8}{10} \downarrow 1,2,1,2,4,7,2,5, = \quad -10669134$

$$\therefore \quad \frac{8}{10} \downarrow 1,2,1,2,4,7,2,5, = \cdot 89880788 = y.$$

The value of ϵ^{-x^2} may be found by two successive operations, thus,

$$100005025 \times \frac{16}{100} = 16000804.$$

$16000804 \downarrow 1,8,1,0,0,6,0,1, = 19059235 \cdot 8$, and
$19059235 \cdot 8 \downarrow 1,8,1,0,0,6,0,1, = 22747964$, to which append the negative sign.

11. *Find the co-ordinates of the curve* $y = \frac{2}{\sqrt{\pi}} \epsilon^{-x^2}$, *when the area is the fraction* $\frac{2143}{4789}$; 2143 *and* 4789 *are prime numbers.*

From the last problem,

$$x - \frac{1}{1.3} x^3 + \frac{1}{1.2.5} x^5 - \frac{1}{1.2.3.7} x^7 + \frac{1}{1.2.3.4.9} x^9 - \ldots.$$
$$= \frac{\sqrt{\pi}}{2} \times \frac{2143}{4789} = \cdot 396572205, \text{ (A)}.$$

$\cdot 4$, may be substituted for x in the left number of (A); then, as in the last example,

400 +	once	+ ·400000 . . .	
64 −	3 times	− ·021333 . . .	
5 +	7 times	+ ·001024 . . .	
341		− ·000039 . . .	
		·379652 . . .	take
		·396572 . . .	from (A).
	341)	16920	(↓ 0,4,9,
		1364	
		3280	

The first part of the value of x is $\frac{4}{10} \downarrow 0,4,9, = \downarrow - \overline{86753752}$

$$\frac{4}{10}\downarrow \mathbf{0,4,9,} = \cdot 420002800$$

$$-\frac{1}{1.3}x^3 = -\cdot 024696492;\qquad -\frac{1}{1.2.3.7}x^7 = -\cdot 000054892;$$

$$+\frac{1}{1.2.5}x^5 = +\cdot 001306949;\qquad +\frac{1}{1.2.3.4.9}x^9 = +\cdot 000001883;$$

$$-\frac{1}{1.2.3.4.5.11}x^{11} = -\cdot 000000054.$$

42000 +	once	+ ·42000	2800
7409 −	3 times	− ·02469	6492
653 +	5 times	+ ·00130	6956
38 −	7 times	− ·00005	4892
2 +	9 times	+ ·00000	1883
		− ·00000	0054
35208)			
...		·39656	0201 take
		39657	2205 from (A).
		1	2004 ($\downarrow$ **0,0,0,0,3,4,1,**
		1	0562
			1442
			1408
			4
			35

$$\therefore\quad x = \frac{4}{10}\downarrow \mathbf{0,4,9,0,3,4,1,} = \cdot 420017122.$$

$$-x^2 = -\frac{16}{10^2}\downarrow \mathbf{0,8,18,0,6,8,2,} =$$

$$\downarrow, \epsilon^{-x^2} = -100005025\times\frac{16}{10^2}\downarrow \mathbf{0,8,18,0,6,8,2,} = -17652824$$

$$\downarrow, \sqrt{\pi} = \downarrow \tfrac{1}{2}\pi', \qquad = -57239371$$

$$-74892195$$

$$\downarrow, \mathbf{2.} = +69318201$$

$$-5573994$$

$$\begin{array}{r} -\quad 5573994 = \frac{9}{10}\downarrow 0,4,9,8,2,6,6, \\ 10\smile +\ 230270081 \\ \hline 224696087 \\ 219733500 \\ \hline 4962587 \\ 3980332 \\ \hline 982255 \\ 899595 \\ \hline 8,2,6,6,0, \end{array}$$

$$\therefore\ y = \frac{2}{\sqrt{\pi}}\varepsilon^{-x^2} = \frac{9}{10}\downarrow 0,4,9,8,2,6,6, = \cdot 945787725.$$

12. *Given, $x \sin x = \cos x$, to find x.*

It is evident that

$$x\left(x - \frac{x^3}{1\frown 3} + \frac{x^5}{1\frown 5} + \ldots\right) \text{ must be equal } 1 - \frac{x^2}{2} + \frac{x^4}{1\frown 4} - \ldots\ldots$$

$$\therefore\ \frac{3x^2}{2} - \frac{5x^4}{1\frown 4} + \frac{7x^6}{1\frown 6} - \frac{9x^8}{1\frown 8} + \frac{11x^{10}}{1\frown 10} - \ldots\ldots = 1,\ (1).$$

Put $v = x^2$, then (1) becomes (2),

$$\frac{3v}{2} - \frac{5v^2}{1\frown 4} + \frac{7v^3}{1\frown 6} - \frac{9v^4}{1\frown 8} + \frac{11v^5}{1\frown 10} - \ldots = 1,\ (2).$$

If $\frac{3v}{2} - \frac{5v^2}{24}$ be put $= 1$, then the value of v is $+ 6{\cdot}4 \ldots$ or $+ {\cdot}8 \ldots.$; therefore ·7 cannot be greater than the value of v. Substitute ·7 for v in (2), and it becomes

$$+ 1{\cdot}050000000 - {\cdot}102083333 + {\cdot}003334722$$
$$- {\cdot}000053594 + {\cdot}000000509$$

+ ·1050	once	+ 1·05	00 .....
− 204	twice	− ·10	20 .....
+ 10	3 times	+ ·00	33 .....
		− ·00	00 .....
856			
		·95	13 ..... take
		1·00	00 ..... from
	856)	4	87 ..... ($\downarrow$ 0,5,

$$\therefore \quad v = \frac{7}{10} \downarrow 0,5, \ldots\ldots$$

$\downarrow$ 0,5,	$\downarrow$ 0,10,	$\downarrow$ 0,15,	$\downarrow$ 0,20,
+ 1·050000000	− ·102083333	+ ·003334722	− ·000053594
+ 1·103560553	− ·112763508	+ ·003871509	− ·000065396

$\downarrow$ 0,25,
+ ·000000509

+ 1103	once	+ 1·103	560 ...
− 225	twice	− ·112	763 ...
+ 11	3 times	+ ·003	871 ...
889	4 times	− ·000	065 ...
		·994	603 ... take
		1·000	900 ... from
	889)	5	397 ... ($\downarrow$ 0,0,6,
		5	334

$$\therefore \quad v = \frac{7}{10} \downarrow 0,5,6, \ldots\ldots$$

$\downarrow$ 0,5,6,	$\downarrow$ 0,10,12,
+ 1·050000000	− ·102083333
+ 1·110198495	− ·114124137

$\downarrow$ 0,15,18,	$\downarrow$ 0,20,24,	$\downarrow$ 0,25,30,
+ ·003334722	− ·000053594	+ ·000000509

$\downarrow$ 1,7,2,2,8,3,4,7	$\downarrow$ 2,3,2,5,2,4,2,7,	$\downarrow$ 2,8,8,5,2,4,7,2.
+ ·003334722	− ·000053594	+ ·000000509
+ ·003941787	− ·000066982	+ ·000000673

+	111019	once	+	1·11019|8495
−	22824	twice	−	·11412|4137
+	1182	3 times	+	·00394|1787
−	26	4 times	−	·00006|6982
			+	·00000|0673
	89351			

·99994|9836 take
1·00000|0000 from

89351) 5|0164 ($\downarrow$ 0,0,0,0,5,6,1,5,
4|4676
5488
5361
127
89
38

$$\therefore \quad v = \frac{7}{10} \downarrow 0,5,6,0,5,6,1,5,$$

By advancing another step, the value of v may be found correct to twenty places of decimals.

$$v = \frac{\dot{7}}{10} \downarrow 0,5,6,0,\dot{5},6,1,5, = \cdot 740173889$$

But $v = x^2$, therefore

$$x = \cdot 86033359 = \text{an arc of } 49^\circ\ 17'\ 36''\cdot 55.$$

The value of v may be found under many forms; for instance:—

$$v = \frac{4}{10} \downarrow \dot{6},4,3,7,5,9,7,4,$$

$$v = \frac{5}{10} \downarrow 4,1,1,0,8,6,5,0,$$

$$v = \frac{6}{10} \downarrow 2,1,9,3,8,9,3,2,$$

$$v = \frac{6}{10} \downarrow 2,2,0,\bar{6},3,4,4,4,$$

each gives $v = \cdot 740173889$. This remark applies to all other equations.

GENERAL DEVELOPMENTS.

ANY quantity or magnitude X, capable of being represented by numbers, may be expressed under the form

$$X = 10^m u \downarrow u_1, u_2, u_3, u_4, \ldots \ldots u_n = \overset{n}{\downarrow} \overline{\pm x}, \qquad (1).$$

u being one of the nine digits 1, 2, 3, 4, 5, 6, 7, 8, or 9.

$u_1, u_2, u_3, \ldots \ldots$ have the same range of values, positive or negative, and zero. x is a whole number, and may be either positive or negative, and $\overset{n}{\downarrow}\overline{\pm x}$, represents X, reduced to the nth position. m is a positive or negative whole number. The design and scope of the present work exclude fractional and other combinations: hence all the numbers employed in developing X, are integers, and may be either positive or negative as the case may require. For example, suppose

$$X = 7276{\cdot}68024, \text{ then,}$$

$$X = 10^3 \times 6 \downarrow 2,0,2,3,\bar{1},5,9,3, = \overset{8}{\downarrow}\overline{889287691},$$

Comparing this particular example with the general development (1), $m = 3$; $u = 6$; $u_1 = 2$; $u_2 = 0$; $u_3 = 2$; $u_4 = 3$; $u_5 =$ minus 1; and so on to $u_8 = 3$. In this example $n = 8$, the number of terms employed in the development, and may be extended to 9, 10, ... to suit any required degree of accuracy. $x = 889287691$, that is, X reduced to the eight position; this ultimate whole number may be employed as the logarithm of X, and treated accordingly; but it must be observed that this ultimate number x, has many other uses and relations, especially in connexion with $u_1, u_2, u_3, \ldots$ and with the function X itself. For instance, suppose that X has to be developed so that the expression may be of the form

$$3 \downarrow 3,3,3,0,0,0,0, x',$$

and yet, to be $= 7276{\cdot}68024$, what number then will x' represent in the eight position. It is readily shown that

$$x' = \overset{8}{\downarrow}\overline{747541336},$$

$$\text{or } X = 3 \downarrow 3,3,3,0,0,0,0,747541336, = \overset{8}{\downarrow}\overline{889287691},$$

The number of forms under which X may be developed, without changing the value of X, or the final number x, are without limit. Again, take another example, and let $X = {\cdot}000401428684$.

$$\text{Then } X = \frac{1}{10^4} \times 4 \downarrow 0,0,3,5,7,\bar{3},\bar{2},7, = \overset{8}{\downarrow} - \overline{782087369},$$

In this state of the function $m = -4$; $n = 4$; $u_1 = 0$, $u_2 = 0$, $u_3 = 3$, $u_4 = 5$, $u_5 = 7$, $u_6 =$ minus 3, $u_7 = 2$, and $u_8 =$ minus 1; hence $n = 8$, and $x = -782087369$.

Let $a =$ the ultimate changeable, but not variable, base

$$1{\cdot}000 \ldots (n-1) \text{ zeros} \ldots 1;$$

and the equation $P^x = Q$, is required to be solved.

P may be made to assume the form $10^m u \downarrow u_1, u_2, u_3, \ldots u_n = \overset{n}{\downarrow}\overline{p}$, and Q to assume the form $10^{\mathrm{m}}\, \mathrm{u} \downarrow \mathrm{u}_1, \mathrm{u}_2, \mathrm{u}_3, \ldots \mathrm{u}_n = \overset{n}{\downarrow}\overline{q}$,

$$\therefore\ (a^p)^x = a^q;$$

then, in any system of logarithms,

$$z \log. (a^p) = q \log. a,$$

$$\text{or, } zp \log. a = q \log. a$$

$$\therefore \quad z = \frac{q}{p}.$$

Also, in any system of logarithms,

$$z \log. P = \log. Q;$$

$$\therefore \quad z = \frac{\log. Q}{\log. P}$$

Hence, $$\frac{\log. Q}{\log. P} = \frac{q}{p};$$

and, consequently, p and q may be employed as the logarithms, respectively, of P and Q.

Let $a_1, a_2, a_3, \ldots.$ be the bases of $u_1, u_2, u_3, \ldots.$ and also of $\mathrm{u}_1, \mathrm{u}_2, \mathrm{u}_3, \ldots..$; then, because

$$10^m\, u \downarrow a_1^{u_1}\, a_2^{u_2}\, a_3^{u_3} \ldots..) = a^p = P,$$

$$\text{and } 10^{\mathrm{m}}\, \mathrm{u} \downarrow a_1^{\mathrm{u}_1}\, a_2^{\mathrm{u}_2}\, a_3^{\mathrm{u}_3} \ldots..) = a^q = Q;$$

$$\therefore \quad P \times Q = 10^{\mathrm{m}+m}\, u\,\mathrm{u} \downarrow a_1^{\mathrm{u}_1 + u_1}\, a_2^{\mathrm{u}_2 + u_2}\, a_3^{\mathrm{u}_3 + u_3} \ldots.. = a^{p+q}$$

$$\therefore \quad \frac{P}{Q} = 10^{m-\mathrm{m}} \frac{u}{\mathrm{u}} \downarrow a_1^{u_1 - \mathrm{u}_1}\, a_2^{u_2 - \mathrm{u}_2}\, a_3^{u_3 - \mathrm{u}_3} \ldots.. = a^{p-q}$$

And further,

$$P^s = 10^{sm}\, u^s \downarrow a_1^{su_1}\, a_2^{su_2}\, a_3^{su_3} \ldots.. = a^{sp}.$$

Consequently, $u_1, u_2, u_3, \ldots.$ and $\mathrm{u}_1, \mathrm{u}_2, \mathrm{u}_3, \ldots..$ to the right of $\downarrow$, may be operated upon as logarithms, with regard to their respective bases. The numbers to the left of $\downarrow$, are acted upon by the operations of common arithmetic; but, as these numbers can always be reduced to digits and powers of 10, the operations of common arithmetic to be performed cannot be difficult.

It may be necessary now to repeat, that in this work $l\overline{u}$ is put for $d u$, the differential of u; $^{2}\overline{|u}$ the second differential of u; $^{3}\overline{|u}$ the third differential of u; and so on. $\overline{|u}^2$ is put for du^2, the square of the differential of u; $\overline{|u}^3$ for the cube of the differential of u, &c. In the same way, $^{2}\overline{|u}^{3}$ represents $(d^2u)^3$, the cube of the second differential of u. Then Maclaurin's, or, more properly speaking, Stirling's, theorem may be expressed as follows:

$$U = \{U\} + \left\{\frac{\overline{|U}}{\overline{|x}}\right\}\frac{x}{1} + \left\{\frac{^{2}\overline{|U}}{\overline{|x^2}}\right\}\frac{x^2}{1.2} + \left\{\frac{^{3}\overline{|U}}{\overline{|x^3}}\right\}\frac{x^3}{1.2.3} + \ldots\ldots \quad (2).$$

$\{U\}$, $\left\{\frac{\overline{|U}}{\overline{|x}}\right\}$ $\left\{\frac{^{2}\overline{|U}}{\overline{|x^2}}\right\}$, &c. are intended to represent, by the use of brackets, what U, and the results of the operations expressed by symbols

$$\frac{\overline{|U}}{\overline{|x}},\ \frac{^{2}\overline{|U}}{\overline{|x^2}},\ \frac{^{3}\overline{|U}}{\overline{|x^3}},\ \text{\&c. become when } x = 0.$$

To develop a^x iu a series by (2).

Put $U = a^x$ then $\{U\} = 1$

$$\frac{\overline{|U}}{\overline{|x}} = \log.\ a\ a^x \quad \text{then} \quad \left\{\frac{\overline{|U}}{\overline{|x}}\right\} = \log.\ a$$

$$\frac{^{2}\overline{|U}}{\overline{|x^2}} = (\log.\ a)^2\, a^x \quad \text{then} \quad \left\{\frac{\overline{|U}}{\overline{|x^2}}\right\} = (\log.\ a)^2$$

$$\frac{^{3}\overline{|U}}{\overline{|x^3}} = (\log.\ a)^3\, a^x \quad \text{then} \quad \left\{\frac{^{2}\overline{|U}}{\overline{|x^2}}\right\} = (\log.\ a)^3$$

&c. = &c. then &c. = &c.

$$\therefore\ a^x = 1 + (\log.\ a)\frac{x}{1} + (\log.\ a)^2\frac{x^2}{1.2} + (\log.\ a)^3\frac{x^3}{1.2.3}\ \ldots\ldots \quad (3).$$

When $x = 1$, (3) becomes (4),

$$a = 1 + \frac{(\log.\ a)}{1} + \frac{(\log.\ a)^2}{1.2} + \frac{(\log.\ a)^3}{1.2.3} + \ldots\ldots \quad (4).$$

(4) being inverted gives (5),

$$\log. a = (a - 1) - \frac{(a-1)^2}{2} + \frac{(a-1)^3}{3} - \ldots\ldots \quad (5).$$

Since $a = 1\cdot000 \ldots (n-1) \text{ zeros} \ldots\ldots 1$

$$\therefore \quad \log. a = \cdot 000 \ldots (n-1) \text{ zeros} \ldots\ldots 1 = (a-1),$$

as the remaining part of (5) after $(a-1)$, has no influence within the proposed degree of accuracy.

For the purpose of illustration, let $a^x = X$, then,

$$X = 1\cdot34985882 = \downarrow 3,1,4,1,2,1,1,3, = \downarrow \overset{8}{\overline{30000000}},$$

which being compared with (3), gives $x = 30000000$,

$$n = 8, \ a = 1\cdot00000001, \ \log. a = \cdot00000001.$$

K	L
10000000	$\ldots\ldots\ldots = 1$
3000000	$\ldots\ldots\ldots = \frac{x}{1} \log. a = B$
450000	$\ldots\ldots\ldots = \frac{x-1}{2} B \log. a = \frac{x^2}{1.2} (\log. a)^2 = C$
45000	$\ldots\ldots\ldots = \frac{x-2}{3} C \log. a = \frac{x^3}{1.2.3} (\log. a)^3 = D$
3375	$\ldots\ldots\ldots = \frac{x-3}{4} D \log. a = \frac{x^4}{1.2.3.4} (\log. a)^4 = E$
203	$\ldots\ldots\ldots = \frac{x-4}{5} E \log. a = \frac{x^5}{1.2.3.4.5} (\log. a)^5 = F$
10	$\ldots\ldots\ldots = \frac{x-5}{6} F \log. a - \frac{x^6}{1.2.3.4.5.6} (\log. a)^6 = G$
(6). 13498588	

$\frac{x-6}{7} G \log. a$ will not increase the period K a unit, the result would fall under L; the values of $C, D, E, \ldots$ under K, are not affected by putting x for $(x-1)$, or for $(x-2)$, &c. Take the term E, for example:

$x - 3 =$ 29999997 Mult.
$D =$ 45000 by

4) 13499 99865000

3374 99966250 . Mult.
log. a ·000 00001 by

$\frac{x-3}{4} D \log. a = 3374{\cdot}99966250 = 3375.$

$x =$ 300 00000 Mult.
$D =$ 45000 by

4) 13500 00000000

3375 00000000 . Mult.
log. $a =$ ·00 000001 by

$\frac{x}{4} D \log. a = 3375{\cdot}00000000 .$

Hence, the result E, within the limits of the required range of accuracy, is not affected by putting $x - 3$ for x, and it is evident that the range of accuracy may be extended to any given limit.

1|0|0|0|0|0|0|0|0 .
|3|0|0|0|0|0|0|0
|3|0|0|0|0|0|0
|1|0|0|0|0|0

1 3|3 1|0 0|0 0|0 .
|1 3|3 1|0 0|0 .

1 3 4|4 3 1|0 0 0
|5 3 7|7 2 4
|8 0 7
1

1 3 4 9|6 9 5 3|2 . . .
|1 3 4 9|7 . . .

1 3 4 9 8 3 0 2 8
. . . . 2 7 0 0
1 3 5
1 3
4

(7). 1·3 4 9 8 5 8 8 1 = ↓ 3,1,4,1,2,1,1,3,

∴ (7) corresponds exactly with (6).

The equality between $\downarrow 3,1,4,1,2,1,1,3,$ and $\downarrow {}^{8}\overline{30000000},$ remains to be established. It will be shown presently, that the ultimate values of $\downarrow 1,$; $\downarrow 0,1,$; and $\downarrow 0,0,1,$ in the eight position, will be

$$\downarrow 1, \quad = \downarrow {}^{8}\overline{9531018},$$

$$\downarrow 0,1, \quad = \downarrow {}^{8}\overline{995033},$$

$$\downarrow 0,0,1, = \downarrow {}^{8}\overline{,99950},$$

$$\begin{array}{lcr} 3 \times 9531018 & = & 28593054 \\ 1 \times 995033 & = & 995033 \\ 4 \times 99950 & = & 399800 \\ \text{and} & & 1,2,1,1,3, \\ \hline & & 30000000. \end{array}$$

$$\therefore \downarrow 3,1,4,1,2,1,1,3, = \downarrow {}^{8}\overline{30000000},$$

and the connexion shown to exist generally is established in this particular case.

ULTIMATE VALUES

of $\downarrow$ **1,** $\downarrow$ **0,1,** $\downarrow$ **0,0,1,** *&c. and of* 2, 3, 4, *&c. in the eight position.*

Referring to the equalities (page 42), and the method of calculation employed (pages 52 and 53), the succeeding deductions are readily drawn.

$\downarrow$**0,0,0,1,**=9999·54 (*d*).

Then, $\downarrow$**0,0,0,9,** = (*d*) × 9 =89995·86
and $\downarrow$**0,0,0,0,9,9,5,4,5,7,** = 9954·57

∴ $\downarrow$**0,0,1,** =$\downarrow$**0,0,0,9,9,9,5,4,5,7,**=99950·43 (*c*).

Then, $\downarrow$**0,0,9,** = (*c*) × 9 =899550·
and $\downarrow$**0,0,0,9,** = (*d*) × 9 = 89995·86
and $\downarrow$**0,0,0,0,5,4,8,7,3,1,**= 5487·31

$\downarrow$**0,1,** =$\downarrow$**0,0,9,9,5,4,8,7,3,1,**=995033·17 (*b*).

Then, $\downarrow$**0,9,** =(*b*) ×9=8955297
and $\downarrow$**0,0,5,** =(*c*) ×5= 499752
and $\downarrow$**0,0,0,7,**=(*d*) ×7= 69996
and $\downarrow$**0,0,0,0,5,9,7,3,** = 5973

∴ $\downarrow$**1,**=$\downarrow$**0,9,5,7,5,9,7,3,** =9531018 (*a*).

Therefore the ultimate values of $\downarrow$**1,** $\downarrow$**0,1,** $\downarrow$**0,0,1,** and $\downarrow$**0,0,0,1,** in the eight position becomes known, and are respectively 9531018 (*a*), 995033 (*b*), 99950 (*c*), and 10000 (*d*.) Ultimate values of $\downarrow$**1,** $\downarrow$**0,1,** &c. in any other position may be found in a similar manner. As multiples of these ultimate values of $\downarrow$**1,** $\downarrow$**0,1,** $\downarrow$**0,0,1,** &c. in the eight position may be found useful, they are here appended.

	$\downarrow$**1,** (*a*).	$\downarrow$**0,1,** (*b*).	$\downarrow$**0,0,1,** (*c*).	$\downarrow$**0,0,0,1,** (*d*).
1	9531018	995033	99950	10000
2	19062036	1990066	199900	20000
3	28593054	2985099	299850	29999
4	38124072	3980132	399800	39998
5	47655090	4975165	499750	49998
6	57186108	5970198	599702	59997
7	66717126	6965231	699652	69997
8	76248144	7960264	799602	79996
9	85779162	8955297	899552	89996

It will be found, on referring to page 54, that

$$2^{\cdot} = \downarrow 7,2,6,0,7,8,2,6,$$

Then, $\downarrow 7$,	=	66717126
2,	=	1990066
6,	=	599700
and		7826
The ultimate value of 2, in the eight position	=	69314718

Again, $3^{\cdot} = \downarrow 11,5,0,4,4,8,6,8,$

Then, $\downarrow 10$,	=	95310180
$\downarrow 1$,	=	9531018
5,	=	4975165
0,4,	=	39998
and		4868
The ultimate value of 3, in the eight position	=	109861229

In a similar manner, the ultimate values of 4, 5, 6, &c. in the eight, or in any other position, may be found and registered for use.

$$2^{\cdot} = \downarrow \overset{8}{\overline{69314718}}, \qquad 7^{\cdot} = \downarrow \overset{8}{\overline{194591016}},$$

$$3^{\cdot} = \downarrow \overset{8}{\overline{109861229}}, \qquad 8^{\cdot} = \downarrow \overset{8}{\overline{207944155}},$$

$$4^{\cdot} = \downarrow \overset{8}{\overline{138629437}}, \qquad 9^{\cdot} = \downarrow \overset{8}{\overline{219722459}},$$

$$5^{\cdot} = \downarrow \overset{8}{\overline{160943792}}, \qquad 10^{\cdot} = \downarrow \overset{8}{\overline{230258510}},$$

$$6^{\cdot} = \downarrow \overset{8}{\overline{179175948}}, \qquad 11^{\cdot} = \downarrow \overset{8}{\overline{239789528}},$$

These ultimate values will often be found useful; for example, let it be required to show that

$$\log. \pi = 1{\cdot}6\tfrac{5}{8} + \log. \tfrac{3}{5},$$

within the limits of the eight position

$$\frac{\pi}{6} = {\cdot}5235987755$$

$$\therefore \quad \frac{10\pi}{6} = \frac{5\pi}{3} = 5 \downarrow 0,4,6,3,1,9,2,9,$$

Then taking the ultimate values of these quantities,

$$\begin{array}{rr} & 160943792 = 5. \\ \downarrow 0,4, \quad = & 3980132 \\ 6, = & 599702 \\ \text{and} & 31929 \\ \hline & 165555555 \end{array}$$

$\therefore \quad \dfrac{5\pi}{3}$ reduced to the eight position becomes $\downarrow \overset{8}{\overline{165555555}}$,

$$\epsilon = \downarrow 10,4,7,1,0,0,3,8, \text{ (see page 123).}$$

$$\begin{array}{rr} \text{Then } \downarrow 10, \quad = & 95310180 \\ 4, \quad = & 3980132 \\ 7, \quad = & 699652 \\ \text{and,} & 10038 \\ \hline & 100000002 \end{array}$$

$$\therefore \quad \frac{165555555}{100000000} = 1{\cdot}6\tfrac{5}{8}$$

$$\therefore \quad \log. \frac{5\pi}{3} = 1{\cdot}6\tfrac{5}{8}$$

$$\text{or } \log. \pi + \log. 5 - \log. 3 = 1{\cdot}6\tfrac{5}{8}.$$

$$\therefore \quad \log. \pi = 1{\cdot}6\tfrac{5}{8} + \log. \tfrac{3}{5},$$

a result easily verified to be correct as far as the eight position.

$$
\begin{array}{rl}
 & 1{\cdot}6555555 \\
\text{Log. } 3 = & \underline{1{\cdot}0986123} \\
 & 2{\cdot}7541678 \\
\text{log. } 5 = & \underline{1{\cdot}6094379} \\
 & 1{\cdot}1447299 = \text{Hyp. log. } \pi.
\end{array}
$$

Magnitudes may be presented under the form

$$2^r\{\ldots w_3, w_2, w_1, \downarrow u_1, u_2, u_3, \ldots\ldots\},$$

in which operative figures stand on the right and left of the sign $\downarrow$, 2^r has a common arithmetical interpretation; but such developments are designedly omitted in the present work. However, to illustrate this matter it is easily shown that

161942·257612 may be represented by

$\{0,5, \downarrow 0,5,5,2,1,2,7,5,$; 30027836·8 by

$2\{0,2,3, \downarrow 1,0,5,2,5,3,6,1,$ and

5341·18272 by $2^2\{0,3, \downarrow 0,0,3,2,2,3,7,3,$

NOTES

TO THE

INTRODUCTORY EXAMPLES.

NOTES TO THE INTRODUCTORY EXAMPLES.

OPERATIONS OMITTED IN PASSING FROM STEP TO STEP IN THE INTRODUCTORY EXAMPLES.

Example I.

$2\,)\,2092118{\cdot}5 = 10^6 \times 2 \downarrow$ **0,4,5,2,3,1,2,0,**

104605925

(diff.)

10|00|00|00|00
|40|00|00|00
|60|00|00
|40|00
|10

104|060|401
|520|302
1|041
1

.1045|81745 . . .
|20916 . . .
1 . . .

10460|2662

3263
3138

125
105

20
20

$10^6 = 1381620486$
$2 = 69318201$
$\downarrow 0,4, = 3980332$
$5 = 499775$
and 23120

1455441914

$\therefore \downarrow$ **1455441914,** in the eight position, $= 2092118{\cdot}5$.

$7)\,{}^{1}78539{\cdot}816 = 10^4 \times 7 \downarrow 1{,}1{,}9{,}8{,}5{,}4{,}4{,}8{,}$

```
  ┌─ 1 1 2 1 9 9 7 3.7
  │   ─────────────────
  │   1|0|0|0|0|0|0|0|0
  │    |1|0|0|0|0|0|0|0
  │   ─────────────────
  │   1|1|0|0|0|0|0|0.
  │    | |1|1|0|0|0|0.
  │   ─────────────────
diff.  1 1 1|1 0 0|0 0 0
            |9 9 9|9 0 0
                4|0 0 0
                      9
      ─────────────────
      1 1 2 1 0 3 9 0 9 ...
              8 9 6 8 3 ...
                    3 2 ...
  │   ─────────────────
  └─  1 1 2 1 9 3 6 2 4
              ═══════
              6 1 1 3
              5 6 1 0
              ───────
                5 0 3
                4 4 9
                ─────
                  5 4
                  4 5
                  ───
                    9
                    9
                   ──
```

$\downarrow 1,$	=	9531497
1,	=	995083
9,	=	899595
and,		85448
		11511623
7	=	194600794
10^4	=	921080324
		1127192741

∴ In the eight position, 78539·816 is represented by $\downarrow \overline{1127192741,}$

Examples II. and III.

In Example III. it was stated that

$1{\cdot}250000000 = \Downarrow 2{,}3{,}2{,}6{,}7{,}3{,}2{,}3{,} = \downarrow \overline{22315476,}$.

```
1|0|0|0|0|0|0|0|0 0
 |2|0|0|0|0|0|0|0 0
   1|0|0|0|0|0|0 0 0
────────────────────
1 2 1 0 0 0 0 0 0 0
```

```
12|10|00|00|00
  |36|30|00|00
     |36|30|00
        |12|10
-----------------
124|666|421|0 ..
   |249|332|8 ..
       |124|7 ..
-----------------
1249|1587|85 ..
    |7494|95 ..
        1|87 ..
-----------------
12499|08467
     |8|7494 ..
       |3|750 ....
         |2|50 ......
           |37 .......
-----------------
124999998
```

The following equations of equality reduced to the eight position are established in the early part of the work.

$$\downarrow 1, \quad = \downarrow 0,10,\ \bar{4},\ \bar{1},\ \bar{9},\bar{5},\bar{1},\bar{3}, = \downarrow \overline{9531497,}|$$

$$\downarrow 0,1, \quad = \downarrow 0,\ 0,10,\ 0,\ \bar{4},\bar{4},\bar{6},\bar{7}, = \downarrow \overline{995083,}|$$

$$\downarrow 0,0,1, \quad = \downarrow 0,\ 0,\ 0,10,\ 0,0,\bar{4},\bar{5}, = \downarrow \overline{99955,}|$$

$$\downarrow 0,0,0,1, \quad = \downarrow 0,\ 0,\ 0,\ 0,10,0,0,0, = \downarrow \overline{10000,}|$$

&c. = &c. = &c.

$$\downarrow 0,0,0,10,0,0,\bar{4},\bar{5}, = 100000 - 45 = \overline{99955,}|$$

```
ten times 99955 = 999550
                    4467 minus
                  -------
                  995083,|
```

```
        ten times 995083 = 9950830
minus four times 99955 =    399820
                          -------
                          9551010
              minus         19513
                          -------
                          9531497,|.
```

2 times 9531497 = 19062994
3 „ 995083 = 2985249
2 „ 99955 = 199910
67323

∴ ↓2,3,2,6,7,3,2,3, = ↓$\overline{22315476,}|$

The values of 2, 3, 4, &c. reduced to the eight or any other position, involving whole numbers only, are easily found as follows :—

2· = ↓7, 2,6,0,7,8,2,6, = ↓$\overline{69318201,}|$

3· = ↓1,1,5,0,4,4,8,6,8, = ↓$\overline{109866750,}|$

4· = ↓14,5,2,2,0,1,1,9, = ↓$\overline{138636402,}|$

5· = ↓16,8,4,8,7,4,4,3, = ↓$\overline{160951879,}|$

6· = ↓18,7,6,5,2,6,9,4, = ↓$\overline{179184951,}|$

7· = ↓20,3,9,8,6,0,1,0, = ↓$\overline{194600794,}|$

8· = ↓21,7,8,2,7,9,4,6, = ↓$\overline{207954604,}|$

9· = ↓23,0,5,0,9,2,9,4, = ↓$\overline{219733500,}|$

10· = ↓24,1,5,1,9,2,9,5, = ↓$\overline{230270081,}|$

By a simple problem in the early part of the work, it is easily shown that ·2 = ↓7,2,6,0,7,8,2,6, which is easily reduced to ↓$\overline{69318201,}|$

$2^2 = 4\cdot$ and $2^3 = 8\cdot$

69318201 × 2 = 138636402
69318201 × 3 = 207954604
8 × 1·25 = 10·

But it has been just shown that 1·25 = ↓$\overline{22315476,}|$

∴ 207954604 + 22315476 = 230270080.

"Again, 10 ÷ 9 = 1·11111111 = ↓1,1,0,1,0,0,0,1, = ↓ 10536581,

```
      ↓1,   = 9531497
      ↓0,1, =  995083
      and       10001
              ---------
             10536581 take
 for 10·    230270081 from
            ---------
 for  9·    219733500
 for  3·    109866750 half
            ---------
```

```
 for 2·    69318201
 for 3·   109866750
          ---------
          179184951 for 6·
```

```
 for 10·  230270080
 for  2·   69318201
          ---------
          160951879 for 5·
```

All the numbers are now established except the number for 7.

```
 7/6 = ┌─1·1666666667 = ↓1,5,9,0,9,3,3,5,
       │ ============
       │ 1 1|0 0|0 0|00|0 0
       │    |5 5|0 0|00|0 0
       │        1|1 0|00|0 0
  diff.│            1|10|0 0
       │                |5 5
       │ ------------------
       │ 1 1 5|6 1 1|10 5|5 . .
       │     1|0 4 0|49 9|9 . .
       │         4 1|62 0|9 . .
       │                9|7 . .
       │ ------------------
       └─1 1 6 6 5|5 7 7 7 1
           . . . .
             10 8896
             10 4989
             -------
               3907
```

```
 ↓1,      =    9531497
   0,5,   =    4975415
   0,0,9, =     899595
   and            9335
              ---------
              15415842
        6· =  179184951
              ---------
              194600793
```

```
3907
3500
----
 407
 350
----
  57
  58
----
```

$$\therefore\ 7 \times \downarrow\overline{194600793,}| = \downarrow 20,3,9,8,6,0,1,0,$$

In example 2 it is stated that

$$\epsilon = 2{\cdot}718281828 = \downarrow\overline{100005025,}|$$

```
e/2 = 1·3591 40914 = ↓3,2,1,0,2,2,1,2,
      ==========
      1 3|3 1|0 0|00|0 0
         |2 6|6 2|00|0 0
 diff.   |    |1 3|31|0 0
      ------------------
      1 3 5|7 7 5|31 0|0 . .
           |1 3 5|77 5|3 . .
      ------------------
      1 3 5 9 1||1 0853
          . . . . 30061
                  27182
                  -----
                   2879
                   2718
                   ----
                    161
                    136
                    ---
                     25
                     27
                     --
```

```
↓3       =  28594491
 0,2,    =   1990166
 0,0,1,  =     99955
and             2212
            --------
            30686824
      2· =  69318201
            --------
           100005025
```

$$\therefore\ \epsilon = \downarrow 3,2,1,0,2,2,1,2, = \downarrow\overline{100005025,}|$$

In the second example it is also stated that

$$\pi = 3{\cdot}141592654 = \downarrow\overline{114478742,}|.$$

$\frac{\pi}{3}$ = 1·0471975 51 = ↓0,4,6,3,1,9,2,9,

diff.

1 04|06 0|40 1|0 . .
|62 4|36 2|4 . .
1|56 0|9 . .
2|1 . .

1 04 6|8 6 32|64 . .
|3 1 40|5 9 . .
|3 1 . .

1 04 7 1|7 73 5 4
. . . .|2 01 9 7
1 04 7 2

97 2 5
94 2 4

3 01
2 09

9 2
9 4

↓0,4, = 3980332
6, = 599730
and 31929

4611991
3· = 109866750

114478741

∴ π = ↓114478741, = ↓12,0,1,0,0,8,2,3,

Example IV.

It was assumed that 497 × 23 = 11431, because

23) 114478742
92

224 (467
207

177
161

G G

Example V.

10596085·33 = ↓0,5,8̇,1,5,1,8,8,

10000 0000 00
5000 0000
1000 000
1 0000
50

105 101 005 0 . .
840 808 0 . .
2 942 8 . .
5 9 . .

10594476 17 . .
105945 . .

10595 5 3562
. . . . 5 4971
5 2978

1993
1060

933
848

85
85

↓0,5, = 4975415
0,0,8, = 799640
and 15188
for 9· 219733500

225523733

diff.

98 × 23

2255 2 3 7430 = ↓0,0,0,5,5,$\bar{1}$,$\bar{1}$,$\bar{2}$,

2254 0 0 00 00 . .
1 1 2 70 00 . .
2 25 . .

2255 1 2 72 25
1 1 27 56
2

2255 2 3 99 83
. . 25 53 .
22 55

298

diff.

$$\begin{array}{r} 298 \\ 226 \\ \hline 72 \\ 68 \\ \hline \end{array}$$

$$\downarrow 0,0\bar{1},4,\bar{2},\bar{5},\bar{1},\overline{11}, = \downarrow 0,0,\bar{1},4,\bar{2},\bar{5},\bar{2},\bar{1},$$

$$= \downarrow 0,0,\bar{1},3,7,4,7,9,$$

Because $\downarrow 0,0,0,4,0,0,0,0, = \downarrow \overline{40000,}|$

and $\downarrow 0,0,0,0,2,5,2,1, = \downarrow \overline{2521,}|$

Example VI.

$$\pi : 180 \times 60 \times 60 :: \text{length} : \text{seconds} = \frac{180 \times 60 \times 60 \times \text{length}}{\pi};$$

but $200000\,\pi \downarrow 0,3,1,0,0,\bar{7},0,\bar{5}, = 180 \times 60 \times 60,$

$$\therefore \text{ seconds} = \text{length} \times 200000 \downarrow 0,3,1,0,0,\bar{7},0,\bar{5},$$

Example VII.

The length of an arc of 1″ = ·000004848136811 ;

·4848136811 ÷ ·48 = ·10100285 = $\downarrow 0,1,0,0,2,8,2,2,$

To multiply a given number, as 3457 by 48 :—

$$\begin{array}{rl} 2\,)\,345700 & 100 \text{ times} \\ \hline 172850 & 50 \text{ times} \\ 6914 & \text{twice} \\ \hline 165936 & 48 \text{ times.} \end{array}$$

Hence the truth of these rules is established.

Example VIII.

It is evident that $\downarrow \overline{16265543,}|$ which is 7 times $\downarrow \overline{2323649,}|$ may be written $\downarrow$ **1,6,7,6,3,8,6,3,** because

$$
\begin{array}{lrl}
\text{Constant } (A), & 9531497\,) & 16265543 \\
 & & \underline{9531497} \; (\downarrow 1, \\
\text{Constant } (B), & 995083\,) & 6734046 \\
 & & \underline{5970498} \; (\downarrow 0,6, \\
\text{Constant } (C), & 99955\,) & \;\;763548 \\
 & & \;\;\underline{699685} \; (\downarrow 0,0,7, \\
 & & \;\;\;63863 = \downarrow 0,0,0,6,3,8,6,3,
\end{array}
$$

SECOND SOLUTION.

8. *Given the obliquity of the ecliptic* $= 23^\circ\ 27'\ 25''\cdot42$ $= 84445''\cdot42$, *find the natural sine and log. sine of this angle.*

$$
\begin{array}{r}
\underline{84445''\cdot4200} \\
42222\ \ 7100 \\
\underline{1688\ \ 9084}
\end{array}
$$

Length of arc $=\cdot40533\ \ 8016 \downarrow 0,1,0,0,2,8,2,2, = .409402949.$

$\cdot409402949 = \cdot4 \downarrow 0,2,3,3,3,6,1,8, = \qquad \cdot4 \downarrow \overline{2323649,}|$

cube $= \quad \cdot064 \downarrow \overline{6970947,}|$

$= \quad \cdot064 \downarrow 0,7,0,0,5,3,6,6,$

fifth power $= \quad \cdot01024 \downarrow \overline{11618245,}|$

$= \quad \cdot01024 \downarrow 1,2,0,9,6,5,8,2,$

seventh position $= \cdot0016384 \downarrow \overline{16265543,}|$

$= \cdot0016384 \downarrow 1,6,7,6,3,8,6,3,$

$\div\ 6 \quad = \cdot010666667$

$\div\ 120 \quad = \cdot000085333$

$\div\ 5040 = \cdot000000325$

	·409402949	+
$10666667 \downarrow 0,7,0,0,5,3,6,6$ =	11436725	−
	397966224	
$85333 \downarrow 1,2,0,9,6$, &c. =	95845	+
	398062069	
$325 \downarrow 1,6,7,6$, &c. =	383	
Natural sine of 23° 27′ 25″·42 =	·398061686	

3) 3·98061686
1·32687229 = $\downarrow 2,9,2,6,5,2,2,1, = \downarrow \overline{28283872,}|$
(Example 3,) 3· = $\downarrow \overline{109866750,}|$
∴ 3·98061686 = $\overline{138150622,}|$

Then 138150622 divided by the constant 230270081 gives ·59995038.

∴ Log. sin 23° 27′ 25″·42 = 9·59995038

2 = 69318201
109866750
179184951 = 2.3.
138636402
317821353 = 2.3.4.
160951879
478773232 = 2.3.4.5.
179184951
657958183 = 2.3.4.5.6.
194600795
852558978 = 2.3.4.5.6.7.
207954604
1060513582 = 2.3.4.5.6.7.8.
219733500
1280247082 = 2.3.4.5.6.7.8.9.
230270081
1510517163

$$
\begin{array}{rl}
1510517163 & = 2.3.4.5.6.7.8.9.10. \\
239801578 & \\
\hline
1750318741 & = 2.3.4.5.6.7.8.9.10.11. \\
248503152 & \\
\hline
1998821893 & = 2.3.4.5.6.7.8.9.10.11.12.
\end{array}
$$

Which may be continued at pleasure by simple addition.

Example IX.

The following simple additions and subtractions may be made before commencing to operate :

$$
\begin{array}{rr}
 & 69318201 \\
 & 138636402 \\
\hline
2.4 = & 207954603 \\
 & 179184951 \\
\hline
2.4.6 = & 387139554 \\
 & 207954604 \\
\hline
2.4.6.8 = & 595094158 \\
 & 230270081 \\
\hline
2.4.6.8.10 = & 825364239 \\
 & 248503152 \\
\hline
2.4.6.8.10.12 = & 1073867391
\end{array}
\qquad
\begin{array}{rr}
 & 109866750 \\
 & 160951879 \\
\hline
3.5 = & 270818629 \\
 & 194600795 \\
\hline
3.5.7 = & 465419424 \\
 & 219733500 \\
\hline
3.5.7.9 = & 685152924 \\
 & 239801578 \\
\hline
3.5.7.9.11 = & 924954502
\end{array}
$$

$$\frac{1}{2.3} = 179184951 \text{ negative}$$

$$\frac{1.3}{2.4.5} = 259039732 \text{ negative}$$

$$\frac{1.3.5}{2.4.6.7} = 310921720 \text{ negative}$$

$$\frac{1.3.5.7}{2.4.6.8.9} = 349408234 \text{ negative}$$

$$\frac{1.3.5.7.9}{2.4.6.8.10.11} = 380012893 \text{ negative}$$

Example XII.

$\cos D = \sin(13^\circ\ 45'\ 13'' + 49513'')$.

10 times length of arc $= 2{\cdot}40045818 + 2\downarrow 1,8,7,6,0,3,1,5,$
$= \downarrow 87570364,$

10^{8} .... $-\ 230270081$
$+\ 87570364$
$-\ 142699717,$ put $= x$.

x^3 .... $-\ 428099151$
$1.2.3$ .... $-\ 179184951$
$-\ 607284102$
10^8 .... $+\ 690810243$
$83526141 = 2\downarrow 1,4,6,9,6,3,8,1, = 2{\cdot}30532$
69318201
14207940
9531497
4676443
3980332
696111
599730
$9,6,3,8,1,$

$\therefore\ \dfrac{x^3}{1.2.3} = {\cdot}00230532$, true to the last figure.

x^5 ...... $-\ 713498585$
$1.2.3.4.5$ ...... $-\ 478773232$
$-\ 1192271817$
$10^5 +\ 1381620486$
$189348669 = 6\downarrow 1,0,6,3,2,4,9,1, = 6{\cdot}64182$

$\therefore\ \dfrac{x^5}{1.2.3.4.5} = {\cdot}00006642$, true to the last figure.

$$
\begin{array}{lr}
x^7 \ldots\ldots - & 998898019 \\
1.2.3.4.5.6.7 \ldots\ldots - & 852558978 \\
\hline
- & 1851456997 \\
10^9 + & 2072430729 \\
\hline
& 220973732 = 9\downarrow 0,1, \ldots\ldots
\end{array}
$$

and will only give a unit in the eight decimal place.

$$
\begin{array}{lr}
+ & \cdot 24004582 \\
- & 230532 \\
+ & 664 \\
- & 1 \\
\hline
\cos 76^\circ\ 14'\ 47'' \ldots & \cdot 23774713 \quad \sin 13^\circ\ 45'\ 13''
\end{array}
$$

$$
\begin{array}{l}
A + B = 67^\circ\ \ 1'\ 37'' \\
\ 90\ \ \ 0\ \ \ 0 \\
\hline
22^\circ\ 58'\ 23'' = 82703''\text{; arc} = \cdot 400955459
\end{array}
$$

$$4\cdot 00955459 = 4\downarrow 0,0,2,3,8,6,8,3, = \downarrow \overline{138874995,}$$

$$
\begin{array}{lr}
10 \ldots\ldots - & 230270081, \\
+ & 138874995, \\
\hline
- & 91395086, \text{ which put } = \overline{x},
\end{array}
$$

$$
\begin{array}{lr}
x^3 \ldots\ldots\ldots - & 274185258 \\
1.2.3 \ldots\ldots - & 179184951 \\
\hline
- & 453370209 \\
10^8 \ldots\ldots + & 460540162 \\
\hline
& 7169953 = \downarrow 0,7,2,0,4,4,6,2, = 1\cdot 07432862
\end{array}
$$

$$\therefore \frac{x^3}{1.2.3} = \cdot 01074329$$

$$
\begin{array}{rr}
x^5 \dots\dots - & 456975430 \\
1.2.3.4.5 \dots\dots - & 478773232 \\
\hline
- & 935748662 \\
10^5 \dots + & 1151350405 \\
\hline
 & 215601743
\end{array}
$$

$= 8 \downarrow 0,7,6,8,1,8,2,8, = 8{\cdot}63573736$

$$\therefore \frac{x^5}{1.2.3.4.5} = {\cdot}00008636$$

$$
\begin{array}{rr}
x^7 \dots\dots - & 639765602 \\
1.2.3.4.5.6.7 \dots\dots - & 852558978 \\
\hline
- & 1492324580 \\
10^7 + & 1611890567 \\
\hline
 & 119565987
\end{array}
$$

$= 3 \downarrow 1,0,1,6,7,7,8,5, = 3{\cdot}3056 \dots$

$$\therefore \frac{x^7}{1.2.3.4.5.6.7} = {\cdot}00000033$$

$$
\begin{array}{lr}
+ & {\cdot}40095546 \\
- & 1074329 \\
+ & 8636 \\
- & 33 \\
\hline
 & {\cdot}39029820 = \cos 67^\circ\ 1'\ 37''
\end{array}
$$

The next term will not give a unit in the eight decimal place.

$$
\begin{array}{lrrr}
a + b \dots & 90^\circ & 0' & 0'' \\
 & 67 & 35 & 41 \\
\hline
 & 22 & 24 & 19
\end{array}
= 80659''; \ {\cdot}391045865 \text{ length.}
$$

$\therefore\ 3{\cdot}91045865 = 3 \downarrow 2,7,4,7,7,1,7,4, = \downarrow \overline{136372319,}|$

$$
\begin{array}{rr}
10 \dots\dots - & 230270081 \\
+ & 136372319 \\
\hline
- & 93897762
\end{array}
\text{ put } = \downarrow \overline{x,}|.
$$

$$\begin{array}{rr} x^3 \ldots\ldots & -\ 281693286 \\ 1.2.3 \ldots & -\ \underline{179184951} \\ & -\ 460878237 \\ 10^3 \ldots\ldots & +\ \underline{690810243} \\ & 229932006 \end{array}$$

$$= 9 \downarrow 1,0,6,6,7,2,7,9, = 9{\cdot}96625116$$

$$\begin{array}{rr} x^5 \ldots\ldots & -\ \ 469488810 \\ 1.2.3.4.5 \ldots\ldots & -\ \ \underline{478773232} \\ & -\ \ 948262042 \\ 10^5 & +\ \underline{1151350405}. \\ & 203088363 \end{array}$$

$$= 7 \downarrow 0,8,5,2,7,1,2,9, = 7{\cdot}6200397$$

$$\begin{array}{rr} x^7 \ldots & -\ \ 657284334 \\ 1.2.3.4.5.6.7 \ldots & -\ \ \underline{852558978} \\ 10^7 \ldots\ldots & -\ 1509843312 \\ & +\ \underline{1611890567} \\ & 102047255 \end{array}$$

$$= 2 \downarrow 3,4,1,5,4,2,7,6, = 4{\cdot}775 \ldots.$$

$$\begin{array}{lr} + & 39104587 \ldots \text{arc} \\ - & 996625 \\ + & 7620 \\ & \underline{28} \\ & {\cdot}38115554 \ \cos 67^\circ\ 35'\ 41''. \end{array}$$

$B = 20^\circ\ 25'\ 10'' = 73510''$, length of arc $= {\cdot}35638656$

$$= \tfrac{1}{10} \downarrow \overline{127090963,}$$

$$\cos x = 1 - \frac{x^2}{1.2} + \frac{x^4}{1.2.3.4} - \frac{x^6}{1.2.3.4.5.6} + \ldots.$$

$$\begin{array}{r}
-\ 230270081 \\
+\ 127090963 \\
\hline
-\ 103179118 \text{ put } = \downarrow \overline{x,}\,.
\end{array}$$

$$\begin{array}{rr}
x^2 \ldots\ldots\ldots & -\ 206358236 \\
1.2 \ldots\ldots & -\ \ 69318201 \\
\hline
 & -\ 275676437 \\
10^2 \ldots\ldots & +\ 460540162 \\
\hline
 & 184863725
\end{array}$$

$= 6 \downarrow 0,5,7,0,3,6,7,4, = 6{\cdot}35056866$

$$\begin{array}{rr}
x^4 \ldots\ldots & -\ 412716472 \\
1.2.3.4 \ldots\ldots & -\ 317821353 \\
\hline
 & -\ 730537825 \\
10^4 \ldots\ldots & +\ 921080324 \\
\hline
 & 190542499
\end{array}$$

$= 6 \downarrow 1,1,8,3,1,3,2,8, = 6{\cdot}721619 \ldots\ldots$

$$\begin{array}{rr}
x^6 \ldots\ldots\ldots & -\ \ 619074708 \\
1.2.3.4.5.6 \ldots\ldots & -\ \ 657958183 \\
\hline
 & -\ 1277032891 \\
10^6 \ldots\ldots & +\ 1381620486 \\
\hline
 & 104587595
\end{array}$$

$= 2 \downarrow 3,6,7,0,4,7,3, = 2{\cdot}8457 \ldots\ldots$

$$\begin{array}{rl}
1{\cdot}00000000 & + \\
{\cdot}06350568 & - \\
{\cdot}00067216 & + \\
{\cdot}00000285 & - \\
\hline
{\cdot}93716363 & \cos 20^\circ\ 25'\ 10''
\end{array}$$

$b = 20^\circ\ 22'\ 54'' = 73374''.$

2) 73374″·00

36687 00
1467 48

·35219 52 ↓0,1,0,0,2,8,2,2, = ·35572719 length of arc

32) 3557271900 / 111164747 = ↓1,1,0,5,8,2,6,4, = $\overline{105848 44,}|$

105848 44
32 = 2^5 346591005

+ 357175849
100 . . . . − 460540162

− $\overline{103364313,}|$ = ↓ $\overline{x,}|$
− 206728626 − 2·
− 413457252 − 4
− 6201858 78 − 6

x^2 . . . . . − 206728626
1.2 . . . . − 69318201

− 276046827
10^2 . . . . + 460540162

184493335
= 6↓0,5,3,3,3,1,0,4, = 6·32709138

x^4 . . . . − 413457252
1.2.3.4 . . . . . − 317821353

− 731278605
10^4 . . . . + 921080324

189801719
= 6↓1,1,0,9,0,1,8,8, = 6·672006 . . .

x^6 . . . . − 620185878
1.2.3.4.5.6 . . . . . − 657958183

− 1278144061
10^6 . . . . . + 1381620486

103476425
= 2↓3,5,5,8,8,5,4,3, = 2·8142 . . .

$$\begin{array}{r}
1{\cdot}00000000 + \\
{\cdot}06327091 - \\
{\cdot}00066720 + \\
{\cdot}00000281 - \\
\hline
{\cdot}93739348 = \cos 20^\circ\ 22'\ 54''.
\end{array}$$

$$\begin{array}{rrrl}
 & 90^\circ & 0' & 0'' \\
A = & 46 & 36 & 27 \\
\hline
 & 43 & 23 & 33 \text{ length of arc} = {\cdot}757341994
\end{array}$$

$$7{\cdot}57341994 = 7\downarrow 0,7,9,0,8,6,7,8, = \downarrow\overline{202474649,}| =$$

$$\begin{array}{rr}
 + & 202474649 \\
10\ldots\ldots - & 230270081 \\
\hline
 - & 27795432 = \downarrow\overline{x,}|
\end{array}$$

$$\begin{array}{rr}
x^3\ldots\ldots - & 83386296 \\
1.2.3\ldots\ldots - & 179184951 \\
\hline
 - & 262571247 \\
10^2\ldots\ldots + & 460540162 \\
\hline
 & 197968915
\end{array}$$

$$= 7\downarrow 0,3,3,8,3,0,0,6, = 7{\cdot}2397717$$

$$\begin{array}{rr}
x^5\ldots\ldots - & 138977160 \\
1.2.3.4.5\ldots\ldots - & 478773232 \\
\hline
 - & 617750392 \\
10^3\ldots\ldots + & 690810243 \\
\hline
 & 73059851
\end{array}$$

$$= 2\downarrow 0,3,7,5,6,7,1,6, = 2{\cdot}07624672$$

$$\begin{array}{rr}
x^7\ldots\ldots - & 194568024 \\
1.2.3.4.5.6.7\ldots\ldots - & 852558978 \\
\hline
 - & 1047127002 \\
10^5\ldots\ldots + & 1151350405 \\
\hline
 & 104223403
\end{array}$$

$$= 2\downarrow 3,6,3,4,0,3,4,8, = 2{\cdot}8353\ldots$$

x^9 ...... − 250158888
1.2.3.4.5.6.7.8.9 ...... − 1280247082

− 1530405970
10^7 ...... + 1611890567

81484597

= 2 ↓ **1,2,6,4,5,0,0,3,** = 2·258 ...

Length of arc = ·75734199 +
·07239772 −
·00207625 +
·00002835 −
·00000023 +

·68699240 = cos 46° 36′ 27″.

90° 0′ 0″
(a) 47 12 47

42 47 13 = 154033″ ·746773057 length of arc

7·46773057 = 7 ↓ **0,6,4,9,8,1,0,6,** = ↓ **201069219,**

+ 201069219
− 230270081

− 29200862 = ↓ x,

x^3 .... − 87602586
1.2.3 ...... − 179184951

− 266787537
10^2 .... + 460540162

193752625

= 6 ↓ **1,5,0,6,0,7,6,2,** = 6·94088166

x^5 ...... − 146004310
1.2.3.4.5 .... − 478773232

− 624777542
10^3 ...... + 690810243

66032701

= ↓ **6,8,8,8,3,4,1,5,** = 1·935361

$$
\begin{array}{rr}
x^7 \ldots\ldots - & 204406034 \\
1.2.3.4.5.6.7 \ldots\ldots - & 852558978 \\
\hline
- & 1056965012 \\
10^6 \ldots\ldots + & 1151350405 \\
\hline
& 94385393
\end{array}
$$

$= 2 \downarrow 2,6,0,3,3,7,0,0, = 2\cdot56974$

$$
\begin{array}{rr}
x^9 \ldots\ldots - & 262807758 \\
1.2.3.4.5.6.7.8.9 \ldots\ldots - & 1280247082 \\
\hline
- & 1543054840 \\
10^7 \ldots\ldots + & 1611890567 \\
\hline
& 68835727
\end{array}
$$

$= \downarrow 7,2,1.2,5,1,2,7, = 2\cdot09 \ldots$

$$
\begin{array}{rl}
\text{Length of arc} = & \cdot74677306 + \\
& \cdot06940882 - \\
& \cdot00193536 + \\
& \cdot00002570 - \\
& \cdot00000021 + \\
\hline
& \cdot67927411 = \cos 47^\circ\ 12'\ 37''
\end{array}
$$

Example XIII.

When the term involving x^3 was operated upon by $\downarrow 5$, the term involving x^5 had to be operated upon by $\downarrow 3,3,1,9,1,9,6,2,$ because

$9531497 = (A) \quad 995083 = (B) \quad 99955 = (C)$

$$
\begin{array}{rl}
& 9531497 \\
& 5 \\
\hline
& 47657485 \\
& 2 \\
\hline
3\,) & 95314970 \\
\hline
& 31771657 \\
& 28594491 = 3\,(A) \\
\hline
& 3177166 \\
& 2985249 = 3\,(B) \\
\hline
& 191917 \\
& 99955 = (C) \\
\hline
& 9,1,9,6,2
\end{array}
$$

∴ When ↓5, represents the cube of a number, ↓3,3,1,9,1,9,6,2, will represent the square of the same number.

Example XVI.

When the term affected by x^7 has to be operated upon by ↓7, ↓0,7, ↓0,0,7, &c. the co-efficient of x^6 must be operated upon by ↓6, ↓0,6, ↓0,0,6, &c.

When ↓0,0,3, becomes an operating figure for the seventh power, the operating figures for the third power are ↓0,0,1,2,8,5,5,9, but the number − 52 composed of two figures, is not altered by this a unit, and is therefore omitted in the operation.

In finding the consecutive numbers to the right of ↓, composing the root of an equation, it may often happen that the leading numbers of the divisor are destroyed, when the addition is performed. In such cases, it will be found convenient to transform the given equation into another equation. For example, take the equation

$$x^3 - 37{\cdot}13394977\,x^2 + 459{\cdot}6430761\,x = 1896{\cdot}482019\ (R).$$

and it will be found, that this equation may be verified by putting $x = 12{\cdot}35843041$, $x = 12{\cdot}3432103$, $x = 12{\cdot}39455496$, or $x = 12{\cdot}3809644$. Yet there is no guarantee that any one of these numbers is a root of the given equation. But there is no room for doubt when the given equation is verified by substituting

↓6,6,3,6,9,6,24,15, for x^3; ↓4,4,2,4,6,4,16,10, for x^2;

and ↓2,2,1,2,3,2, 8, 5, for x; Because

↓6,6,3,6,9,6,24,15, is evidently the cube of ↓2,2,1,2,3,2,8,5,

and ↓4,4,2,4,6,4,16,10, is evidently the square of ↓2,2,1,2,3,2,8,5,

If 10 be substituted for x in the given equation, then

+ 3000	3 times	+ 1000·00	
− 7426	twice	− 3713·39	
+ 4596	once	+ 4596·43	
* 170)		1883·04	take
		1896·48	from (R)
		13·44	

* The leading figure of the divisor being destroyed, it is convenient to transform the given equation into another in which the leading figure of the divisor is not cancelled in the addition. Let the roots of the given equation be diminished by ↓ **2,2,**

$$
\begin{array}{rl}
 & -3{\cdot}713394977 \\
\downarrow 2,2, = & +1{\cdot}234321 \\ \hline
 & -2{\cdot}479073977\ (p). \\
\downarrow 2,2, = & +1{\cdot}234321 \\ \hline
 & +1{\cdot}244752977\ (r). \\
\downarrow 2,2, = & +1{\cdot}234321 \\ \hline\hline
 & -\ {\cdot}010431977
\end{array}
\qquad
\begin{array}{rl}
 & +4{\cdot}59643076\dot{1} \\
(p)\downarrow 2,2, = & -3{\cdot}05997307036461 7 \\ \hline
 & +1{\cdot}536457690635383\ (q). \\
(r)\downarrow 2,2, = & -1{\cdot}536424739323617 \\ \hline\hline
 & +\ {\cdot}000032951311766
\end{array}
$$

$$
\begin{array}{rl}
 & -\ 1{\cdot}896482019 \\
(q)\downarrow 2,2, = & +\ 1{\cdot}896481993162757 \\ \hline\hline
 & {\cdot}000000025837243
\end{array}
$$

∴ $x^3 - 10{\cdot}431977\,x^2 + 32{\cdot}9513117\,x = 25{\cdot}837243$ is the transformed equation when its roots are multiplied by 1000. This last equation is easily operated upon, and roots found that may be relied upon. Further observations on the introductory examples are deemed unnecessary. The following examples illustrate a new method to find the sine, cosine, &c. of an arc without the use of tables, employment of impossible quantities, or the powers of the arc.

Let θ = arc of 20° = ·349065851 = ·3 ↓ **1,5,6,4,1,9,3,** then

+	100000000	put	= A
+	34906585	= A ÷ 1 × ·3 ↓1,5,6, . . .	= B
−	6092350	= B ÷ 2 × ·3 ↓1,5,6, . . .	= C
−	708877	= C ÷ 3 × ·3 ↓1,5,6, . . .	= D
+	61862	= D ÷ 4 × ·3 ↓1,5,6, . . .	= E
+	4319	= E ÷ 5 × ·3 ↓1,5,6, . . .	= F
−	252	= F ÷ 6 × ·3 ↓1,5,6, . . .	= G
−	13	= G ÷ 7 × ·3 ↓1,5,6, . . .	= H

Hyp. log. 1·41774258 = ·34906585

$$\log (A + B + C + D + E + \ldots) = \theta$$
$$\cos \theta = A - C + E - G$$
$$\sin \theta = B - D + F - H$$

1·00000000 + = A	·34906585 + = B
6092350 − = C	708877 − = D
61862 + = E	4319 + = F
252 − = G	13 − = H
cos θ = ·93969260	sin θ = ·34202014

The consecutive terms A, B, C, &c. are easily found, take for example, (F), the work unabridged will stand thus:

```
5 ) 61 86·2  (E).
    ---------
    12 37·2
          3
    ---------
    37 1 2
     37 1
    ---------
    40|8 3
     2|0 4
        4
    ---------
    42 9|1 . .
       2|6 . .
        |2 . .
    ---------
    43 1 9 = F.
```

The operating numbers employed being $\downarrow$1,5,6,4, the remaining numbers are not required.

Let θ = an arc of 23° 27′ 25″·42 = ·409402949

·409402949 = ·4 $\downarrow$ 0,2,3,3,3,6,1,8,

+	100000000	put	= A
+	40940295	= A ÷ 1 × ·4 $\downarrow$ 0,2,3, . . .	= B
−	8380537	= B ÷ 2 × ·4 $\downarrow$ 0,2,3, . . .	= C
−	1143672	= C ÷ 3 × ·4 $\downarrow$ 0,2,3, . . .	= D
+	117054	= D ÷ 4 × ·4 $\downarrow$ 0,2,3, . . .	= E
+	9584	= E ÷ 5 × ·4 $\downarrow$ 0,2,3, . . .	= F
−	654	= F ÷ 6 × ·4 $\downarrow$ 0,2,3, . . .	= G
−	38	= G ÷ 7 × ·4 $\downarrow$ 0,2,3, . . .	= H
+	2	= H ÷ 8 × ·4 $\downarrow$ 0,2,3, . . .	= I

Hyp. log. of 1·50591836 = ·409402949 = θ

1·00000000 + = A	·40940295 + = B
8380537 − = C	1143672 − = D
117054 + = E	9584 + = F
654 − = G	38 − = H
2 + = I	
cos θ = ·91735865	sin θ = ·39806169

Let θ = arc of 5° 27′ 39″·14 = ·09531018 = ·09 $\downarrow$ 0,5,7,5,8,

+	10000000	Put	= A
+	0953102	= A ÷ 1 × ·09 $\downarrow$ 0,5,7, . . .	= B
−	45420	= B ÷ 2 × ·09 $\downarrow$ 0,5,7, . . .	= C
−	1443	= C ÷ 3 × ·09 $\downarrow$ 0,5,7, . . .	= D
+	34	= D ÷ 4 × ·09 $\downarrow$ 0,5,7, . . .	= E
+	1	= E ÷ 5 × ·09 $\downarrow$ 0,5,7, . . .	= F

Hyp. log. 1·1000000 = ·09531018

$$\text{Log. } (A + B + C + \ldots) = \theta.$$

$$\cos\theta = A - C + E.$$

$$\sin\theta = B - D + F.$$

```
         1·0000000 + = A            ·0953102 + = B
             45420 − = C                1443 − = D
                34 + = E                   1 + = F
        ___________                 ___________
cos θ = .9954614              sin θ = ·0951660
```

The quantities C, D, and E, have only to be determined, for A and B are given, and it is easily observed that F = 1. The following unabridged work shows that C, D, and E, are found in a few minutes.

```
 4765·51            454·20           4) 14·43
       9                 3              ______
 _______            ______               3·61
 42|89|0 .          13|63                   9
  2|14|5 .            |68               ______
   | 4|3 .            | 1  .             32| . .
 _______            ______                2| . .
 450|78             143|2 . .           ______
 ·· 3|15              1|0 . .            34 = I
      23               |1 . .
      4 .           ______
 _______            1443 = D
 45420 = C
```

Given θ = ·225154191074 *an arc of* 12° 54′ 1″·3855975, *to find* sin θ *and* cos θ *to twelve places of decimals.*

$$\theta = \cdot 2 \downarrow 1,2,3,2,5,8,7,6,2,3,5,$$

+	1000000000000	=	= A
+	.225154191074	= A ÷ 1 × ·2↓1,2,3, . . .	= B
−	25347204876	= B ÷ 2 × ·2↓1,2,3, . . .	= C
−	1902443160	= C ÷ 3 × ·2↓1,2,3, . . .	= D
+	107085855	= D ÷ 4 × ·2↓1,2,3, . . .	= E
+	4822150	= E ÷ 5 × ·2↓1,2,3, . . .	= F
−	180953	= F ÷ 6 × ·2↓1,2,3, . . .	= G
−	5820	= G ÷ 7 × ·2↓1,2,3, . . .	= H
+	164	= H ÷ 8 × ·2↓1,2,3, . . .	= I
+	4	= I ÷ 9 × ·2↓1,2,3, . . .	= J

log. 1·252515934056 = θ.

$$\text{Log.}\ (A + B + C + \ldots\ldots) = \theta.$$

$$A - C + E - G + I = \cos\theta.$$
$$B - D + F - H + J = \sin\theta.$$

1·000000000000	+ = A	·225154191074	+ = B
25347204876	− = C	1902443160	− = D
1070858855	+ = E	4822150	+ = F
180953	− = G	5820	− = H
164	+ = I	4	+ = J
·974759700190	= cos θ.	·223256564248	= sin θ.

The operative figures ↓**1,2,3,2,5**, ... fall out of use, one by one, as the results C, D, E, &c. decrease; for example, in finding H, only ↓ **1,2,3,2,** are required.

```
G = 18095·3
         .2
   ─────────
7) 36191 .
   ─────────
    5|1|7|0
     |5|1|7
    ───────
    5 6|8 7| . .
        1|1 4| . .
           1| . .
    ───────
    5 8 0|2 . .
        1|7 . .
    ───────
    5 8 1 9| . . . .
          1| . • . .
    ───────
    5 8 2 0 = H.
```

The sum of the series

$$\frac{2}{\sqrt{\pi}}\left(x - \frac{1}{1.3}x^3 + \frac{1}{1.2}\frac{x^5}{5} - \frac{1}{1.2.3}\frac{x^7}{7} + \frac{1}{1.2.3.4}\frac{x^9}{9} - \frac{1}{1.2.3.4.5}\frac{x^{11}}{11} + \ldots\right)$$

may be found in a similar manner (see Example 10, page xxi).

$\frac{2}{\sqrt{\pi}}\,x =$ ↓ **1,1,8,5,7,2,8,5,** = 1·12056087

$x^2 =$ ·9 ↓ **0,9,1,9,1,2,3,** which put = ·9 ↓ u,, . .

1·12056087	$+ = A$
·36836583	$- = A \times \frac{1 \times \cdot 9}{1 \times 3} \ \downarrow u_1 \ldots = B$
·10898475	$+ = B \times \frac{3 \times \cdot 9}{2 \times 5} \ \downarrow u_1 \ldots = C$
2559080	$- = C \times \frac{5 \times \cdot 9}{3 \times 7} \ \downarrow u_1 \ldots = D$
490734	$+ = D \times \frac{7 \times \cdot 9}{4 \times 9} \ \downarrow u_1 \ldots = E$
79194	$- = E \times \frac{9 \times \cdot 9}{5 \times 11} \ \downarrow u_1 \ldots = F$
11016	$+ = F \times \frac{11 \times \cdot 9}{6 \times 13} \ \downarrow u_1 \ldots = G$
1342	$- = G \times \frac{13 \times \cdot 9}{7 \times 15} \ \downarrow u_1 \ldots = H$
146	$+ = H \times \frac{15 \times \cdot 9}{8 \times 17} \ \downarrow u_1 \ldots = I$
13	$- = I \times \frac{17 \times \cdot 9}{9 \times 19} \ \downarrow u_1 \ldots = J$
1	$+ = J \times \frac{19 \times \cdot 9}{10 \times 21} \ \downarrow u_1 \ldots = K$

·83980247, area of the curve

x^2 and x may be developed under many forms, and the series summed in a similar manner; for example, x^2 may be put $= \cdot 8 \downarrow 2,1,8,6,7,1,2,8$, and the same result obtained.

THE END.

CPSIA information can be obtained
at www.ICGtesting.com
Printed in the USA
LVHW100444110522
718424LV00003B/222

9 783375 006495